Rowan Metcalfe (1955–2003) is a direct descendant of Mauatua and Fletcher Christian, and describes *Transit of Venus* as 'a meditation on my ancestors'. In 1974 she won the Katherine Mansfield Short Story Award (for young writers) and in 1997 won the BNZ Katherine Mansfield Short Story Award. Owen Marshall writes that she 'created short fiction of special power and intensity'.

Transit of Venus

Rowan Metcalfe

First published in 2004 by Huia Publishers,
39 Pipitea Street, PO Box 17-335,
Wellington, Aotearoa New Zealand.
www.huia.co.nz

ISBN 1-86969-083-4

Copyright © 2004 Rowan Metcalfe
Literary agency services provided by Dr Susan Sayer

All rights reserved. No part of this publication may be reproduced, stored in a retrieval system, or transmitted in any form or by any means, electronic, mechanical, including photocopying, recording or otherwise, without prior permission of the copyright owner.

National Library of New Zealand Cataloguing-in-Publication Data
Metcalfe, Rowan
Transit of Venus / Rowan Metcalfe.
ISBN 1-86969-083-4
NZ823.3—dc 22

Published with the assistance of

I dedicate this work to all the descendants of the Bounty, *including my own children, and my kind father, and to all my* Bounty *cousins I humbly offer these words, in the hope that they may help to understand our ancestors' deeds and lives.*

And to the people of Tahiti, I also offer this work, in tribute to all our tupua vahine, our glorious foremothers.

And let me not forget my own mother, who first put a pen in my hand, or my numerous dear friends all over the world who have assisted me in many ways, or Creative NZ for financial assistance.

This work began as a meditation on my ancestors. I didn't realise when it started how much they would have to say, or to teach me. Accompanying them on their journey, I found them guiding me on mine. It was a journey in time and space, leading out of the rich, dark complexity of pre-European Tahiti, into the pure light of the Absolute Truth. By the mercy of the Lord, we can all be forgiven and redeemed.

Contents

Cast of Characters ix

Maps xiv

Prologue xix

I Red Feathers 1

II The Ship 155

III The Talk of Women 235

Epilogue 273

Glossary of Tahitian Words 285

Cast of Characters

The *Bounty* story teems with fascinating characters. When I began this work I did not expect so many of them to demand my attention, but I soon realised that they all had something to contribute to understanding the mutiny and events that followed.

For those interested in the history of Tahiti, all the relationships and genealogies mentioned are drawn from historical fact.

Bounty descendants will be able to identify their own ancestors among the crowd. The unrelated reader may enter into the story without being overly concerned with the many details of relationship. The important people will stand out.

It has often been said that Mauatua was a 'chief's daughter', or, by the romantically inclined, a 'Tahitian princess'. This is not strictly true, but there is no doubt that she had close blood ties with the ruling powers of the time.

I took the liberty of inventing three characters: Hinuia the priestess, Maunu, the mahu servant, and Rehua, Mauatua's Tahitian lover. I did this to elucidate the events and fill gaps in the history.

Apart from these three, every other character mentioned was an actual person.

Note that in Tahitian, as in all Maohi languages, the words for cousin and sister, or cousin and brother, are the same. Also note that it was common practice for Tahitians to change their names, usually to mark an important event or change in status. For example, the chief Tu changed his name to Taina after the birth of his first son, and Mauatua changed her name to Maimiti around the time of the mutiny. Most of the characters in the book changed their name at least once during the course of events, including the mutineer Aleck Smith, who mysteriously became John Adams on Pitcairn.

Adams
The name adopted or reverted to by Alexander Smith, ABS on the Bounty. *Died on Pitcairn in 1829.*

Aimata
lit. 'Eater of Eyes', traditional Tahitian name of Pomare Vahine, Queen of Tahiti in 1831.

Aleck
Alexander Smith, see above. On Pitcairn was known as John Adams.

Auo
Younger sister of the chief Tu/Taina, of Pare. Cousin of Mauatua/Maimiti.

Ari'ipaea
Younger brother of chief Tu/Taina.

Eti
Edward Young, midshipman on the Bounty.

Fataua
Older sister of the chief Tu/Taina, of Pare. Cousin of Mauatua/Maimiti.

Hinuia
A priestess in the service of Mauatua/Maimiti's grandmother.

Itia
High chiefess of Pare by her marriage to Tu/Taina.

Mai
A native of Huahine who travelled to England with Cook and returned to Tahiti two years later.

Manari'i
A young Tahitian man who accompanied the Bounty *to Pitcairn. Murdered there in 1793.*

Maoiti
Birth mother of Mauatua/Maimiti.

Mareiti
Mauatua/Maimiti's father's second wife.

Margaret
A granddaughter of Mauatua/Maimiti, daughter of Charles Christian and Sully, born in 1822.

Mauatua
A young woman of the chiefly family of Matavai, with blood connections to the high chief Tu, of Pare. Later known as Maimiti, or Mainmast, and by Fletcher Christian as Isabella. Died on Pitcairn in 1841.

Maunu
A personal servant of Mauatua/Maimiti's grandmother, and later of Itia.

McCoy, William
A Scottish ABS on the Bounty. *Died on Pitcairn in 1797.*

Nari'i
An aunt to Mauatua/Maimiti by marriage.

Niau
A Tahitian boy, killed on Pitcairn around 1793.

Oha
A young man who joined the Bounty *at Tupuai, as companion to Titahiti.*

Pani
Joseph Banks, scientist and gentleman, Cook's patron on the Endeavour *voyage.*

Parai
Captain *Bligh.*

Purea
A high chiefess of southern Tahiti who was seeking to extend her power and prestige during the first visits by European ships.

Quintal, Matthew
A Cornish ABS on the Bounty. *Murdered there in 1799.*

Rehua
Mauatua/Maimiti's lover, from the island of Aimeo (Moorea).

Sully
The daughter of Teio, who was born on Tahiti and went to Pitcairn as a baby. Died on Pitcairn in 1826.

Taina
Name adopted by the chief Tu, of Pare, after the birth of his first son.

Tapuetefa
An uncle to Mauatua/Maimiti.

Tararo
A chief from Raiatea who joined the Bounty.

Tatahe
Mauatua/Maimiti's younger cousin, son of Tapuetefa and Nari'i.

Tautoia
Oldest uncle of Mauatua/Maimiti, who inherited the chiefdom of Matavai but died in battle.

Te Aha Huri Fenua
Father of Mauatua/Maimiti.

Teio
A girl from Pare, known on Pitcairn as Mary. Died there in 1829.

Teraura
A girl from Matavai, bond sister, or closest friend, of Mauatua/Maimiti. Known later on Pitcairn as Susannah. Died there in 1850.

Tetua Avari'i
Mauatua/Maimiti's maternal grandmother, born on Aimeo.

Tevarua
A girl from Matavai, known on Pitcairn as Sarah. Died by falling from the cliffs there in 1799.

Thursday October
The first child born on Pitcairn, in 1790, son of Mauatua/Maimiti and Fletcher Christian. Died on Tahiti in 1831.

Ti'ipari'i
Mauatua/Maimiti's maternal grandfather, old chief of Matavai and Haapape.

Tinafanea
A young woman from the island of Tupuai, who joined the Bounty.

Titahiti
A Tupuaian chief's son who accompanied the Bounty *to Pitcairn.*

Titriano
Transliteration of Christian. Fletcher Christian, Manxman, first mate on the Bounty. *Murdered on Pitcairn in 1793.*

Toofaiti
A girl from the island of Huahine, known on Pitcairn as Nancy. Died on Tahiti in 1831.

Torano
Transliteration of Solander, Cook's botanist on the Endeavour.

Tu
High chief of Pare, cousin of Mauatua/Maimiti, later known as Taina, then King Pomare 1.

Tuaonoa
A young ari'i woman of Tahiti. Her full name was Teehuteatuaonoa. Known on Pitcairn as Jenny. Left Pitcairn aboard a whaling ship in 1817. No descendants known.

Tupaia
A priest of Tahiti who sailed with Cook to Aotearoa but died en route to England.

Tute
Captain Cook.

Vaetua
Younger brother of the chief Tu/Taina, of Pare. Cousin of Mauatua/Maimiti.

Vahineatua
A young woman of Matavai. Known later on Pitcairn as Prudence. Died on Tahiti in 1831.

Vehiatua
Chief of the Taiarapu peninsula, often at war with the other chiefs of Tahiti during Mauatua/Maimiti's childhood.

Williams, Jack
ABS on the Bounty, *native of Guernsey. Murdered on Pitcairn in 1793.*

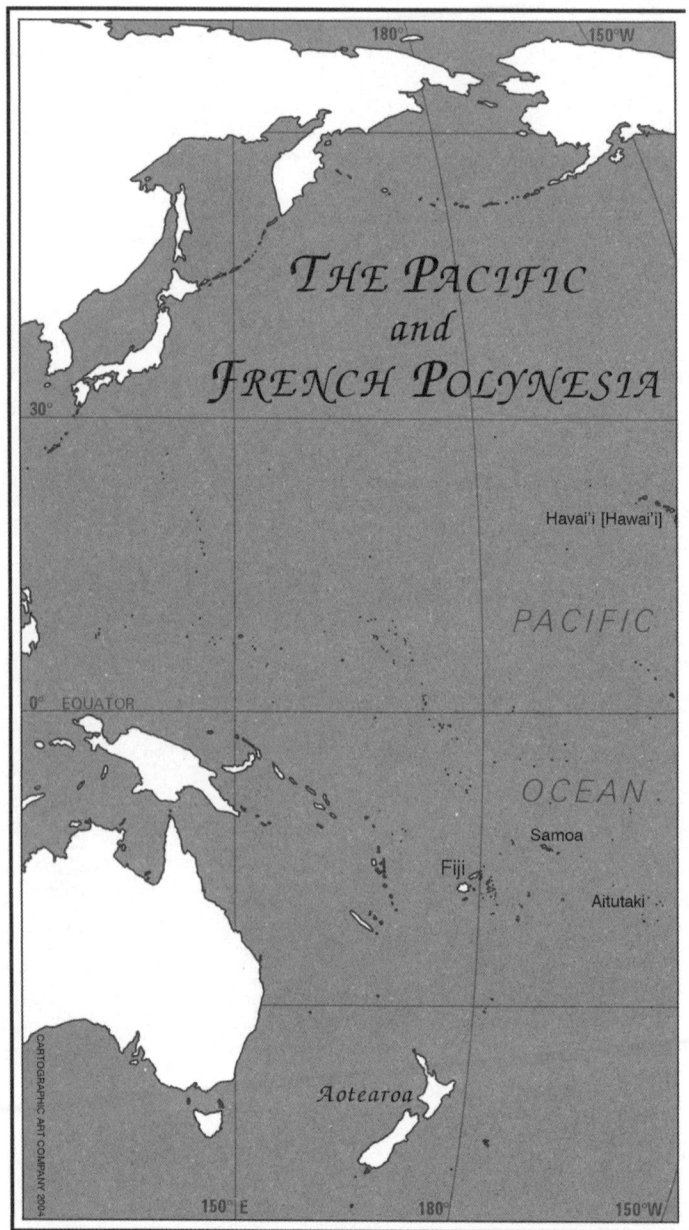

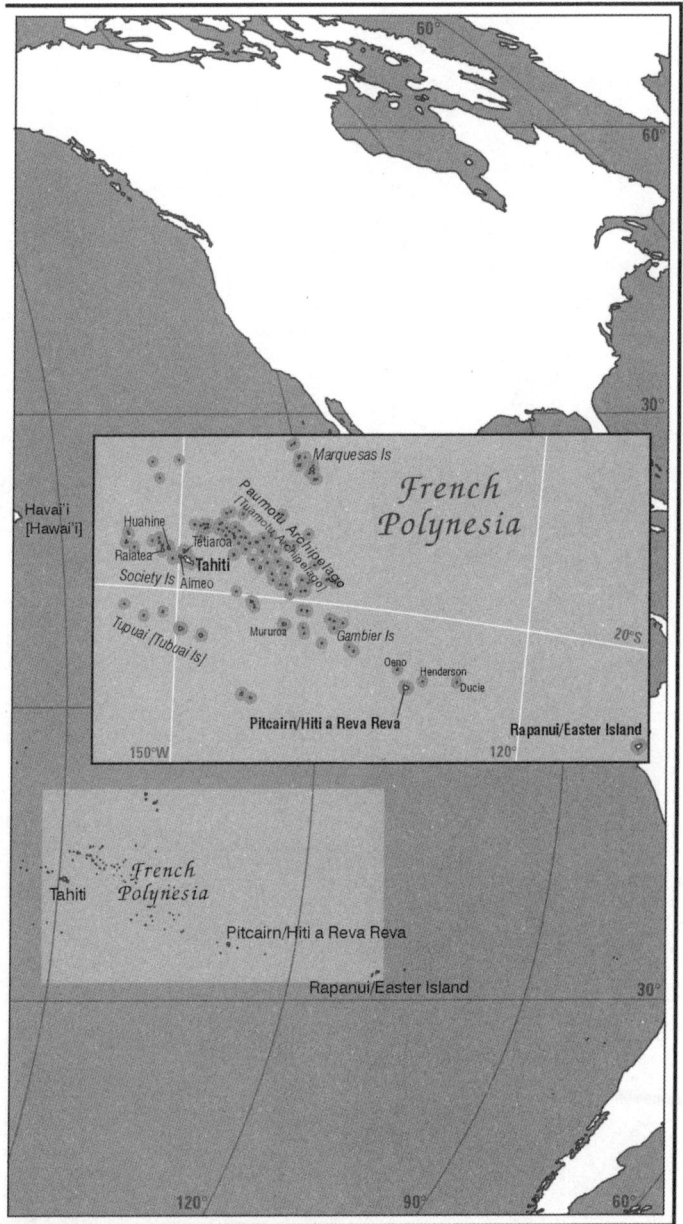

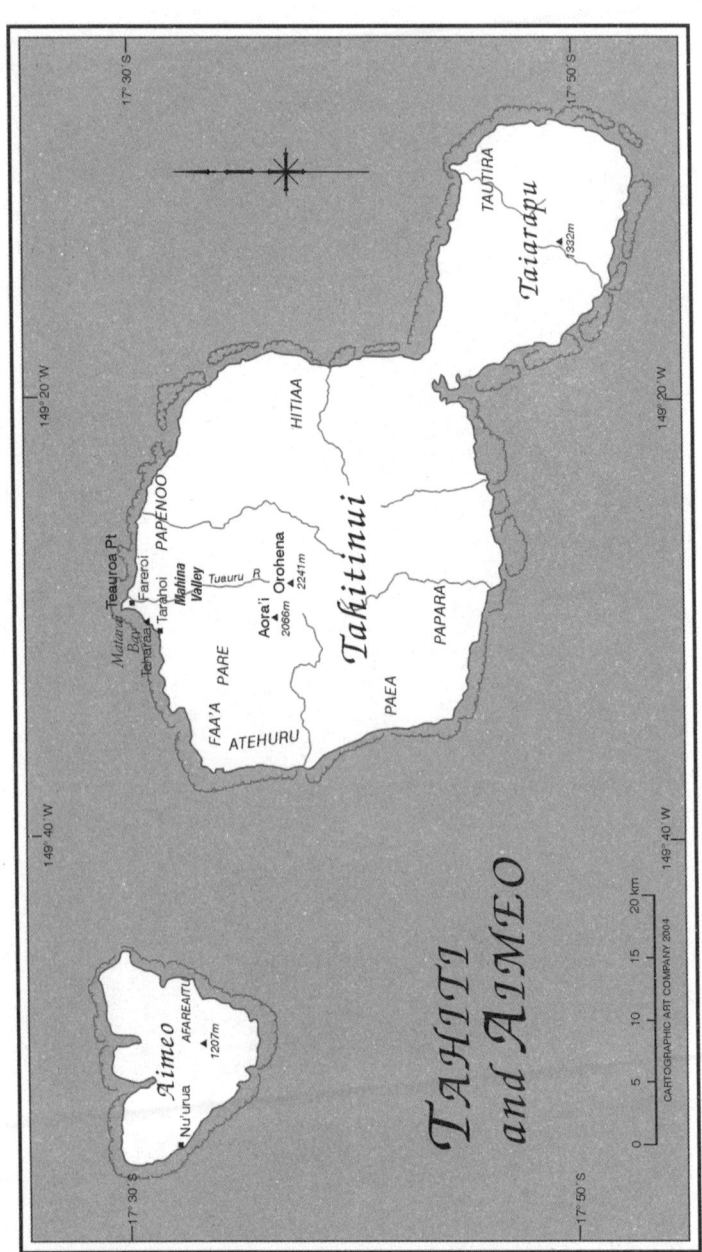

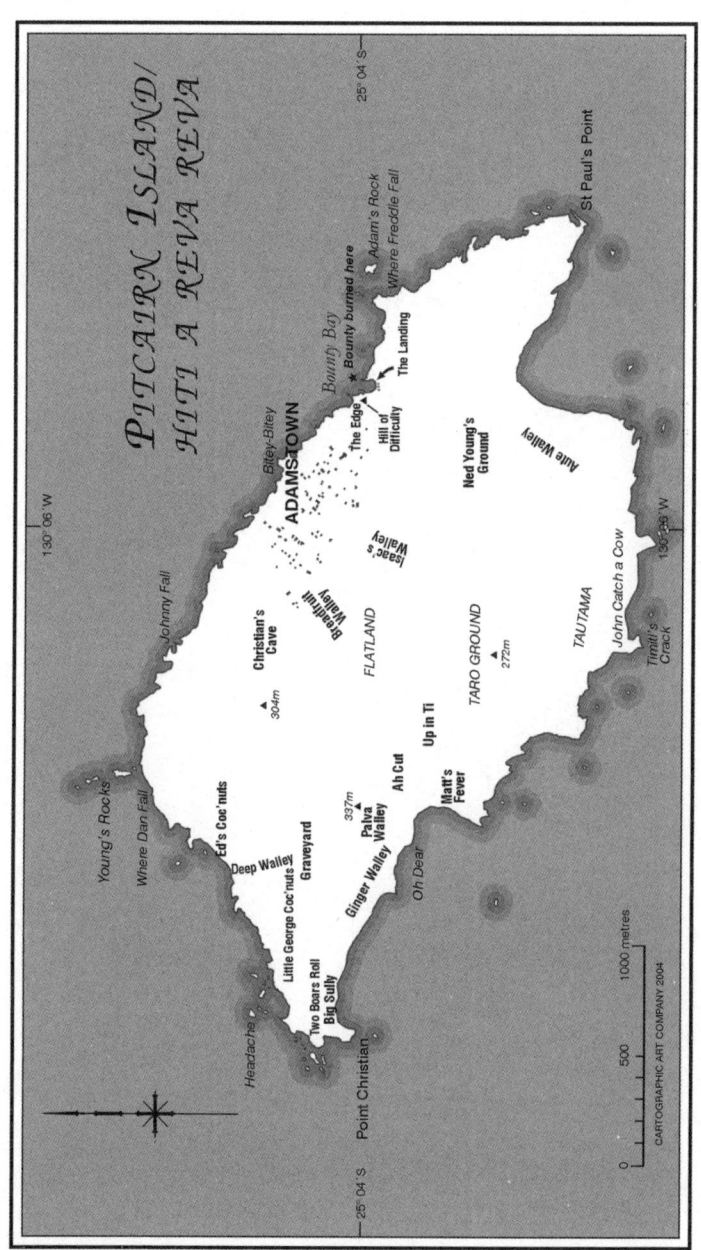

Prologue

Year of Our Lord 1831

O my land standing forth!
Now hide your face
Be lost to view!

To the white god, the young people.

Garnered like a sheaf on the decks of the *Lucy Anne* they stand, our daughters, our sons, their sons and daughters, and theirs again. Our hina tini. Brown eyes and blue eyes, girls with arms entwined, young men firm footed on the rolling ocean as their grandfathers before them.

Our island home slipping away behind us, all falling silent, turning with one gaze to its vanishing. Even the little children stop rushing like puppies among our legs, stand witness as the only land they know dissolves into the light of the rising sun.

But before any doubts can be expressed, Mr Nobbs leading us into song.

Immortal love forever full, forever flowing free!

Our voices boldly raised into the wind. *Forever shared, forever whole, a never-ebbing sea!*

Who are we to fear a sea voyage or a far land? Our legs will soon remember the roll of the swell, the salt spray be as meat and drink to us, the masts our trees, the decks our land!

Our outward lips confess the name, all other names above.

The name of Jesus Christ. Iehu Tireti! Even our tongues have been twisted in order to pray to the white god, and the little ones can whisper the name of Jesus like birds in a bush.

Love only knoweth whence it came and comprehendeth love.

But do not forget the ancient demons of this ocean! How often in the years gone by we heard of Puna's beastly sea gods, the devouring ones, who threatened Rata on his famous journey to redeem his parents from slavery to foul Puna.

There are just four of us left now, of the thirty who came from Tahiti on that weary ship, seeking like Rata across the trackless ocean. The others who were with us are long gone.

Aue, all the dead men. Already we have wept enough.

Toofaiti and Vahineatua, Teraura and Mauatua, those were our Tahitian names.

We are the only ones still living. We remember, and we performed our own rituals before leaving Pitcairn, secretly leaving offerings on that hidden altar, out of sight of white men's prying eyes. The white Lord is very good, but we are still Maohi.

Do not neglect the old gods, e hine, they are the source of your being. They flee to the highest pinnacles, but returning in triumph, they gather our people on the winds ...

Tahiti! Teraura and I hardly dared speak of the old friends, the sisters and cousins we hope to find still alive. We hear Tahiti is a Christian island now, like Pitcairn, with churches and preachers of the white god.

We too, have our white preachers, Mr Nobbs and Mr Buffet, whose children are my grandchildren, boys with names from the book. Thomas, John, David and Reuben. Of Christians there are a Joseph and three Marys, two young Fletchers, two Pollys ... too many to count. Fletcher would be proud, after all. From our blood springs a people worthy of his Island of Man, worthy of the fenua maitai which appeared when hope was gone, just as he had promised.

When we looked again, our island home had vanished.

The *Lucy Anne* lifted her skirts and began to run before the wind. The people settled to enjoy the ride.

'Sit over here Granma, sit over here. Put your bundle here. How's this ship, Granma, es good'un no?'

Unroll the comfortable mats. The children are in all directions, the babies are set down among us. 'Granma, watch me! Granma, Joseph is gwen up a mast!'

Lucy Anne slides over the waves. It's good to be at sea again. Going home at last. She is more comfortable than *Bounty*. A few chickens sticking their heads out of baskets here, but *Bounty* had creatures sticking their heads out every hatch. So many smelly creatures the Englishmen wanted to bring with them, all manner of four-legged absurdities. It was a floating sty with stinking bilges. Refusing to make love, we banded together in the great cabin. Na, we unrolled our mats there and lay down together like this to talk, with sandalwood smouldering all night and day against the stink.

Lucy Anne pitched and the creak of timber set memories spilling.

Margaret Christian crept closer to her grandmother, reaching for her hand. Secretly, holding it in her lap, her fingertips would trace the mysterious messages written into the weathered skin. Silently, listen.

Tahitinui is the land,

Teauroa is the point,

Fareroi is the marae.

From Teauroa you will see Aimeo, with the sun setting beyond it.

Above stands the mountain Orohena, and beside it, Aora'i. Nobody can reach the top of those peaks. They are tapu.

I'sa listening, Granma, Margaret's fingertips replied.

'From Hema was born Tahaki of the golden skin. From Tahaki was born Vahieroa. From Vahieroa and his wife Mata Mata Taua, the highest chiefess of sunward Tahiti, was born Rata, who rescued his parents from foul Puna's land. This is not to be forgotten.'

'And Rona-nihoniho-roa, Granma?'

'Rona, the long-toothed man-eater! Tahaki's great-grandmother. Her daughter Hina was his grandmother, No'a his grandfather.'

'In Noah's ark?'

'Kaue kaue, e hine.'

'Mr Buffet says Noah is my ancestor.'

'Mr Buffet does not know your grandfather's genealogy, so he's wrong to say such.'

'Is Captain Cook my ancestor?'

'No, but he had a ship of animals like Noah.'

'Are there dogs on Tahiti?'

'Yes, dogs that bark, bark, bark, and cats that meow.'

The babies looked around at those strange sounds.

'Horses, Granma?'

'Our chiefs and chiefesses had strong men to carry them, no horses. Captain Cook brought those animals.'

'Mr Buffet says the queen of Tahiti rides in a horse and carriage like the queen of England.'

'Then she invites you to ride with her, for your great-grandfather and hers were half brothers.'

'Is the truth, Granma?'

'Would I tell a story?'

'Are we cousins with all the Tahiti people?'

'Many, many, Margaret Christian. Your great-great-grandmother, Tetua Avari'i, made me remember the names of all our family. Everything must be remembered. No paper to write on then.'

'You wrote on your hands Granma.'

Her own small hand was almost as dark as the old one's, and already calloused from climbing and scrambling, grating coconut and gathering firewood.

But the back was plain. Empty. She had tried scratching patterns there, using a feather pen and schoolroom ink. One morning Mr Buffet had caught her with pen in hand and her tongue between her teeth. 'What have you done girl?' he exploded, seizing her wrist. 'Has the devil possessed you, or are you a heathen through and through?'

'Please Mr Buffet, the quill jump up and write on me!'

Mr Buffet's face hair had seemed to stick out horizontally. 'I knew it! We shall have to thrash the devil out of you!'

She had shrieked and eluded his grasp, his roar of laughter following her all the way down the hill to the spring.

By the time she had washed her beautiful patterns away, everybody knew.

Margaret Christian a heathen!

She prayed harder than ever. She could not be a heathen if she prayed so hard.

Her grandmother, smelling of coconut oil, was combing Margaret's hair, snipping lice between her last remaining teeth.

Safe under her hands, Margaret lay back and listened to the creakings and strainings of the *Lucy Anne*, her eyes wandering upward into the enchanting web of canvas and ropes. At last a ship! The *Lucy Anne* was her prayer come true, she was going on a real journey. Like Rata. Like the men from ships who rowed ashore to Pitcairn. They who climbed up the Hill of Difficulty and ate as much food as there was to give them, their ships lying out beyond her reach.

Her grandmother would find her gazing at that distant beacon while the other children were singing hymns to the guests. Embrace her there, above the raw ocean. The wind singing up off the surf.

She heard the other children laughing. For no matter. Granma holding her. Now the story would begin.

'Tell me again how Grandfather came to Tahiti to find a wife.'

'Ssh. Listen now. It's beginning long long afore that. Before Tute came, the priests foretold everything. A canoe without an outrigger, carrying the children of a glorious princess! That is what Pau'e the seer predicted. The people would be covered from head to foot, he said.'

'Like Mr Buffet and Mr Nobbs.'

'Ssh. This Tute was a mystery. Maybe an ancestor. Maybe an atua. Na, the children knew. Tute was chief of a land of wonders. He sailed a ship full of gifts. All the little children getting something! I had a comb, but I wanted scissors. When he departed I was wild because I'd missed the farewells. Maybe Tute made one more gift of scissors, and where was I? Far up the river path with my own granma, chasing her escaped piglet. Who's wilder, the pig or me, I didn't know. Tute's sailing away and all the other people are down at the beach.'

'Why you not let the pig go, Granma?'

'For when that pig runs onto any land belonging to a man, pau, it's lost to the woman. No sweet little pork dinner. Belongs to the man. When it runs onto the marae, the same. Belongs to the priests.

'That pig was like an eel, this way and that way. We falling in the mud, our good clothes all stained. Finally got it cornered in an aute plantation. Then poooum! The cannon goes! The pig's bolting and I'm bolting too ...

I
Red Feathers

Tute
1769

At the sight of the pig running Mauatua too began to run, ignoring her grandmother's shouts, following the path back to the beach, her heart pounding wait, wait, wait for me, furious at her grandmother for dragging her away when everyone knew the ship was leaving today, the great white ship and the white men, Tute the chief of the white men, and all the wonders on board.

She hardly saw the people on the shore, their legs were only a forest she had to run through, darting and ducking, until she could find a place to see from, hearing only the voice of her heart, wait for me, wait for me! At last she could see, increasing her vantage by scrambling up a leaning palm trunk, and just at that moment came the bright flash of fire across the water, the boom of the cannon, and the answering thunder from high up in the mountain peaks.

Aue! The women were wailing. Aue! Already the great ship was nearing the gap in the reef, its sails were filling like clouds with sunlight, its deep belly still freighted with treasure, the white men guiding it away, away, like a bird on the wind, calling to Mauatua.

Aue! It has gone without me! It has gone without me! She leapt and her legs began running again, they carried her across the sand to the water's edge, splashing into the warm water. She threw herself forward and began to swim, the ship calling to her. An adult's arms caught her and pulled her up. 'Where are you going, little one?'

It has gone without me! The white ship, and the sea-eyed men on it, whose tongues so deftly wrapped their slippery, hard-edged language, whose supply of toys and curiosities seemed endless, whose stiff-legged, loose-armed dances were already the craze of all her playmates.

'Ho'i mai, ho'i mai!' she heard the women crying all around her on the beach. 'Come back to us!'

Some of the people were leaving now, running along the shore to reach Tahara'a, the point of land across the bay from where they could watch the ship gliding away through the pass. Mauatua wanted to run that way too, but now across the waters of Matavai came the great double canoe of Purea, returning with the ari'i who had gone out to farewell Tute. High on the shaded rear deck they sat, above the paddlers' flashing shoulders. The men's turbans and mantles were white, but the women were all darkened and streaked from cutting with their paoniho, drawing their sacred blood to show the gods their strength of feeling. The lofty headdresses of two high priests, radiant with white tropic bird feathers, stood above them all, and even higher, twisting and rippling at the tops of the curving stern posts, tassels of sacred red feathers proclaimed the authority of all the chiefs and priests aboard.

Slowly, led by one voice, then another, the women waiting on the beach turned their weeping to song, pulling down the folds of their barkcloth wraps to bare their shoulders and breasts in respect. As the canoe drew closer Mauatua could see among the nobles her uncle Tautoia, the warrior chief of Matavai, and close to him sat Te Aha Huri Fenua, her birth father. Beside him sat his new wife Mareiti, the sister of Purea, the high chiefess. Next to them sat Purea herself, who had stayed at Matavai since war had laid waste her own district of Papara. The white men had paid court to her at the royal guest house of Matavai. Now her white gown was richly bloodstained, but her head was high in triumph, for they had treated her as if she were the most important chief of all Tahiti, and the great guest house was strewn with the strange and wonderful gifts they had pressed upon her.

Mauatua would have run towards the canoe, but again a hand checked her. 'Show respect,' cautioned Tetua Avari'i, her grandmother, who had caught up with her on the beach. 'Your father's new wife is of higher rank than us.'

Purea's bearer waded out to the canoe. He bent his back for the high chiefess to leap upon and carried her up the beach on his shoulders. They passed so close to Mauatua that she could smell Purea's sandalwood oil and see the fine patterns of stars tattooed on her feet. Behind the chiefess came the rest of the royal party – the tapairu, the waiting maids, crowned with leaves and ferns; noblemen and priests in sashed gowns and turbans; the drummers, whose maro revealed their tattooed buttocks; and the married women with blood-streaked faces like fierce masks.

Tetua's hands were firm upon her granddaughter's shoulders as she recited each name and blood bond to her. 'There is Amo, Purea's husband, and Teri'irere, their son, the rightful inheritor of the high chiefdom of Papara. His grandmother, Teroro e Ora, is the aunt of your grandfather, and thus may he sit upon our marae with your uncles. There go the sisters of Purea – Mareiti, and Teraematatea ...'

So many names. Mauatua looked back to the sea, but the ship had vanished from sight. Across the bay people were scrambling to the crest of the hill Tahara'a to watch it disappear. Obeying the impulse of her limbs she ducked away again through the crowd and began to run along the sand.

✵ ✵ ✵

'They do not recognise her,' said Mauatua's mother, Maoiti. 'She is running loose among the commoners' children.'

'You too have seen the belly of Mareiti,' Tetua Avari'i reminded her. 'She is of higher rank than you, and her child, when it is born, will take precedence over Mauatua. You will not be well thought of if you try to promote your daughter to a higher status.'

'Are my daughter's uncle and cousin not both chiefs,' Maoiti said.

'But your line is weaker than Mareiti's, this you must remember.'

'Is her father not uncle to the young chief of Pare!'

'The chiefs of Pare descend from Paumotuan commoners. They are not true ari'i, no matter how much power they accrue by their alliances.'

'Speak you thus of her father's blood?'

'He was not my choice for you, and now he is with Mareiti he doesn't even acknowledge your daughter.'

'If she runs loose with the common children how is anyone to acknowledge her? How will her noble blood be known and what marriage will she make?'

'You may leave her education in my hands, my daughter, she shall have a suitable match when the time comes.'

✖ ✖ ✖

Mauatua slipped between the coconut-frond wall panels of the guest house. Her cousin, Tatahe, squeezed tight behind her. It was cool and dark inside. Glimmering stars of light danced all across the matted floor, shimmering and twisting like those that play across the bed of the lagoon. At the other end Purea's women sat resting in the open doorway, facing the light. The murmur of their voices blended with the constant whisper of the breeze through the palm leaves and made a soothing music that emboldened the two children. Carefully they tip-toed among the scattered finery, among withering strings of flowers, coconut cups of scented oils and discarded wraps, in search of Purea's treasure. Deep in the shadows, Mauatua beckoned. 'Look, here Tatahe!'

Some of the things they wanted to see were spread on a tray which pooled the subtle light like water across its hard surface. Coloured beads, like pearls of the rainbow – but every child had seen those by now, and been given a handful that had been scattered in the sand or lost under the floor matting indoors. A fan that folded and unfolded, made of bone finely pierced and carved, and flower-painted cloth. They took turns opening and closing it and fanning themselves. There was a selection of the tools the white men used to eat their food, hard, bright things, which Tatahe tried to lift to his mouth the way the white men did, almost stabbing himself in the ear as he missed.

'Like this,' whispered Mauatua, taking the thing delicately in her left hand and turning it towards her lips. 'Feri kuta,' she mimicked, 'tanku tanku, feri kuta.' She rolled her eyes as she chewed and completed her act by wiping her mouth on a corner of bark cloth robe. From under the robe appeared the tiny pink feet of the white-woman image. Tatahe pulled at it and the little image emerged, staring at them with wide-awake eyes. Mauatua gave a shiver of fear. 'I think it is a ti'i, for sorcery,' she said. 'I don't like it.'

'No,' said Tatahe, 'it is the wife of Tute, see, a lady of Peretane. It can't hurt you.' He stroked its stiff, whitish curls, then he began lifting its layers of soft skirts and petticoats until he reached its naked wooden fundament. 'Look,' he pointed, 'she has nothing here, the Peretane lady.'

Mauatua looked and it was true, there was not so much as a groove between her legs. She could have no magic power then, which was reassuring. Tatahe wanted to play with it and make it dance, but Mauatua had seen something else – a wooden box which she knew held a special treasure. She opened it and carefully lifted out the paoti that lay snug within. It was cool and shiny, a single thing, with a long, sharp point. She pressed the sharp point against her finger tip. A one thing that was two things. She put her finger and thumb into the two loops, pulled them apart, and it became two things, two things like the two-legged garment worn by the white men. Two things sharp, like the tail of the frigate bird. She had seen Purea and the women cutting each other's hair with it. She had seen Tute cutting a piece of cloth with it. One thing, two things. The two legs opened and closed with a cold sound, a sound her tongue couldn't say. When they came together they bit like a jaw with that swift, fierce sound, and the thing was cut. She pulled a curl of her hair down and, pulling it out tight, she held it between the two legs of the paoti and snapped them together. She and Tatahe looked at each other as the curl fell loose from her fingers. 'Let me do it!' said Tatahe, reaching for the paoti.

'It's only for girls,' she rejoined, snatching it back.

'Tute did it, you said.'

That was true, she remembered. She handed over the paoti. 'You should cut my hair,' she said. She pointed to the side of her head. 'Very short here.' Then to the top. 'Let it be long here.'

She heard the paoti snapping near her ear. They both started to giggle. 'It's easy!' declared Tatahe, and the paoti snapped some more. She felt hair falling down her neck and onto her shoulder and then on the mat round her knees. 'We have to gather it up,' she reminded him. 'We'll bury it, I know where.' She reached up to feel her scalp, the hair short and rough.

At that moment one of Purea's attendants stood up and turned to come towards them. Tatahe threw down the paoti and they had leapt up and squeezed back out between the wall panels before the woman's eyes had time to adjust to the darkness. All she found there was the scissors lying on the soft pandanus mat amid the scattered curls and she bent to gather them up for safe disposal, muttering charms against sorcery.

The women's fans and fly whisks fell still when the children finally reappeared, and those who were plaiting moia looked up from the rhythm of their hands. 'Aue, what have you been doing?' cried Grandmother Tetua. 'Turn your head around.'

The little girl slowly swivelled her ragged head, looking sidelong at her grandmother's face.

'How did you do this?'

'With the paoti of Tute,' answered the child boldly.

'With the paoti of Purea,' Tetua chided her. 'And why have you made a hairstyle for mourning, nobody has died.'

'The white men have gone,' said Mauatua. 'Tute has gone!' And she opened her mouth and began to wail.

'He will be back,' said her grandmother, loud to still her child's voice. 'The white men will be back. With all their trouble,' she added.

✘ ✘ ✘

'Why are they coming here, so far from their own land?'

Mauatua's eyes opened again, even though she was so sleepy. The candlenut lights were still burning and she could see the men sitting and lying at the other end of the fare. Grandfather Ti'ipari'i had his warm dog-hair cloak on against the cold mara'amu breezes that would suddenly arise at this time of year. Her uncles Tautoia and Tapuetefa were there too, and other important men of the district of Mahina, Tautoia's relatives and appointees. They had been drinking 'ava together.

'They say Tute came to look at the stars. With their long eye they could look at the heavens even during the daylight. They saw Ta'urua e hiti i Matavai crossing the sun.'

'Don't they have stars in Peretane?'

'Different ones, they say, but Ta'urua they know from their own heavens.'

She lifted her head from her sleeping mat to listen better. Her cousin Tatahe sighed in his sleep beside her.

'They are men then,' said her grandfather. 'If they were gods they would need no tools to look at stars.'

'But their tools are very fine. Through the long eye I looked upon the body of Hina te Marama, so close she filled my eye, though my feet remained here on Tahiti. Others looked at the land and saw people on the shore at Papenoo. Upside down!'

A lizard chirped in the thatch and the candlenut light shivered and spat.

'They are learned men. It takes learning to know the movements of the stars.'

'True,' agreed Tapuetefa. 'And great skill to sail their ships so far. Ten moons it took them to sail here from their country.'

'We could sail so far ourselves with tools and iron and sails like theirs,' said another. 'We could take a ship to their country and taste their women as they have tasted ours, and eat of their food as they have eaten of ours.'

'Thinking always of your stomach and your ure my friend. It is only their iron we need. Their women and their food must be no good, that they want ours so much.'

'And what of the iron? Does it not come from their earth? Could we not make it from our earth?'

'They take it from their earth and they put it to fire.'

'They cook it?'

'Ae. But it is not like yams. It comes only once from the earth, it is no good to put it back for it will not grow again, as many who planted the nails of the Farane ship already know.'

Mauatua heard them chuckle softly as they remembered the foolish people of the district of Hitiaa who had sown some nails and waited for nail plants to grow.

'Like the Raiateans,' someone added, 'baking their paoti.' The story of the people of Raiatea who had put their scissors in the oven to try and make them cut again was already a famous joke, embellished by the best wits, and mention of it always raised a laugh.

Mauatua herself had watched one of the Peretane men fixing the iron tools that people brought to him, holding them to a circle of stone from which sparks showered as he turned it. Tatahe had dared her to dart through the sparks. It didn't hurt, you couldn't feel them. The man had frightened them away, waving the big knife that had been spitting sparks on the stone. Tapuetefa had asked for one of these stones to be brought for him on the next ship from Peretane, since the sailor had refused to part with his.

'Easy to laugh,' cautioned Ti'ipari'i, 'but we were not so wise ourselves a short while ago.'

'There must be plenty of iron in their earth for so many nails, so many tools.'

'Ae, we must hope for them to come back here and bring more for us.'

'They will come back, but it is not only nails they bring,' said Ti'ipari'i. 'Purea is taking advantage. The Popa'a still favour her and she is inviting trouble on us all. Vehiatua of Taiarapu watches with covetous eyes and may next attack this side of Tahiti. He is envious of the gifts and prestige Tute brings to our districts. If it was not enough that Purea brought disaster on her own people with her plans for grandeur, now she invites trouble by staying here. Vehiatua is very jealous.'

'Now that her priest Tupaia has sailed with Tute perhaps she and Amo will return to Papara and live humbly. Many hundreds died upon their shores by the weapons of Vehiatua's warriors, their lands are laid waste and their people are in need of good government.'

'Purea is not a woman to be humble.'

'It was Tupaia who encouraged her ambitions.'

'An artful priest who has now fled the scene of the disturbance he caused, e, let his journey be long.'

'Let Vehiatua attack then,' Tautoia spoke like a warrior. 'Together with Tutaha and the forces of Pare we can repel him easily.'

'You speak fearlessly of bloodshed,' said Ti'ipari'i. 'It is since Tupaia brought Oro the war god from Raiatea that these troubles have begun. How many more will die for Oro? They say the beaches at Papara were piled up with the slain and the fishes of the lagoon take possession of their skulls. And all this because Vehiatua would not honour Oro according to the commands of Purea and Amo and their troublesome priest. Shall the valley of Mahina also be piled with corpses?'

'Some say it is the white men who bring these troubles. That their gods do not accord with ours ... '

'But the Popa'a ship has been our salvation, for if Tute had not arrived Vehiatua would certainly have ventured an attack already.'

'And now that it has gone his retribution will quickly follow. We need the Popa'a weapons. Who has the white men's guns shall be unassailable, even as the Popa'a themselves are unassailable.'

'I have heard it said that the Popa'a are capturing the spirits. They copy every plant and creature and make images to carry away with them on the white leaves. They mark down everything with this paper tattoo. They make pictures even of us. You, my brother, how do you know that the high chiefs of Peretane will not soon be looking at your image on paper?'

'And what if they have a long eye that allows them to see us from Peretane?' put in another.

At this a few of the men laughed. 'And what if they have a long gun that can fire at us from there?' said one, even as he laughed.

Hearing them laugh, Mauatua was reassured. She had seen the white sheets covered in tiny black figures, like tattooed bark cloth. She had seen one or two of the Peretane men studying these sheets for long periods, and other men making such marks themselves upon the paper, and she understood that they must hold knowledge and secrets, just as a tattoo upon the skin holds the secret power of its wearer. Slowly, the tattooed pages turned before her eyes, one after the other, and their ciphers spoke a silent language in the darkness.

Oro

Mauatua

Many were the bleaching bones upon the marae and upon the beaches of Tahiti in the years following Tute's first visit. It was said that Vehiatua had built a marae at Taiarapu entirely of skulls of the warriors he had slain.

At Matavai the sea was red with blood and the sharks came to feast there while Hina te Marama shrank in the heavens. At Matavai, the shore of my ancestors, Matavai below mighty Orohena.

We were up the mountain. We had followed the valley of Tuauru since morning. Tetua Avari'i knew the path, she'd followed it many times.

How many of us were there? There were all the women of Tetua's household: Hinuia, our priestess, my mother and her sister, my uncle's wife, the teu teu women who gathered our food and cooked for us, who tended our taro plots, whose husbands and brothers fished for us and now were gone to paddle the war canoes. There were the children of the household: Tatahe and I, and two babies who were carried by the teu teu women under their cloaks. My older cousins, whose circumcision and tattooing ceremonies had been delayed by the constant state of war, walked together behind, as if unwilling to follow. There was also Maunu, who was mahu. He carried the food gourds strung from a pole across his shoulders, walking mincingly, for he kept his ure bound up tightly in barkcloth.

We crossed and recrossed the mountain streams while the rain never ceased to fall. The women wore lacquered capes of fig-tree barkcloth, but we children were all naked although we had been rubbed with coconut oil before we set out and the water streamed off our skins as from the leaves of the banana palm.

My great-grandmother, Ti'ipari'i's mother, who had not left the fare for many moons, had refused to come with us. I remembered her as we climbed. 'I am leaving this world,' she whispered to me from her shaded corner. 'My eyes long only to see the ancestors in the place beyond.' Her dry hand clasped my wrist, her dark eyes burning in darkness. 'The Popa'a gods are coming and I do not wish to meet them. But you are already taken, child, and your children and your children's children and their children will have to serve them.'

Like fire at the bottom of a dark pool her eyes burn before me, her words stay with me.

We did not see her again.

Before night we came to our sheltering place, a rock cave under the netted roots of a purau tree. From nearby came the splashing roar of a cascade pouring down from above, and in front there was a flat platform of rock, and the stones of a small marae, overhung by the dripping trees. Tetua and Hinuia went first to lay an offering, a portion of the morning's fish parcelled in a young banana leaf. Hinuia unwrapped it on the altar and knelt to say the prayers, bowed over in the rain.

Thunder resounded in the high peaks all night and we lay rolled tight in our mats, close together, teu teu and ari'i, while the priestess chanted and lightning flooded the glittering marae stones and the waters gushed from the slopes. At dawn we were afraid too, for then the sound of the great drums of war could be heard from the valley far below, followed by the rattling beat of the to'ere, the slit gong, which announced the human sacrifice.

The teu teu women were all afraid. Any husband or son could fall to the man slayer, marked out to him by some inadvertent wrongdoing, and be carried slung on a pole to the marae. Oro was demanding and the priests were zealous in those times. The breaking of any tapu, any act which displeased the gods, any careless insult or neglect, could mark a man for sacrifice. And when the drums fell silent we were also afraid, for then came the distant blare of the conch shells that announced the call to battle.

The vapours which filled the valley as the sun climbed the heavens reeked of blood and fire. All day Hinuia chanted and we stayed close to the shelter. We did not cook, but ate only plantains and fermented breadfruit paste, sitting wrapped in mats at the lip of the cave. It was not safe to stir about there, we children knew. Even the babies lay still and quiet, passed from arm to arm, song to song.

Only Maunu went away, and came back with sticks of sugar cane. They soon made our lips sticky and loosened tongues. Maunu began to relate his adventures on Tute's ship, how he had danced on board with the Peretane men, who thought he was a real woman. He showed how, pulling up Nari'i to whirl around, clasping her at the waist, his legs stiff, in the Popa'a way, even pretending to kiss her on the mouth in the Popa'a way, until we children were laughing and pretending too and smacking our lips against each others. Finally, with a shriek, he demonstrated how one of them had squeezed him, discovering his ure bundled up tight between his legs and then they all wanted to squeeze him because they didn't believe he was not a real woman.

Then he brings from inside his cloak a woven pouch, and he opens the pouch and inside it is, look, a very small thing, and look closer, it is made of the shiny iron, and four-legged animals with trees on their heads are on it, around the side of it, and then it is in the hand, look, and on the top is another animal, with a man riding on its back, all in colours. The man has red clothing, very small. Then Maunu shows how it opens, it is a container, and inside is a powder, earth coloured. 'Like this,' he says, takes a pinch in his fingers and puts it in his nostril, rolling his eyes. 'Popa'a medicine.'

Tatahe is reaching for it.

'E, Maunu, did you find that in the garments of your dancing partner?' laughs Nari'i.

Tatahe is taking the pinch.

'It was a gift to me,' replies Maunu. 'A gift to Maunu from Torano, e.'

All the women are laughing and Tatahe is sneezing and coughing, and laughing. 'Strong medicine,' he manages to say.

When the mists lifted and the sun was dropping behind the mountains we could see the reef again from our ledge. We were glad to see it still there, the sheltering reef, protecting us from the great ocean of danger, the familiar reef we could see from our own home in the valley. But Maunu went away to a place where he could see better and when he came back he said, 'The blood of the warriors is being sucked from the bay of Matavai by the departing water! Aue, the great ocean is drawing it into the night, and the sharks are swarming at the gateways of the reef to drink of it!'

Hinuia let out a cry and returned to her prayers, and the gloom of night fell swiftly.

Fearful were those nights of war, and the days long without the smell of the oven, and the chanting of the priestess was a solemn weight upon us. But we had time to get used to the Popa'a medicine and we learned how to sniff it without hurting our nostrils. I studied the medicine container every time, the man-carrying animal and the animals with trees on their heads, which could have been sacred to the Popa'a, perhaps guardians of the medicine's potency.

We knew that in Peretane there were creatures we had never seen before. The foreign ships had brought them, the visiting Popa'a chiefs had gifted many to Purea. Curious birds had strutted about among the people like dogs, making strange noises. Some of these had already died or been carried away by visitors. Stranger yet had been a round-eyed animal with smooth hair, softer than a dog's, and a voice like a bird's. It stole food and it chased and killed the hatchlings of the curious birds. I had liked it though, for its hair was smooth to touch and when I touched it kindly it had a different voice in its throat and would lie down at my feet to play. That animal, too, had been carried away by visitors.

We came down at last from the mountain. The sea was clear again, but the smell of death rose to meet us as we came towards our home, and all the scented herbs we had woven into wreaths for our temples could not disguise it. The priestess went ahead of us, chanting, chanting. The common people were also returning and they came wailing to Tetua Avari'i as we passed, naming and numbering their losses, and forming a train behind us. Someone cried out that the warrior Tautoia, my mother's brother, had fallen, and worse, that his body had been carried away by the enemy.

Thus we came to the shores of our land with much lamentation and clamour, until we were within hearing of the great marae, the marae of our people. There we stopped in awe and fear, for the priests were performing the rites for the slain warriors, and seeking omens. At such a time no woman or child or commoner would want to approach the forbidding black stones of the marae. Even my grandmother, the highest ranked woman of Mahina, would not step upon them, or touch the sacred stones of the walls.

Led by Tetua, the women brought out their paoniho and began to cut themselves, and so began the grieving of those times, in which all the gods were called upon and the spirits of the dead were farewelled into the world beyond the light, a time when the spirits crowded, thickly, intertwining with the songs of the living, seething like eels within the dark pool of woe.

Sometimes we children stayed close to the women, bound with them into the common wreath, as the fern is bound with the ti leaf into the mourning crown, pulled tight by the ties of our blood. At other moments, suffocated by that close bondage, we crept away, as children do, and made our own funeral rites over a dead rat, crouching among the thickets in our own secret places, muffling our laughter at the foolish incantations of our own 'high priest' for his praise of the rat's ancestry, its valour and deeds and noble death.

By night there came to us distant cries, then the leaves of the ni'au palms would rattle, the timbers of the house would shiver and shadows tremble against the palm leaf walls. 'It is the mourners in Pare that we hear on the wind,' we heard.

'The chief mourner roaming the shore for the death of Tutaha.'

'Tupapau!' we heard, and crept close to one another. The dead overwhelmed the living in those times.

At Pare the old chief Tutaha, my father's uncle, had at last been slain by Vehiatua's warriors, and his body was carried back to his marae for the full funeral rites.

I went along the coast to Pare with Tetua. The far ocean burned with a white fire on that day, as if to consume the odours of death which drifted from the land.

There were so many relatives in Pare and it was cousin Vaetua who led me to the fare tupapau, to see the corpse of our great-uncle Tutaha. Great was my fear as we approached that sacred place, near the marae of Pare, but Vaetua was bold.

'Tread as I tread,' he instructed, and I trod so close our skin was touching. 'It is tapu, but we are family,' he reassured me. Alone, I would have feared to be seized, strangled or devoured. Yet none of these things happened and I knew it must be Vaetua's mana that was protecting us from the jealous spirits and watchful atua which lurked in the leafy shadows. Even accustomed as we were become to the smell of death in our nostrils, with each step it was harder to breathe the foul air in that tapu place. Finally it was the chorus of flies that announced the house of the dead.

There sat Tutaha, looking at us from the shade of garlanded awnings. I almost cried out with fright and fled, for I thought he was still living. A turban of white cloth was on his head, baskets of food were close to him, flowers were strewn upon the bier. Of the miri, the embalmers who constantly attended and anointed the corpse, only one sat alone there, sleepy in the heat, waving a big plaited fan which he flicked at any settling fly. His murmured prayers hovered and circled like the insects.

We gazed at the old man until our bellies were full of that strange, stinking sight.

'They have pulled out all his flesh and his entrails,' Vaetua informed me.

'Yet he looks as fat as ever.'

'They have stuffed his skin with oil-soaked cloth.'

I thought of the white-woman image given to Purea by Tute, whose body was stuffed with cloth in such a way and whose limbs had rested as stiffly as Tutaha's.

'When his skin falls from his bones, then they will carry them to the cave in the mountains,' Vaetua went on, in the voice of his boyish pride. 'Up there,' he pointed to the highest peaks. 'But his skull will be kept close by so his spirit can return and the priests consult with him. Now my brother Tu will be chief! Great will be the glory of Pare when the white men's ships return, for we shall get all the iron they bring. Even Vehiatua will come to make peace with us, for the white man's iron. This is said. The priests are divining even now to know the duration of the peace.'

My cousin Tu, who was no warrior, had fled to the high mountain passes to escape the bloodshed, but even then, as we came along the shore, the news of his return was being called among the houses.

But my uncle Tautoia did not return to Matavai. Grandmother Tetua grieved long for him and made many offerings at our family marae. Parcels of sweet coconut poi, necklaces of rare blossoms, small glittering fish from the lagoon, each day some new gift to the ancestor goddess who watched over us, and who delighted in the sweet things of te ao marama, the world of light.

Hinuia spent many hours in prayer and consultation with Tetua and sometimes my mother and I were called to join them. Yet Tautoia did not return, either dead or alive.

It was a terrible thing for the body of a warrior to fall into enemy hands. Misfortune would come upon the family line, causing it to die out. This is what my grandmother feared, though I knew it not, small child as I was at that time.

The great guest house on the shore of Matavai had been burned, the wreckage of broken canoes cast ashore there, and the trees had been stripped of their fruits. The few remaining pigs and dogs were carefully guarded and it would be many months before the men ate flesh again.

To restore the supplies of food my grandfather Ti'ipari'i declared numerous rahui upon the land. At every turn ti'i images and poles topped with pennants of white cloth reminded us of the restrictions. For many weeks we ate only fermented breadfruit from the storage pits, a little fish, and plantains carried down from the high slopes. The days of feasting and dancing we had known during Tute's visit were like a happy dream, gone in the morning.

Yet I learned to follow my own footsteps into a hidden world inhabited by the people of Tute. I walked among them, hearing their voices. The colours and fastenings of their garments, the styles of their hair, their gestures and rituals, all these I saw, and they spoke to me and called me to them, and I knew that I loved them.

It was Grandmother Tetua who understood this and would let me lie in her lap. She sang to me of forbidden loves, of lovers torn apart, and voyages to distant lands, while her fingers gently massaged my limbs. Her songs guided me onto the silent paths of my life, borne on the living breath of the ancestors. Grandmother Tetua, I call to you now from the world of light! I call to you that the blood of our ancestors shall live forever, though it be carried by children with sky-coloured eyes! Ours will be the people of the new world Tetua, children of the new gods, who will go beyond the visible horizon and take birth in the Popa'a lands, rich with their wealth and bringing glory to our tribe!

Tohu

Mauatua's hand was in the flame. The young girl's whole impulse was to snatch it away, yet her grandmother held her tight against her arm's urge to pull, against her legs' urge to kick and run, her voice's desire to cry out. She opened and then closed, opened and then closed her eyes, seeing alternately the pitted depths of the night within, then the pierced shade of the tattoo house, the stars of light that flickered and trembled among the thatch, then blistered like sores on the raw flesh of darkness, dark, light, dark, light.

This way she was distracted from the burning pain for a little longer, a little longer, while the tahua tatau beat rhythms into her flesh, tap tap tap with the sacred bones of the tattoo tool, igniting a ring of fire, flame by flame around her wrist.

Tetua Avari'i pressed the bloodstained cloth down on each new flame, absorbing it, yet still it glowed like the oven stones and the sacred bone teeth struck the next alight, aue, she must bite her tongue as it flared forth, brightening the night within, while the priestess chanted the prayers, calling upon Tohu, the god of tattooing, who gave the fishes of the ocean all their colours and designs.

It is the red blood of Mauatua, of Marae Fareroi, that flows,
The red blood of the mother Maoiti,
The red blood of Tetua Avari'i of Marae Nu'urua.
It is the sacred red of the spiralling cords,
Red of the woman's canoe
Bringing life, bringing life!
Now the sign is formed on her skin,
The sign recognised, the sign given,
The sign known in the world of light,
In the world of darkness.
Here is Mauatua, here is the daughter of her people,
She is the river of her people's valley
That carries the sweetness of the mountains to the ocean!
She is the doorway of her people,
She is the home of her ancestors,
And the place of leaving,
She who comes to womanhood,
Behold the sacred flow of red!

Now the journey begins. When she stands she feels faint. Where are her legs, her feet? Her hand has been bathed in oil, bound with soft cloth. The priestess lets her lean, the tahua tatau is wrapping the tools in cloth. It is just beginning.

They step out into the light. 'E, hine,' murmurs Hinuia, whose voice is more often heard by gods than by humans.

Above the long sand spit of Teauroa, by Matavai, boys' kites swim and swerve, flying up where breath of ocean meets breath of land, coiling, dancing, diving. She takes the first breath of her womanhood. In the voices of light new songs may be heard, that only women know the words of. What music denotes the shivering and fluttering of light among the leaves of the tou tree, what stories pass among the rasping ni'au palms? A lizard with a glittering tail darts from the path, vini birds clamber among fruiting branches. Now it is no longer the world of childhood!

Hinuia brings the little ark of the goddess from its shelter at the family marae. Grandmother Tetua Avari'i still brings her gifts in memory of Tautoia, the warrior son, whose bones have never been returned to his marae, but today the altar stone is cleaned by the morning's rain, polished by the sun.

First she prays to the ancestor goddess to be with her, and then she asks of her the things it is proper to ask. That she may bring honour to her family, that her body should be sweet for love, for skill at cloth beating, for protection from the sorcery of disease. All the things it is proper to ask. Before she dares to make her secret request. 'Atua …' still she hesitates, whispers, 'Atua, bring a canoe with no outrigger, with white sails, this is the wish of my womanhood.'

And she places before the goddess the white man's medicine container, the tiny box given to her by Maunu, with the mysterious Popa'a animals worked on it. It is no longer shiny, but has grown dark as if it had some mysterious life in it. Only the tiny clip which opens it has remained bright, and inside it is still pale. She has hidden it in secret places, she has placed secret wishes into it and closed them tightly. The small, sacred things of childhood have fitted neatly within it. Her fingers have begun to rub the colour from the tiny red garment of the rider. Resting on the altar stone it could appear to be no more than an odd-shaped stone, with a dab of redness. 'Here is my offering to you,' she says.

※ ※ ※

The feast was spread in the shade of the fare nui, the great guest house of the district of Pare. At last a time of plenty had come again after the years of warring and restrictions. Ovens for pigs had been dug, fires had blazed all morning to heat the oven stones and the feast-day smoke had sent the signal far and wide. Today, for the first time, the newly tattooed girls would be allowed to taste the baked pork, normally forbidden to all but the highest born of women.

The breadfruit trees of Pare and Matavai had been plundered and the fruits roasted on the open flames until their coarse green rinds were charred black and the white flesh would melt in the mouth. Coconuts had been grated to extract the sweet milk, some for a dipping sauce, some to be mixed with plantain fruits and grated taro root and cooked with hot stones dropped into the sticky paste. Sprouting coconuts had been split open and the spongy navel of the developing roots, the uto, had been baked in the oven as a special delicacy.

Dishes and baskets had been woven from palm fronds, banana leaves had been spread, flowers strewn. Yet Mauatua's mother and Grandmother Tetua had quarrelled over this feast, a feast called by Tu to celebrate the tattooing of his young sister Auo. Auo had not only received her first tattoo, but she and her youngest brother had been in the fare ha'aporo, the fattening house, this season and were as sleek as porpoises.

'Why shouldn't Mauatua join her cousins' feast day?' asked Maoiti. 'Is she not good enough? Yes, she is of the same blood as them, and has not her grandfather Ti'ipari'i been Tu's advisor ever since old Tutaha died, and has his chiefdom not prospered under his guidance? All Tahiti should see that Mauatua is the equal of her well-born cousins, let them see my daughter sit side by side with her father's people.'

But Tetua had tried to persuade her otherwise. 'Are you not afraid to humiliate your daughter by elevating her beyond her status? Auo may be high ranked enough to sit upon her father's paepae and comb her hair, but Mauatua must learn the skills of a less-elevated destiny. Let her have her feast day at home among the local girls. You are too proud, Maoiti.'

'I am proud, ae,' agreed Maoiti, 'and if her father should be there with Mareiti and their children I want him to see her among her cousins and know she is as good as Mareiti's children and worthy of a high-ranked suitor when the time comes.'

'And what if she should be scorned for your attempts to raise her up? What attentions do her cousins pay her, what regard do they hold her in?'

'She is of the same blood, and it shall be as I wish for her,' Maoiti had declared.

And so it was that Mauatua and her cousin Auo came side by side to the feast, dressed in clean new cloth, their heads heavy with garlands, their new tattoos still smarting on their wrists. Yet Auo was rounder and fatter than Mauatua. Her skin was pale, for she had been kept in the fare ha'aporo for three weeks. Kept in the shade, not permitted to walk about, to play or dance, only to rest and sleep there, and eat specially prepared food – huge bowls of poi made from bananas and taro and coconut mixed with breadfruit; the freshly grated meat of several coconuts each day; bunches of finest fe'i baked in the oven to sweet yellow pulp. Auo was as soft as a pudding, as if she would melt, her breasts and belly creamy as banana flesh.

'What was it like in there,' Mauatua wanted to know.

'It was boring,' said Auo, 'and I was tired of eating, eating, eating. My arms and legs were twitching to dance, but they wrapped us so tightly that I could hardly even walk. All we could do in there was talk, when our mouths weren't full of food.'

Mauatua was glad that she had not been fattened, as her mother had wished, but she saw how her cousin's swelling breasts and padded hips were admired, and although Auo wore cloth no finer than her own, beaten almost transparent, the dyed and printed borders of Auo's were more elaborate, and the deep red patterns bespoke her belonging to a family of the maro ura – the red-feather insignia of the highest chiefdoms of Tahiti.

But she looked at the frizzy puff of curls around her cousin's shining face and remembered Grandmother Tetua's quiet words to her as they had arrived. 'All that frizzy hair they have only proves their descent from the Paumotuans. They may raise themselves up to the loftiest place and pray upon the highest marae in the land, but they are not true ari'i. Remember this, and look to your mother's blood for such nobility as courses in your veins, Mauatua.'

✹ ✹ ✹

'It is a strange gift that Mauatua offers to our ancestress,' said Tetua.

'Is it fitting?' asked Hinuia.

'It is a thing of the white man. Is that a fitting thing?'

Hinuia thought long before she answered, 'Who can say what our ancestress accepts as a fitting thing? Who can say what it is that the gods wish for us?' Then she added, 'But let us throw the first blood in the ocean.'

So the blood-scorched cloth was bundled tightly, bound with coconut fibre, and placed inside the clean chamber of a clam shell; and the clam shell was bound together round and around. In the early morning Hinuia paddled out beyond the reef and cast the clam shell towards the farthest horizon, making the right prayers as it vanished into the body of the sacred ocean.

✳ ✳ ✳

Mauatua

Three rainy seasons had passed now since a white man had stepped ashore at Matavai. That man was Tute himself, back in command of two ships which were journeying to a land far behind the setting and rising of the sun, a land the sun did not warm. On that journey he had taken with him Hitihiti, and on the second ship had travelled Mai, both young men from the sacred isle of Raiatea. Tute had brought Hitihiti back from those distant lands, but of Mai, and the second ship, no more had been seen. Although Tute gave his word that that other ship had returned to Peretane, with Mai aboard it, some believed that, like the priest Tupaia who had gone with Tute the first time, Mai would not return alive to Tahiti.

But Hitihiti, what stories and boasts he brought back with him from his travels on the white ship! He told of the land of Aotearoa where the people of Kupe the voyager had travelled many generations ago and now occupied two great islands. 'But the eating of human flesh is common among them,' he had recounted, and aue, we of Tahiti shuddered to think of this horrible practice. Then he had travelled even further to a place where the sun never left the sky, yet it was so cold that no plants or fruits could grow. 'That land was all white, white,

white,' he had said, and rocks of solid water floated in the ocean and the land was covered with a white substance which turned to water in the hand. To far Rapanui, the navel of the world, he had also travelled, and seen there enormous statues erected by the ancient ones with their eyes looking out to sea. All these tales and more he told.

Next had come two Popa'a priests who lived on the peninsula of Taiarapu with their servant. I never saw them, but it was said they quarrelled constantly. They were disliked, for they had taken stones from a marae to pave the floor of the house they built – so well they might live in fear with those sacred stones beneath their very feet and the wrath of the gods of that marae close upon them.

Their Popa'a servant, who was called Ma'imo, travelled around Tahiti alone and was popular everywhere. The ari'i would greet him as one of their own. He was invited to eat and sleep in the guest houses of the highest families and he learnt to understand and speak the Tahitian tongue.

When he passed through Matavai he was invited to eat with my uncle Tapuetefa. My cousin Tatahe and I were among the children who followed Ma'imo to the men's eating house. When we had become quite a crowd around and behind him, he turned and laughed and asked us all our names and then he repeated them to us, remembering every one correctly, from which we then made a game of exchanging our names to confuse him, telling him, 'No, *this* one is Tatahe, *that* one is Hiarahi, *there* is Mauatua,' and so forth until he threw up his hands in despair and we hardly knew ourselves who we were any more.

Crouched a little distance from the men as they sat eating, we were intrigued first by Ma'imo's curious way of speaking our language, then by his delicate, surreptitious manner of eating, then by the turns of the men's conversation as they discussed the similarities and differences between the women of Tahiti and the Popa'a women of Ma'imo's country.

At last Tapuetefa stood and gestured us to run away. 'Are you little rats that you sit watching us at our meal?' he cried. 'Show some respect for our guest now!' And indeed we were as little 'iore rats that scampered away into the undergrowth, only to creep back closer to the scene of the repast, whiskers quivering.

※ ※ ※

Long and deep were the discussions in the men's houses and the voices more numerous than the morning cockerels as the coming of the white men dawned. A small thing then, with wide-open eyes and ears, was this Mauatua.

In the fishermen's houses they praised the sharp iron nail which was swiftly bent upon a hot stone into the form of a hook. The ringing of that sound was new upon our ears and less often was heard the rasp of coral on bone, of bone on shell, as hooks were shaped and filed. 'It is good, the white man's nail, quick to bend in the fire. And do the fish caught upon it not taste as good as any other?'

And the tale of the first nail was told again.

'Blown from his course by a great storm was the chief Tepourai, cast upon the shore of an unknown place, an island far from the courses of navigation. His canoe was wrecked by the storm, and he said to his men that they would have to build a new canoe, or perish there in that place.'

'Hei, there were trees on that island, lucky for them.'

'And coconut fibre was there, to lash together the body of the new canoe. But what was missing, what tool had none brought with him to that place, what small point that bores the lashing holes? No awl of bone, no sharp splinter of leg bone had they to pierce those holes, aue!'

Here the listening child's eyes opened wide. Aue!

'The bone of a reef fish, will that pierce the hull of a canoe? The beak of a seagoing bird, will that bore a hole in timber?'

The child guessed that it would not.

'So someone must die, one of those brave and noble men must die to give the sacred bone of his leg to that necessary purpose.'

'And how shall that man be chosen, when all were equals and brothers to each other there?'

The child waited to know.

'Here is how. One marked stone was put into a coconut shell, with many others, the same size and shape. And each man put his hand into that coconut and drew a stone. Behold, the marked stone was drawn by the chief Tepourai! And so he must prepare to sacrifice his life. Aue! But wait, what thing was this lying near his feet upon the shore?'

'A nail!'

'A nail! Some white man's ship had foundered there and left no trace, but only this small length of iron, to save Tepourai's life.'

'It was a sign, a sign that the white man's iron is good for Tahiti.'

'It is a sign that the Maohi man is cleverer than the white man, ne?'

'How so?'

'The white man needs many nails to make his va'a. The Maohi man needs only one! Hei, it is good.'

At the chiefly houses the 'ava was passed solemnly from mouth to mouth. 'The priests say the diseases are the manifestations of the foreign spirits brought by the Popa'a, come to destroy the people of Tahiti so the white men can live here on the wealth of our land.'

'They have wealth of their own, lands of their own.'

'So what do they want then?'

'If it is our women, they shall take them, if it is our food, they shall eat it, for with their weapons we can deny them nothing.'

'They are unclean, their skins are unwashed, their teeth stink of rottenness. The spirits of disease cling to such people.'

'But our own people are clean, and they suffer worse from the new diseases than the Popa'a.'

'The spirits of disease are hungry when they arrive at Tahiti, those foreign spirits attach themselves to our people and we know no remedies to repel them, our own gods do not yet recognise them.'

'Even now the priests are making a sacrifice at the marae and asking our gods to fight those foreign spirits of disease.'

'What are they sacrificing for this?'

'It is a pig and a plantain tree, a man-long banana which lies in the stead of a human man.'

'What use is that? Only the white man's gods can cure the white man's diseases. The foreigner Ma'imo knows the medicine of his people. When the young chief of Taiarapu was dying of a fever brought by the foreign ship at Tautira, it was Ma'imo who cured him. He would not let Vehiatua go to bathe in the cooling water, he forced him to lie there panting and sweating, and he gave him medicine he had brought with him.'

'But did the priests there not sacrifice a man to the gods for restoration of his health? Who is to say then, whether it was Ma'imo's medicines or the priests which saved him?'

'Vehiatua was saved, but what of the others who have died of that sickness? Who will sacrifice a man for them?'

'The 'ava Peretane, the foreign drink, that is the medicine for me. It burns like a cleansing fire within. Our own 'ava is as water beside it. Pass me the cup.'

✸ ✸ ✸

Mauatua

At the women's house we were puzzled by the itchy red bumps that were appearing on our bodies during the night, with an itch and suppuration unlike the bite of any fly or mosquito we knew. 'It is some Popa'a thing, a foreign creature come to plague us.'

'But what creature is it, where does it live, silent and unseen?'

'Here,' said Hinuia, and she squatted down by a dog that was lying nearby. With her hands she parted the hair on its belly. The dog, which was an ugly one much petted by my grandmother, looked up curiously for a moment then dropped its head back to the earth and rolled further onto its back. 'It is the same thing which is making the dogs scratch,' and she showed us the marks on the dog's belly, among the knobbled teats there. There crawled a black creature shiny as a tiny seed. 'A louse!'

'A louse, but like no louse of Tahiti. Look, it jumps,' and sure enough when she tried to catch it between her fingers it jumped, and was gone.

'A foreign louse, aue.'

'From the Peretane dogs that came here with Tute. They have jumped upon our dogs.'

Some of the women began looking in the children's hair for that Peretane louse. 'We have never seen it on our bodies or our heads,' they said to each other.

'It multiplies here,' explained Hinuia, and she patted the earth. 'Under our floor mats, in the soft grasses of our beds it lies waiting for us to sleep.'

How many were the silent powers of the Popa'a man to change our lives! The thoughts of the women were as one.

'This is why the Popa'a prefer to sleep off the ground,' exclaimed one. And as one they realised what that meant, but none spoke this thing. In Tahiti we had always slept on the earth. That was the way of our people.

But even the dogs were changing. The tall thin dogs which had come ashore from Tute's first ship had liked to run, racing each other like children, and now at Matavai were born certain tall, thin dogs that liked to run. Nobody had yet eaten one of those foreign dogs, they had a different spirit from Tahitian dogs. They played while their brothers slept, they ran where their brothers ambled, and they barked as if to speak while their brothers let out at most a sleepy growl. At night by moonlight those dogs called to each other along the shore and they woke the cockerels which crowed all night long for the dawn of the white man.

Year of Our Lord 1831

At dawn the *Lucy Anne*'s sails were set for the first hint of breeze.

Some of the young ones had stayed awake all night on deck, waiting to sight the land that the grandmothers remembered.

Now that land was before them. Lost in the breath of its gods, which cloaked the high mountains from peak to shore and lapped across the oiled water with tongues of a thousand fragrances.

'Smell it Margaret! Tahiti, Tahitinui Mare'area! Breathe deep.'

You will know the smell of our ancestors' bones.
The colour of our blood, salt of our lagoon.
The flowers that open at dawn for us.
The odour of death.

An eerie silence on that rich breath. No early beaters at the cloth boards, no fishermen at the reef to raise the welcome. No paddlers racing out to hail the ship.

The woman held her granddaughter close.

Lucy Anne slid along on the morning wind. The sun rose behind them and the land was inflamed in a radiant haze. The young ones stood silent until some of the girls went on their knees and Mr Nobbs began prayers.

Her lips refused the sticky English words. The old Maohi language welled up like a spring in her throat and began to run like a stream into dry parts. Grief and joy pounded in her breast. Only the dignity of age prevented her from leaping out to swim. Soon they would hear the drums, surely, to welcome them home.

They saw the land emerging slowly from the withdrawn breath, the narrow beach, the knotted fringe of palm and ironwood, the houses along the shores of Taiarapu and of Papara and Paea slipping by. Now, instead of drums, a bell rang out from the land. Its iron voice cleared the last shreds of golden haze from the treetops and they could see the people on the shore, moving among the trees, all going in one direction. 'Hallelujah!' cried Mr Nobbs. 'We are in a Christian place.'

The Tattooed Hand

A girl with the first tattoos on her wrists and hands was becoming a woman. No longer allowed to run naked to the bathing pool in the morning, she folded and knotted her skirt with care. Together the women plunged into the dark, pulling body of the pool, which seized upon their awakening skin, causing the day's first cries of delight.

Now the pigeons flew up noisily from the trees. What fruit would be ripe today?

Mauatua kept with her friends whose tattooing was also begun. They compared the work of the tattooists, admiring the delicate patterns of spirals and fronds encircling their wrists, twining down their hands, the vines and stars and circlets which announced their family, tribe, birthplace and status. Courage and beauty were the standards. The hours of pain were worth this.

It was no longer the world of childhood. In their dancing their hands were like paired birds, attracting all eyes. Over the cloth-beating boards the tattooed hands flashed new patterns as they beat the old rhythm. In weaving, the tattooed fingers directed the pandanus ribbons into more complex designs and followed them to the end. How could a woman grow if her hands were not tattooed? That woman would be incomplete.

After noon, while their elders rested in the shade, they would walk together in sinuous lines along the shore. They shredded pandanus leaves as they walked, weaving them into small balls which they tossed in the air, or to each other, and at boys whose attention they sought but who would find it difficult to identify which girl had thrown the inviting missile.

At the favourite groves they gathered a mat full of flowers and leaves and sat to garland making under the trees. Among the blossoms and fronds the tattooed hands flitted like butterflies, like creatures patterned to hide among foliage. Swiftly the leaves were twined and bound and the ornaments set admiringly upon their hair.

Such beauty was made for dancing, for love! Their feet began to seek the day's rhythms and their songs would attract boys whose hands burned to strike the sharkskin bellies of their pahu to raise Tane, the god of pleasure. For Tane's pleasure the girls' pareu would slip at last to their hips, caught there by swaying belts and sashes. The command of the drums and the confidence of the new tattoos set their hands flying free in newly acquired gestures, sending new messages. The drums beat harder, faster, the tattooed hands began inventing and inviting. Aue, they said things a girl would not whisper! She must stop and turn to her friends for the cover of their laughter.

In the evening, after small children had gone to their sleeping mats, the games were conducted by moonlight and the flare of spear fishers' torches reflected in the lagoon. Shrieks and laughter soon gave way to the lulling of the night insects and the lap of the quiet waters.

Maoiti was gone to live along the coast with her new husband, but when she visited her family at Matavai she still scolded Tetua. 'Mauatua spends all her days with the common girls – what will that lead to? Are the sons of fishermen and canoe builders suitable mates for my daughter?'

'She is a good girl, she comes when she is called.'

'All the more will some son of a taro planter want her. Let her go to Tu's household at Pare and keep company with her cousins. You should go too, and join your husband there in Tu's household. What is the use of staying here at Matavai? Our family is nothing any more, only our connections with Tu's family raise us above the ordinary people. My father is wise to attach himself to the fortunes of Pare, for that is the future of our people. Why stay here grieving for Tautoia. You know he will never return?'

'Your father wants to keep peace among the tribes, thus he proffers his wisdom and knowledge to the young chief. Myself, I have no desire to live among the frizzy hairs. Our marae is here, it is the place of my children's birth. Should I abandon it now? Someone must stay to serve our gods or they too will abandon us.'

'Then send Mauatua at least.'

'Mauatua will be safer here with me, I keep her close by. She has no inclination to run to the wrong man, this I sense in her, unlike her mother.'

⁂

Mauatua opened her eyes to the light that came sliding and stretching in between the bamboo walls. Close to her ear a mother hen and peeping chicks were scratching and fussing. From the paepae Tetua was calling her to wake.

In the early sun her grandmother sat waiting, her bad leg stretched out in front of her, her stick in her lap.

'Today we go to the bathing pool together,' she said as Mauatua came out yawning. 'Your young arm will be better than any stick to lean upon.'

The path to the pool was long for the old woman, and even longer for Mauatua that morning. Her bare feet knew it well, its tripping rootlets, its hanging vines, its slippery corners. The young trees alongside it had grown with her, their leaves wove the familiar patterns of morning. Tetua too had walked that path many times, but now one of her legs was swelling with the fe'e fe'e sickness, kept carefully concealed by long skirts of barkcloth.

By the time they reached the pool the other girls were already wringing out their hair on the bank. 'Ehi, Mauatua!' they cried. 'Where were you? We thought you had the fever!'

'Today I am accompanying my grandmother. What fever?'

'The fever of love!' Their laughter sprang as if from one source, like flowers of one tree.

'Foolish girls,' replied Tetua. 'Be careful lest that fever strike you for it has no cure.'

'Only one!' retorted the first speaker, and the laughter blossomed again.

'Then cure and disease are the same thing,' said Tetua. 'How wise you are for girls with their first tattoos! Run to your chores now and be careful of the temptations of Tane.'

She unwrapped her long skirts and, careful of her footing, entered the shallow part of the pool. 'Give me your hand, e hine,' she said to Mauatua. They waded together up to their waists. There was a rock under the surface which Tetua liked to sit on.

Mauatua's friends were already planning their afternoon's fun as they dressed and combed. She dived deep so not to hear them, just hear instead the voice of the water. She held her breath as long as she could, longer, longer, until she felt the unbearable desire to breathe.

Tetua sat on her rock, cleaning her hair with the foamy juice of ginger stems picked along the path. The priestess Hinuia had arrived at the pool with Mauatua's aunt Nari'i. The small children ran to the water naked, the teu teu women unfolding their garments from their strong bellies. Mauatua's oldest cousin, Tetuaraenui, tall and graceful, was ready to leap from the overhanging rock.

She had been asked for, Tetuaraenui, as a second wife for nobody less than high chiefess Purea's brother Auri. It seemed to please everybody but Tetuaraenui herself, for Auri had already a slackening in his belly and grizzled streaks in his topknot, and she was accustomed to the young men of Matavai for her dancing partners. To Auri she would be bound though, for it was agreeable to both families that she should be the ornament of his marae at Faa'a.

Mauatua could see that her cousin's displeasure was just a pretence, hiding the pride of her new prestige. 'How many babies will you have with that old man?' she teased her, splashing.

'Hei, be careful little sister, or Tuna the eel will have you for himself,' she replied and dived so swiftly beneath the surface that Mauatua struck out in fright. Something slid against her leg – the hand of Tetuaraenui, or was it Tuna himself, uncoiling from his underwater cavern to seek her as he had sought the beautiful maiden Hina, to be his wife? Her heart beat wildly as she swam for the shallows.

When she gained her footing by her grandmother's side, the old one said to her, 'E hine, why are you afraid of Tuna? Tuna sought Hina in love. For love of Hina, Tuna sacrificed himself, and remember what grew from his sacrifice. The ni'au is Tuna's gift to us. Remember whose face you see on your drinking nut.'

But although Mauatua had seen Tuna's round eyes on every coconut and supped sweet water from his mouth every day, still she was afraid of his brother eels.

'You will come to love him,' Tetua assured her, 'Ae, love him as Hina did, even though she too was afraid at first.' She scooped up a floating purau flower. 'Look at this flower,' she said, 'Tell me what is in the centre there.'

It was freshly fallen. Yellow petals lapped its deep red mouth, red tipped its seeking yellow tongue. Mauatua knew what connection to make. 'It is the ure of the purau,' she replied.

'The ure of the purau, ae, that is at the centre, always at the centre, for it is the part of the flower which is ever giving life. From the purau flower, the purau tree, from the bodies of men and women, the generations to come. From the centre of beauty springs love – that is the lesson of the purau flower.'

She tossed the blossom back into the stream, to follow its course to the salt water.

From the sandy groves of breadfruit and palm and pandanus along the shore rose the first ringing rhythms of the barkcloth pounding. Fresh from bathing and prayers the women came to take their places at the boards.

Mauatua had her place there, close to her grandmother, where she had sat since babyhood, first watching, then taking a mallet herself, making her first strikes on the wet edge of the work, learning how to beat the pulpy material evenly, stretch it finely, thin it to a moist skin which would dry to stiff tissue able to be softened, cut, patterned, dyed.

The aute saplings had been brought from the plantations by the men and the bark had been slit lengthwise, carefully peeled, and soaked. Women sat half submerged, working the wet layers with sharpened shells, scraping the thick outer away from the soft inner tissue. Yesterday's strips, laid out to dry on carpets of banana leaves, were carefully transferred to the pounding board, where they were soaked again, and subjected to the binding forces of the toa wood beaters.

It was marriage cloth for Tetuaraenui they were beating that day, fine wide cloth for the exchange of gifts, long sheets that took all the saplings of an entire plantation, days of peeling, stripping, soaking, scraping, layers lapped and beaten across the boards. It was marriage that Aunt Nari'i raised her voice to sing of, spreading the finished cloth before the eyes of Auri's people with her verses. Fine cloth from the plantations of Mahina, beaten by the sisters and aunts of Tetuaraenui by the flowing waters of Tuauru. The mallets flew, melding fibre to fibre, binding the sinews of the aute into a gift that, carefully rolled and scented with sweet oils, would bring them honour when it was presented on the marriage day.

The tattooed wrists kept a steady rhythm. The music of cloth beating rose like smoke above the trees, drifted out across the wide bay, and was heard by fishermen returning with the night's catch and by travellers arriving on their canoes.

It was heard by the messenger from Pare, carrying news that had come from Papara. Swiftly he brought his canoe around the point of Tahara'a and saw ahead the dark crescent of Matavai, its long hook of black sand with wind-tossed palm heads lifted high above the shaggy ironwoods along the shore. Above the thick, fruiting groves and the plumes of cookhouse smoke, his eye rose up to greet the cloud-tended heights of mighty Orohena, whose peak was lost in the realm of the gods.

'What is the news?' called a fisherman as he pulled close by, his shimmering catch still flickering at his feet.

But the messenger had been instructed to take the news only to the household of the chiefess Tetua, and he paddled on silently, with the sound of cloth beating for his guide, the sound of cloth being beaten for the marriage of Tetuaraenui of Matavai, to Auri of Faa'a.

It was Maunu who finally brought the news to the cloth-beating place. He came quietly, like a timid girl, as was his way sometimes, and dropped on his knees before Tetua Avari'i. 'There is news,' he said, and at once the music of work ceased.

'What news is there?' asked Tetua.

'There is news that I have been asked to bear to you, from the Pare messenger who brought it from a messenger of Papara.'

'There cannot be war now, what news is this?'

Maunu bent his head lower, he spoke to the ground, his shoulders trembled and his voice was neither woman's nor man's. 'The death bird was heard in Papara last night near the house of Purea, and when her women went to her in the morning it was only her body that lay rolled in her mats. This is the news I was asked to bring to you.'

Tetua dropped her mallet. 'Aue, no more shall we beat this cloth!' she cried. 'A marriage shadowed by death! Call Hinuia to me, Maunu.'

It was Mauatua who crept close to cover her grandmother's grief. She knew it was less for Purea – whose power had waned as Tu's had increased and who had become an old woman among old women, deserted in the valley of her grand aspirations – than for Tetuaraenui, whose marriage was now cast in the inauspicious shadow of this death.

And for her grandmother's terrible certainty that it was the bones of her warrior son Tautoia, cursed on the enemy marae, which were being used to bring misfortune upon her family.

Maeva!
1774

The altar under the miro trees at the family marae was seldom visited anymore by Tetua Avari'i. Hinuia the priestess went alone there, passing hours in prayers and chants, in a cloud of smouldering sandalwood.

Tetua instead stayed on her mats in the fare shade, leaving only to bathe, and accompanied only by her granddaughter. The pain and swelling of her leg she mentioned to no one except Hinuia and Mauatua, and she kept herself covered with long lengths of cloth, letting none see the shame of affliction.

She spoke no more of her lost son Tautoia and made no enquiries into the affairs of the district, or of Tu's household at Pare. She no longer beat cloth or joined the singing by torchlight after dark, though she would send Mauatua to these activities.

Hinuia massaged the swelling leg, used poultices steeped in tamanu oil, and medicines distilled from the nono fruit, but the fe'e was a sickness without cure, and Tetua's was a grief without respite, although she never mentioned the curse upon her family to Mauatua. When her husband Ti'ipari'i died suddenly at Pare, still in the service of Tu, Tetua ignored the formalities left the priests at the high marae to decide upon the matters of mourning.

Ti'ipari'i's anointed remains were still lying upon the bier in the sacred grove on the day that Tute returned.

The word had been circulating for some days already that Tute was back, that he was at Taiarapu, befriending the old enemy Vehiatua, that Mai had returned with him, and his ship was loaded with more strange animals. Anxious in case Vehiatua should claim all the glory of hosting the great white chief, the people searched the horizon daily, looking for the sail that would announce his return to Matavai.

Mauatua was fanning her grandmother to the soft drone of Hinuia's chanting when they heard the shouting begin. 'Sails, white sails! It's Tute! Heiii, Tute's coming!'

The fan fell still in Mauatua's hand and Hinuia's chant trailed away. The girl's legs made to leap up and run but the looks of her elders kept her seated. Joy and anticipation leapt up in her belly. Long stillness had been the mood, like a day without wind or sun, but now the shade of unspoken grieving lifted and melted like morning cloud. As the drums began to call she looked with a silent plea from the eyes of Tetua to those of Hinuia.

'You must go,' said the priestess.

She sprang to her feet, dropping the fan.

'But you will not go aboard the ship, e hine. Do not let it come to my ears that you have swum out to it. Remain upon the shore, e hine. Keep away from the foreign men. There should be no stain of Popa'a disease upon your blood, remember your noble ancestresses and hold fast to their purity. Now go!'

Stopping only long enough to pluck two red fau blossoms for her hair, Mauatua joined the crowds that hurried shoreward. Around the houses the morning's work lay abandoned. Coconuts half grated, chickens half plucked. Weaving tossed aside, tools scattered. Even the sleeping dogs looked up and raised their ears at the unwonted commotion, and two of the tall, thin foreign dogs which Tute had left last time came bounding to join the throng, yapping and springing as if they could smell their Popa'a cousins coming across the water.

At the water's edge the people were gathering. Already one big drum was calling for a partner, striking loud, trembling notes that vibrated though the crowd. People were arriving with arms full of plants to weave garlands, the priests had found time to fasten on their tallest headdresses and finest belts as they hastened from the marae, babies were carried at their mothers' breasts. Another drum joined the first, setting up a double rhythm which fanned the fire of excitement.

Along the beach canoes were being pushed out now, and anyone whose relative or friend owned one was seeking a place, even clinging to the outriggers. Some bold swimmers, young men accustomed to the depths beyond the reefs, were stroking out into the bay. The drums set Mauatua's body alight. Her eyes were fixed on that trembling imminence across the water.

Soon they saw Tu's great double canoe, the *Rainbow*, with many paddles flying in harmony, round the head of Tahara'a, skimming across the water from the Bay of Pare. 'Tu hastens to meet the white men, whilst at Matavai we no longer have a royal canoe to greet our guests,' rose the lament, for the great canoe of Matavai had been destroyed in the wars against Vehiatua and no new one built. But that regret was soon forgotten again in the approaching excitement.

The long-haired dogs leapt and bounded among the people on the sand, running in and out of the water, barking loudly, and someone called out, 'Listen! The dogs on the white ship are calling to their cousins of Tahiti!' Everyone listened for the voices of those foreign dogs arriving across the water, even before the men were visible on the decks, and this was a new wonderment.

Soon the men could be seen climbing up the tall masts, rolling up the sails and fastening them as if to the branches, whose many limbs were like a tall forest afloat, with the ropes hanging down like vines. At the rear of the ship the red flag of Peretane was reflected in the lagoon, and a man in the big hat of a Peretane chief appeared at the prow. The one with the sharpest eyes saw first, but soon the word was passing along: 'Tute!'

The word becoming cry, the cry becoming song – 'Tute, Tute, it is Tute!' the drum beat underlining these words. 'Haere mai, o Tute no Peretane, haere mai a Tahitinui Mare'area! Welcome to our land once more, may the rain of Tahiti fall softly upon your shoulders, may the food of Tahiti give you strength. Welcome, welcome, return to our land!'

The girls were flinging off their pareu and plunging into the sea, keeping their garlanded heads above the water. 'Peretane! Peretane!' was the call.

'Mauatua, come with us!'

But she did not run to join them. She remembered the noble blood of her ancestresses.

Now they could see the cannons being primed on the ship. Those who knew put their hands to their ears, and those who did not know cried 'Aue!' and 'Hei!' as the lightning flowers exploded from the cannons' black mouths and the sound of thunder filled the valleys up to the peaks, and the mountain gods gave the answering drum roll.

The best dancers were gathering, pressing forward with songs and steps of welcome ready, and other women pushed in beside them, their hands beginning to fly to express their joy. Haere mai Tute!

They watched the great anchor of metal falling swiftly on its metal rope into the bay of Matavai, and one voice announced, 'Here is the anchoring place of white ships, only here at Matavai is the water deep enough and the harbour sheltered enough for the Popa'a vessels. Let Matavai welcome Tute!'

But it was the double canoe *Rainbow*, with Tu of Pare in command and feathered pennants flying, which hovered under the tall prow of the foreign ship, and it was the high priest of Pare calling out the greetings to Tute.

A boat was lowered and Tute – in his two-legged garment, his glittering hat and coat – climbed down into it, while the people in the canoes and the girls in the water threw flowers and held up choicest fruits, calling to the white men on board who were holding their arms out to welcome those girls and help them climb up.

The press upon the shore was tight now and Tapuetefa's men pushed the people back to make a space on the sand, a space for Tute to approach the land. Mauatua pushed closer to her uncle Tapuetefa, chief of Matavai, who waited dressed in his finest robes with a gorget of feathers and pearl shell shining on his breast.

Someone had identified a man with Tute in the small boat, a tall man dressed in foreign clothing, a three-cornered hat pressed down on his curling black locks. 'It is Mai! Mai has returned to Tahiti.'

'Aue, he will be full of tales and racked with pride, that stripling, for being the only one who has seen Peretane,' said another.

'Look at him, dressed like a Peretane chief, he who was but a priest's apprentice, failed at his calling.'

Yet a thousand eyes scanned his amazing costume.

The foremost dancers now came to the front, their performance coming to a final crescendo in time with the drumming. *Rainbow*, carrying Tu, was beached first, and he came ashore. What was Tu wearing! A splendid coat of thick foreign cloth, a new gift from Tute, closed from his chin to his knees, and stiff with metal fastenings and ornaments. In admiration they made space now for him, the great friend of Tute, which made him the most powerful man on Tahiti at this moment. Shoulders and breasts were respectfully bared, murmurs of awed approval ran through the crowd.

Now Tute's men pulled the small boat up the sand. Profound silence fell as Tute stepped onto the land, accompanied by Mai, done up from head to toe in tight foreign clothing.

It was Tu who claimed the honour of the welcoming ceremony, who made the long speech with its many references to the glories and riches of Tahiti. It was Tu who was greeted first in reply. Only then could Tapuetefa step forward to extend his own welcome, which should have been his honour by right, for it was his territory that Tute had landed at.

Mauatua's eye took in the foreign chief with all the hunger of one who loves. His nose was sharper and harder edged than any Tahitian nose, this she had remembered. He had taken off his big hat and it dangled from one hand, his elaborately curled hair did not move in the breeze but remained stiff around his pale face. He spoke slow, careful words of Tahitian, inclining his head respectfully to each of the ra'atira and priests.

When he had greeted all the high-ranking men his eye turned upon the crowd and glanced from face to face as if seeking. It fastened upon Mauatua and he moved towards her. His smile was one of recognition. 'It is Mauatua,' he greeted her.

Swiftly now, the chief Tu stepped up and pulled her forward, saying, 'My cousin Mauatua – has she not grown since last you saw her, o Tute? Gladly will she be yours. She is of noble birth, an ornament to her family here at Matavai. Gladly will she be hostess to such a great chief from across the ocean, a man hungry for the delights of our land ...'

But Tute held up his hand to stay this invitation, and he addressed only Mauatua when he spoke. 'Ah Mauatua, you are grown like a flower of your people,' he said kindly, and in his eyes she recognised something, something she knew from watching her grandmother. The silent shadows of grief.

So when he said to her, 'My own daughter, she is this tall now,' indicating a girl about the same size as herself, she knew that the daughter he spoke of was no longer in the world of light, but gone, gone where Popa'a children go to after their deaths.

Now she must reply, and she could not be seen to struggle. Words must not fail her, but leap forward as gracefully as a dancer between them. 'Welcome o Tute!' she began, and then the words sprang lightly to her tongue. 'Welcome to Matavai! O Tute, if your daughter were here in Tahitinui she would be as a sister to me. Our land, our river, our mountain peaks would be hers, and she would be as blood of our own blood, the daughter of Tute. Welcome!'

She took the red fau bloom from above one ear and reached up to fix it behind his, and then the people pressed forward without restraint, and so many wreaths and garlands were thrown upon him that soon he was up to his ears in flowers and leaves and his brow was overhung with every sweet blossom of the land. 'Maeva, maeva, maeva!' they called, and Mauatua, following his every move and look, saw tears brimming in his narrow eyes.

'Aroha, arohanui!' she cried. 'Great love have we for you, o Tute!'

※ ※ ※

From the coconut palms on the waterline to the plantains of the highest mountain slopes, soon all kinds of fruits were being stripped from the trees and carried to the cookhouses, or out to the ship to trade. Pigs were driven in from every distant quarter and squeals of slaughter rent the air. Although it was not the season of the great ocean fish, the smaller fishes of the lagoon were chased into nets to fill the ovens.

Tu presided over the festivities at Matavai and at Pare, and all the nobles and chiefs of the two districts, and all their families came to eat and mingle and to see the white men. Tu came in person, with two of his attendants, to invite me to the heiva. Grandmother Tetua received him on her mats in the shade. She was sitting up, suffering the pressure on her leg which caused her pain, but she had not bared her shoulders as a sign of deference to him, an omission which could have offended.

'Chiefess,' began one ra'atira, speaking on Tu's behalf, but he did not berate her for any discourtesy. Instead he gave her all the many titles and distinctions of rank which belonged to her family. 'It is right for you to be proud, a woman of your status. Your husband was a man of honour and duty, your son died as a warrior of the highest rank. Let me tell you that now your granddaughter Mauatua has been favoured by Tute.'

'How so?' she asked, although she had already heard it all from my own mouth.

'She was chosen by him, and she did honour to both our families in her reply. It would be fitting for her to be at the guest house for all the festivities.'

Only now did Tetua lower her robes and reveal the shrunken shoulders and fallen breasts of her old age, a sign of capitulation at long last to a power she had disclaimed for all the time of my childhood.

'She may come,' she replied, 'But she should have pride of place, for she represents both our families.'

'Nothing less.'

'And our priestess, Hinuia, must accompany her. Mauatua has come to womanhood and will have high-ranking suitors soon. She should not be polluted by the foreigners. I fear they bring diseases and bad spirits among us.'

'She shall be protected as my own sister. But will you not accompany Mauatua yourself Tetua Avari'i?'

'Grief does not permit it,' she replied. 'Would it be right for an old woman to be feasting and revelling with foreign guests while her husband's corpse still lies in the ghost house? No, Tu, your family has arranged all this hospitality, even though my son Tapuetefa stands as chief of this district. We alone could not provide lavish entertainment, alas. Make free with our land, and let our families be at peace with each other, and our people be as one, so we may all have benefit of the foreigners' gifts without quarrel.'

✖ ✖ ✖

Mauatua

So I came to be at the great guest house of Pare, on soft mats next to my important cousins, plump Auo of the frizzy hair and Vaetua, now a handsome youth with an indolent, careless gaze. Tu himself was slick with perfumed oils and dressed in arresting combinations of Tahitian and foreign garments, bristling with feathers and braid and boar's tusks.

After the feasts, there was oratory and music, and the nights did not end until the last dancers fell exhausted. Until the reed torches were burnt to ash, and people slept where they lay, men and women coupled in the darkness and the early cockerels crowed. Night after night it was so.

The Englishmen went back to their ship to sleep, or to the houses of white cloth they had erected on the sandspit of Matavai, and the girls crept away with them. Hinuia would reach out for me, and we would relish the comfort of the fine mats beneath us as we lay down to rest. Hinuia's cloak enfolded me and in the darkness the soft roar of surf on the reef became one with the people's breathing, the gently rolling swell of sleep, the mingled moans of couples. Cradled against Hinuia's protecting flanks, a sweet lull of happiness poured over me, but the thrill of anticipation kept my blood so alive that I could hardly sleep. On those nights was conceived the new Tahiti. The life of the white men had entered us and we embraced it in careless ecstasy. I had no fear, then.

Mai

Mauatua

For the fullness of one moon and more the glorious ship lay in Matavai Bay, and there the people of Tahiti came to see the white men.

The shores were a constant throng of activity. To be among the white men, that was everyone's desire; to go on board the ship and see and touch, to get some new toy or tool. Everyone wanted to be bond friend, taio, of a sailor, to go on board. For girls it was easy, night and day they were climbing up and down the sides, and they vied with one another for the most gifts. Necklaces and fans, mirrors and combs, were easy to get. They passed quickly from hand to hand, swopped and exchanged, borrowed and begged. A roll of foreign cloth or a metal blade required more attentive dedication, even tricks. Hiro, the god of thieves, was much in favour. The men, disadvantaged in this exchange, begged their sisters and wives to get for them the things they desired and could not acquire for themselves.

Every day there were new entertainments. People flocked to see the animals the ship had brought. There were all sorts of waddling birds, including one with a long tail that opened like a fan, but the children ran after it for its feathers. There were four-footed animals, some with tusks upon their heads, dropping trails of tiny dung balls everywhere they walked, with voices we had never heard before, seeming to speak the Popa'a language themselves, talkative, noisy animals. Everyone was amazed and astonished – such creatures could not even have been concocted by magicians. Nobody understood what they were for. Tute was purported to have said that you could drink their milk, but nobody could believe this. 'It surely cannot be fit for people to drink the milk of animals,' it was declared.

Tute also said that the hair of the frizzy ones could be made into cloth, such as his clothes were made of, but it seemed an unimaginable task.

There was one kind of animal, however, that everybody admired. They were a pair, male and female, and as they stepped from the boat onto the sand, rolling their big eyes and tossing up their heads, I recognised the same animal shown on the medicine container I had offered to the ancestor goddess after my first tattooing. It was the va'a with white sails I had asked for, complete with the sacred animals of the Popa'a! I went to the marae and bowed down before her that day, in recognition of her arrangements. Yet I told no one, not even Hinuia.

They were powerful, those animals, sacred. They had strong necks crested with fine, flowing hair like a woman's, and a tail the same. They walked on tall, sinewy legs, and they allowed a man to ride on their backs.

When the white men mounted them and commanded them to run by a strap around the animal's head, then we had a sense of their difference from us, we were awed. They were masters of the creature. They looked down us from up there, running faster than a man, with their feet above the earth. When Mai tried to ride on one, it flung him from its back. We laughed at him because he prided himself so much in his foreign acquisitions, but the horse was not fooled by him. The horse knew Mai was not one of its masters.

'This is not a good horse,' he explained. 'In England I rode many horses, the chiefs and nobles all ride, and the noblewomen are pulled behind the horses in rolling canoes.'

Rolling canoes! We were incredulous. But among the things he had brought from England was a toy in two parts, a horse made of wood which attached to a rolling canoe fashioned in iron. It passed from hand to hand, children attached a cord to it and pulled it along the ground. Soon they were imitating the sound of horses as they ran.

'Peretane is a very large island,' Mai told us. 'They have built paths across the whole land for the canoes to roll on. It would take many days to travel from one end to the other.'

How many tales Mai had to tell. When small children pulled at his curious clothes and women wanted to try them on, he told of the terrible coldness in that country where such thick clothing must be worn night and day, even garments to cover his feet and his hands, made from the skins of the foreign animals. 'So cold the people make fires inside their houses, and the houses have solid walls built of stones, many rooms inside, and even rooms built on top of rooms, one above the other. Some rooms even below the ground. And so cold is it that they sleep on beds filled with feathers and have thick mats upon their floors made from the hair of animals, dyed in many colours ...' Many people did not care to believe him of course. They said to one another that houses could not be built of stone, they would be too dark, and rooms could not be built on top of each other, for it would offend all decency for one person to walk above the head of another, and that a fire in a house would cause too much smoke. They took the stories away and passed them from mouth to mouth, and the details became more and more remarkable, until the foreigners were sleeping on the roofs of their houses like chickens, with coloured feathers to keep them from the cold. Soon the children had invented songs about Mai's amazing adventures, illustrated with mimicry. They tied their feet up in pandanus leaves to imitate his shod step, they raised and lowered banana-leaf hats and kissed one another's hands.

The girls teased him constantly. 'Mai, Mai!' they called, rolling their eyes. 'Can you do it the Peretane way? Are the

Peretane women prettier than us? You should have brought one to Tahiti!'

But Mai was pleased with himself, he shook back his long curls. 'The gentlewomen were generous to me,' he assured them, 'and far too well bred to bring among hoydens like you.'

Instead of a foreign woman he had brought with him two companions from Aotearoa. One was the son of a chief of Aotearoa, and he was a guest in my uncle Tapuetefa's household. Toa was his servant, and shared the quarters of Tapuetefa's servants, but he went from place to place as freely as a bird, ignoring boundaries and tapu as if he were himself a chief of Tahiti. He was about the same age as myself, that Toa, and he wished to make love with me. He would wait secretly near our house. He followed me, pressing small gifts on me, once an ornament of bone he had carved himself, feathers of sea birds he had collected during his passage on the ship, and a red one he had got, he said, at the islands of Tonga. At night I heard him blowing on a nose flute he always carried, which whispered to me on my pillow, small songs easily understood.

He spoke like us, yet not. The women and girls made fun of him as they did of Mai, and laughed at his affection for me, but he didn't care. 'Toa, Toa, ma'a ta'ata o Aotearoa! Man-eater!' they teased him, biting on their forearms to show their meaning. But he was not put out by their insults. He began searching his head as if for a louse, and mimed the eating of it. 'Kaikutu no Tahiti! Louse eaters!' he responded.

'Why not?' he would ask me when I hesitated to go away with him alone among the trees. 'We are not brother and sister.'

'It would not be proper. I am waiting for chiefly suitors,' I replied.

'I am chief in my own country,' he would lie. 'Much land, great forests, deep bays. Come with me and I will show you.'

'How will we go there?'

'We go on Tute's ship, first to Peretane with him.'

This game appealed to me. 'What will we do there?' I asked.

'We will visit all the chiefs of that land and the king will give us gifts to bring back. Horses, weapons, iron tools ...'

'Will we wear English clothes?'

'Hats, shoes, coats with buttons, we will be stiff with clothes.'

'And will you eat any Englishmen?' I couldn't resist asking him.

His anger flared up. 'You too mock the ways of my people! Louse eaters,' he said. Then he added, 'It was another tribe who ate the ten Englishmen. Toa eats no man flesh.'

'Ten!'

'It was a big meal.' He laughed and rubbed his belly. 'Then we will visit all my friends on all the islands we visited on Tute's ship,' he went on. He named them all, friends and islands. 'Everywhere they will welcome us, Toa and Mauatua.'

'But what if we want to stay in Peretane?'

'We stay, we go, we are travellers under the wind. Mai says there are hundreds of ships even bigger than Tute's in Peretane, and many other lands to visit.'

Now we were among the trees, away from watching eyes. Toa put his arms around me, and his hands were no more afraid to roam than he was.

'Kiss me in the Peretane way,' I asked him.

'The Peretane way?'

'Yes. Mouth to mouth.'

He did not hesitate. We pressed our mouths together, awkwardly, not knowing how it is done. Our lips slithered and tangled, met and unmet. Our tongues darted to taste, and retreated, like two eels in a cave. I closed my eyes and imagined I was kissing a handsome Englishman, but it was no good.

He wiped his lips with his hand. 'Urgh, like two sea slugs together,' he said. 'The Maohi way is better.' His fingers began to explore again and his eyes darkened with desire. His breath was on my cheek, soon the ure of this man-eating servant boy would be pressing into me, this I knew.

'I hear my grandmother calling me!' I cried, and I leapt up and ran away before he could stop me. For the journeys of Toa were not what I was waiting for.

His red feather I took to our marae and slipped it under the stones there, in the sacred place.

Red feathers were among the things in abundance on that ship. Such feathers had always been sacred to our people – they represented the gods. They could usually only be got with great danger from the tails of tropic birds nesting in the cliff faces of Taiarapu, or traded in dangerous voyages to distant islands where red-feathered birds lived in the forests. They were the ornament of the highest chiefs and priests, and necessary in the rituals on the marae. Yet the white men had arrived with bags stuffed full of them, and Mai, too, distributed them generously, until commoners were wearing red feathers in their hair and the priests were clamouring for prohibitions.

Hidden in his English clothes Mai carried another kind of mystery, a handful of small metal discs which rang together sweetly. He would bring them out on his palm. 'With these, I can have anything there in England,' he said, boastfully we thought. 'If I want new clothes I give some of these to a man who makes clothes, and he makes them. If I am hungry, I give some to a man who has food and he will give me that food which I need.'

We did not understand. Did food not grow in Peretane for whosoever was hungry? What were the metal discs for, and who made them, and how did a person get them? It was too much of a mystery for us and Mai could give no better explanation. One by one the discs found their way into the hands of the children, who exchanged them among one another, talking of what they would be able to get with them when they went to Peretane as Mai had. Their illusions were broken when Tatahe asked one of the sailors to give an axe for the disc he had. 'Pah!' cried the sailor, 'you need fifty of those to exchange for this axe.'

Then Tatahe was angry and threw it into the waters of Matavai, but already another child was splashing out to dive for it, so intrigued were the children by those metal tokens.

At the formal feasts, in the company of Tute and his officers, Mai made eloquent speeches. He praised the generosity of his hosts, he eulogised Tute's navigation, describing the horrible storms, the hazardous shoals, they had experienced. He extolled the wonders of Peretane. The richness of the clothes, the sumptuous houses, the music of singing instruments too many to describe, the styles of dancing, the foods so many and varied that it would be possible to never eat the same meal twice. He told of places where the houses joined one to the other in row upon row as far as the eye could see, with multitudes of people swarming in the thoroughfares and the earth paved with stones for further than a man could walk. Of great bridges crossing rivers as broad as the ocean, and huge temples roofed with stone. So great were the wonders of that land that people began to yawn behind their fans. 'Truly, it must be a remarkable place,' they said. 'How lucky that Mai has been there and can tell us all about it. It is a wonder that he wanted to come back to Tahiti at all when things are so fine there.'

When there were no Popa'a present, when only a few people were around him, Mai's tone altered. 'Hear these words,' he would say, drawing them close.

'This is what I will tell you. The Popa'a say their god forbids killing. They say human sacrifices would cause their god to be angry, but everywhere in that land I saw strangled men hanging from poles, and women too. They are careless of their god, yet they have all manner of riches in their land, and the noblemen live in splendour, and their god is bountiful to them.'

'But this you should know, that while the chiefs feast and sport, the common people are hungry. Children die of hunger there in that cold place, and the noblemen permit it, taking no care for the common people.'

This we found strange, for if a chief of Tahiti were to neglect the people's welfare, he would have no mana, and be no chief at all.

'Listen to this also. Many are the sicknesses of that country. There is a season of darkness when the sun is weak, the plants withdraw into the earth, and the nights are longer than the days. Then the people are afflicted with sickness, their lungs are consumed by coughing, they take fevers and die, covered in disgusting sores.'

Thus we learnt that what we already knew of foreign sickness was only the beginning, there was more to come.

'In those paved thoroughfares where the houses are built one joined to the other there is no cleanliness. They pass ordure within walls and then throw it out into the common pathways. But the nose accustoms even to such a stink! The rats there are as big as this and run among the houses at night.'

Now we began to understand why the foreigners wanted to come to Tahiti, and it was like a bad smell to some, and they got up and left. Others wanted to hear more and questions tumbled from their mouths faster than he could answer them. What of their women, were their children born the same way as ours, was their lovemaking the same? What did they do with their dead, in what attitude did they pray to their god, what sacrifices did they make? His answers set them rolling their eyes, shaking their heads, laughing.

'Their women, ah, the noblewomen feign the ways of young girls and affect not to understand a man's desires.' Here he turned his head, lowering his eyes, and put up his hands as if to refuse a proposition. 'But their moans of pleasure are much louder than their protestations! As for their children, they come the same way as ours, and their dead, they place in wooden boxes and bury near the temples. They pray like so, with their hands together, but they make no sacrifices at all. Rather, they say that their god sacrificed his only son for them.'

'Sacrificed for them?' This was novelty. 'How, why?'

'The god allowed his son to be born as a man, and then killed, like this.' He stood with arms outstretched to demonstrate the manner of the son's death. 'They pray to the dead son for eternal life beyond this world.'

The listeners were awed at this. In Tahiti the people must make sacrifices to the gods, not the other way around.

'Ha!' said one. 'Then they are fools. What use would it be to pray to a corpse?'

'You see,' said Mai. 'The more I tell you the less you will understand. Such are the ways of the foreigners.'

At last I was left alone with Mai. We squatted near to each other in silence. Torchlight reflected on his broad features, another world glittered far away in his eyes. I waited until he spoke again.

'You are curious, Mauatua, but hear my words. The ways of that country are narrow and slippery, and whosoever falls is lost. It is a treacherous place. The people look at you, but they do not see you. They are like the rooms in their houses, closed with doors, and what is behind the doors, they do not wish you to see. Aue, it is hard for a Maohi to understand. They are not like us. Different spirits stalk that land.'

'Were you afraid?'

'Not afraid, for I am strong, and my atua protects me. My hosts were generous to me, they gave me everything I needed, everything, and I became accustomed to their ways. But they are not like us. I longed for my people. Now I'm back, but I'm not like you any more. I am a stranger on Tahiti. Where will my home be?'

'Stay here. Has Tu not invited you to join his household? Here will be your home.'

'Tu is a high chief, surrounded by people with noble blood. What can I be in his household? When all the gifts I brought have been given and all the stories told, then what will I be? A servant among servants.'

Then Mai laughed. 'Too much sorrow! In England I learned how they make the foreign 'ava, from a fruit that clusters on a vine, and I have plants to grow that vine. The foreign 'ava is good to drink – you will be happy even when you are sad. Hei, it is good!'

But it was not the foreign drink which I was curious about. 'Tell me about the tattooed leaves,' I said.

Mai was surprised. 'What does a young girl want to know of such things?'

'What are they for, what do they mean? Did you see many, did you learn how to make them?'

'Hei, in the noblemen's houses are thousands and thousands of those leaves, bound into bundles covered with animal skin. Rooms full of them!'

'What are they for?'

'The Englishmen can look in them and find knowledge. There are stories in them, and memories, but it is hard to understand. They can speak those tattoo marks out loud, or they can hear them silently just by looking at them. Stories of their god and his son can be found in one, which is kept in the temples, and the priests speak their words from it.'

'It is sacred then.'

'That one is sacred, others are not. Some contain knowledge, others tell stories, and some have images. Even music can be played from certain marks. Tomorrow, I'll bring one for you, it will be my gift to you.'

When Mai put it in my hand I felt the awakening of a new desire. The book was smaller than the ones I had seen in the hands of Tute or the other officers of his ship. Its cover of animal skin was soft, like a woman's. The leaves were so fine and white, they ruffled in the air like finest reva reva peeled from unborn fronds of niau and arranged in the hair of a court dancer.

'Like this,' said Mai, and he showed me how they opened one leaf after another, in order to follow the story they could find in the markings. The signs followed each other, thousand upon thousand, laid out in line after line in black patterns on white. And Mai assured me that thousands of such books filled whole rooms in people's houses in England!

'Each sign has a sound,' he explained, 'and each group of signs is a word, see, a word that can be spoken aloud like any other word, or kept silent.'

'Show me,' I insisted, and he put his finger to the paper and tried to draw an English word from the signs there, twisting his tongue and furrowing his brow with the effort.

'It is hard,' he said. 'For English, the mouth must perform tricks. It takes long to learn. These are the words the priests say in their temples, this is their sacred book. Here is the name of the son of their god that was sacrificed, look. That word I know, they showed me.'

Then before me for the first time was the name of that man, Jesus Christ.

'How do they say it?' I asked him.

He pulled back his lips in a grimace, then he pursed them, they worked around the invisible word, performing tricks until a sound like a whistling groan escaped between his teeth. He tossed his head in frustration. 'Too hard!' he declared. 'Make it like, Iehu. Iehu Tireti.' He rolled back on the sand where we sat, he laughed, like sobbing. 'Hei, it is good! Iehu Tireti!'

Year of Our Lord 1831

'Aimata is my name. It means, "Eater Of Eyes."'

A drowsy sadness filled the queen's own heavy lidded eyes. A carelessly twisted wreath of leaves had slipped askew on her temple. She lifted a bottle from beside her and sipped thoughtfully from its long neck.

'Eater of Eyes,' responded the grandmother politely, her own eyes on the uptilted bottle, remembering. 'Only the highest chiefs were offered the eye of the sacrifice.'

Aimata smiled now with lazy lips. 'No more eating of eyes. It is good. Missionaries, very good. Tahiti is a Christian land now.'

'You have the good book?'

'The book, yes, we have it written in Tahitian, the people are learning to read it.'

'Then we are all Christian people.'

She gave a soft, easy laugh. 'They say we are cousins too,' she said.

'Your grandfather was my cousin. Your grandmother knew me when I was as small as this child.'

'Then truly you are the one Grandmother Itia called the Matavai virgin! They said she sailed away with a white man and nobody heard of her again.'

'Now she has returned.'

Then they looked from one to the next, eye to eye to eye, the queen, the grandmother and the virgin, and what they saw was their own blood, and all of Tahiti written in it, hot and dark.

'It is very good that you have returned,' said the queen. 'I will give you land, all your people, all you need.'

'That is the generosity of a true ari'i, your majesty.'

'Tahiti is your home, cousin.'

Now the gaze of Aimata wandered again, out into the fierce haze of day, the palm tops burning in the wind, the island of Aimeo lost in it. She took another sip from the bottle and sighed. 'E patea, you have been gone a lifetime. Tahiti is not the place it was in my grandmother's time. Now we sing only hymns and the missionaries speak over our dead. A Christian land.'

She stood up suddenly, her dress of blue rustling around her hips. 'Come with me, come.' She carried the bottle, her skirts sweeping the floor around her bare feet. People were crowded on the verandahs of her palace. Some sat singing, some were drinking from bottles, some were lying sick, being fanned with leaves. They all looked up to her as she passed by. 'Aimata! Aimata our blessed queen, our ari'i nui!'

She greeted them all by name. Aimata, they begged her. My husband is made to work on the road and we have no food. Aimata, all my sister's children are sick of the fever. Aimata, my brother was chased and beaten because he did not go to the church on Sunday. Their laments turned to smiles when she greeted them.

'The ovens are full today,' she told them. 'Come and eat, there is plenty for everybody.'

She swept on across the grounds of the palace. Everywhere, people were lying and sitting under the trees. Some got up and followed behind her, an old woman wailing with a blood-striped face, a hobbling man with sores all over his legs, a row of little children in ragged shirts chanting English songs.

'Plenty for everybody!' she repeated.

Aimata! Eater of Eyes!

Outside the long guest-house, built of palm trunks and thatch, the people sat down to wait while she took her guests inside.

'Here,' she gestured to them. All was shadow. 'Here are all the gifts sent from the foreign kings and queens.'

The contents of a fleet of white ships appeared around them. Slowly the eye could pick them out, tossed about as if a great wind had shaken a magic tree.

The queen picked up a mirror and handed it to Margaret. 'For you,' she said with a shrug.

Ahi

Mauatua

The banana palm waits for rain.
Long is the pause of heaven!

Clouds gathered, but rain did not fall.

'The atua of the white men is disturbing our seasons.'

'It is the ancestor spirits of the foreigners challenging the mana of our own.'

'When the foreigners have left, rain will fall and the soil become ready for the new plantings.'

'Only then will the rivers gush again with food for the lagoon fish, bringing the great creatures of the outer ocean to feed at the gateways of the reefs.'

Such were the sayings of the old people, of the priests and soothsayers of those times.

War canoes slipped along the coast and were drawn up at Pare. Their tall stern-posts filled the bay like a forest and warriors thronged the shores and groves, practising their skills with their weapons to the low beat of drums, eating, oiling themselves, bathing in the men's pools, sleeping.

Tu had asked Tute to join with him and his friend To'ofa, chief of Atehuru, in a raid on the chief Mahine of Aimeo. Long had this raid been planned and deferred, canoes been gathered, rites performed, negotiations prolonged. So long that nobody expected a raid any longer. But now Tute might be persuaded to take To'ofa's side, to turn his guns and cannons on the warriors of Mahine, and end the uncertainty. The drums beat louder and faster, the messages spread like ripples on water.

To arouse the war god, Oro, a man was sacrificed, but still Tute refused to take part in the raid. To'ofa made the raid alone, and was unsuccessful, so he had to make a truce on bad terms. He promised to seek revenge against Tu for deserting him. Word spread that he planned to attack as soon as the white men had gone, but Tute said that he would return to avenge such an attack.

So while some said that the white men were a curse upon Tahiti and wanted them to leave, others argued that they were a glory to our tribes and would protect us and bring great prosperity. 'First, the Popa'a tools, and soon his weapons. Truly is the time of Oro come! Conquering with fire, sacrifice will be rewarded.'

Foreign banners were attached to the stern posts of the war canoes, or pieces of coloured cloth and abundant quantities of the red feathers that had been brought by the foreigners then dedicated to Oro by the priests of Tu's marae. Oro of the conquering fire! A new aspect was seen of that fearful god. Even Mai got himself a canoe – bartered from To'ofa for a bunch of such feathers – and hung it about with flags and pennants. 'Like a girl just come up from below decks,' I heard it said, so laden with foreign finery was that canoe.

I was but a girl myself, kept close by my grandmother's side. Hinuia and Tetua spent more and more hours together in prayer, and then I could put down the fly whisk or the fan, creep away from their muttering and chanting and go out among the people, always listening and watching.

The ship was ready to leave now. Its men had repaired masts and sails, hauled on board wooden casks full of water, nets full of coconuts and breadfruit. They were folding up the cloth houses they had erected on the shore at Matavai, loading up the complicated equipment that they had kept under guard there. And still their friends in Matavai were feeding the men and letting them sleep in their houses with their women.

While the drums beat along the coast at Pare, with a soft rumble of menace that kept all attentive to the sound, lest it should change. While the sailors waited for the wind which would flick their white sails to life. While the banana palm waited for rain and the drooping groves grew bare of flowers.

Tu arranged more festivities for Tute, to please him, perhaps persuade him even yet to swoop upon Aimeo with thunder and flames, and again Hinuia and I were invited to Pare, this time to prepare a play to present to the white chief. My cousin Auo, her older sister Fataua and I were to be the players, along with four comedians, friends of Fataua. Fataua was herself an actress. She lived and travelled with the arioi, those people who dedicated themselves to music and dancing and entertainments of all sorts. Fataua and her arioi friends had come to visit her family at Pare, and to see Tute whose presence had been heard of far and wide throughout the islands. The story we were to enact was an old one, telling of three sisters all wanting the same man.

The battle drums were allowed to fall silent at last, and the drums for our heiva were struck up instead, the pleasure drums of Tane. Threats and uncertainties were forgotten, the rhythm of performance picked us up and the music drew us along the well-worn path of that story. We looked to one another and saw ourselves not as Fataua the actress, not shiny cheeked Auo, not skinny Mauatua the Matavai cousin, but those other three ancestral sisters, and then again the world was but a surface of light thrown across the crowded depths of the past, where we swam like fish amid the shoals of our ancestors, knowing ourselves by them.

From the direction of Tu's house, when the drummers rested, we could hear the steady knock and scrape of metal on wood, the rasp of metal cutting. Tute's woodworkers were making a box for Tu, we heard. It was to be a box big enough to hold all the gifts and treasures Tu had received from Tute, big enough for two men to sleep upon and guard all those riches. We three went to see the men working on it, perspiring under the palm thatch, and we admired the long curls of shaved wood that fell from their blades. We brought drinking nuts, and Fataua and Auo pushed me forward with them. The men stopped to drink, passing words and laughter, looking at us three, also laughing. One of them beckoned to me.

'Go, go to him,' urged Fataua and Auo, pushing me forward again, and I went, feeling all the men's eyes upon me, and their cheering laughter loud in my ears. The one who had beckoned drew me to his side. Afraid to look up and see his face, I pointed instead at his work, the tool laid on its side on the smoothed timber, and to my surprise he picked up the tool and put it into my hands. It was heavy, with a flat blade beneath. Then he put his arms around me and guided my hand with his. The blade pushed, unwillingly at first, then with sudden swiftness, along the plank, a shining curl emerging from the top, while the other men roared, and my cousins all cheered with delight. I wanted to do it again. But then I smelt the white man's sweat and in a moment my girl's body was set alight by it. All their eyes were upon me, everyone would surely see that flame ignited. Suddenly I was afraid: I ducked out from under his arm and ran. We ran together, Fataua, Auo and I, but when we returned Hinuia was waiting for us.

'This is the smell of a white man you have on you!' she said to me immediately. 'Where have you been?'

'Only to see the men building Tu's box,' Fataua explained, 'and one of them showed Mauatua how to smooth wood with his tool.'

Auo began to giggle.

'Go and wash yourself,' said Hinuia. 'Clean yourself before the gods. Your grandmother should not hear of this.'

I went alone to the running water, but before I washed my skin I smelled one more time the white man's strong odour, mixed on my own skin now into something new. Then I knew that it was more than nails and mirrors and knives that the other girls were trading for on the ship at night, and I felt a woman's fire begin to burn in me.

Obediently, however, I washed myself, and returning to the others, rubbed myself afresh with scented oil, ready to step back onto the mats to rehearse our performance. But now I could not leave the shining surface of the world. The distant rasping and tapping of the white men's tools distracted me, my hands and feet were disconnected from each other. The depths resisted me, my eyes were enchanted by light that glanced among the palm leaves, my ears by the white men's voices. I lost my step, forgot my words.

'What is this now!' exclaimed Hinuia, who was watching us. 'Go again and wash yourself, e hine! Go before the gods and make yourself clean, with the correct prayers. What foolishness to be going among the white men at such a time. You should know better!'

And so again I went to the water. Hinuia came after me, her strides were long. At the water's edge she stopped. She plucked out the comb of human bone which fastened up the hair never cut from her sacred head, and that hair fell like a cape across her shoulders. No royal red tiputa had ever clothed Hinuia, only the girdle of her mana, which now, as she stepped into the water, coiled around her like a spectral wind, a wind such as those that pass among the sacred trees, giving the leaves to murmur the names of the gods, causing the flesh of mortals to shiver with dread.

I sank up to my shoulders, fearful of her anger, my eyes fixed on hers as she came towards me. She came down to me until we were eye to eye. Those eyes were fierce. They pierced me in an instant, saw everything that was not said. They saw the woman's fire burning in me. They saw my love of the white men, held close since their white ships had first entranced my baby eyes. She saw their sacred book, which was wrapped in cloth, lodged among the house rafters, deep in the shadiest corner where a breadfruit tree hung over the roof. I felt her eyes would surely ignite that book even in its hiding place, and the whole house would burn down from the anger of the gods issuing like flame, and every tree in Matavai would be roaring with fire, from whence it would race up the valleys to the very mountain tops and engulf all of Tahitinui. Aue, for the burning girl!

Then, even as my secrets roared like flames in the wind of her seeing, I was submerged. Hinuia pushed me beneath the surface, she held me there, her hands on my shoulders. I let her hold me, as I had let Tetua hold my arms for the tattooist. I did not struggle, though voices roared in my ears, a stone and water chorus whirled around me, sighing and groaning. She held me until she knew I must come up, until my limbs wanted to leap from the water and run, my throat crying with relief. She emptied me of secrets. Without words she drew them out of me like brands and cast them burning on the water around us, flashing and glancing around the black centre of her fearful gaze.

When she spoke, her voice was harsh and low. 'Do you let your cousins push you into the arms of a white man, a stranger? Are you their servant, to take their wrongdoing upon yourself? Remember who you are, e hine, hear my words. The foreigners are dangerous, they are full of secrets, full of tricks. You are a Maohi, and your ancestors will protect you, but only if you are attentive. Attentive to our gods, attentive to your ancestors, attentive to your grandmother and your family, attentive to your learning and your work, and to your dancing and singing with your cousins. Come now, keep them waiting no longer.'

The ancestors were strong, their guardianship enclosed me. I learned the steps, the movements of the arms and hands. My behaviour was correct.

Before the feast, when all the people were gathered, Tute also put on a show. Two of his men came carrying a large box between them, and they set it very gently on the ground, as if it contained something alive. The people crowded forward, expecting more of the foreign surprises, novelties and tricks, but Tute's men gestured them back, forming a large circle. There was something dangerous in the box, we understood. Some hid their faces in fear, some even ran away before the box was opened.

The objects inside it were small, no more than tightly wrapped packets, but they were handled with great care. 'Foreign atua!' it was exclaimed, for they were like the carefully bundled gods of our own marae, brought out for sacred occasions. The men guarded the objects while darkness fell, and we waited, gathered. Tute came. He called for a flame and a man with a reed torch came forward. Tute lit a twist of cloth with the flame, and, as a murmur of astonishment ran through the crowd, he set alight one of the packets. People who had pushed forward to see now pressed back again as sparks began to shoot up from the packet – not ordinary sparks, but coloured sparks, green at first, then blue, more and more of them. People shrieked in terror and began to run in every direction, crying that we would all be killed by the foreign atua. The sparks popped and hissed, growing higher and higher, gushing up and throwing an unearthly light on astonished faces, on figures fallen to their knees and covering their heads.

Tute lit another bundle, and this one shot up from the earth into the heavens with a ghastly howl, bursting into a mass of red stars which lasted but a moment in the sky before falling into blackness, quickly followed by cascades of green and orange, while on the ground more and more were alight, gushing fire and coloured smoke, crackling and flashing.

In the crowd, as nobody had fallen dead or wounded, the cries of terror gave way to admiration and pleasure. It was, after all, another of the white men's amazing tricks which they liked to play on us, and we began to laugh with delight at our own foolishness, and at the foreigners' extravagant cleverness. Tute too, was laughing, his face flickering with coloured light, laughing at our laughter.

After this our little play seemed unexciting. Our audience was small. Tute watched attentively however, the way he watched everything. He was seated on the frontmost mat, next to Tu, who leaned toward him now and then explaining the story. Near to them, propped up and wreathed with garlands, was Tute's image. The image had been created with colours and brushes by a servant of Tute's whose work, it seemed, was to make images of everything he saw. Mountains, clouds, war canoes, dancers, priests, whatever that man looked at, he could depict with his colours. My cousin Vaetua had taken him as taio and accompanied him on walks up the valleys, carrying his boxes of colours for him, and was very vain of his friendship with the image renderer. Tu had asked for an image of Tute that he could keep near to him. Now two Tutes beheld our performance, one alive and vivid, his eyes bright by torchlight, the other rigid and flat, but with watching eyes also.

How long he would watch over us, how long.

At last the white men departed. They were going first to Aimeo. Mai went ahead, in his new canoe, with his friends from Aotearoa, all gaudy as flowers in their foreign clothes. Others left aboard the ship, girls with their lovers, determined to follow them for as long as possible. Whole families accompanied them in a fleet of canoes, to return under other winds and other moons.

But at Matavai the feasting was over, the dancing was over, the storytelling and play acting were over. No more were heard the foreign voices calling across the water, the foreign laughter, foreign songs, foreign anger. The clang and clatter of foreign tools, the thunder of weapons, the bleating and snorting of the foreign animals, all were gone from our land. The shores were empty, the paths through the groves were deserted, the trees and plantations were stripped of food.

Many other things remained, however.

Te Oho Matamua

At Matavai foreign plants had emerged to greet the light of Tahiti, sprung from the seeds of another world. Mauatua had seen them in Tute's gardener's hand, numberless as stars, rolling in his palm.

Later she had crouched to see the minute specks of life that hatched from them, while he named them for her. Squatting at the edge of the plot, she had watched him work. He had worked hard, but the spirits of the plants were unwilling and many had shrivelled back into the earth, leaving only a few survivors. Now that he had gone, it was these she came to tend. She found that he had left behind two tools, one with a metal blade, the other with spaced teeth, hidden among the bushes near the plot. She tested them in her hands. Their long handles were suited to her height and she quickly learned to use them.

She came in the hour of sunset when other girls were making garlands for the evening's games. By lagoon light she whispered the prayers necessary for plants to grow, carried water to them, and picked insects off their leaves. By their names, she encouraged them. Pumpkin. Pea. Bean. Cabbage. Turnip. Her tongue crushed the names, tasting their foreignness, over and over. The iron tools scratched the soil.

When the rain came it weighed down their fragile leaves. Some withered and collapsed and were dragged back into the earth. A loose pig trampled in the night, and the strong weeds of Tahiti grew more swiftly than she could restrain them. Yet day by day small flowers began swelling into long pods, strange roots swelled beneath strange leaves and foreign vines stretched out across the steaming soil with curling tendrils that grasped for their anchorage upon Tahiti.

Mauatua was a tall girl, it was a sign of her noble lineage, there had been gods among her ancestors. Great gods who came among humans, made love with them, and passed their knowledge and secrets to their earth-born sons and daughters. Some, like Tahaki, were giants, golden skinned, with magical powers, bestriding the world of light above and the world of darkness below. Some were terrifying sorcerers, man eaters and shape changers. They peopled her history, surrounding her like an invisible crowd. They were present in her limbs. Long limbs, long hands, inscribed with the ancient signs of her people. The tattoos had reached her fingers, entwining them like vine tendrils. She saw her hands in the soil, as plants. Her fingertips were tapered and long, for her grandmother Tetua had been careful to encourage these qualities by rolling them between her own fingers when she was a baby, day after day, rolling and stretching the baby's fingertips. Just as she had pressed her granddaughter's nose a little each day, to encourage its flattening, for a nose is more beautiful if it is slightly flattened, and fingers are more beautiful if they are long and slender.

    She knew that her mother Maoiti would say, if she knew, 'Why is Mauatua working in the soil like a teu teu? This is not work for my daughter. Let her weave and plait, or beat and decorate barkcloth. Those are proper occupations for her hands.'

Even her grandmother might forbid her to tend the plants if she knew. But she did not know. Nor did Hinuia know, she thought, that she came here alone. It was not proper for a girl to be alone. Alone in Tute's garden. Alone at the hour of sunset. Alone without protection from the evil spirits which waited for such times to harm their victims. Tupapau! Varua'ino! Spirits with long teeth! They would spring, they would place some evil seed within her! Leaves rustled, grasses stirred. Sometimes she threw down the tools and ran from that shadowy place where none other came.

Other times she would remember the goodness of Tute, and feel sure that his mana would protect her from harm here in his garden, tending his plants.

One evening she looked up and saw Teraura watching from the edge of the plot, as she herself had done. The two girls stared at each other. Teraura was younger, smaller, darker. She was the daughter of Ta'upo, a ra'atira of Matavai who was a friend and ally of Mauatua's uncle Tapuetefa. Her mother was a manahune. Teraura was of lower rank than Mauatua, to the same degree that Mauatua was of lower rank than Auo. It was important to understand these things. Therefore it was Mauatua who spoke first.

'Do you come to watch my work or to join me, Teraura?' she asked.

'What work is it that you do here alone?' questioned the other.

'Caring for the plants left by Tute. This is Tute's garden.' Mauatua struck with the blade and severed the stem of a weed cleanly with it.

'I knew you were not coming here to meet a boy. The other girls are guessing who it is.'

Mauatua smiled. 'Here is my boy,' she said, holding out the long-handled tool.

The other girl laughed, piercing dark eyes beneath thickly arched black brows. Above her right ear the white star of a tiare flower glowed.

'Let me try at that work then,' she said, rising. 'Let us care for Tute's plants together. Aren't you afraid to be here alone at this hour?'

'With my boy?' asked Mauatua. She put the hoe in Teraura's hands. 'I am not afraid. I feel Tute's spirit will protect me.' She bent and lifted some leaves to show Teraura. 'See these yellow flowers? And see here the fruit that set from them? That is called pumpkin. English food.'

'Will you eat that food?'

'We will all eat it.'

Light was slipping from the breadfruit leaves which had carried it all day in their living basket. The nature of all things began to change as the shadows darkened. Teraura mastered the hoe before she spoke again. She looked around the clearing and drew close to Mauatua.

'Did you go with the white man who gardened here?' she asked.

'He did not desire me,' said Mauatua, surprised. 'He treated me as a child, not a woman. If he had desired me I would have run away. He was too hairy.'

'With legs as crooked as a dog's!'

They had to muffle their laughter as they remembered him, the thin, crooked, hairy man.

'You knew him also?'

'Ae. As a woman.'

Mauatua was startled. 'Aue! Was it by force that he took you?'

'He did not force me. I desired him. I desired a white man.'

'Do others know?'

'The other girls would not believe me. They thought I was making it up. They said I took the three nails he gave me from my older sister.'

'What was he like, the thin hairy one?'

'It was only once, but he was strong like a man, and he was kind. Some of the girls said the white men they went with were rough and crude. Not this man. With him I was a woman.'

'I too have desired a white man,' said Mauatua.

'What was he like?'

'I dared not go with him. I ran away.' Mauatua looked around anxiously into the darkening groves. 'Hide the tool here,' she said. 'It's too dark now.'

First they walked, then they ran, pushing through the narrow path back to the open ground, the sea shore. The first of the evening's drums awoke ahead of them. They could hear the distant voices calling with joy, awakening the spirits of music. Soon a faster drum joined the first, pulling the girls' feet towards the dancers. The dark wavelets of Matavai teased at their ankles.

'I have seen Hinuia the priestess watching over you,' said Teraura. 'You will have to accept the husband they choose for you.'

'I may have lovers.'

'They will choose your lovers too.'

'Mauatua will choose her lovers, and her husband too, you will see. The priestess knows my desires. She will help me.'

'They will have a chieftain for you, a man from Huahine or Raiatea looking for a wife from Tahiti.'

'It is a chieftain I will choose,' said Mauatua. 'Nothing less.'

The first fruit was for the gods. Light shone back from the pumpkin's glossy skin. She had watched it swell like a pregnant belly under its sheltering leaves, day by day. At the altar she placed it carefully, and at once she felt the crowding round, the watching spirits among the trees. Birds fell silent as she began her prayer, the leaves were thick with listeners.

'Atua, I offer you this new food. Fattened by the soil of Tahiti, swollen by the rain of Tahiti. Atua, the foreign seed wishes to grow in Tahiti.'

'I will not eat that,' said Tetua, when she saw the sweet-smelling yellow flesh, steaming from the earth oven on a fresh purau leaf.

Mauatua helped her grandmother to food. She broke the soft uru into bite-sized morsels, dipping each into the bowl of salty coconut sauce before she lifted it to her grandmother's lips. She scooped the melting fei banana from its skin. She divided the white fish from its backbone. Only the pumpkin was left. She began as if to break a small piece, in case her grandmother should change her mind.

Tetua raised her hand. 'I have finished eating,' she said. 'The rats will enjoy what is left.'

Hinuia spoke next. 'The food was grown by Mauatua's own hands,' she interjected.

Mauatua's hand poised motionless above the food at these unexpected words. She glanced away from Hinuia's gaze. Truly there were no secrets from the old priestess.

'Is this true?' asked Tetua.

'It is true, but ... '

'You have been tending the white men's plants?'

'They are the plants of Tute, who left them here for us, as a gift.'

'As a gift? Or did he leave those seeds behind to feed the foreigners who will be coming here in other ships?'

'I tended them properly, none the less, for Tute is my friend.'

'Everyone is Tute's friend.'

'Should we be enemies, Grandmother?'

'Who would dare to be the enemies of such men? But there are some who worship him like a god, looking for their own advantage. Such advantage will be short. Let me taste one tiny morsel then, only to know how it is, the yellow food of the white man.'

She leaned back then and let Mauatua put it in her mouth. Closing her eyes she savoured it slowly, but when she spoke at last, all she said was, 'Your mother will complain that your hands are soiled, e hine.'

Of more than soil stains were Maoiti's complaints. 'Why is Mauatua kept here among old women?' she asked. 'Why is she not going to the dancing master with her royal cousins at Pare? Should she be fetching and carrying like a teu teu? Look at her, she is too thin! She should be kept in the fattening house for a month, to fill her breasts. What nobleman will want such a narrow wife?'

'Mauatua is needed here in her grandmother's household,' replied Hinuia. 'She is the companion of her old age. Who otherwise will care for your mother now, e Maoiti? The years have been long, the wrinkles hang down, an old woman stays in the house. What your daughter learns by her grandmother's side will be just as valuable as dancing lessons.'

To this there was no reply a scolding mouth could properly make.

After a long lapse the sound of cloth-beating mallets was heard again at Matavai, hesitantly at first, reluctantly. For now many wore garments, given by the sailors, that lasted longer than barkcloth, and could be worn in the water without disintegrating. 'Why beat barkcloth when we wear these foreign clothes?' it was asked, but the habit was strong. Even the sound of one mallet called the women to the beating boards as irresistibly as the blowing of the conch shell called warriors to their weapons. Many beaters were still absent, the hands of women and girls who had followed the ship to Aimeo and not yet returned. The younger girls took their places at the boards.

Mauatua had inherited Tetua's mallet, now that her grandmother came no more to beat cloth. Each of its four sides was cut with grooves, graded from coarse to fine. To begin, the coarsest side, to beat the fibres of the bark apart. To end, as the cloth thinned and grew, the finest grooves, the lighter touch, to bind them back together. Across the beating board sat Teraura and through the interweaving rhythm of the beaters the two girls heard each other. Even the meeting of eyes was not necessary to convey those messages which rang from each blow. Mauatua! Teraura! Mauatua! Teraura!

Later, weaving garlands side by side, they crowned each other, and exchanged names. On the dance ground they stepped up together and danced as one. Occasionally we still stole away to Tute's garden and harvested the vegetables that had survived there, biting into raw roots and snapping open pods. Our eyes were ever roaming the far horizon, but our wait would be long.

Te Hau

Mauatua

Our tattooed hands rubbed oil into the soft flesh of Tetua's back. Her spine was stiffening now, giving in to the pain and immobility of the fe'e sickness. It was hard for her to stand, she must have someone to hold on one side, on the other her stick.

Her face was clenched with discomfort when I walked her, even a little way through the trees to relieve herself.

I would help her lie down for the massage, stretching her stiffening limbs. Then Hinuia and I would massage together. Hinuia instructed, her hard fingers drove the pain from its hiding places, her knuckles rolled, her fists pressed in upon the darkness of Tetua's night.

But Tetua was old and grief was her companion. If pain left her, it soon returned.

When they chanted together, Hinuia's voice was high and light; it was a voice like a quavering spirit's, like a kite caught on the wind, a voice of the air. Tetua's was of the earth, the sounds came from the rocks of the earth, from the soil and roots.

It was old prayers that they sang, old chants of Tetua's family marae, the great marae of Nu'urua on Aimeo. Songs of Tetua's ancestors, in the language of the ancestors, which is full of strange twists and turns of meaning, almost forgotten in these times now. They were like the knotted strings that the priests prayed with on the marae, those songs. They ran from knot to knot, ancestor to ancestor, travelling across marae and mountain, waterfall and peak, entering caverns, valleys, pools, mists; they climbed into the highest clefts of the mountains where only the spirits dwell, lifting like tropic birds on the updrafts of the ocean, rolling like rocks to the feet of the slopes.

My aunt Nari'i, and Maoiti, both came to Tetua's side, and my cousin Tetuaraenui came from Faa'a, big bellied. The rafters hummed with female voices again.

I was exempted from the fetching and carrying, for Tetua had expressed her wish that my tattooing be finished. I was to spend time at the family marae, or to work at weaving the mat I had begun. I was not especially skilful at weaving, but it was required that I persist. It had begun as a mat of Stars Crossing the Heavens. The stars were woven into its border, and at each one my fingers hesitated, crossing, uncrossing, seeking yet again the correct pattern. Frayed edges and splits marked my clumsy forgetfulness. So many the strands of that mat, thousands fanning out from its working edge, each one to follow its determined direction, to join with the others in the endless pattern spreading out before me. The mat of The Dying of Tetua it became to me, with the sound of the old chants woven into it, and the voices of the women under our roof, singing in harmony. The stars crossing heaven would soon be crossing my hips also, tattooed indelibly into my skin, mine until death.

At the family marae Hinuia was preparing the dye. Carefully she had selected tu'tui nuts and plucked them, with the proper prayers. On a small fireplace of stones, she burned them one after the other, letting the soot gather on a chimney stone above them, watching the smoke and flames for signs, auspicious or inauspicious, the soot thickening on the chimney stone until finally there was enough to be scraped into a stone bowl and mixed with pure water from high in the mountains. In this the tahua tatau would dip his sacred bird-bone chisel. The turmeric Hinuia prepared also, grating the fibrous root into coconut oil, releasing pungent soothing juices, to be rubbed into the broken skin.

'Look for the signs,' Hinuia told me. 'Listen, you will hear.'

I waited for the first strike of the bird-bone chisel into my skin.

'In the beginning there is darkness,' began Hinuia. 'It is the blackness of te po.'

How soft and formless my waiting flesh. The black band around the curve of buttocks would be made first, the punctures would be many, many. My mother and Nari'i were here in the softly rustling fare tatau. Someone held the skin taut. Let the bones of the sacred bird pierce me now, let the blood flow. Let me wear my tattoo like a woman. Aue!

'Ta'aroa revolved in the shell of darkness in the void. No sun, no moon, no mountain, no ocean was there. There was only the void. Then Ta'aroa opened the shell, he broke it apart and he called out, "Who is there?" He called to the void, "Who is there above, who is there below?" And none answered...

Many are the regions of darkness. In the depths of the farthest caverns dwells the lizard, Te Mo'o. The keeper of sacred memory. He may show himself to those he chooses. A young woman alone in the searing valley of the tattooing pain, on that towering plain of black rocks, to her he may show himself. His eyes glow like stones from the fire, his jaws and cheeks are marked with mysterious patterns, aue! With his fiery eye he glares, then he is gone.

'Ta'aroa raised up his shell for the sky, and he commanded the rocks to appear, but none appeared, and Ta'aroa was angry. He made a mountain range of his backbone, he pulled out his flesh for the earth and his entrails for the clouds, and in his anger his blood grew hot and flowed away to make the red of the sky, the red of the rainbow, the red of earth.'

The earth grinds its jaws, hot liquid bursts up from below, surely the blood will cook in the veins, surely the brain will explode!

'All that is red is Ta'aroa's blood! Sacred! Ta'aroa called forth the gods then. He brought forth Tu, the artisan; Atea, the moving sky; Hiro, the evil one; Oro the warriors' god. Tane, lord of the forests, of the insects, of the flowers was created. Tane, the bringer of sacred knowledge, Tane, god of beauty, who dwelled among humans.'

The women sing together. Their voices recall the world of light.

Many are the delights of a woman in this world,
A woman who wears the noble girdle,
The girdle of black soot made sacred
Made sacred by the holy fire.
For her will be the delights of Tane!
Tane who clasps the beautiful woman to him,
Tane who knows the ways of pleasure,
She will be the one to please him,
Tane the beloved.
Tane the ever-erect, who strews flowers on the shore,
Tane who calls the dance!
A woman of the tattooed girdle is known in the land
In all the lands of our people her worth will be known
Her ancestors will be known,
Their deeds will be remembered
By the signs upon her body.
In the lands of the gods the woman is known
Captivated by her beauty they will favour her
The woman adorned, the woman who stands tall
In the land of her forefathers!
Children will slip easily from her,
As fish through the gap in the reef
The best of food will be for her,
The sweetest of oils will be her perfume,
Many are her pleasures in this world.
But for now she must lie on her belly in the shadows.

Night and day were woven together, the cocks crowed by moonlight; burning tu'tui nuts flickered and hissed until dawn, the fragrance of sandalwood infused the darkness. Someone fanned her, nono leaves were pressed upon her hips and buttocks to cool the flaming garland she now wore there. The medicinal oils prepared by the priestess were rubbed in, specially prepared food was placed between her lips.

Was it by night or by day that two lizards fell from the thatch where they had been fighting, landing as loud as a coconut on the mat near her head. They were black and scaley, long as rats. She glimpsed only their tails as they ran quickly to cover.

'What sound of war was that?' cried out Tetua, startled.

'Only two lizards falling from the thatch,' was the reply.

'Does the spirit of Tautoia return? Is he released at last from the sorcery of Vehiatua's evil doers?'

Up rose the chants again. Only the priestess could interpret the signs. Only the songs could banish dread, embracing with familiar words and rhythms, running on and on like a swift and steady canoe across the trackless depths of the ocean, skimming the invisible barrier between the worlds of light and darkness, life and death – a safe vessel, riding homeward, in this vessel all together, one people, one knowledge, one memory, one song.

We were not divided, then.

Tetua had long stopped eating. She took only coconut water.

When the scabs on my hips were healed she looked at the work of the tahua tatau.

'It is well begun,' she said. Her breathing was slow and laboured. 'It will take you far, if it is finished as well as it is begun.'

She bade me come closer, lie down at her side. Her voice was like hot stones raked from the ashes. 'E hine, I am devoured. The curse of Vehiatua has destroyed me. The Paumotuans at Pare conspire with the white men. Our mana has been stolen and evil times befall us.'

'Aue, Grandmother,' I made to comfort her, fearful of all this talk of curses and conspiracy.

'It is too late for me. Who will restore our mana? You too may be cast away from this land of Tahiti, from Matavai and Orohena. Then you must take your ancestors with you, e hine, do not forget us.'

'Unto your hina tini, the grandchildren of your grandchildren,' I reassured her.

'Our mana must be restored.'

Suddenly she clasped my head in her hands and pulled me close to her. 'When I go you will take my breath, e hine,' she rasped. 'You, because you must take it with you when you leave.'

Dread seized me. 'I am not leaving, Grandmother!' I protested.

'Because you must take it with you,' she repeated.

The time approached. The designs on my hips and buttocks were complete: I was a woman. The band of black was smooth flowing and clean edged. Above it revolved the stars, as within the dome of the sky; below, the waves encircled me with their secret language. When Tetua saw them completed, she said nothing. She was beyond speech, beyond gesture. She only breathed, and the last breath was coming closer, closer. Still we fanned and chanted, and sometimes whispered as if Grandmother was one of us, giggling like girls on the river bank. But Grandmother only breathed, the girl in her finally gone. Kneeling there, I finished the mat, weaving in the last ragged ends to the sound of her breathing. Which was worse to bear, the sting of grief, the stone of dread, the thousand-time punctured skin, or the thousand ends of fara that had to be woven in, is not to be remembered. I hoped she would change her mind and choose someone else to receive the last breath, such as my mother, or my uncle. I hoped I would begin to bleed so that I would have to be secluded in the women's menstrual house for three days.

Yet the sturdy canoe raced on across the infinite waters, carrying us all on its decks, and nobody could leave it. There was no escape.

The time was coming. Tetua's breathing was ragged, small gasps died away, the tu'tui lights shuddered, flaring and dimming, lighting up sometimes the ribs and rafters of the roof, then closing us into a glimmering circle. A drum was being beaten along the shore and its circular rhythm became a soft mat for me to lay my head on.

I slept, and woke with Hinuia holding me by my hair. She was pushing me down. 'Open your mouth,' she commanded.

Te hau! The breath! My mouth was opened onto Grandmother's, my skin seemed to shrink upon me as I realised. From the depths of a blood-hot darkness something was rising. The breath! Approaching like a tupapau on the wind, stinking of death, and yet I could not close my mouth or turn away but was held in the grip of that thing while my stomach sickened with horror and it entered me. Te hau!

It lodged in my lungs. In panic I struggled up, and Hinuia pushed me down a second time, a third time, until my grandmother was empty of breath. As the last groan escaped her, Hinuia pulled me away and clasped me to her. She held me close so I could not vomit up that terror from my stomach or sob it out of my lungs, for that unknown entity which now sought to possess me contained the living breath of my ancestors, their knowledge and mana and history. It was te ihu, the living spirit of my line, that Tetua had passed on to me with her dying breath. Aue.

The word went out that the soul of Tetua Avari'i was taking leave, and the people began coming. For three days her soul would remain near her body and she must not be left alone. When the embalmers had finished, she was wrapped in thick layers of white bark cloth, perfumed with oil, so that none would see, even yet, the hideously swollen leg with its festering sores. But nothing could hide the smell of the disease.

Wearing garlands of sweet-smelling ferns and flowers they approached her, kissed her, touched her, bowed before her, offering prayers. The manahune, the fishermen's wives, the planters of taro, the carriers of bananas from the mountains, came to mourn their chiefess. Soon the cutting began and from one to another it spread like fever. All around were the faces of women wailing, mouths open, eyes closed, with the blood of their self-inflicted wounds glistening on their cheeks, as red as the feather amulets in Tetua's lifeless fingers. At each new cut a cry went up, and was joined by another as the first died away, a pattern of rising and dying that began to resonate in the air, enclosing us all in an eerie cavern of sound. The smell of blood rose quickly on the seasonal heat while the pile of red-stained cloths mounted at the foot of the bier where the mourners left them. I heard my own voice join the others, but the horror remained lodged in my breast. Then I envied the married women their shark-tooth blades and filed shells.

Hinuia guarded me. She kept me at her side, close to Tetua's head. Hinuia did not weep. She remained bolt upright, unspeaking and unseeing under wreaths of maire ferns. She was waiting to see Tetua's soul depart.

For three days there was no activity permitted in the valley – no fishing, no cloth beating, no lighting of ovens. The only movement was around the house of mourning. But canoes began to arrive. From Aimeo they came first, from every chiefly family of that land, all connected by blood or by marriage to the marae of Nu'urua, the place of her birth.

The manahune went back to their homes and the visiting nobles filed in, chiefs with fly whisks, with tassels of red feathers on their fingers, with round bellies, women with pearls hanging from their ear lobes. I felt their eyes were all upon me, possessing me, because I was the vessel of Grandmother's breath, pitying me for the curse on our line. Wondering why grandmother had chosen me, looking for something on me, a sign maybe.

The wailing began to rise again, spinning like a circular wind in my ears, whipping the stench of death into a nauseous pit. I rushed past the servants, who formed a gossiping crowd around the outside of the house.

I stopped to gasp the fresh air, choking on the fetid odours that filled my throat. Dodging fallen fronds, crab holes and nuts hollowed out by rats, I ran through the coconut groves towards Tute's garden, the charnel pit hot on my breath. The rain came from behind me, soaking into my pareu and pasting fern fronds to my brow. I ran in under a purau tree, but the rain followed me in as grey shifts stormed across the lagoon, twisting and warping. The smells of ocean and earth fumed in their wake, and then the rain came harder, wetter, drumming on leaves, rattling fronds, until the only smell was water. Gratefully, I inhaled, feeling the rain run down my face, washing away the clinging effluent.

In the black flash of an instant he was there, glinting like a wet stone. Te Mo'o. When I looked at him he melted away, but I knew him now. I knew he would not desert me, not leave me alone choking on Grandmother's ihu, wearing her death like a skin that had attached itself to me. His lizard skin reminded me of the book, hidden away in the house roof above the mourners. The black shiny book full of silent words. For a moment I was shocked to remember it there, secreted away above the sacred heads of chiefs and nobles. Or had Hinuia found it and taken it to dispose of, probably out in the ocean, where dangerous influences are lost in the holy spaces of saltwater? It would be days before I could know, yet I could see it now, floating above me, open like a door, with white light spilling from it, covered in black signs, like crawling insects.

When I opened my eyes to the world again I noticed something near my foot. It was the white feather of one of the foreign birds that Tute had brought, lying there. A wing feather, and I sat looking at it, trying to remember which bird it could have come from. Yes, the big white one that flapped and honked. The feather lay on the black sand, like a back to front shadow. I remembered how Mai had told me the Peretane people make the signs in their books. Like the tattooist, with the cut point of a feather, dipped in dye. I had only to reach out for it.

Meanwhile someone had come, and was waiting a little way from me, crouching under the twisted purau boughs, looking out to sea. Teraura. But before I could call her name, the shadow of the mourning house fell back upon me. The taste and smell of death welled back up from inside me, from within myself, filling me with ghosts. If I opened my mouth she would hear them speaking, if I went close to her she would smell the decay. So I let the rain keep falling between us.

No longer the world of childhood, this, but filled with contesting spirits, with unfamiliar entities, a host of conflicting deities, things roaring out of the void, soaring, clattering, wailing, gasping, the unburied. The unburied! Aue! My uncle Tautoia, his bones tossed into the charnel pit of Vehiatua! Fallen to me now that appalling burden, passed on in Grandmother's breath. To me, a girl newly tattooed, who should be playing with her friends and dancing to the drums of Tane. My throat called out to Tetua, cried out to her through the noise of rain, begging her to return, and not leave me with those cursed bones. But she was gone. The red canoe no longer held her. It was Grandmother who had escaped.

Teraura had brought a fresh pareu for me, rolled up in waterproof matting, and a gourd of monoi perfumed with tiare to redress my hair. She opened a coconut, still immature enough for the flesh to be a sweet white jelly, and she peeled me fruit. She showed me a new way to make a wreath from green and yellow purau leaves. 'Because now is our tau' arearea, our time for pleasures and love,' she said. 'You should wear yellow to remind all those old people in the mourning house that you are young and full of life.'

She massaged my back, which ached from sitting so long at the head of the bier. 'Don't be afraid,' she said. Her sinuous fingers followed my spine. 'All that talk of spectres and omens, it's for the old ones. We are young, beloved of Tane. Aue, Mauatua, your tattoos are so fine!'

When we came back to the mourning house Tetua's spirit had already left. It was being said that it had departed tranquilly, accompanied by two spirits in the form of white birds that had been seen to swoop in from the storm and take shelter in the breadfruit tree that overhung the thatch. By now it would be ascended to the peak of Rotui, the mountain on Aimeo from whence all souls depart. It would have leapt across the ocean to the peak of Temehani, on Raiatea. From there it would go either upwards to Rotunoanoa, the perpetual pleasure gardens, or be thrown down into Temehani's crater, there to remain a captive of the gods, their servant until they released it. The red-feather amulets might protect her from that fate, or they might not.

Either way, she was beyond our assistance. Her corpse was no more than a corpse now, the living becoming accustomed to its lifelessness. The women began to gossip among themselves, the guests to move about, greeting relatives and friends from afar. Canoes from along the chain of farther lands were being pulled up on the shore. From Huahine, Ra'iatea and Maupiti they would come, as the word carried outward on wind and current.

Tapuatefa ordered a platform to be built high above the ground near the family marae, and the bier lifted up there. He called for the oven fires to be lit, for pigs to be prepared for the ovens, and the heaping up of food to begin. A period of forty days of mourning was considered correct, and all the guests must be fed.

Year of Our Lord 1831

Margaret had difficulty keeping up with her grandmother. The old woman seemed to have regained the stride of youth.

'Run after Granma Christian and look after her,' her aunts had told her. Gladly she had run away out of the house of sick people.

The road was full of fascinating sights. Missionary men on horseback, English ladies with waisted gowns and ribboned bonnets. They were not lying in their houses groaning with fever, no they were going home from church in full health, with their prayer books and bibles swinging on cords. The English children ran along beside them, also carrying their bibles, and they looked sideways at Margaret with eager curiosity, some smiling, some scowling like the missionary fathers.

Granma kept walking, the bottom of her long dress reddening with mud, her bare feet soiled to the ankle.

There was so much to see on Tahiti! The ships floating on the mirror harbour, the horses with their different colours, women washing clothes in the running streams. Why must granma walk so fast? By the side of the road was a man beating a dog with a stick. The dog was crouching, yelping there on the dirt. The old woman pulled her close as they passed. 'No look, e hine, is a bad thing to see. Tahiti is full of wickedness.'

Then they heard noisy laughter and squealing from a house beside the road. Beside its doors and along its verandah white men were lounging with bottles, their feet up on the rails. Their muskets were on their laps. Granma walked ahead with her back straight. 'Turn your eye from wickedness,' she instructed. 'Stop your ear for no hear it.'

They began to climb the slippery hill that separated Pare from the next bay. When they reached the top the old woman stopped at last and let her granddaughter rest. The surf was running in that black-lipped bay below them, dark rollers were curling on the long sand spit. 'Look now,' she said. 'Look now at Matavai. Matavai, home of our ancestors. This where your grandfather's ship came, look, look! Remember! That where your mother Sully born, in a big storm. That the place, there, by that one big cocknut tree, didn't blow down in the storm, still standing though your mother gone already from this world.'

She sat down on the grass, clasping at her breast, and her lips began to form the old language, which Margaret could but half understand, words rushing from her throat in a torrent. Out of her dress pocket she withdrew something Margaret had never seen, a comb perhaps, with a row of pointed teeth. As her voice rose, she raked it across her scalp and rivulets of blood began to flow.

'Granma, what you doing, you hurting yourself!'
'Aue, e hine! Aue, aue!'

Tau' arearea

Mauatua

In their years of tau' arearea, young people were permitted all pleasures. The gods delighted in their experiments and adventures. Nothing was forbidden between them. A mother would be proud for her daughter to attract many boys and have many lovers, for it showed how desirable she was, a compliment to the mother and her ancestresses. Accomplished in the skills of lovemaking, her attractions would become famous and powerful men would seek her out. These were the fond hopes of mothers.

Teraura was such a girl. Tane could not resist her flashing eyes, her sharp-edged smile, which lured them like a pearl-shell hook spinning on a line.

She and I had declared ourselves name sisters, friends for life. After Grandmother's death she came to live in our household, and spread her sleeping mat next to mine. Many nights she returned late, some nights not at all.

For me, there were no meetings along the torch lit shore, no nights in secluded groves. It was not boys which claimed my hours of darkness, but something else, fierce and persistent, that came looking for me, night after night.

It began with the scratching and fluttering in the breast, began quietly, like the pecking of a chick within the egg. But quickly increasing and spreading, feather and bone soon scrabbling at the ribs, twitching in the limbs. Bird, rat, bat, spirit inhabiting, pecking, clamouring, breathing. Breathing. Louder and louder, rattling like stones, breathing my name, clutching, reaching, pulling. Mauatua, Mauatua!

Rolling on my mat as I woke, I flung them off like spiders. They leapt out into the guttering candlenut light that burned all night, they fizzled and expired in the shivering flames, but they left the smell of death in my nostrils, smoking in my lungs.

I would look across at Teraura, lying on her back with her arms flung up. She smelt of pleasure, of coconut oil and sweat, and she smiled in her sleep. For comfort I would creep closer to her, inhaling her perfumed heat, and imagine the pleasantness of her dreams. Her ancestors did not harass her, they let her sleep in peace. Sometimes she woke and reached out to me with a sigh like a baby that has fallen asleep at the breast.

At the marae Hinuia kept vigil, receiving the visiting mourners who still arrived. The place filled me with dread. Pursued by it at night, I kept away from death by day. But each morning the priestess called me there. 'What are your dreams, e hine?'

'They pursue me with their heated breath, it's always the same.'

'Your ancestors are looking to guide and assist you. You must forget the white men e hine, forget, forget, forget. Listen to the spirits, let them manifest, or they will become angry and try to harm you.'

I grew impatient under her endless prayers.

When Tetua's body was taken down and placed in the burial chamber, Hinuia made me look one final time at Grandmother's tattooed hands. 'That is how you will recognise her in the afterworld,' she reminded me. The flies were buzzing eagerly and I dared not cover my nose with a cloth.

I looked instead at my own hands. That is how I will recognise myself. By those same patterns incised into my skin.

'These shall be your keepsake,' she said, and she took up a split bamboo and began tweezing out the corpse's fingernails.

'Not me, Hinuia,' I begged her. 'Let Maoiti have the gift of her mother's nails.'

'First, you will clean them in the ocean,' she instructed. 'Then shape them with a coral rasp, then polish them with monoi, then bore them with a shark's tooth, then attach them to a cord plaited from your grandmother's hair.'

'We wear necklaces of coloured beads now,' I protested. 'I'm too young to wear death mementoes.'

Hinuia reached out and snapped the thread of my necklace with a movement so swift I scarcely felt it, showering beads across the mat. I glimpsed them running away into the cracks of the flagstones.

'The white man's cord is weak,' she said. 'Don't be fooled by their playthings. This is the ihu of your grandmother we speak of, this is the mana she found you fitting to receive. Now is the time to cleanse these foreign influences from you, to look for your guide, to follow the wisdom of your ancestors. You must be absolutely pure, you must bear no stain, no hara, offend no spirits or deities.'

How could I tell our priestess that my guide had directed me to copy the white man's sacred signs, placed a feather in my hands.

The metal blades had nearly all found their way into the hands of men since they were first traded for. The men treasured them, some had learned to shave the hairs from their faces with them, like Popa'a men. They consecrated them to their own gods, wearing them strung on their hips in pandanus sheaths.

It was well known that foreign medicine was necessary to treat any wound made by those foreign blades. And likewise, a foreign blade would be necessary to cut the quill of the foreign bird and turn it to such outlandish purpose.

A sharpened shell, used to scrape aute bark for cloth making, or to split and cut pandanus leaves for weaving, was not sharp enough. Nor was a sliver of bamboo, though it could quickly slit the belly of a pig for the oven. A shark's tooth, cunningly fitted to a handle so as to tear open human skin, was unsuitable. A stone, ground to an edge for hewing timber, too clumsy.

Along the shore fishermen and net menders were gathered.

'What do you want a metal blade for? asked one of them.

'To cut the shaft of a feather.'

'Why do you want to cut that feather?'

'For making patterns on barkcloth.'

'A woman's purpose. This is a fisherman's knife, it would be unlucky to turn it to women's work.'

'But it is a foreign knife, and our gods have no jurisdiction over it.'

'It makes no difference, a man does not let a woman use his tools.'

This set the younger men glancing and giggling like girls.

'A white man would let me.'

'E, a white man would let you, but can a white man spear fish as we do?'

The laughter mounted.

'The white men speared all the prettiest fish on Tahiti!' claimed Teraura, who never missed a chance to flirt.

The men hooted with delight at this reply. 'Take these,' said one of them, throwing a string of coloured lagoon fish at her. 'When can I come fishing at your house?'

Teraura broke into a dance, flinging the fish around her hips. Other girls were arriving, attracted by the laughter.

It was Teraura who borrowed a knife from one of her lovers, perhaps without him knowing it. The feather was cut easily then. Together we prepared the dye from burnt tu'tui nuts, scraping the soot to mix with water in a coconut shell.

The book itself was where I had hidden it, still tightly wrapped. Teraura sighed with admiration as the layers of cloth disclosed it. She turned it around in her hands, caressing its soft skin, marvelling at the smooth edges which fanned out into a thousand white whispering leaves. 'What is it?' she asked.

'It is the sacred knowledge of the white men, all told by signs.'

'Aue! What will you do with it?'

'Watch and you will see.'

At first the dye spilt from the eye of the quill in black droplets and spoiled the white cloth. It was necessary to shake them out first, and seek the grip which would apply just the right amount of pressure. Then it was easy. But the marks in the book were so tiny, so many, and I did not understand how they could have been made so small except with the tip of the tiniest feather. My first attempts were clumsy and disfigured. I began by tapping dots, the way the tattooist works, before I realised that it was possible to form the shapes with a single line. By the end of the afternoon I had copied the first word many times, each time more completely than the last. The mystery of it stared from the rough barkcloth. They were like a mask that hides a sacred face, those seven signs. GENESIS.

After Teraura had come to live in our household, our bleeding soon began happening at the same time. We stayed three days each time at the women's house, among all the other women whose moon cycle was the same, and we did not work, or touch food in this time, but drank only water, and bathed in running water, and stayed away from all others. Children and men did not seek us there; we kept to a separate part of the shore and had a bathing pool of our own where our blood could be washed away safely. Tuna, the eel, was guardian of that pool, and grew fat there in return for protecting us from evil spirits, for Tuna loved the woman, Hina, so much that he gave his life for her.

Yet the white men had left bitter traces of their passing. Rashes of spots and blisters that broke out on women's breasts and bellies and shoulders, sores in the most intimate parts. At the women's house these signs were discussed and examined, medicinal treatments trialed and recommended. Some women were grieving the loss of babies born half formed; others, in fear, had gone to the tahua mori to massage out a white man's child, or to the tahua ra'au, to mix a secret remedy. There was weeping and whispering.

'What have we done that the gods punish us with these sorrows?' it was asked.

'Evil spirits of the white men,' it was murmured.

'They leave their sicknesses with us, they leave their children to die in our wombs. Death is in their embrace.'

Teraura and I pressed tightly together as we heard the stories murmured there.

'The gardener was a kind man,' said Teraura. He carried no bad spirits with him.'

'Tute, also, is good.'

'Next time I will go with them,' she said.

There were other girls who were interested in the talk. Mareva and Faahotu were cousins, the daughters of manahune sisters. Mareva's mother had been a servant in my grandmother's household. They were strong-legged and broad-shouldered, and both had spent time on Tute's ship, and learnt some of the Peretane language. They liked to retell the stories of those times, about nights squeezed into the swinging nets the sailors slept in, with the white men snoring all about while the girls lay joking and talking in the swaying belly of the ship. They acted out the tricks that had been played on the men, incorporating white men's snores, white men's angry voices, the sounds of their pleasure. We burst with laughter at these tales. Some of the older women were disapproving, but our eyes strayed constantly to the distant horizon, where the white sails would reappear.

Vahineatua, like Teraura, came from a ra'atira family. The work of her hands was always fine. From her grandmother she was learning how to bleach and scrape purau bark to make fine skirts and mats, and how to treat the pia stalk to get the soft white ribbons used to decorate dance costumes. She had a soft voice and a quiet laugh and she would draw near to me and Teraura in the women's house. Her family had kept her close to home all her childhood, but now she was a woman, free to follow her own inclinations. Like me, she was pirimomona, a virgin, and had heard only stories of white men's love.

By night, circled in her glowing orb, glorious Hina sat straight-backed among the stars with beater raised, pounding an endless sheet of white barkcloth. It was for Ta'aroa, god of the ocean, that Hina herself had given her life, in that distant time when the gods dwelt on earth. She was working tirelessly at the beating board, making a cloak for him. All night and all day her mallet pounded, but Ta'aroa wanted to sleep. He sent a servant to ask her to cease, but she only laughed and said cloth beating was soothing to sleep to. He sent his servant again to command her to stop, and still she refused. 'Tell him to block his ears,' she replied.

Ta'aroa was furious, and he sent the servant one last time to stop her. He pleaded with her, but she said, 'You will have to kill me if you want me to stop.'

The servant, afraid of his master, snatched Hina's mallet and hit her on the head with it. Now at last, the beating stopped, and Ta'aroa could sleep in peace. Then Hina's spirit left the world, it flew up into the sky. It occupied the moon, and she sits there beneath a heavenly tree, with her mallet ever raised to her work, and appoints herself the guardian of women's occupations.

This is the stubborn and fearless Hina who cannot be extinguished by command of even mighty Ta'aroa, but takes to the realm of stars and resides in an orb of light, like an unborn babe in its water sac.

Again and again she dies and is reborn in an endless reflection and echo of te ao marama, the world of light inhabited by humans. It was Hina we praised and Hina we prayed to, the Hina of ages, Hina the goddess, Hina the protectress, Hina the maiden, Hina the old one. We are her daughters, her servants; she commands our wombs and showers the night with her subtle radiance. Even the ocean must obey her.

To Hina the girls prayed for a cure to the foreign afflictions, weeping and singing the old songs, sung by the grandmothers and their grandmothers, retelling the stories of Hina's goodness. Hina, do not desert us.

While others said that only a foreign medicine could cure the foreign disease.

The symbols began to flow easily from my feather tip. Hooked sticks and coiled lines, circles and crosses, dots and loops. I kept the patterned sheets rolled up among my mats, not daring to let Hinuia see how I passed my time. She thought that I went with the other girls to dance and swim in the afternoons. Often I did. In Matavai Bay the coral head of Hiro's reef was always raised above the water, inviting us to swim out to it. The small waves scrambled around it, tangling and crossing as they met each other. As we played and dived there, the gods looked down favourably upon us from the peaks of Orohena, from the slopes of food springing forth. We were their favourite daughters – they would grant us fertility, grace and strength. We admired one another's breasts and bellies, and our tattoos, nearly all complete, which gave us secret patterns such as the birds and fishes wear.

Sometimes we dived to the seabed to look for things left behind by Tute's ship, which had lain at anchor near the Toa Hiro. There were still nails to be found, and the metal discs. Teraura, who was a good diver, found a metal fork lodged in a crack of coral. 'My sister must have dropped this in her haste,' she declared. 'When she sees me eat so nicely with it she'll want it back.'

'Did she drop this also?' asked Mareva, tossing her a bottle.

'Aue, the white man's crazy water, and the stopper is still in it.'

They gathered around quickly, holding the bottle up to the light and pushing at the bung.

'There was a special tool for pulling out the stopper,' Faahotu remembered.

'We'll have to push it in with a stick.'

Teraura carried it ashore, but she could not hide it from the boys who were playing on the sand. 'What have you found?'

'Only a bottle.'

'Is it empty? Let us see.'

'It is ours, we found it.'

'It's full! My brother has the tool to get the stopper out.'

'Tell your brother to bring it to me then.'

'Let me take it to him.'

'Go now and get him to bring it to me.'

'He is gone up into the valley, cock fighting.'

'Then tell him tomorrow.'

She kept hold of the bottle and later we hid it in a crab's hole under a purau tree. Next day it had gone already, and the boys were crazy.

'You stole our bottle,' Teraura accused them.

'No, it was the thieving land crab that must have taken it,' came the reply, and they laughed, and invited us to dance with them.

In the years of tau' arearea young people were permitted all pleasures. Nothing was forbidden between us. But it was a different hand which guided me, the unseen which crowded at the borders of the known world, beckoning me.

Upa Upa

Flying pennants and tassels like coloured birds above, the canoes came in through the pass to Pare. The sound of the conch shell trumpeting across the water set the lonely bull, left there by Tute, to bellowing in excited reply, the mixed-breed dogs began to bark and people rushed to the shore wondering what they would see.

'Arioi! Arioi!' the cry ran back.

A ripple of excitement had been spreading out from Pare. The long-stagnant atmosphere of suspense was stirring, for Tu planned marriage, and the new chiefess would be Itia, the niece of Mahine, the warrior chief of Aimeo. The wild drums and ululations of the arioi announced a holiday of feasting and revelry at Pare, the lifting of tapu restrictions to celebrate the marriage. Paddles dipped in time to the drum beat, and on platforms raised across the decks of their canoes, dancers began to shake and gesture, calling forward to the people on the shore, sunlight bursting from their raiments of shining yellow leaves and red dyed cloth, their shimmering plumes, their trailing garlands.

Some held it to be a great alliance, this marriage, ensuring safety from the forces of Mahine. But as always there were others who shook their heads and cautioned. It would be seen as treachery by To'ofa of Atehuru, who had long sought to involve Tu, and Tute too, in his own battles against Mahine. Treachery was seldom left unavenged.

For all the seasons that had come and gone since Tute's departure, Tu had been invoking the invisible cloak of Tute's promised protection against his enemies. The portrait of Tute took pride of place at all the ceremonial occasions at the Tarahoi Marae. His pale gaze and rolled white hair were the first thing any guest to Tu's royal household would see. The image was freshly garlanded, like a ti'i, each day. 'My friend Tute, the chief of Peretane,' Tu always referred to him as, and, as if that alone was enough to protect his lands and subjects from any harm, he had left Pare in the charge of his brother Ari'ipaea, to travel with the arioi for months at a time, roaming from island to island with those masters of pleasure.

Itia herself had also been living with the arioi. She was known among them as a champion arm wrestler and surf rider. Her shoulders were like rocks and her legs like the trunks of trees. Her belly was wide enough to carry three babies at once. She stood as tall as her husband, and bolder in her stance. When she came onto the marae on the day of her marriage the people gave a gasp of awe and delight to see one so truly a queen. Her immense stature was wrapped in cloth richly stained with dark red and yellow, chains of yellow shells swung from her girdle, and she wore a crown of red and yellow leaves whose long points radiated around her head like the rays of the sun. The discussions of her lineage had been flying for weeks. Now the people tore the garments from their shoulders and breasts in reverence. With such a wife, Tu would be a great chief indeed and the fame of the district of Pare would spread far and wide.

Mauatua was there with her Pare cousins for the marriage ceremony. The perfumes of flowers and oil and freshly made barkcloth rose up above the crowd. The ni'au palm tops glittered in the balm, throbbing to the drum beat that rang throughout the valley and resounded from the slopes.

Brought out from secret caches, the skulls and bones of Tu's ancestors had been set up by the priests upon the altar stones, their empty sockets staring from atop the crossed piles of thigh and arm bones, and from the front row of the assembly the pallid image of Tute looked on with an impassive gaze. The cloths were spread there before the altar, pieces specially beaten by the women of each family, and Itia and Tu were seated on them. Tu's headdress was huge with feathers, scarlet tropic bird-tail quills fanned out from its heights, and from behind, the shining, curling, plumes of cockerels black and white sprang out trembling in the light.

The two faced each other in the closed circle of their sacredness, fixed in the collective gaze of the living and the dead. The high priest began to call upon the spirits to approve the union, and, as the sound of his arcane chant arose, some looked up and saw, coiling upward through the mists that clothed the peaks of Aora'i, a spiralling vortex of dark air, and the eyes of the crowd rose to follow that auspicious sign as it wavered on the sky, followed by a murmur of approval and relief.

By the time the bowl lined with miro leaves passed Mauatua, the mixture of cane juice and coconut milk in it was purpled with the blood her relatives had drawn from their brows with shell and tooth blades and let fall into the liquid. Carefully, the priest stained the sacred cloths with it, mingling the bloods of the two families drop by drop, a symbol of union to be secreted among the other holy relics of the marae.

Only the final rite remained to be performed. The tall drums were struck up again and their sharkskins pounded the message into the thick air. Another great sheet of cloth was unrolled and tossed across the couple, covering them completely, and the drum beat came heavier and faster, finding the rhythm that sets the blood racing with pleasure. All eyes watched the movements muffled by the cloth, the skin of men and women glistened with moisture, the indrawn breath of anticipation flowed like a stream from one to another. Mauatua felt light, her body hungry, her mouth dry. She began to ache as if with fever. The hot sunlight danced overhead and desire swelled in the heat like a fruit about to burst. The voices of the people began to urge on the climax, crying, chanting, cheering, singing, in a frenzy of passion.

Torchlight blazed all around the open sides of the fare upa upa, the great performance house. The important people sat on soft mats around the arena, the commoners thronged the grassy slopes beyond, jostling for the best view. The musicians sat ready, the beaters of tall drums, blowers of flutes. The fatu upa upa, the master of ceremonies, stepped forth.

Stepped forth, ha ha hoi! High stepping, proud chested, like a cockerel. Black eyes darting forth from red-dyed face, he scanned the audience, great chief and servant alike, man, woman and child, stilling and silencing them so that when he flung up his arms the long leaves of his armbands could be heard to rustle. Orange flames danced on his oiled breast and belly, his legs were blackened with the tattoos of the highest rank of performer.

'Ha ha, indeed, it is I!' his words sprang forth. 'I stand! I stand to take my place on the assembly ground of this mighty chief, Tu Nui e A'a i te Atua. Here, on the projecting point of Utuhaihai where it reaches forth into the food-providing bay of Pare ... '

Thus it began, thus it always began. The long recitation of names and references, everything placed in its relation to everything else. The chief in relation to land and sea, in relation to the gods, in relation to the commoners, all things beginning at the chief, weaving around him like the radiating strands of a basket begun from the centre, a basket to hold the bounty of Tahitinui, all its food and wealth and goodness. Thus it always began.

And was always different. There was license to say anything, freedom of all subjects. Today the jests would be on the new chiefess, everybody knew that.

'Hei! Such a treasure will our chief Tu be able to offer his bond friend Tute when that great one returns to Tahiti.' He gestured slyly towards Tute's silently watching image, crooked his knees and pretended humility before the foreign chief, then he leapt up to imitate him, with stiff walk and unbending spine, raising and lowering his invisible hat, greeting and turning. Stiff armed, he approached Itia and he bowed from the waist. 'May I remain erect in your service your highness,' he said, and the people cheered with delight. Itia herself was a mountain of laughter, a shaking mountain of laughter – and the people were happy to hear the new chiefess laugh – and now the laughter must not stop, it should be louder and wilder, it should fill the night and drive away all spirits of darkness and fear, it should shake every breast and fill every throat, snapping the bonds, loosening the constraints of propriety. So that when the dancers, the fire jugglers, the mimics, the actors, the wrestlers came out into the magical circle of wavering firelight, there should be no barrier between the people and the pleasures of their senses.

For one beat, one blood, one breath to expand from each human core, a single ecstasy embraced every man, woman and child. For the feet to applaud the mats, the arms speak poetry, the tattooed limbs and painted torsos become bodies of gods, ancestors, demons, shining armatures of colour entwined in streamers of flame and feathers of man birds, with eyes burning in the black sockets of now, then, forever, like stars in the navel of night, the legends living again, generations begotten anew.

Dances began slowly, with hands drawing down the stars, then sending them back, whirling, with steps that whispered on the mats with one voice, navels filled with flowers, praising the moon, causing the perfume of aroha to bloom so the men would spring from their haunches, their thighs bending like the niau in the storm, oiled rods their ure, stiff with the seed of ancestors bursting, and the bellies bending together, hip following hip, arm attracted to arm, one beat, one blood, one breath. So that even a virgin woman, seated among her highborn relatives, would know the gathering force of love, the need of man for woman, seed for soil, soil for rain, and the fires of love running her through with that exquisite pain, that powerful longing – so how beautiful the glistening dark crevices displayed, the invitation of the thirsty flower, beneath the dance skirts lifted in unison.

Then the lead dancers show the way, enacting every move of love, summoning the ecstasies of desire. Even a virgin might be swept into the glowing orbit of this worship, abandoning all her senses to it. Wild cries wing up, circling the circling couple, the drums echo their every step and turn, their flesh like food for the gods, for every woman recognises the rapture of the womb, opening unseen, and every man remembers in an instant the exquisite narrowness of enclosure. Wetness is on their skins, flowers fall around their quivering limbs, garments are cast away. Everything is revealed, consumed, the backs are arched, the trembling ure enters every woman as it presses into the one. Even the virgin will know its purpose, its perfection. And voices begin to cry out for pleasure, and the drum echoes each thrust with steady beat, firelight twisting on the limbs that contort in the consuming dance of love, ablaze across the tattooed loins that press the pleasure home.

Even as babes slept in arms and laps, even as old men nodded with approval, even as chiefs were honoured and virgins aroused, young men were pushing at the edge of the crowd, wide eyed, and the aspirants, those who would be arioi themselves and worship with equal fervour, the aspirants danced on the edges of the circle, tossing their bodies into the postures of unrestrained frenzy, lost in the upa upa, the infinity of pleasure.

For three days nobody worked, except those who were preparing and cooking the food, but they laboured hard at the fires in the heat of the afternoon to prepare the evening's feast, while others still slumbered in the shady guest houses and groves, resting before the night's fresh revelries.

A young man came weary to the performance house after sunset. He was tired from the firing of the oven stones, tired from the lifting of the hot baskets of fish and plantain fruits, from the husking and breaking of man-high heaps of coconuts. Yet the drums soon began to beat fresh blood into his veins, new fire sprang into his belly. His arms felt light again, the sinews of his legs pulled him towards the pounding centre of the dance, the musk of pleasure filled his fire-dried nostrils. His smoke-stung eyes began to look, searching among the women and girls for one who might be his partner that night, and as the dance began mounting to its peak, the flare of a torch showed him the enraptured gaze of the virgin Mauatua, seated there among the ari'i, with the highborn wedding guests. Again and again he sought her above the surging motion of the dancers, casting his desire towards her until at last he caught her eye. He opened his own eyes wide, showing her all the whites of them, and she, she smiled in return, with open lips, her face aglow.

Then he could hardly wait for the dancing to end, impatient anticipation tightening his intestines, manhood leaping. For only at such a time, with all the rigorous rules of class suspended for the upa upa, would a cookhouse servant get a chance to make love to an ari'i virgin.

All through the laughing, coupling crowd he sought her afterwards, afraid he may have misunderstood her look, if such a look could be misunderstood. When they found each other it was with startled recognition. She smiled again, put her hand to her mouth, turned to her friend, the pretty dark one who went everywhere with her, her name sister. The name sister, Teraura, was already famous for her tricks, but it was the highborn girl he wanted, the tall one like a lissom sweet cane to suck the juice of, slender and smooth haired, she who walked with her head above the others, her eyes seeing further.

The three of them went along together, not as if they were going anywhere in particular, among the singing, flickering shadows of the unsleeping night, weaving among the crowd, until Teraura saw a friend of hers and went away with him.

Then they were alone.

'Come, Mauatua,' he said. 'This way, I know a place.'

All thoughts of white ships were gone from her head, it was something hotter than an oven stone that filled her being, drawing her to him to relieve her of it, and she followed without hesitation.

The broad hands of breadfruit leaves were sheltering her from the morning sky when she woke. The smell of cookhouse smoke was on her skin, bringing a hot flood of memory. She reclosed her eyes and waited expectantly to feel his strong thighs reach over her again.

But he was long gone. It was Teraura who sat there waiting for her friend to wake. She had been up early along the river and came back with an armful of fragrant jasmine strands and purple ti leaves. Her fingers were binding them together, and at the same time she was finding the words for a song. The pleasures of the upa upa were its subject.

'Who is that handsome boy, does he have a name?' she asked. 'Shall I call him Stoker of Oven Fires? Servant of Hungry Virgins?'

Her friend stretched herself, smiling. 'I could call him Food Tasted in Darkness. Have you seen him this morning?'

'He spoke only to me, and told me where to find you. He is walking like a chief today.'

'Aue, everyone will know, Hinuia will hear of it.'

Teraura shrugged. 'Tau' arearea. It is permitted. You told me long ago that you would choose your own lovers. This is for you.' She held up a finished garland. 'Ti'ura, the purple ti which smooths the water for fishing and tafifi, the perfume of desire. Was it good, the food you tasted?'

'It was good.'

'Wear this and you will taste it again tonight.'

'Should I be as greedy as you?'

'A girl should eat when she is hungry. Aue, but you smell of the cookhouse, come to the bathing pool.'

Year of Our Lord 1831

With renewed energy, like a young girl, the old woman pushed through tangles of vines and weeds, holding aside branches for her granddaughter to follow her, lifting her feet over mossy stones and rivulets.

'Where we going, Granma?'

'Follow me, e hine.' She started to sing, not hymns, but a soft monotonous crooning in the old tongue. The thick foliage bent back behind them like a trap. Sinking into the greenery around them were collapsed and rotting walls and roofs. Her singing grew louder, and suddenly stopped.

They were on the edge of an open space. A tumble of stones surrounded it, thick with the long weeds of neglect. She pulled Margaret to her knees beside her. 'Te marae,' she whispered. 'This where your ancestors prayed. No church then e hine.' Tall stones poked up through the rank grass in the middle. Out of habit Margaret began to say the Lord's Prayer. When she got to lead us not into temptation, something made her open her eyes. A rat moved without haste along the overgrown wall. She watched its tail disappear through a hole, and her tongue dried up on the next words of the prayer. It was the eye hole of a skull. A pile of skulls, with baby trees sprouting through the sockets. One had been lifted up by a growing tree and grafted onto its sapling trunk.

'Death is everywhere, come to everyone, come to all these ancestors,' said her grandmother. 'No look any more.'

They moved on again. They were climbing now. Sometimes through the trees she caught glimpses of the bay where her grandfather's ship had lain and where her mother, that they all called Big Sully, had been born in a storm. Tahiti was so much bigger than Pitcairn. The mountains seemed to be towering above her, reaching into the clouds. The sound of water was continuous. She followed her grandmother's bare ankles, up and up, over roots and rocks and cold streams, sometimes using their hands to pull themselves up. Halfway to the sky they stopped to eat some bananas, and saw the bay far below. Granma lifted up her skirt, stretching her muddy legs into the sunshine. 'One day come up here with your aunt Susannah. Teraura her name then.'

'What for you coming up here so far, Granma?'

'Come with me, you follow me now e hine.'

The cave was invisible to Margaret's eyes, all overhung with greenery. But Granma knew it was there, she pulled away vines and branches. 'Stay here,' she instructed before she crept in under the hanging leaves.

Margaret sat down on the warm rock. She watched a little lizard come back out of the grass where it had run for cover. Then she saw lying among the leaves at the cave mouth a curve of light, a big old pearl shell whose moon shine was bleached by sun and rain. She wondered why the shell was so high up the mountain, so far from where any people lived. She picked it up and applied its sharp edge to the mosquito bites on her legs. It was a perfect scratcher. Then she scratched white patterns on the backs of her brown hands until they were sore and she was sleepy. Resting her head in the shade of a bunch of ferns, she closed her eyes to wait for Granma.

Itia

The chiefess Itia was being carried over the hill of Tahara'a which divides the districts of Matavai and Pare. She had two bearers, even stronger and taller than herself, who took turns to carry her on their shoulders, for her sacred feet could not touch any ordinary ground without rendering it equally sacred. Those feet, tattooed with ascending spirals, were crossed above the breast of her bearer, her hands rested nobly on her braced thighs. The two of them made a godly height, a tall vision. The second bearer went swiftly ahead, setting the pace, his naked buttocks flexing with his uphill strides, setting to motion the intricate patterns of his tattoos. A third man came behind, carrying a roll of matting, her fan and fly whisk. Yet a fourth followed him, the pole across his shoulder bending with the weight of food and gifts.

At the crest of the hill they paused, and Itia looked down upon the ruffled waters of Matavai, clasped by the long headland, fringed with a dark feathering of ironwoods and waving palms. She saw the deep calm water where the white men could safely bring their laden vessels. For this sheltered water, the bay of Matavai, was the envy of every chief of Tahiti, and soon, she knew, it would be entirely under the control of her husband Tu, for the chiefly line of Matavai was broken by the curse of Vehiatua. The bones of the old chiefess Tetua had been scraped and buried, her second son, Tapuetefa, had been lost on a fishing expedition, and his young son Tatahe was yet unconsecrated to take his place. Nari'i, and the priestess Hinuia held the remnants of the family together, and were sure to be searching for a suitable match for the girl Mauatua, a man who would assist young Tatahe, scarcely circumcised, to protect their claim to Matavai.

Alas, the girl could not marry into Tu's family. She was too closely related to them. The fault of her headstrong birth mother, Maoiti, who had thrown herself at the first high-born man she could, but had quickly been rejected on account of her scolding ways. It was to be hoped that the daughter had not inherited her sharp tongue, for Itia knew of young men further afield, and her desire to see her own husband stand as supreme chief on Matavai's black sand when the next white ship arrived filled her with eager anticipation.

Her second bearer backed up to the first. She stretched forward to clasp his bent shoulders and leapfrogged onto them as easily as a little child. He gripped her crossed ankles, and the first bearer took his place ahead to begin the long descent.

Itia noticed that the house of Nari'i and Hinuia was in need of repair. The palm-leaf panels were withering and would let in the cool south wind. The chickens scratching at the edges of the mats were not shooed away. It was the old priestess who presided, her hair almost all white, but crowned by the tall comb made of her ancestress' bone. A tremor of fear ran through the chiefess' bosom at the sight of this tapu bone. Then she remembered that this was one who presided over a dying line, whose endless prayers and incantations had failed to restore

Tautoia's bones, failed to protect her mistress from the hideous fe'e disease. Whose magic was dried-up and useless. Itia had her mat spread to sit upon and she called for the gifts to be presented.

Then, at the right moment, she mentioned her business.

※ ※ ※

Hinuia kept her countenance. During the night, while others slept, she had seen a single bird fly across the face of the moon. A sign. She looked hard into the smile of the chiefess, whose teeth were as white as her barkcloth shawl.

'It was the wish of her grandmother that Mauatua should remain at Matavai. It is my wish that she should remain at Matavai. We have need of her here and we hope to see her children born here.'

'She can return as soon as she has found a husband,' Itia replied. Many young men are visiting us at Pare now, canoes come from Aimeo and Huahine, even from the Tuamotus. I myself have cousins who seek a wife … '

'She will not marry a man from the Tuamotus,' said Hinuia.

Itia chose to ignore this well-placed insult. 'In our household she will be able to take dancing lessons with her cousins, grow fat eating the best of foods. Among the other girls her beauty will blossom. I have chosen the prettiest girls of Tahiti and Aimeo to be my waiting maids, and men will flock to meet them.'

The chiefess lifted her feather-edged fan and stirred the air with long slow sweeps. She lowered her voice a tone. 'As the girl is no longer a virgin, it will be harder for you to attract so many prospects here,' she suggested delicately. 'Her loveliness may go unseen. It would be a waste, and I hear she is very clever … '

'She took the dying breath of Tetua Avari'i. She is no ordinary girl. A great responsibility is her burden. She is our future. Think of this before you entice her away from us.'

Itia seized eagerly on this new objection. 'It is in the very memory of your mistress Tetua that I make this request, for was Tetua not born at Nu'urua as I was myself? Was Tetua not my grandmother's cousin?'

'This I cannot deny,' said Hinuia, 'but Mauatua belongs to Matavai.'

'Shall we ask her her own desires?' Itia put it.

Hinuia did not move a muscle. Her eyes burned. Without turning she called to the servant who hovered nearby. 'Where is Nari'i? Where is Mauatua? Bring them here.'

They waited in silence.

✻ ✻ ✻

Mauatua heard Maunu calling to her, and she hid away the piece of cloth she was copying signs onto before she replied.

'The chiefess of Pare is here to see you,' he announced excitedly, rolling his eyes up. 'She is seated on her mat in the house face to face with Hinuia, and,' here he came close and whispered in her ear, 'she is asking for you to be one of her tapairu!'

Nari'i came hurrying from her work and they took their places on the mat beside Hinuia. The chiefess was beautiful in spite of her broad features and masculine form. Her dark, intelligent eyes fixed a kindly attention on the young girl opposite her. She was said to be as generous and benevolent as she was bold and handsome and Mauatua, the object of her gaze, felt sure this was true. Straight away she knew that she would like to live at Pare, in Itia's busy household which, she had heard, was always full of music, laughter and noble guests.

'The chiefess Itia of Pare has come to issue an invitation,' began Hinuia. 'You will listen to her and give your answer.'

Mauatua listened with the proper respect, saying nothing, but already her thoughts were racing. To be a tapairu in the highest household of Tahiti – what girl would refuse this offer? She imagined the dancing and singing, the days spent in gentle pleasures, the admiring crowds of young men who always sought the attentions of such girls. The Matavai household, whose losses seemed to follow each other like beads on a string, had become a place of sadness since Tapuetefa's death. There were too many ghosts in the empty spaces and she shivered on her mats at night. Teraura was always out with one of her lovers, Hinuia was constantly at her prayers, and no white sail ever appeared on the horizon.

Yet how could she leave now, when her family's shoulders were heavy with grief. She glanced at Nari'i, who was like a mother to her, strong and tireless, but with grey in her hair and creases down her cheeks since she was left a widow. At Hinuia, old bones creaking, who had guided her hand since babyhood. She looked at the chiefess, whose thick black hair was pierced with a single red tropic-bird feather like a swift dart thrown there.

She gave the politest answer. 'I thank you for your invitation. You do me great honour, but I cannot give you my answer without consulting with my elders,' she said. 'My family needs me. This is my home.'

She felt Hinuia sigh. An invisible wave of relief seemed to flow out around her.

✂ ✂ ✂

Itia made her farewells and left that day without achieving her wish. But within one moon she returned. This time she had made sure that the mother, Maoiti, had advance notice of her intentions and would be there too. Itia had chosen the finest of gifts to bring, and she had sent ahead of her two servants who were already at work cutting palm fronds and plaiting new wall panels for the house. For Mauatua she had brought a mirror from Tute's ship, backed with shining metal and engraved with foreign symbols. There was no mistaking the delight in the girl's eyes as they lit upon it. To add to that, there was a pair of scissors with a tassel of foreign red thread, soft as hair, attached to one loop. She saw the admiration and envy in Maoiti's expression as her daughter received such valuable gifts, and she knew the priestess would be defeated today.

Hinuia sat straight backed as ever. All day Maoiti had raved at her, reminding her of her impotence. When she had protested that Tetua would have wanted the girl to stay at Matavai, Maoiti had poured scorn on her. 'And now does my mother's servant tell me what is best for my daughter?' she had said. 'Should she stay here in this place of ghosts while her youth fades? What whim of foolish old womanhood is this? Let her go and take advantage of this great opportunity. She will make a fine match and she will come back wearing red feathers.'

Hinuia knew that red feathers were not Mauatua's destiny, that the girl had strange, unnatural habits, was too often alone, that she had secrets and unspoken longings. Perhaps, after all, it was safer for her to go to Pare where her oddness would be rubbed away by the company of other girls and the activities of the royal household. Perhaps if she stayed at Matavai it would be her destiny to become a crazy spinster. Perhaps by leaving she would escape the curse of Vehiatua which was cutting her family down one by one. She let Maoiti's scolding tongue run its course. It complained of the bad company Mauatua was keeping, of Hinuia's carelessness in letting her lose her virginity to a servant, of what people were saying about Matavai on the other side of Tahitinui. She held her own tongue.

And when she saw the gifts laid out, and the new palm-leaf panels for her house mounting up outside the walls, she knew that Itia could not be refused. Even so, Mauatua should be seen to make her own decision. 'Speak, e hine, and let us hear your wishes now,' she said, when Itia had repeated her invitation.

Mauatua's request was not so surprising. She saw her mother's eagerness and Hinuia's resignation and knew she could accept. But there was one person who must come with her. 'I have a bond friend, Teraura, who is as a sister to me. If I am to live at Pare, then I would wish for her to come also.'

Itia considered. The girl Teraura was known even at Pare for her wild ways, but she was also known to be accomplished at hand work, a weaver of beautiful garlands, good tempered and cheerful. If the price of Mauatua included Teraura, then so it would be. A place would be found for her too.

Tapairu

Mauatua

It was Maunu, not Teraura, who came with me to Pare to be a tapairu at the court of Tu and Itia.

Teraura had not come to the women's house that moon, and everyone soon knew that she had found the man who could strike to life a child in her womb.

His family at Hitiaa wanted the child to be born to them, so she rolled her mats and bundled together her treasures, some cloth that I had patterned with the quill for her, her secret amulets and the pearl-shell earrings she wore when she was dancing. Nari'i gave her a roll of fine white cloth. Hinuia's ritual was for the safe delivery of her new life. Her mother gave her the paoniho, to draw the blood of grief and joy.

She was happy, smiling, when she climbed into his canoe; he was handsome and proud. The women were pleased for her. They approved of his family and the correct way the arrangements had been made. Talking all at once, they anticipated a healthy son, congratulated her mother on such a successful match.

I went alone to weep. Aue, I wept for my solitude.

Ever more the woman, Maunu, yet on the way up the slopes of Tahara'a the day we left, he was like an uncle, keeping pace behind me, guiding my steps upward, not letting me stop until we reached the top.

There we gained our breath and viewed the two chiefdoms, the one behind us, the one ahead. When I saw the smoke rising from the cookhouse of my old home my throat began to tighten, to think of Nari'i and Hinuia left there alone.

'No, look this way,' said Maunu, turning me gently.

The smoke from numberless cooking fires was drifting up the valleys of Pare. Large canoes were beached along the shore and we could hear the mingled rhythms of drums and tapa beaters.

'Hei, they are making a big welcome for us!' he said. 'This is our big chance, Mauatua – we'll be the belles of Pare!'

'You, maybe, Maunu.'

'They'll soon fatten you up. No more tears, e hine, the feast awaits us. Maunu's time has come!' He headed off downhill, shrieking and giggling, hardly waiting for me to keep up with him.

When we arrived he regained his decorum, put on his haughtiest manners to impress Itia's servants as they took us to her.

'I come with Mauatua, and her mistress is to be my mistress,' he told her.

She smiled her wide generous smile. 'Turn around,' she commanded.

He turned gracefully, enjoying being on show. The other girls began to giggle. One threw a flower at him.

'Is he not a fine man, girls? Better he came than that firebrand Teraura, ne?' Her laughter came from deep in her chest, like something bubbling up and overflowing, shaking her breasts. 'This one, I keep for myself.'

After this he was always near her. She took him for her taio and gave him a high position as guardian of the tupu, the sacred cast-offs of her body. The clippings of her nails, the hair cut from her head, her worn-out or discarded garments, it was Maunu's job to take them all to the tiri a pera, the burial pit on the marae, safe there from any kind of malicious tampering, or sorcery which could threaten her life. It was the position of greatest trust.

The tapairu shared her house. We had a wing of our own, and no ghosts assailed me there. No, it was full of the dreams and vanities of young women, gossip, laughter, songs and games. It was a difficult place to keep anything hidden. Before I had been there two nights everyone knew about the book rolled up in my sleeping mat. 'It was a white man who gave you this?' they asked.

I told them it was Mai who had given it to me, but of course some did not believe it. They passed it round, fingering and exclaiming.

'What is it? What do all these marks mean?'

'The stories of the white men's god, told by the white men's signs.'

Soon they had seen the pieces of barkcloth I had patterned with the signs and the word was out that Mauatua was making new designs on cloth.

The girl called Tuaonoa was the first to ask me to put those designs on a pareu for her. I agreed because she was ari'i, from the chiefdom of Paea, higher in rank than myself. She brought me the piece of cloth, larger than any I had patterned before, soft and smooth. First, I used my new scissors to trim the rough edges. Their cutting beak was so swift and sure it guided my hand as if it were a living thing, snipping this way, that way, until it had made a border like sharks' teeth, as sharp and fine as the handsome features of Tuaonoa herself. Then I mixed the dye and began to draw the signs along the borders, one following the other, around and around. I opened the leaves at random, and copied what I saw.

And it shall be, when thou art come in unto the land which the LORD thy God giveth thee for an inheritance, and possessest it, and dwellest therein; 2 That thou shalt take of the first fruit of the earth, which thou shalt bring of thy land that the LORD thy God giveth thee, and shall put it in a basket, and shalt go unto the place which the LORD thy God shall choose to place his name there.

When Tuaonoa wrapped herself in this pareu she appeared as no woman of Tahiti had ever appeared before. The clipped edging and border of silent black words created an effect that everyone turned to see, and desired for herself. More and more cloth was brought to me to decorate. One day Itia called me to her. Maunu was cutting her hair for her: already he was her most personal attendant. He pulled up the glistening black curls one by one and snipped the ends, looking at me over her head and raising his eyebrows, grinning. He was very happy at Pare. Sharing Itia's mat was the old woman who had come with her from Aimeo, a servant from her childhood, swinging a fan entirely covered in tufts of tiny red parrot breast feathers. Itia smiled at me lazily. 'Ah Mauatua,' she said. 'Sit, sit here beside me. Tell me about this beautiful cloth you're making. Is it true that you are decorating it with the white men's signs?'

'It is true. I copy them from the book given to me by Mai, who brought it from Peretane.'

'Sacred signs they say.'

'It is a book of sacred signs.'

'It is good then, very good. We shall be ready for the white men when they come back.'

'Let us hope they come back soon.'

'Indeed. And the white men's sacred signs would only be understood by persons of high birth, would they not, by priests and noblemen and chiefs?'

'That may be so.'

'So you should make them only for persons of high birth. Not for servants or commoners.' She let these words linger between us.

Maunu pursed his lips, pulled out a curl and snipped. The old serving woman gave a sigh, as if she was falling asleep, her head nodding.

'You may make such cloth for me, Mauatua,' Itia went on. 'You may colour it with mati and re'a, the fig and turmeric that give the colours of royalty. It will be the finest cloth on Tahiti.'

She lifted a mirror that lay beside her and viewed her hair. Her laughter welled up from the deep spring of her satisfaction. 'The best cloth,' she repeated. 'Yes, it is good, very very good. Only the best at Pare, ne?'

To make dye from mati figs required much patience. Many baskets of the small yellow fruits must be gathered. They must be pinched and squeezed for their milky juice, which was dripped into water. Broad leaves from the tou tree were laid in the water until they absorbed it, spread out on banana leaves, gently turned and shaken. Slowly, their veins began to turn red, so when the leaves were twisted in bundles of coconut fibre, the fibre was soon wet with redness. The colour of the sacred blood which flowed to us from the gods. Red clothes were a long labour.

Yellow was less troublesome to produce. There were trees and plants which would give up their yellowness, for the trouble only of grating a root or soaking some bark. Several other girls came to the work with me, and Itia sent her old servant, who was skilled in the selection of plants and preparation of dyes and would sit stripping bark all day in one corner, praying only for brown, for the deep dark brown that would confirm her expertise.

Sometimes Itia herself came and sat among us. She was extravagant with red and we would have to send for more mati figs. Day after day we sat in the shade among the heaps of leaves and fruits, bowls and graters around us, the lengths of cloth spread out before me. Cloth for pareu and ahufara shawls, for tiputa cloaks and dance costumes, for Itia not only wore these garments herself, but gave them away to important guests and favoured friends, and the cloth we made must have eventually arrived on the farthest islands.

We began to press ferns and leaves and mosses into the dyes and onto the fabrics, making flowery patterns like the ones stamped onto the lengths of foreign cloth which had come from the ships, and I copied signs from the book among the leaves, letting them become tendrils and buds, or building them row on row into stripes and squares dividing the flowers. Red on yellow, brown on red, yellow on white, different combinations emerging each time we began a new piece.

With the red stain on my fingers I was exempt from all other forms of work. I did not have to prepare food or grate coconut. My fingers were no longer tormented by the counting and remembering of fara weaving, and I did not even have to beat tapa any more if I didn't want to, although often I took up the mallet for the pleasure of it. The best food from the ovens was my portion and many gifts came from Itia. Feathered fans, shining necklaces, mats and belts, gourds of monoi. For the first time in my life I was arrayed like an ari'i, like the highborn girl Maoiti had always insisted I was.

Other girls grew fat and smooth-skinned, and none more so than my cousin Auo. The tattoos on her buttocks had taken twice as long as mine, so ample were they, and the pareu I made for her took twice as long to dye and pattern. Entire bowls of monoi were rubbed into her belly. Her radiant fatness was the summit of her achievement, first choice was hers among the ari'i and ra'atira men who came seeking wives. She was almost too big to even dance by the time her marriage arrangements were made with Metuaro, a relative of Itia's from her marae on Aimeo.

It was easy to be content at Pare. Every day sumptuous foods were brought to the cookhouses: sweet fe'i carried down from the high valleys, tuna fish as big as a man, nets of jumping shrimp. A constant stream of carriers was kept busy and the aroma that filled the valley of Pare when the ovens were opened was famous in all Tahiti. There was no shortage of anything. Music called from every garden and grove and in the heat of the day we bathed at the springs and gossiped in the shade among the murmuring green pigeons. In the evening torches were lit, canoes pushed off from the sand and laughter was heard from the shadows. At Itia's house the tapairu were practising their newest dance and children darted among the musicians or copied the girls move for move.

There were always young men visiting. The sons of underchiefs, whose homes were in the valleys, came for their training in the arts of war or the secrets of the high marae. They attended the schools of navigation and genealogy, dancing and oratory. Like the girls, they chose their skill and developed it under the tutelage of the experts. The old ways of Tahiti were still strong, even though there were knives made of metal now, shirts of foreign fabric, and foods grown from foreign seeds.

At the centre was always Itia, constantly surrounded by servants and waiting maids, guests and relatives. The burden of sacredness which had been hers and her husband's had been transferred to their first-born, a boy, who henceforth carried the full rank and title that had been his father's, Tu Nui e A'a i te Atua.

He and his younger brother and sister lived unseen across the river, closed off and protected from the world by a maze of stone walls. They were cared for by a crowd of sanctified servants and elders who were the only persons allowed to touch the children's tapu heads and limbs, or prepare their food, those children of the maro ura, the red-feather girdle.

His name and sacredness passed to his heir, Tu had the high priest announce a new name for his own new status. Taina. Freed from the constraints of tapu, which had even prevented their feet from touching unsanctified ground, he and Itia enjoyed their guests to the full. Everyone came to Pare in those years. The feasting and dancing, the tournaments in archery and wrestling and surf riding, came one upon other, as if we were all already in Rotunoanoa, the heaven of eternal pleasures.

My birth father, Te Aha Huri Fenua, was often among the guests in those times. He greeted me correctly, as a woman. His frizzy Paumotuan hair was going grey, and he wore a boar's tusk at his throat. My half sisters also came on a visit from Papara, and for three days they followed me everywhere, making me garlands like Teraura used to, and weaving me a belt studded with shells, singing songs of sisterly affection, as they wove.

Our sister is as tall as the bamboo
That sways on the mountain side
What is it that your eyes see from up there sister,
Looking out across the sea?
Will you think of us when you wear this gift we weave?

I promised to make them new pareu for their tattooing feasts.

For what was my hunger in those years?

'Come!' the other girls called to me, with welcoming smiles. 'Come to the tapa board, come and beat with us, our work is not complete without you. Here is your beater.'

They moved over for me. My hands fell willingly to the work of forgetfulness. My arms began to sing with the rhythm, in my ears beat the women's drums which have beaten for generations, calling out. Grandmothers, aunts, foremothers, all can be heard in the rhythm, calling to one another down the generations. The gods are familiar with our sound, the canoes bear home to it. They do not ask me what I long for. Women beat. Women long. Women sing. Cloth flows from the board as words from the lips.

Patterns and designs flowed from my hand like roaming thoughts, reaching out to the edges of the known world, piling up like clouds at the horizon. Ships in sail began to appear on the borders, blown over billows of silent words.

But there the glorious LORD will be unto us a place of broad rivers and streams; wherein shall go no galley with oars, neither shall gallant ship pass thereby. For the LORD is our judge, the LORD is our lawgiver, the LORD is our king, he will save us. Their recipients marvelled at these works and wanted more.

But for all the advantages of wealth and high standing the book had brought me, still I sometimes feared the unknown god it concealed. When I looked at the completed work, coloured and trimmed, draped around the shoulders of the chiefess or the waist of a dancer, I was in awe of its unknown power.

I returned frequently to the marae at Matavai to make prayers and offerings to our ancestor goddess. The gifts on her altar were few now: weeds sprang from between the paving stones and fallen leaves lay undisturbed on the walls, but I did not neglect her for I knew she had guided my hand, that she had brought the white ships I longed for, showed me the gifts that would bring me what I desired. I offered to her not only flowers and food, but fragments of cloth with their secrets rolled tightly within them.

At Matavai I would sit with Hinuia for a while. Her look was dark, as if a shadow had fallen on her. She had heard, of course, of my work. 'E hine, I fear the white gods are stealing your soul,' she sighed. 'This book you copy from, it is full of their secrets is it not? Can the spirit of your grandmother come to you and guide you while you surround yourself with their power?'

'I believe it is the will of the gods, priestess,' I answered her.

'How is it that a girl so young knows the will of the gods?' She started up suddenly. 'Was it the will of the gods that your grandmother died of the fe'e? That your uncles died in their prime? The work of spirits of darkness and wickedness, servants of our enemies come to lay waste our marae and cast down our mana! Taking even our daughters from our houses, filling them with foolish fantasies ...'

'The curse of Vehiatua has no power over me, patea.'

'Is that what you believe, e hine?'

'The new gods are already among us, the white man cannot be turned away, these are new times ... '

'There will be death and disease, this I see. There are demons among the white men too. When will you learn?'

She softened. Her hands reached out to me, protecting. The prayers began to slip from her tongue, the old words, the known words, the words of the generations passed from memory to memory. The voice of the wind in the aito trees I heard, the distant roar of the reef, the lullabies of my grandmother. Then my heart was heavy.

'E hine,' she said, 'when you were born your grandmother wanted your cord buried under the house posts in the usual way, so that you would bring prosperity to your family. But I had a dream which instructed me, and it was I who paddled out to cast the cord into the outer ocean, just as your first blood was also thrown there.'

In my own dreams the white men were walking and talking. Their mysterious, measured voices told me things that I understood, but could not remember or translate when I woke. There was one, clothed in a robe of black which reached the ground, who always beckoned me to follow, and led me between long walls, turning now and then to encourage me on. To either side there were doorways which he opened, just as Mai had described to me, onto enclosed rooms, and in the rooms there was every type of toy and tool of the Popa'a, so many things that there would have been no room for anyone to stand. He explained everything in an unknown language as we went, opening door after door, until the last one. Behind that one was none other than Mai, standing wide armed, eyes staring, as when he had demonstrated the sacrifice of the white god's son, nailed to a wooden cross. The door closed again. My guide had vanished.

There were other dream men whose behaviour was less mysterious, who pressed themselves against me, I against them, feeling their bodies beneath their strange clothes, they mine. How frustrated and disappointed I was when I awoke, grasping at nothing.

During the afternoons, while we oiled and perfumed ourselves for the evening, plucked the hairs from our bodies (that endless task), combed and arranged our hair, chose our decorations, I would be imagining the attentions of a white man. Many of the young ra'atira with whom we danced and flirted in the evenings would make suggestions to me. Sometimes I responded, if there was one who appealed to me, but often they had to accept my refusal. Other girls became attached to particular young men with whom they shared all the games of love. There was constant gossip and laughter about the men, all their attractions and defects were discussed, their skills as lovers compared in detail.

'What about you, Mauatua?' someone would turn to me and ask.

'It is only a moment's pleasure,' I would reply, and this always caused so much merriment that sooner or later someone would ask me again. 'You should ask him to go longer,' someone would soon suggest.

'You must be doing something wrong.'

Then the advice would begin to flow.

'Grip firmly his testicles'
'Seize hold of it and pull away before he comes.'
'Make him drink nono juice.'
'My lover has no need of such assistance,' I assured them.

But speculation was a favourite pastime. First it must be the cookhouse servant, Tasted in Darkness. Then a visiting chief who had four wives with him. Next an old widower who, toothless as he was, was yet famous for enticing young girls to his sleeping mat.

Often I longed for Teraura's tacit complicity. I dreamed of her too. Showers of printed white leaves fell around her as she held up a child with shining pale skin and curls the colour of turmeric dye. As she turned away he stared back over his shoulder at me. A man would take me by the arm, as the foreigners did, we followed ankle deep in a lagoon made red as if by the sunset. Suddenly a curtain lifted, and there sat Tetua on a mat, waiting for me, smiling. She unwrapped her skirts and showed me her leg, healed at last.

By day I covered sheets of cloth with colours wrought from the plants and the soil. By night I wandered in another world, consorting with the shadows of the dead, the living and the unborn, strange familiars.

Ahia hia

Mauatua

Dogs bark at night, and secrets speak,
The black ti'i
The white man's warm blood,
The hanging-down banana flower.

Tahitinui began to feel small. Its shores too narrow, its peaks too high, and beyond, nothing to be seen but the distant horizon. Beyond that horizon, somewhere, were the white men. Their world, that Mai had spoken of, full of riches and mystery. The life we lived seemed but a dream of the past. The new world was within us. The sound of tapa beating, the drumming and singing, were like fragile remnants of an old pattern on decaying cloth.

One day I looked up from my work and found Teraura there. That was always her way, to appear unexpectedly. The white flash of her smile flew like a spark to me. We leapt to embrace, and to mingle our breath, and call each other sister once more. I had to bend to her now and I realised at once how tall I had grown, and how much I had missed her.

She admired my pearl necklet, my reddened fingers. 'Hei, what riches!' she exclaimed. 'Your cloth is famous all over Tahiti. You and your book of words. But they say you have no man. How can that be, you should have a lover.'

'I can live without one. And there are plenty of men ... '

'I know what you're waiting for.'

'Itia has every little chief of the islands here to look at us.'

'You should choose one. A tall one with a big canoe. Make love to him! It may be long before the others return, the white ones. You may have wrinkles down to here when they come.'

'I am waiting for your sons to grow up. Then I'll choose.'

'Hei, they will be too short for you, Mauatua!'

'Where are they?'

'With my mother at Mahina. Come to see us there. Today I come alone to tell you.'

'To tell me what?'

'Mauatua, at Hitiaa the men are practising with weapons. They say that Tute will not be coming back, and Tu cannot protect himself. The priests and warriors are holding counsel on the marae.'

'But Tu has many friends and allies.'

'He should not trust them. I have heard my husband speaking of it. They say he gives himself too much power and raises himself too high. It is an affront to their mana.'

At Matavai, Hinuia too spoke with foreboding. 'Hiro is abroad, the dark one, the whirring god of thieves and evil doers, who incites envy and greed in men. Then Oro, that bloody god, will be quickly aroused by the priests. The weapons will be tested again, the to'ere will rattle for sacrifice.'

A wind shuddered through the house walls. I felt the lizards wait motionless on the rafters, and my arms shivered with dread.

'You feel that wind?' she said. 'It is the wind Mauriuri pe'e va'a, the wind that detaches canoes, the wind that brings war. E hine, I am going up there.' Hinuia gestured to the cloud-wreathed peaks.

'To the mountains?'

'E, up into the mountains.'

'Who is going with you, patea?'

'I go alone.'

'Who will care for you?'

'The gods will care for me, the spirits will be my companions.'

'E patea, who will care for me? Who will be left here to praise our ancestors and keep the weeds from our marae?'

She brought out of the shadows the canoe-shaped box of our family ti'i, and placed it before me. 'She whose cord is buried in her people's land will be rooted there,' she said. 'But she whose cord is cast into the water will follow it, and nothing can keep her from her journeys. I cannot keep you from your desires, this is seen now, but this must go with you. For there is no prosperity here, all is gone. Where are our heirs, where are our warriors? Itia and her wily husband have taken advantage of our weakness.'

'Was it not the curse of Vehiatua?'

'Truly this valley has been cursed, and outsiders come to trample over our mana.'

Her voice began to rise and tremble to commemorate those griefs, and I too. Aue! For the bones of our dead, secreted in the mountain caves, and for those whose bones are lost, and whose spirits wander unprotected in the labyrinths of te po. Aue!

She embraced me. She was skin and bones beneath her robe, but her ihu, the life force which animated her, had not shrunk. It burned like an invisible flame around her. 'Hold fast to your ancestors,' she instructed me. 'Beloved of your ancestors you must be, and they will protect you.'

It was from the marae of Nu'urua on Aimeo that the black ti'i had come, with Tetua Avari'i when she married Ti'ipari'i. It was to Nu'urua she returned now with me. Her bulging eyes sealed, her mouth close lipped. Her squatting knees resisting the downpulling earth, her long fingers clasping her belly. Blackness her age, her mana, the years of her knowing. I alone now had the power to summon her spirit with prayer and offering. To connect with the ones who went before.

We put to sea before the plundering chiefs of Hitiaa and Paea and Atehuru came, the ti'i wrapped carefully among my bundles. Taina had fled into the mountains with his priests and servants. Our canoe was crowded with women and children, bundles of food were crammed into every space, a litter of puppies clambering over everything. On a separate canoe travelled Itia and Auo and their children, with their servants, including Maunu.

Beyond the reef we turned to look back at Tahitinui Mare'area. When we saw a rainbow, arcing up from the mist-filled bowl of the highest valley of Aora'i, we prayed. We understood that Tahiti was the abode of gods. What men can reach those highest places? Only the bone carriers reach there, into the arms of the gods, there where the sky descends.

But we didn't look back for long because Aimeo awaited us, afloat in the haze of afternoon. Now we felt the wind that sucked between the two islands tugging roughly at the matting sail, the long feather pennants at the mast tip writhed on the eddying breezes. The helmsman braced himself at the steering oar, and from the curving prow our companion, Teio, leaned forward into the splashing spray as we plunged across the wildly dancing water, throwing a chant up to the gods that govern the many winds.

With the lowering of the sun the slopes of Aimeo quickly darkened ahead of us and thick shades of purple blackness bloomed on them, like banana flower. Wings of great birds were sweeping above the reddened crests when we came through the pass of Vaiare at dusk. The sail was brought down, the paddles manned, and only fishermen on the reef would have seen our canoes slip around the coast, heading silently towards the safety of Nu'urua. We arrived there by starlight, the tall black stones of the marae looming on the point.

The lagoon embraces Nu'urua. The breath of the sea comes to meet you. It is like a mother, the smell of the mother, humid and familiar. Aimeo is circled by that warm, liquid embrace, the reef protecting, the lagoon providing. One day is the same as the next there, the same flower opening, the same leaf falling, the same fruit ripening. From Nu'urua, Tahiti cannot be seen.

The news from Pare was not good. The raiders had overcome Taina's warriors and the valley had been stripped. Not a plantain was left uncut, every breadfruit and coconut was gone, Taina's white Peretane pigs were slaughtered, his long-legged foreign dogs were stolen away, all his foreign tools and trinkets looted. So we stayed at Nu'urua and Aimeo fed us.

Often we women had only each other for company for days on end. The men stayed on the other side of the marae. They had their own activities there and kept to themselves. The priests of the marae were vigilant. Every protocol and tapu was strictly observed there. There was seldom opportunity to meet alone with a man, although Rehua had watched me from the day of our arrival.

It was by the water's edge at sunset. He came and sat near to me, a little behind me.

I waited for him to speak, night coming swiftly, the reef encircling with its fine line of light, stars emerging.

'It's no good for fishing tonight,' were his words at last.

I waited for whatever foolishness would follow.

'But it is a good night for sailing to Raiatea. Feel the wind – Matari'i will be clear in the heavens.'

'You are sailing to Raiatea tonight?'

'No, I'm going fishing. Maybe I will be lucky.'

Rehua the navigator. I laughed. 'Why didn't you come to Pare when the fishing was good there?' I teased him.

'I was studying, not chasing women. And I knew you would come to me.'

Rehua too, dreamed of sailing white ships. 'But not as a slave of the white men. One day we will capture a ship and take it for ourselves. We'll do it in the night when the ones supposed to be on watch are sleeping.' He drew his finger across his throat.

My blood surged. 'Would you kill them all by stealth? What about their guns?'

'We need to take them, then the power is ours.'

'It will be difficult,' I said.

'It can be done.'

'There may be better ways, without killing.'

'What ways are those?'

'The ways of women.'

'Trickery!' Rehua said. 'Then we will tie them all up and hold them prisoner while we sail their ship around the islands, plenty of trading. Then we send them on their way. Don't come back or next time you will die.'

'It is impossible to stop them coming. We should befriend them and travel with them.'

'They are too dangerous, too unpredictable.'

He told me that when Tute had come to Aimeo he and the white sailors had rampaged across the island, smashing canoes and burning houses for two days after someone stole one of his hairy animals that were grazing near the ship.

'Is it true? Yet he was always peaceful and friendly on Tahiti,' I protested, wanting to defend my old friend.

'As if possessed by demons. The old ones were terrified. They are still talking about the white devils.'

Rehua was as vain of his tattoos as of his navigational skills. His belly was ocean girt, the prow of a canoe pierced his navel. On his thighs were engraved concentric circles of symbols, fitted to the contour of muscle beneath as perfectly as if they had grown there. Between them hung the black flower of his manhood, the folds of his scrotum plucked and oiled, foreskin smooth as petals, the shaft of Tane rising like a ti'i ... Of this too he was vain, and pleased with my admiration of it.

Itia encouraged me too. She spoke of a marriage ceremony, there at Nu'urua. 'I will speak for you as a sister,' she said. 'It is a good match, your grandmother would be pleased. You will bring fresh blood to Matavai, a new chiefly line. Why don't you marry him? You're as crazy for the sea as he is, you can travel together … '

I delayed and demurred. I used the insufficient excuse that Rehua and I shared a great grandmother in common. How could I say that I was waiting for another man, a stranger?

When our son was born he was given over to his father's people. He grew happily among his cousins, but although I spent time with my son and his aunts there, I never lived in Rehua's household. I remained attached to Itia's, travelling from Nu'urua to Pare and back to Nu'urua according to the whims and wishes of that chiefess, according to the growth of pigs and breadfruit to feed her moving chiefdom, according to the priests and prophets consulted by Taina, who remained hidden in the mountains and installed his brother Ari'ipaea to keep watch over the ruins of his chiefdom.

All the while Rehua went on men's voyages, extending his studies of navigation, memorising the pathways from island to island. Of sea currents and winds and stars he seemed made and his body tasted of salt.

It was Rehua who brought the news from Huahine that Mai was dead, and his two friends from Aotearoa also. The white ship seemed further away each day.

Under the trees, along the beach in the afternoon, creeps the melancholy. The melancholy is the air of the afternoon, it is the spirit of the hour. The lagoon lies still, it hardly moves, only small questions. It is the rustle of the leaves, the dark shade from which the streams run out, murmuring to each other. The silent ti'i speaks of generations. The present is only her dream. When will we awaken from it?

'Ahune
Mauatua / Maimiti
1788

A group of young boys, who had been playing on the sand spit of Matavai, came running with the news. 'A ship, white men, a ship!'

It was the first Popa'a ship they had seen. Even the adults had almost stopped speaking of such things and little remained at Matavai to remind anyone except a few rusty tools and worn-down blades.

The message flew out in all directions and canoes were already arriving from Pare and Papenoo by the time the ragged ship, with sails hanging in tatters, a few exhausted-looking wretches of men heaving on the ropes, crept into the bay. People watched with dismay as the sailors collapsed on the decks, unable to stand to greet those who were climbing aboard from the canoes.

'They are sick,' the word came back. 'They have been blown off course and have run out of food.'

'Pah, that ship is stinking!'

'Food will make them well again. Bring plenty of food!'

'Are they Peretane?'

'Where is Tute?'

'This is not his ship. Tute is dead they say.'

'That great chief, dead! How?'

'Killed at Havai'i!'

'Eaten!'

Aue! A woman began to wail. A row of gaunt white men watched them from the rail of the ship. A ship of ghosts!

The discussions and arguments raged night after night. Some believed the ship of starving white men was an omen of death and destruction, but Taina's priests assured him that the signs indicated another, more fortunate, vessel would arrive soon. So Taina installed a deputy, Poino, to oversee Matavai, and built him a new house there, ready for the long-awaited foreigners.

Now at Matavai I was a guest at my own birthplace, and understood the destiny of a woman whose cord has been thrown into the ocean. Vehiatua's curse had returned, it seemed, with that ghost ship, and it was to haunt me long after it had sailed away. I walked up into the mountains, following the steep slippery paths to Hinuia's cave, and came down again with her incantations hanging on me like garlands of stones, her admonitions flaying my ears, and a new name.

'You with your painted cloth, you by your white man's words, you have brought this ship of death! Do you see now that it does not please the gods if you worship the white man's gods and idols? Tute is dead, they say? Tute has been dead for years, news travels fast in the spirit world. Tute is dead, and the white man is a liar. More war, more disease, more death, that is what the white man will bring. Turn your eyes back to your own land and your own people. Mauatua – Cling-to-the-gods – was the name we gave you. But you should have another name, a name for a woman who waits on the shore. Maimiti – Sickness-for-the-sea – should be your name. May the ocean atua protect you, for you will need them.'

I was at Nu'urua with Rehua and our son when the message arrived that the predicted ship had anchored at Matavai. Rehua commanded a canoe and we sailed back together. From Pare we paddled inside the lagoon and joined the busy traffic of canoes rounding the point of Tahara'a.

And there lay a ship, at last.

Afloat on the singing light of noon.

In a moment I had stripped off my pareu and leapt from the canoe. I dived down and when I came up it was still there. I trod water, laughing, then I swam without stopping, ducking and diving among the canoes which crowded about it, the greenery and flowers strewn on the water, until my fingers were touching its timbers. I swam all around it, and wherever I looked up the men were laughing in the sky, the masts were full of people, girls were diving from the rails, scrambling up the ropes, hands were beckoning to me. From the tip of the prow, where a war canoe carries its ti'i, a carved woman leaned out as if to point the way forward across the waves, her cloak blowing from her shoulders. At the rear a great banner of red cloth was hoisted, pronouncing its origin, its holiness. Peretane! Below it, painted across the stern, framed with flowers and fruits and leaves, were the six signs of the ship's name.

BOUNTY. A shining silent word, speaking to me.

I kicked back out to the clear water where I could float on my back and see everything. The dog's-tooth peak of Orohena piercing the everlasting mantle of cloud, dark shadows drifting slowly up and down the valleys. A frigate bird going over slowly, rising and falling in its passage, tipping its head to look down at the new ship. The shining word written everywhere, on the sparkling water, on the sky.

BOUNTY.

From then on I watched. I counted at least forty foreigners, all men, as usual. I was glad.

The chief was easy to identify in his elaborate clothes and big hat, calling orders in a strident, impatient voice. He was quickly recognised as Parai, who had been one of Tute's underchiefs on his last visit to Tahiti, a friend of Tute. Tapitane Parai, he was called, as if he had taken his dead friend's place and title. Was he the chief for me, or would he refuse women, as Tute had done?

But he was short, too small for a woman my height, even if he had been attractive. Not Parai then.

Poino came to escort them to his house. Poino the pretender, acting the part of a real chief; Parai followed by two of his hatted underchiefs, their faces running with sweat. Mats were spread. The people crowded around the house curiously. I remembered when Tute had sat here the first time with my grandfather, and I was a little child gazing at him from my grandmother's lap.

The formalities were long and the white men began to look ill – their clothes were clearly too hot. Poino knew few English words, Parai remembered some Tahitian ones, with difficulty. Poino asked about Tute, the great chief, dead?

I watched Parai carefully. He had large eyes, like a woman's, and a small, soft mouth. There was fear in them as he looked around at us, blindly. 'Cook is not dead,' he said. 'No, he sends his greetings.'

This caused a stir, a ripple of unease. The white man lies.

Or maybe not. Does it matter when Matavai Bay is full of people and food, when important guests are honouring you, when there are speeches and firing of guns, dances, feasts to prepare for, novelties of every sort, tricks and surprises? It was better than the arioi. Upa upa Peretane! The people rushed to embrace their new friends. 'Taio, taio!' was the word. It was a race to claim a taio. Brother friend, to exchange names with, exchange gifts. Honoured guest, honoured host. Taio.

There were plenty to choose from. Tall, short, hairy faced, balding, pale, dark. Even two men dark as ourselves, both in the clothes and decorations of underchiefs. Some scarcely out of boyhood. Others ugly, scarred, toothless, strong to smell from eating dried meat for months. Some noisy, others shy. One who appeared to be blind. All smiling, smiling, happy to see us. 'Taio, taio!'

It did not take long to see that although Parai was the chief there was another man who was better respected. One of the dark-skinned ones, a strong, handsome man. I marked him well.

Long after sunset people sat watching the lights on the ship, the shapes of men passing across them. Drums were beating again in Matavai, and no one slept yet.

Taina and Itia crept back into Matavai that night, he overland, she by water, in the stealthy manner they had adopted since Pare was ransacked. At dawn they sent to the ship that they had arrived, and were arraying themselves in the best of their remaining finery. Taina had had a pig slaughtered and Itia had managed to appropriate a long sheet of cloth that had been beaten at Nu'urua for a wedding. She chose Vahineatua to be wrapped in it as a gift to Parai. I helped to wind it around her waist until she was padded out so far she could barely move.

'A nice small girl, she makes the cloth look big,' said Itia approvingly. 'We will make the English chief happy.'

'I think he'll be difficult to please,' I said.

'There will be something he wants, or he is not a man. Hurry with those wreaths, girls. Where is Maunu to fix my hair?'

Parai's boat, manned by four sailors, was pulled up on the beach waiting to take us to the ship. They stared at us in wonder as we climbed aboard. Taina and Itia went first, not knowing whether to sit facing forwards or backwards. Then there was a scramble for places. Vahineatua, wrapped in the cloth, almost fell into the water. The pig went in with its trotters tied around a bamboo cane, sticking up between Taina's knees. Maunu, who had managed to get aboard, wearing a headdress of cloth ribbons and fluttering reva reva made especially for the occasion, immediately began to flirt with one of the sailors, and the boat was in an uproar before we had pulled away.

'Mamu!' Quiet! We turned to look at who had spoken, standing in the prow. It was the dark one, the chief who was not chief. How did he know our word already? He was smiling at us. 'Mamu!' responded Taina, and we all began to laugh again.

'Pull away, lads!'

'Aye aye Mr Christian!'

The small boat was heavy with our desires. Taina and Itia's for the iron and weapons they knew would be aboard, the girls' for clothes and trinkets. Mauatua's whole desire stood behind her in the prow. Wedged between Vahineatua and Maunu, she could not see him. Only feel his eyes on the back of her head.

It was a game to get aboard in our long robes. Now I saw why the foreigners wore those two legged garments. Vahineatua, in her bundle of cloth, was carried up on a sailor's back, but no sailor was game to put Itia on his shoulders. She had to manage the tiny steps, shouldered from below by Taina, losing half her skirt to the sea.

Parai was waiting, the sailors standing back against the rails to make way for us, all eyes upon us. Overhead, the dizzying masts were festooned with more ropes than could be counted.

The greetings were enthusiastic on both sides. Taina and Itia embraced their saviour like a long-lost brother. 'Taio!'

They presented their oven-ready hog, several baskets of breadfruit, and then called on me to unwrap the gift of barkcloth. Vahineatua and I stepped up before Parai, and as Vahineatua slowly turned, I began to draw the cloth from her, unwinding it arm length by arm length. A murmur of anticipation began to rise from the men as they recognised the intention, and as her nakedness approached it grew to a roar of appreciation. I smelled a wave of masculine lust and remembered the white man at Pare. How I had run from him. Vahineatua stood revealed for only a moment before I enclosed her in her own pareu.

'All right lads!' It was Parai shouting this time.

He dismissed them back to their work and invited us to follow him down a narrow staircase into the belly of the ship. Down there it was a goblin world. There were tiny narrow passageways and openings, which Itia kept sticking in. Nowhere could I stand upright. In one place there was a huge metal firebox where two men were stirring food in metal dishes. We could smell the taro and pumpkin that had been traded on board yesterday. Parai showed us to a room large enough for us to all press into. He presented Taina with boxes of metal tools of all kinds, which rendered him and Itia almost speechless with satisfaction, but when Itia received only necklaces and ear drops for herself she soon regained her tongue. 'Are a child's playthings a gift for the highest chiefess of Tahiti?' she said, passing the trinkets to us. 'I also need axes to cut trees and build houses, tools for the canoe builders, metal for hooks and blades. Do not dishonour me, e friend Parai?'

We saw that Parai did not understand. She pointed to the gifts he had given Taina and said to him, 'More. For Itia.'

Everybody laughed, she winked at us. 'Which one of you will bring me the contents of his coat pockets tomorrow?'

'Maunu,' suggested someone in a whisper. 'The queen of pocket thieves!'

I remembered how Tute had terrified the people of Aimeo when his goat was stolen. The Peretane do not admire a cunning theft.

While everyone was admiring the gifts and speculating on the value of the many different blades and items of iron, I slipped away and retraced the narrow passageways to the staircase, intending to see what was happening on deck. As I approached the steps a pair of legs was descending them. Entranced I watched the ankles clad in soft white cloth, the thick breeches, the jacket encrusted with glittering metal, the throat ornament of pleated white cloth. And the smiling face of Titriano. He made way for me, removing his hat and bowing slightly from the waist. 'Madam,' he said.

Like a simple girl, I began to laugh, with astonishment and happiness. 'What is "madam"?' I asked.

'A name for a woman of high rank, madam.'

'What is man of high rank?'

'Mister, madam.'

'What is the name of this ship, mister?'

'The name is *Bounty*,' he said.

'*Paunti*?'

'*Bounty*. Means much much goodness, enough for everyone.'

'Plenty. "Ahune."'

'"Ahune."'

'Maitai roa.'

'Very good.'

'How did you learn our language?'

'From Captain Bligh.'

'Is he a good chief, Tapitane Parai?'

'Very good. My friend.'

'Taio?'

'Like taio.'

In the dimly lit space, the whites of his eyes showed, and his teeth. I was close enough to hear his breathing. 'In Tahiti we do this,' I said. I came closer and pressed my forehead and nose against his, to exchange our breath. In height we were equal, heart to heart. His ihu flowed into me, I inhaled it deeply, smelling the unfamiliar sharpness. The ship creaked in its timbers as it rocked gently beneath us. His hand on mine was firm, and moist.

'Maitai roa,' he said into my ear.

They were the words of a long-ago poet of our people that I whispered in reply, too ancient and vague for him to understand. 'I am the woman of your longing,' I told him.

It was a charm, a simple thing. A Tahitian man might have thrown it back at me, laughing, but the white man, the white man was lost. I lifted the wreath from my head, to his. 'Maeva, maeva, welcome to Matavai.'

Within days Matavai was swarming with people. Envy and craftiness arrived by the canoe load, curiosity came down every path from the valleys, while Taina and Itia and Parai exchanged gifts and visits with endless ceremony. From land we could hear the laughter and cheering long after dark, the firing of guns, the visiting chiefs from other districts invited too, drinking foreign 'ava through the night.

Finally Parai's desire was revealed. He wanted young breadfruit plants to take to his king. Only breadfruit plants! Of those Tahiti had more than enough. People were pleased when they heard this: It was a good exchange, breadfruit plants for iron, and good to think of the king of Peretane eating Tahitian breadfruit. Taina was elated. The men began coming on shore, putting up their sailcloth houses. Titriano was in charge, but he stripped to the waist like the men and worked under the hot sun.

I watched other women begin to vie for his attention. The sailors had quickly chosen manahune and teu teu women to pair with, but the underchiefs, the officers, were for the high ranking women to choose from. As there were only nine of them, the competition was strong, and more women were arriving every day. Titriano liked to flirt and play and I watched to see if any other woman had tried to break my spell on him. I was extra vigilant with tupu, careful to leave nothing that could be used in a spell against me, not a hair or nail.

I cleared away the vines and weeds that had grown over my old family marae and returned the atua to her altar there. Turning up the secret stones I uncovered the sacred relics of our family: locks of hair, red feathers, and parcels of bones, crumbling like things abandoned. I cleaned them, replaced them wrapped in fresh cloth. The altar was within sound of the white men working. The black ti'i listened. It was what the gods wanted: they wanted to meet the white atua that strode in from another sky.

Year of Our Lord 1831

On the walls of the mission church danced patches of blue painted light, and the ocean breezes played in the flickering blinds. From the roof's high beam hung palm fringes and pandanus tassels twirling on the rising draught, and the smell of coconut oil both sweet and stale was very strong.

The missionary ladies in their bonnets and ribbony gowns led the first hymn, but they were soon outsung by the rest of the congregation.

Higher than everyone, alone on the pulpit, stood Mr Henry, the black-clad missionary man, with his cheeks grey as iron. Margaret tried hard to understand the preaching, but his manner was so different from Mr Buffet's or Mr Nobbs that she couldn't follow at all and her attention began to stray.

Among the other children it was Matthew Henry – aged twelve as he liked to inform everyone – who caught her eye so fast she could not look away. Now and then he narrowed his attentive gaze fiercely, then reopened it very wide. She wasn't sure if it was a friendly signal or a hostile one and wanted to laugh.

She felt her aunt Mary's sharp elbow.

'And God so loved the world,' the missionary, Matthew's father, was saying, 'that he gave his only begotten son. And whosoever!' He looked all about from face to face causing Matthew to suddenly compose himself. 'Whosoever shall come to him, shall not perish but have everlasting, EVERLASTING, life.'

Some said 'amena', and other voices rose to wail for the dead. The missionary had two begotten sons, Matthew and James, both alive, and from his expression it was clear he did not approve of the women wailing in church. He held up his hands as if he could stop it.

But it was Thursday October Christian who was to be buried that day.

When Margaret and her grandmother had finally returned from the places of the dead ancestors, they heard the weeping from far away and found all the aunts and sisters on their knees crying to the Lord.

Grandmother had refused to come to the church for her son's burial. Aue, aue! cried the women, at Granma's face striped brown with her own blood.

Now Matthew Henry was crossing his eyes and sucking in his mouth like a fish. Uncle Thursday was dead of the fever that was raging in every house and hut. But she, Margaret Christian, had seen the place of skulls. Everybody was going there, with the ancestors. Same as her mother Sully, whom they had wept for at home on Pitcairn when Margaret was a little girl.

Suddenly, as if somebody else was operating her face, she stuck out her tongue at Matthew Henry, as hard as she could.

'We must be gone,' the mothers and aunts declared, 'we must find a boat to carry us back to our home, aue, aue!'

The night was disturbed by cries and groans that floated abroad. Then came the voices of the women, hush now, hush, singing lullabies in the mother tongue. Hush now!

Tupapau!

The missionary people coughed, but they did not die of the fevers. 'Because we pray to God,' Matthew Henry explained proudly. 'He is our protector. You are heathens, that's why you will die.'

'It's not true, we pray three times a day at home!'

'Then why are you all sick? And why was your uncle named for a day of the week?'

'Days of the week are in the Bible!'

'My father says there is not one reference to October in the whole of the Bible. He declares your grandfather must have been quite mad, as well as very sinful.'

Margaret looked at Matthew Henry's freckled forehead one more time before she ran at it, even though he was taller and she had to jump at him.

'Fiend!' he shrieked, as he tumbled backwards. 'Heathen!'

II
The Ship

Hina'aro

Rehua came along the black sand spit in the afternoon heat. There was only one man on guard at the Popa'a camp, his gun hanging at his side and a piece of white cloth knotted on top of his head. He straightened up as Rehua approached and watched him intently.

'Good afternoon to you,' said Rehua, speaking the foreign words with practised care.

The man grinned and returned the greeting.

Rehua stopped to look at the plants the white men had carefully uprooted. Hundreds and hundreds of them, neatly lined up in rows in the shade of white cloth awnings. He was amazed at the dedication of purpose, to sail for ten moons across open ocean to fetch plants for their king. And the men themselves, some of them so puny and sickly looking that it was a miracle they had survived the journey. Their skin naked and hairy, reddened by the sun like roasted pigs. Yet the women were clamouring to make love to these unwholesome savages. And they had guns. Not only were they skilful navigators, but their gods must be very powerful.

The white man spoke again. 'Good tattoo,' he said, admiringly.

Rehua let him admire, vain of the powerful symbols that braced his calves and circled his shoulders.

The white man began to indicate things he recognised on Rehua's body, naming them with his language – island, canoe, turtle, ocean – those words full of tongue and spittle. 'I want tattoo,' he began to announce in gesture.

'Tattoo! For you?' Rehua laughed. 'Tattoo is for the gods. Tattoo is blood and pain.' Then he had an idea. 'You give me gun, I take you to tahua tatau.'

The white man laughed heartily, then looked at him slyly. He lifted the gun to his shoulder and eyed Rehua along its length. 'You want gun?' he said.

Rehua stood his ground, even put his hands to his ears, waiting for the flash of fire and thunder. But nothing happened. It was his turn to laugh. 'Friend,' he said.

'Friend,' repeated the white man. He lowered his weapon.

Along the shore Rehua came upon other white men lying in the shade with a group of women and youngsters attending to them, decorating them with flowers, caressing their limbs and dancing for them. If he was amazed by the white men's purposefulness, he was equally disdainful of his own people's adulation of the scruffy strangers, and fearful for their gullibility. Only yesterday he had been aboard the ship, up on the deck among the crowd, admiring the fine timberwork and ingenious gadgets, when a startling sight had appeared in one of the openings from below – a head of yellow hair, elaborately dressed and stuck with glittering ornaments. Everybody had turned to look as the pale, smiling face of a white woman emerged, her stiff body draped in a colourfully decorated garment. Rehua had realised straight away that it was nothing but a fake, made up with cloth and hair, for amusement, but some people had been fooled by the trick – an old woman rushed forward to offer gifts of food. Such humiliation. To cover his embarrassment Rehua had laughed as loudly as the sailors when Parai seized the fake head by the hair and tossed it into the crowd while the women shrieked with horror.

But he had felt the same disappointment as they did, afterwards. He would like to meet one of their women. The infamous Mai had boasted of his exploits with them, during his sojourn on Aimeo in Rehua's boyhood.

'Why you bring no women?' he had turned to ask of the man at his side, the chief they called Titriano.

Titriano smiled wryly. 'You take women on your war canoes?' he asked in return.

Rehua had been startled by this seeming admission of the ship's real purpose, and phrased his reply with care. 'Not on war canoes. But when we go to find new land, we take women.'

'New land, yes. Tahitinui! Very good land, plenty of women!' Titriano had joked.

Rehua tried to follow the white man's mind, to judge whether his jokes had a more serious meaning, or were meant to confuse him. It was true what Maimiti had said – that the foreigners would be difficult to overcome – but he didn't believe that it would be impossible. Women were their weak point, this much he understood.

He continued along the shore, taking the path towards Itia and Taina's encampment. At Poino's house he stepped in among a gathering of men drinking 'ava. He took his place among others of his rank and the cup came to him in turn. They had all tasted the Peretane 'ava by now and knew its fiery potency. It had already made their own brew of chewed root seem less appetising. 'The Peretane rama is made of sugar cane,' Taina announced. 'We must find out how.'

'I have heard a tahua say that the Peretane drink begins to kill you from the first swallow,' said one of the older men.

'The sailors drink it every day, they look weak and small, but they have great strength and fortitude. It's said they held the ship into the wind in a terrible storm for forty days, and not one man died.'

The magnitude of this feat was neither unappreciated, nor quite believed.

'The rama sustains them when they have not enough food.'

'And when their chief orders them to be beaten.'

Rehua had not been present when Parai had commanded a man to be beaten by one of his shipmates with a thong of skin and metal that flayed open his flesh. He'd seen the scars on their backs though. They were not beautiful, like a tattoo, for which pain must also be endured.

'Their 'ava gives them the ferocity of wild beasts.'

'They are men of iron.'

'With no women.'

'Obviously, they are afraid to bring their women here in case they are too admiring of our manhood.'

'Or they mean to steal our women.'

'There are some they would be welcome to.'

'Others not, my friend.'

At this talk of women Rehua remembered why he had set out in this direction, and got up to leave. He found Maimiti among Itia's women, combing and oiling in the shade. It would have been improper for him to enter the women's area, so he stood a little aside among the trees until he caught her attention. Her green eardrops flashed.

'A woman should wear the ornaments her grandmother wore,' said Rehua. 'Where are Tetua's black pearls?'

'Hei, you speak like Hinuia!' said Maimiti.

'Guns would be more useful than eardrops,' said Rehua.

'You will have to be patient.'

'They may be intent on taking over our land and women.'

'Just like Hinuia.'

'Are you mocking me?'

'Come,' she teased. 'Come with me, let me massage you, e tane?'

She led him away into a secluded place, spread her pareu on the ground and invited his head to her lap. 'There is one man we should pay attention to,' she said, tipping up the gourd of oil she had brought and spreading it from her palms to his shoulders.

'Titriano?'

'Titriano. He's the key to everything we want.'

'You are a clever woman,' he said.

'You should make him your bond brother.'

'Does he not already have a taio?'

'You're a more fitting taio to him than any other. He is a navigator too.'

He felt her hands begin to ease the tension he had been carrying in his shoulders, dissolving the knots of distrust and anxiety that had developed. He smiled to himself as he recognised Maimiti's motives. She was lustful, and curious, like all women, and if he became taio with the white man she would have the privilege of making love with him, as any woman may, according to custom. As it was the white men's custom to give gifts in return, it could be advantageous. And it put the white man in a position of weakness, for he had no woman to offer in return.

He watched a pair of blue vini birds land in the nearest ni'au palm, where they liked to feed. When he closed his eyes he could hear them murmuring to each other. Pigeons were chanting: nothing had changed. The woman's hands were bringing memories of his childhood, of his grandmother's hands, comforting and slow. He let sleep fall over him lightly, her hands still lulling the surface of dream. The ship was riding over a seamless ocean, rising and falling, the vini and u'upa still crooning among the forest masts. He stood at the wheel of the ship, but no effort was needed to hold the rich vessel on course. It skimmed the waves like otaha, the frigate bird.

The white woman came up from below decks, tossing sunlight through her yellow hair. Pulling down the shoulders of her gown she exposed skin of a pale, melting translucence, and as she came closer he saw the embellishment of living insects in her hair, blue and green dragonflies that darted from curl to curl, and dazzling, long-legged beetles that flashed in the light. It was her dainty fingertips sliding over his skin now, knowing exactly where to press, where to stroke, closer, loosening the binding of his loincloth, and closer. He set his course to a distant spot in the blueness of her eyes, a dark tunnel of desire opening wide to admit him until his standing ure was embraced by her full liquid grip. The world of light hummed in his ears a song straining to breaking point, while the ship rolled under him on an ocean bucking with delight.

With ease will a man ride the elements and raho fly willingly to him. This Rehua now knew, for such a dream was about more than one woman's playful desires. That evening, in the flaring light from a blaze of dried ni'au fronds, Rehua saw the blind man take up his curious instrument and balance it under his chin. He caressed its strings with long, soft strokes, and the instrument seemed to moan a little, as if waking, which startled the children. As his caresses increased and quickened, the instrument replied with quickened rhythm. When he slowed again its voice vibrated on the edge of sorrow. The people were held as if by a spell, mesmerised by its unearthly keening and reeling, their stomachs warmed by swigs from a bottle of rama that was passing from hand to hand in the dark. Rehua watched the dancing begin, in Pcretane style, with kicking up of the legs and linking of arms, and a satisfied lassitude overcame him. He was happy to watch them dance till they fell.

Not until later, when the instrument was being tried from hand to hand, protesting with horrible shrieks and groans, while a young girl guided the blind musician's fingers to other places, did he get up and walk on down the shore until he could see the ship.

It sparkled like a new galaxy there, the work of new gods, fallen from the sky. A gift, a sign, a curse. Sailed into the storm for forty days and not one man lost. No amount of scorn could diminish his awe and admiration.

Tane

Maimiti

Teraura was back from Hitiaa, alone. I knew the look in her eyes. As soon as she arrived, she talked me into following the ship's boat when it left the breadfruit camp the next morning.

Skirting along the rocky coastline toward Papenoo, we kept among the trees, the boat sparkling ahead of us as the water lifted by their oars caught the morning sunlight. Canoes belonging to the men's taio skimmed playfully back and forth in its path.

When they landed we crouched hidden under the purau trees, among land crabs scuttling into their holes. The boat crunched onto the sand and we watched the men roll their garment legs up to their bony knees before they jumped into the water.

The two officers, Titriano and Eti, who was even darker skinned, pulled off their jackets and three-cornered hats and stowed them in the boat.

He was broken toothed and wiry haired, the one they called Eti, but so jaunty and wry mouthed that women were quickly drawn to him. The jokes he told in English did not need to be understood to be funny. He was always first to join the dancing, not stiff legged like the others. I knew that Teraura would like him.

Titriano was taller, strong as any Maohi man. All were commoners beside him. 'He's the one I like,' I said to Teraura.

'He's handsome,' agreed Teraura.

'He's noble. See how he walks, he has mana.'

'What about the other one?'

'Eti. Would you have him?'

'But he's not very white.'

'Neither are you, e, princess of Hitia'a.' She laughed so loudly that I thought they had heard us. Their Tahitian taio looked about suspiciously, and grinned at each other.

They walked away along the beach, calling noisily to each other, their digging tools across their shoulders. They were barely out of sight among the trees before Teraura was pulling me toward the boat. 'I want to try that backwards paddling,' she said.

'Parai had a white man whipped for letting something be stolen,' I reminded her.

'We're not thieves. Titriano and Eti will like the joke.'

The backwards paddling was more difficult than it looked. We circled out into the lagoon like beetles, our arms and oars in all directions. Back on the shore we saw two men come running, attracted by our shouts and laughter, but it was too late, we were away from them and gaining a straight course as they splashed out, thrashing their arms.

'Don't stop, Maimiti! Now you have the rhythm,' Teraura shouted.

I knew her eyes were shining with excitement, but I could only see the back of her wild head. 'Where are we going?'

'Listen over your shoulder!'

The sound of the sea on the reef grew louder.

We stopped and rested many times before we arrived back at Matavai. We called some boys to haul the boat up where the sailors would find it, then we fastened on the men's jackets and arranged their hats on our hair.

The women were eating. They dropped their food as they saw us, the young ones with admiration, the old ones less approving. For a moment I saw Tetua's face among them. *Remember your noble ancestresses. Let there be no Popa'a stain on your blood.* It was a crowd of ghosts looking up at us. *Why so, strangely clothed e hine?* Teraura danced triumphantly beside me. *Take care!*

Later, we had to tell the whole story.

Every afternoon, as we waited for the heat of the day to pass, there was another tale to be told of the white men. All we talked about were those men.

Tuaonoa was showing off her new tattoo that day. *A.S. 1788.* The tattooist had turned its loops and lines into an elegant armband. I admired his hand.

'What does it mean?'

Everyone wanted to examine it.

'It's Aleck's sign. Here is "A", beginning "Aleck". The other hisses behind the teeth. "Smith."'

'What are those signs?'

'The time since the birth of the nailed-up one. One thousand, seven hundred and eighty eight.'

Many generations. Perhaps as many as could be counted back in Tuaonoa's family line, which would have as been as long as any on Tahiti. She carried strong blood and her family were known for their fearlessness and bravado. I knew by the tattoo that she meant to come with us to wherever *Bounty* would take us.

Someone else was thinking of this. 'Is Aleck also a chief in Peretane, that he is chosen by Teehuteatuaonoa?'

'Who knows. Perhaps they are all chiefs,' she replied.

'They are servants of their king.'

'Titriano is the chief.'

'Only Parai is left unclaimed then. Who will have him?'

'Parai does not like women.'

'He has a wife and daughters in Peretane.'

'He only likes to frighten and amuse. Bam! His gun goes off. Everyone lies down on the deck and laughs. Itia plays him for a fool. Have you seen the box full of his gifts she and Taina keep on the ship?'

'He treats the sailors like his worst enemies. Why do they beat each other at his orders? Men are killed by such blows. Aue.'

'They say it makes them stronger, like the rama they drink.'

'The scars are ugly.'

'Their circumcisions are ugly.'

'Their foreskins are uglier!'

The roof would have lifted off with the laughter, the ringing frenzy of our powerful longing.

Teraura and I suffered the itchy weight of the jackets and hats all afternoon. We dared not take them off lest someone else be wearing them when their owners came to claim them.

They appeared near sundown with their shirts stuck wet to their chests. Titriano stepped forward and bowed to us, Eti quickly imitated him. They were better than an arioi comedy, those Englishmen. Their foolish smiles only added to their charm.

Titriano's lips were blistered from the sun and I realised that he did not even know how to make a green palm-frond hat to shelter his head. They had walked back bareheaded. I felt embarrassed for my carelessness.

But Teraura had other considerations. 'Shall I take this one to the river and wash him, girls? Do you think I can find the white parts of him?'

She took Eti's willing hand, the other girls urging her on, and led him away towards the river, beckoning us to follow.

Titriano hesitated. He said, 'I must look at the breadfruit plants before night, madam. Do you come with me?'

Behind us they began to sing a song about the skills of white lovers. Titriano may not have understood the words, but he surely knew the meaning of the laughter which followed us.

We walked along the rows of breadfruit slowly. He looked at each plant, sometimes pressing a finger into the soil to feel for moisture, not speaking. I watched him, noting everything. I saw the unspoken thoughts on his brow, and how the impulsive lips were held in check. I saw him finger a leaf with affection, then flick it away.

'Are all these plants for your king? Are they to feed the people of Peretane?' I began.

'They are for the king.'

'Mai told us how cold your country is, causing the leaves to fall off the trees. The breadfruit will not grow without leaves.'

'The king has other islands, warm like Tahiti, far away.'

'Do Peretane people live there?'

'Ae. And also dark-skinned people.'

'Like Maohi people?'

'Darker. Black. Ask Eti. He was born there.'

He lifted a wilting plant from its soil and examined the root. 'What is your word for a man who is in bondage, like a prisoner?'

'After war, a captive?'

'One who cannot leave. He works without freedom.'

I puzzled the meaning of such menacing references. 'For such prisoners there is no longer any word,' I replied. 'Those were other times. On Tahiti we are free.'

'Maitai roa' he said. 'It is good.'

Now my suspicions were aroused. 'Are you such a man yourself?' I asked him.

'I am a servant of my king,' he replied. Again the unspoken thoughts chased each other silently across his brow.

'Yet you are a chief of your own lands, are you not?'

He discarded the sickly plant abruptly, a gesture of disgust, or anger. 'A chief with no place to stand can only be a servant,' he exclaimed.

Now I began to see the source of his situation. His land and title lost to him, he retained his status by service to Parai, as I to Itia.

'He may be an honourable servant,' I said, adding, 'until such time as he must leave.'

He turned to me and I saw the power of my claim on him, there in his eyes. We were perfect equals.

'True, madam, he may be an honourable servant, even in the service of a fool.'

'On *Bounty* an honourable servant; on Tahiti, a chief.'

'Does Maimiti say so?'

'Everyone says so.'

· He raised my hand with soiled fingers. 'In England we do this,' he said. He put his blistered lips to it, his eyes lifted to mine.

Night was falling as we walked side by side to the end of the sand spit. The air was still, Aimeo's silhouette was rimmed with fire and *Bounty* was black on a flood of red, as fierce as a new tattoo.

We watched the sky darken. I was impatient for him, but now he kept apart from me. It was true that he needed to bathe, but the smell of sweat and soil was like the sauce on a dish of sweet food to me.

Soon the bright star alighted winking in the void, drawing our eyes to her.

'We call her Ta'arua e hiti i Matavai. She who rises shining over Matavai. She is the one Tute looked at with his long eye.'

'We call her Venus. Goddess of love.'

'You have a goddess of love?'

'There were many gods and goddesses. Many.'

'Tell me about this goddess. Was she the mother of Iehu Tireti, the nailed-up one?'

'No.' I heard the amusement in his voice. 'His mother was a woman of this earth, a, how do you say it, she had been with no man.'

'Pirimomona.' A virgin. The mysterious Popa'a gods. 'Do all white men believe this?'

'All Christians believe it.'

'And you are Mister Christian.'

'It is only a name.'

'Like Mauatua.'

'Mauatua?'

'It means, "Cling-to-the-gods". But names can change. Our priestess, Hinuia, has also given me the name Maimiti, "Sickness-for-the-sea". On Tahiti you are Titriano. Tell me about Venus.'

'Her father was a sky god, whose ure was cut off by his own son and thrown into the ocean. More beautiful than any woman of earth, she was born out of the surf and was carried to an island of trees and flowers. Every man who saw her, god or mortal, loved and desired her.'

'So she had many lovers.'

'And husbands.'

'And did the men fight with each other?'

'One god turned himself into a boar and gored a mortal man to death, for jealousy of Venus. Wars were caused by her, ae.'

'In Tahiti we say, for women and land, men are lost.'

He was silent for a long time and I wished I had not spoken those words. I ached with my desire for him. The stars were in the heavens and the water lapped softly near us, but something was holding him back. I guessed at another woman. Not any Tahiti girl, but one who was far away.

'Do you have a wife there in Peretane?'

'No. No lands, no wife. I see the light in Captain Bligh's cabin, look. He will be expecting me.'

An English man is not a Maohi man, I realised then. He does not use the same charms, his desires will show themselves in contrary ways.

'Wait, it is my turn to tell a story,' I said. 'You take our breadfruit with you, so you must take the story of the breadfruit too. Those who eat it should know how it came to grow on Tahiti.

'It came about when the people of Tahiti were starving, driven to eat the red earth of the mountainsides. It was a long time ago. All the foods were not growing then and the rain did not fall. One man had a dream. When he awoke he told his wife that he would become food for his family. "How can this be?" she cried.

'"You will eat my head," he told her. Aue. He left the house and went away. In the morning she found a new plant growing nearby, with fruits as big as a man's head. All the people of the valley came to see the tree, with leaves like hands and a head that could be eaten. But the first fruit must be offered to the chief. When the chief saw the tree he ordered it brought to his garden.

'The widow was left with no food again. Then she saw that from the broken roots of the tree new shoots were growing.

'That is how all of Tahiti is covered with breadfruit. Twelve kinds, we are never without it. Every child knows this story.'

Now we could hear the blind man's music from among the trees. 'Come to the dancing with me,' I suggested.

'Captain Bligh expects me, madam, and I am an honourable servant,' he said.

He bowed, and kissed my hand again before we parted.

Later on my sleeping mats, excitement and desire kept me wide awake. Rehua came to me and I wanted him as never before. There are gods worshipped by the act of love. The sounds of our pleasure are like nectar to them and it is wrong to deny them. They have their purposes.

Long after he had fallen asleep I was still retracing my conversation with Titriano, remembering his voice and his smile, and all our talk. The mysterious virgin mother, the unidentified captives, the countless breadfruit trees being taken to the islands of black-skinned people where Eti was born. And the goddess of love rising out of the waves.

On Tahiti it was the masculine Tane who brought men and women together for love. Now Tane and the white goddess were to meet. Their lovemaking would cause great upheavals in the realm of the gods, resounding like echoes in the world of light. This much I knew.

Aita Peapea

Maimiti

The wind began to blow from To'erau, the sky slammed down on the ocean and the sea rolled into Matavai Bay, throwing heavy breakers onto the beach. It was a night of rushing water, and voices were drowned out by the tearing of wind, the rain pouring from the thatch ends, the creaking and shuddering of our walls and roof. Teraura and I lay awake side by side, our ears straining for any sound of calamity, smashing timber or white men's voices, but there was nothing to hear above the roaring darkness except Itia, who was beside herself, wailing and cutting herself all night so nobody could rest. At first light she and Taina were pushing off a canoe to go out through the surf to the ship, desperate to convince Parai that he should come on shore to safety.

Down at the breadfruit camp men were struggling in the wind to dig a channel for the overflowing stream. Canoes were overturned, branches and trunks thrown to the ground, but our houses were all safe and nobody was hurt.

And there had been a child born. She was the daughter of Teio, a Pare girl who, like me, had been with Itia for years. The baby had come without the protection of the proper rites or the sacred birthing house, so swiftly amid the din of the storm that we had not even heard Teio cry out.

The old women were already shaking their heads about it – a sign, they said. Every day since the white men had been here, tapu had been broken and ignored. Teio's baby was another sign of trouble, arriving as if deposited by the wind.

We knew Teio had delivered alone so that nobody would be able to kill her baby for the dangerous circumstances of its arrival. Its fate had been under question since her belly had first become evident. The father had not declared himself, and the gossips had plenty to guess at. Was he a manahune boy of no consequence, a man with another family, a cousin? Any prohibition could have been broken: the child was inauspicious. And if it died before claiming its first breath of this world, it would be better. Puaru.

But she had survived, drawn breath and claimed her ihu, her spirit.

'Help me to protect her, Mauatua,' Teio whispered to me.

I looked at the baby's eyes, wide open to the world of light. 'She is one of us,' I said.

It was to the ship instead, that death came. It was a man we never saw on shore, a medicine tahua, who died, it was said, of drinking too much of their 'ava. They put his body in a wooden box and buried him in a hole in the ground with very little ceremony, for there was no woman to wail him.

'If we buried every body in the ground on Tahiti we would have no room left to stand.'

'Peretane must be a very big place.'

'Or they are all walking over dead people.'

After the storm Taina and Itia spent days persuading Parai not to go to Aimeo to seek a safer harbour, but to stay nearby. They fed him copiously, and took their relatives on board to flatter him. They accompanied him on walks up in the valleys where the manahune people came out to look at him and the children ran after him. They told him he would be robbed or murdered on Aimeo, which may have been true, for they were not as fond of white men on Aimeo as on Tahiti.

When Parai decided to move the ship only as far as the shelter of Toaroa, next to Pare, adjacent to the sacred house where their children lived, they were overjoyed. Once again, the whole household rolled its mats and returned to Pare.

It seemed everything was going Taina's way, for now the To'erau winds set in, beating and ripping at any sail that dared to be unfurled. Parai would have to stay at least another moon.

New houses were soon erected and people came to spend the rainy season in the interesting company. Parai and the chiefs entertained each other night after night, on the ship or at Taina's house, while the sailors began to sleep in the people's houses and eat from our ovens. On long days of overhanging cloud the tahua tatau was kept busy as the men came to him one after the other for tattoos, the tapping of his bone chisel speaking its secret language, darting like a lizard through the rain.

Sometimes Teraura and I hid ourselves and watched the men working together. They wore loincloths now, even Titriano, their new tattoos on display on their chests and arms. They were fattening up at last, their women rubbed them with monoi, and they sometimes sang as they laboured, in voices rough as bark.

When Parai came among them there was an uneasiness. They worked harder under his eye, but less willingly. Bent backs were striped with scars. Titriano didn't look up to Parai, he addressed him as an equal, it was in the way he stood, without deference. He looked almost like one of us. Parai was still as pale as a root and never seen without all his heavy clothing. I did not believe they were friends. There was something amiss. The strange talk of slavery, the scars.

Teraura liked to speculate endlessly on their different attributes, their bodies, their voices, their strength. She changed her mind many times about which one she wanted. 'Stay with Eti,' I told her. 'Eti is Titriano's friend. We will all remain together.'

'When?'

'When it happens. Something will happen. Rehua wants to take the ship.'

'They are crazy, those men!'

'Aimeo men. We can't trust them. If they get the guns it will cause big trouble.'

'We have to trick them.'

I could trust Teraura to think of a trick.

Who are these people?
We don't know them.
Popa'a, the strangers. Who were their grandfathers?
From this land, from that land, our grandfathers never knew of them.
Strange spirits they have brought among us,
The priests warned us,
Goblins!

Sons of women, arousing fierce desires. Rehua enjoyed the heat of the flame, we burned it hot under the gnashing palms, matching each other like wrestlers. Wordless.

And the other thing grew in me like a ni'au palm breaking forth.

'We will kill Parai. Titriano will be with us.'
'I'm staying with you.'
'We'll climb up the anchor cable.'
'Hush, someone can be listening.'
'At dawn the birds leave for the fishing grounds.'
'Make him your taio.'
'Be patient, woman.'
'Someone else will claim him.'
'Your haste is indecent. I enjoy your lust for him. Let me feel it again.'
Rehua.

In the morning it was Titriano my eyes hungered for. I looked for him secretly, and when I let him catch sight of me, I saw that his hunger was equal. He flirted with other women under my eyes and made love with one or two of them, but it did not change the way he looked at me. We watched each other.

Then three men escaped. Their taio helped them, gave them a va'a and food and told them the direction to sail for Tetiaroa.

Taina sent ra'atira off in all directions to capture them for his friend Parai.

'Why must they come back? Are they not free?'

This I asked Titriano under dripping leaves at nightfall.

'We need every man to sail the ship.'

'You can take Tahiti men.'

He spoke some words in English. There was anger in them. He struggled in Tahitian. 'England is not like Tahiti. We must obey our chief,' he said.

'You are angry. Parai is angry. Anger between friends is a bad thing.'

'You are right. He is a good man. I know his children.'

I pictured the white children, playing there beyond the horizon. 'Maybe he misses them. He doesn't like Tahiti as much as you do.'

'He wanted to come here. Tahiti, Tahiti. It would make him important. A big chief, like Cook.'

'He needs a woman.'

'He is a fool.'

The floggings were next. At Teraura's insistence I went out to *Bounty* that day. We were not allowed on board and we crowded on the canoes below. The men all stood in ranks on the deck in silence, their eyes like stones. When the first blow was struck they did not react.

The weapon was raised again, and the victim's woman broke the silence with her outcry.

Again, and we saw the flesh peel under the blow.

For the first time, I dragged the shark's tooth across my scalp, knowing the satisfaction of its bite, and let anguish pour forth as the blows resounded. The sun was darkened and blood rained from the sky.

'Soon,' said Rehua. 'There will be nobody to defend Parai, he'll die alone. You and Teraura will go on board with Itia's women. Drink with them, eat with them, and steal the thing to open the gun chest.'

'What if we can't find it?'

'It's the man who works iron that keeps it. Make love to him while Teraura steals it. Wait on board until we come. I will come first, up the anchor cable under the prow where the watch cannot see. The lazy dog will be sleeping. Be ready for me.'

'When?'

'Tomorrow night.'

I hoped Teraura had thought of something.

'Aita peapea,' she said, 'no trouble.'

'What must we do?'

'Wait until tomorrow.'

There was a commotion on the beach before the cocks had stopped crowing next morning and we rushed down to see what had happened.

Parai was standing remonstrating with Taina. His face was bright red and he raved in a mixture of savage English and ragged Tahitian, gesturing wildly with a pistol in each hand. He was a head shorter than Taina, but I could see the alarm on my cousin's face. He'd always been easily frightened.

Titriano stood beside Parai, dressed in his full English costume, his neck cloth soaked with sweat. He was trying to intervene, to explain to Taina what the captain was trying to say, but he was silenced by Parai's spitting fire, and stood back wooden faced.

At last we understood what had happened. *Bounty*'s anchor cable had been cut during the night, almost through.

'I know nothing of this!' cried Taina. 'It was not our people. We are your friends!'

Some people turned and ran then, taking to the hills in fear of the guns.

'I left one strand,' Teraura told me later. 'So the ship would not break free. Nobody will be climbing up the cable now. Look.'

On the forepart of *Bounty* we could see men already at work, building an extra platform so the watch could stand higher and see better.

'What knife did you use?'

'Eti gave me one.'

'Rehua will guess it was us.'

'I have heard already that it was Ari'ipaea that did it, because his taio had been punished for allowing something to be stolen.'

'Ari'ipaea, that fool. The ship could have been wrecked on the reef!'

Titriano came looking for me. I let him find me alone, near the river and the sound of water rolling on stones.

'Who did it?' he wanted to know.

'Some men from another island. They wanted guns.

'Which men? Did they intend to kill us?

'They intended to take the ship. It was a woman who cut the rope, to prevent them climbing up it.'

'Is this true?'

'It is, because the men will be dangerous with guns. It's good that they did not succeed.'

'They'll try again.'

'No, we'll protect you from their trouble. We are your friends. Come, I'll show you where the best jasmine grows.'

I led the way up the narrow path, clambering ahead. The effort of climbing prevented him from asking any more questions.

There was a place there, a dry rock near the jasmine grove. The stones roared beneath the water. At last I was alone with him, away from the chattering girls and the demanding captain.

I wanted to ask him. 'Is your own home as fine as Tahiti? Are there waterfalls and streams there too? What is the name of the place where you were born?'

The Island of Man, he said it was called.

An important name. The island of sharks, the island of turtles, the island of man. Places we had only dreamed of. He described its shores and mountains to me, its harbour full of ships, and the house made of stone where he grew up. His family had been chiefs there for generations, he said. But now his chiefdom was taken by others, and his mother lived humbly.

'At Matavai it is the same,' I explained. 'It was my family's chiefdom, but now Taina has taken it. I too must be an honourable servant.'

'He took it by war?'

'He needed no weapon. There was no man of our family left to oppose him.'

I looped a long strand of tafifi round his neck, admiring the new tattoo on his chest, a many pointed star that beat above his heart. Venus, the star of Matavai we had gazed at together. 'Now you look like the chief of Matavai,' I said.

He laughed, more lover than chief.

'I do not play, Titriano. With you at my side we can take Matavai back.'

He looked at me startled, a flash of lightning in his eyes.

'We would have the guns, the men would be with us,' I continued. 'It is the ship they desire. We could chase my cousin Taina back to Pare and live as chiefs on our own land, as befits our status.

'Does not Rehua have that claim upon you, madam?'

'Rehua does not wish to be the chief of Matavai. He is a navigator, like you. He knows all the stars and can sail to any island. Together, how strong we'll be, the proudest tribe on Tahiti, with our land and ship, travelling wherever we wish, trading and visiting…'

I watched his thoughts begin to follow that enchanting path. Only to find it blocked. A new look came into his eyes

'There is but one man who stands in the way,' he observed.

'Then that man is in a dangerous place,' I replied.

He looked around at the mountain scene, the water pouring down over the stones, the rainbows hovering above us. 'God help us, for we are all in a dangerous place,' he said. He leapt up and began to cry out in English. To his god perhaps. He struck himself with his fists. It was wrong for me to see and I turned away.

The stones roared beneath the water, water that had poured over the lip of Hinuia's cave, high above, drowning out his cries.

'Ata

Maimiti

Laughter was running wild like a vine in a thicket. Everywhere Parai went, it sprang up and caught people in its playful grip, causing them to drop everything and give in to the delightful hilarity, the joy of seeing the little Popa'a in mounting perplexity. The more we laughed at him, the funnier he became. The very sight of Parai, let alone his speeches or antics, rendered us helpless.

'He won't shoot at us for laughing at him surely?'

'No, look, he's smiling, he's lifting his hat.'

At the most unexpected moments it would happen.

'We looked up and he was there.'

'Observing us!'

'We were mourning our sister's child.'

'He didn't know to avert his eyes. He lifted off his hat.'

'It was she who started to laugh.'

'I could only think of him naked!'

'A white Peretane flower!'

'We laughed so hard, aue, the grief came back redoubled.'

'As if we had seen a tupapau, heiii!''

Was it true that Maunu had seduced him, and been thrown out of the cabin when the white man had laid hold of Maunu's ure? We didn't know, but we wanted it to be true. Taina arranged a heiva at which three men famous for tricks and contortions with their ure performed before Parai. When he asked for it to be stopped, in great alarm and confusion, our suspicions were further confirmed.

The story and the laughter fermented like rotten shrimps in coconut milk, a favourite Tahiti sauce.

Everything was turning back to front, as in an arioi comedy. Taina parading in English clothes and practising shooting on the deck; Titriano fishing on the reef by torch light.

The moon waxed and waned, and waxed again; the English seed was deeply sown, and the old people's dreams were full of portents. Tapu were broken easily and it was a festival without end. Until one day a sailor carried away a branch from a sacred tree growing on the marae, and out the priests came flying with pronouncements and plantain leaves, sending people scattering, demanding retribution from Parai.

It was one trick for another, scare for scare, mana for mana. After the sailors told us that Parai wanted to claim all the pigs sent on board for them and apportion their flesh himself, the people cut the pork into small pieces and hid it wrapped in leaves beneath gifts of fruit and vegetables.

Then the women followed the meat aboard and ate it in the company of the men, discarding the oldest rules of our foremothers.

It was hot in their floating house. Of overcooked food and of rotten sea water, there was a stench which even our heated perfumes of flowers and oils could not relieve. The men were loud, the rama was hot to swallow from the tooth chinking cup, the playing cards were flying across the table. Soon the men's voices began to sound like barking dogs, like the sawing of metal teeth in a tree trunk, their features sliding now from face to face. Teraura was smiling, but her eyes looked as though she had been hit from behind with a rock.

'I am going above,' I managed to tell her. I felt giddy and nauseous. The ship was disjointed and groaning, the floors slithered under my feet. I was looking for Titriano. I hadn't seen him for days. He had avoided me on the paths among the houses. He had avoided me on the shore. I didn't know where to find him.

Instead I was in a corner where hundreds of shiny brown insects with long feelers were crawling in and out of the timbers. I began to vomit, I could not stand, and I lay down on a pile of ropes to die.

Parai bawling orders was the next sound I heard, followed by feet thudding swiftly above my head. Had we sailed away already? Where had I been? I sat up in surprise and hit my head, tumbled out of the swinging bed I'd been lying in. I was sitting in a corner again, holding my ringing skull, when Titriano entered. He was upon me in a moment, on his knees before me with such a look of womanly concern in his eyes that I began to laugh.

He put his finger to my lips. 'Mamu,' he whispered. He had brought a fresh coconut. 'Rama is very bad for woman. Makes her sick. Drink this.'

Tuna's gift had never tasted sweeter.

'Only one sip of rama next time,' he said. 'One sip is good.'

'Is that what English women do?'

I began to remember the scenes that had passed. The night before? Some other night? The roaring confusion of voices and the lights in transparent vessels swinging above. Like somewhere visited in a dream. 'Are we in England now?' I asked.

'No, madam. At Matavai. Teraura is waiting for you with a canoe.'

'Let her wait. She will go back when the ovens are opened.'

Now it was he who laughed. Then his eyes took me in with the glance of authority that I'd seen the other men obey.

'No, you must go ashore. Later I will meet you.'

I looked for him in vain during the afternoon, and walked on the paths among the houses, and along the sand spit watching for the boat which would bring him.

At night, Rehua's body seemed too familiar. The father of our son no longer reached the depths of my desire. It was the white man's seed I ached to receive, the white man's voice in my ear.

For Rehua, it was the wind in *Bounty*'s tasselled sails he longed to hear, blowing him to glory all around the islands, while I would be a woman with two fine lovers and a life of adventure. These were the desires that kept us turning on our sleeping mats in those dripping nights before the wind changed.

'The mara'amu will soon be blowing. Parai must be killed before the voyaging season returns.'

'How? He is always protected, by guns or by Taina's men. And he sleeps alone.'

'When Tute died at Havai'i it took many men, they say.'

'Or a powerful tahua, to kill a white chief.'

'A woman could kill him.'

'He takes no woman. Not even Maunu.'

'That clown. He should have had a weapon.'

'Their king will send another ship looking for them if they don't return.'

'With our guns we will take that ship too. Will they send another?'

'Taina will be angry if Parai is killed. Parai is his taio and he will take *Bounty* for himself. But you will have equal claim if you take Titriano for your taio.'

'The wisdom of women! Do you think of nothing but pleasure?'

'Desire is stronger than force. The gods of war may stand aside for Tane.'

'We will see then what your raho can achieve, woman. Can it steal a ship from the white men?'

Rehua gave a laugh of satisfaction as he put his hand to it, as if the deed was already accomplished.

Teraura came with me into the mountains to see the priestess Hinuia. We followed the paths trodden by fruit gatherers and taro growers, through freshly slashed banana groves with new growth piercing the sappy wounds, by plots abandoned to vines, over the sprawling roots of mape trees, up stairways and passages of rock and clay, under the soft purau which overhangs the tumbling water, the boulders loudly splashed with shadow and spray, pausing now and then to refresh ourselves under the roaring torrents.

From the high meadows above the first tree line, where stands of fe'i held their reddening hands to the sky, we stopped to rest. Our legs and lungs ached and my shoulders were bitten by the unaccustomed weight of the heavy poles of drinking nuts we carried – the very finest, brought in a recent canoe load from Tetiaroa. We drank one each, and cut a juicy cane to chew.

Below us, the long-tailed mauro birds were drifting on the sultry exhalations that rose up the valleys. We could see the shadows of clouds crossing the mottled face of the lagoon, and the long folds of the outer ocean fraying along the reef. Further yet, before the known world vanished into light, the islands of Huahine and Tetiaroa floated in radiance.

Teraura's eyes searched the distance. 'Eti says you can reach Peretane by sailing to the sunset or to the sunrise,' she said. 'He says this world is round like a breadfruit. If a ship goes in one direction it can sail back to the beginning. Around!'

This made us laugh so much that we were light-headed and fell asleep.

The track into Hinuia's precinct was through a dense grove of ofe, huge clumps meeting each other high overhead, difficult to find the way through.

The old one was in her usual place, on the rock terrace of her cave. She did not seem to notice me at first, then she called out.

'Haere mai, haere mai e hine. You come to me at last. Granddaughter of Tetua Avari'i, sit here, this place here is reserved for you. Are those fresh coconuts I can smell?'

'Fresh from Tetiaroa.'

As I laid them beside her, I saw that the sight of her eyes had vanished, as if into cloud. She was looking at me from somewhere else.

'You did not carry all those alone.'

'No, Teraura is waiting for me.'

'I see you are all in it together.'

'In what, patea?'

'In the ship, e hine.'

Truly, her eyes were everywhere. 'Then I have no secrets, patea,' I admitted.

'Not many, since my sight has gone ahead of me from te ao marama.'

More terrible than the all-seeing eyes that had pierced my girlhood, these white orbs.

'Do you come to me looking for magic spells and sorcery? There is mischief everywhere.'

'We are afraid, patea. They speak of killing Parai.'

'Who does?'

'Rehua, men of Aimeo.'

'What is the Paumotuan chief doing, Taina, that famous upstart?'

'Feasting and drinking with Parai. He and Itia are begging him to stay longer, to give them guns.'

'The white men should leave. They should take Taina with them and deposit him in the land of their king, and leave him there.'

'The women want their lovers to stay.'

'Trouble, a ship full of trouble. And you? What does the granddaughter of Tetua Avari'i desire? What brings her up into the mountains to find an old, blind woman?'

'There is one man, Titriano …'

'One man. You see only one man, but there are two, e hine. They want to destroy each other, do they not?'

'Titriano said Parai was his friend.'

'The very worst kind of enemy.'

'Titriano is like one of us.'

'And you want him for yourself.'

'Not for me alone, patea, for Tahiti. To rival Taina and rebuild the chiefdom of Mahina. To father the children of Matavai.'

'A Popa'a chief!'

'He is a chief's son in his own land. You have always known it is what I want, Hinuia. He's the one.'

'He will want to take you back to his own land.'

'His land has been lost to him, as Matavai to us.'

'Mischief everywhere! There will be nothing but trouble for Tahiti from this ship, for it will be divided in two by the passions of those men.'

'Two ships, patea! Now I remember, I dreamed of two!'

Like a flame licking out to engulf a scrap of dry coconut fibre.

'What dream?'

'We stopped in the cane meadows to rest and I fell asleep. Two boats I saw, sailing in opposite directions. But the world is round as a breadfruit and a straight path leads in a circle!'

'Is that the sacred knowledge of the white man?'

Her white eyes gave nothing away when I dared to look at them. Something rustled through the ofe stands. As if a ghost had asked me that question.

But then her hand sought my shoulder, her bony fingertips entering my flesh. 'E hine, I have seen the foreigners too, I have seen them wearing dresses to their necks, on their knees in rows, praying to their nailed-up god. Peretane children! They will be here soon. Come closer to me, let me feel your face. What taint is that on your skin? Have you been drinking their poisonous 'ava? Ahime! The work of malevolent spirits!'

All night at the entrance of her cave the old one is sitting awake. The pearl shell twists on its fine cord, turning, turning, turning, catching and throwing the light of the moon.

Calls and whistles drift like mist. Something chirps, something groans, a breath is felt. Her chants spin so fine a web at first, her voice wanders like a lost child, she weaves a path, circling and returning, calling again, until they begin to answer her, merging their voices with hers one after the other. A thousand spirits gathering now, called up by their myriad names, the darkness leaping and wriggling, like eels in a trap as they speak one upon the other in a whispering, moaning din that rises like a whirlwind gathering force.

Teraura, wrapped in her mat, sleeps peacefully, but the ghosts walk over me with pattering feet, they tweak at my hair and growl at my throat. The twirling shell spins faster and faster, flashes like a pulse until I am blind as she, and my bones are melting into the black heart of te po, the infinite night.

Hina

Watch the moon, for Hina will instruct you.

Crowds were gathering, people from the valleys and around the coast. In the disorder and excitement, Taina's men patrolled with watchful eyes and weapons ready. Taina's moment was coming. Rumours were rife. Who would go to Peretane with Taina and Itia if Parai would take them?

Who would strike the first blow against him if he was left behind?

Endless delaying tactics eked out the anxious parting. The breadfruit plants were being loaded onto the ship and each night could be the last.

The cloth beaters had fallen silent and the women wore English cloth, in colours new to Tahiti.

Only Hina-te-marama's i'e remained ever upraised, beating at the cloth of light above.

Should a woman be empty handed? Maimiti went to the neglected mulberry plantations and cut saplings. She stripped the bark from them, soaked and scraped it herself, then she took up her grandmother's toa wood i'e and beat it into white 'ahu cloth.

Many girls and women were making parting gifts for their lovers at that time. 'Maimiti, what are you making for Titriano?' they asked when they heard the lonely voice of her beater.

'Cloth,' she answered them.

They left her alone, guessing it was not ordinary cloth.

It was the night the fishermen call Hotu, the moon at its fullest. What large-eyed children would be born under such a light, and the fish running by their thousands into the nets set to face the ocean.

Three days she had been confined to the women's house, purging with sea water until the tuauru would have run through her like a stream bed. 'You must be pure,' the old one had said. 'Clean, clean, clean, do you understand?'

She trembled to every breeze, and the moonlight went through her like a leaf.

While the new cloth stained with her own blood, she rolled it into a tight bundle for its secret purpose.

The moon reveals the shadows of the atua. Look up and you will see.

Honu, the turtle. Honu swimming slowly from a school of cloud fish. Honu veiling the stars.

Along the shore the reverberating shark skin, still calling the pleasures of love.

Let others dance. Turn your eyes to Hina and make yourself her servant.

Aero, the ray, on graceful wings.

The long snout of Parata, the shark, gliding slowly with upright fin.

The shadows of atua. The enduring ones, of whom the varied creatures of this world are but the brief substance.

When all was quiet, Maimiti took a canoe from the sand and paddled out to where the ship rode impatiently on the rising swell. It was the darkest part of night the moon had set. When the man on watch saw who it was he only smiled and stepped aside for her to pass.

The heat and smell of sleeping men rose to meet her as she descended into the body of the ship. There, between the stairways, where they would pass it a hundred times a day and never see it, she stowed the tight roll of cloth, wedging it into a crack even a rat could not enter.

Her heart jumped when she realised what she had done. She tried to pull it back, but it was fast.

She made her way through the narrow passageways – how strange these closed walls that could not be seen through, but must be smelt through like a lizard. 'Titriano!' she whispered.

Light was burning softly in its transparent globe, there were tattooed pages spread over his table. He was wearing only a pareu round his waist, his hair loose, curling on his neck. The tattooed star was black on his breast.

Adhere to your purpose, e hine. The time will come for the pleasures of love.

'The wind is changing, Titriano. It will soon carry you away from us I fear.'

It seemed impossible that he could leave. How empty Tahiti would be without him. 'Will you not stay here with your friends?'

'You know I cannot.'

'We can hide you.'

'Then I would be hiding forever.'

'Is Parai your friend that he keeps you captive? On Tahiti we are free. Even the highest chief's servant may leave him.'

He turned away, the muscles of his back alive in the flickering lamplight.

'I will come back!'

'Will you be a free man then?'

'Let's not speak of these things.'

'All Tahiti has already spoken.'

'They are wrong, madam!'

'Then we will wait for you, Titriano.'

In his eyes there was a hunger. It was a hunger for the land, a hunger for everything he could have if he seized it now. But he could not allow himself. He was like a bow stretched to shoot. She wanted to give him the comfort of love, the forgetfulness of desire, but the arrow must not be fired yet.

Instead she looked about for something to take back to Hinuia, some secret thing for her to work her magic with. Her eyes took in greedily the papers and books which lay scattered around, all their thousands of words secretly encoded within. He followed her gaze, and picking up a book it fell upon, opened it to a place marked with paper.

'Look,' he said. 'This is Venus, I wanted to show you before we leave.'

It was a tiny image, engraved in black on the white sheet. The goddess of love was represented, borne on the ocean waves by a floating seashell, just as he had described, her round breasts naked, her long hair gathered across her raho to modestly shield it. Behind her in the sky some people were puffing out their cheeks as if to blow her along. On land her tapairu awaited her with a cloak and flowers, as if she were truly coming to Tahiti.

'Let me take this book,' she said to him. 'To remember you by.'

For a moment he seemed undecided, then with a swift movement he tore the image from the book and handed it to her. 'Never will I forget you, Maimiti,' he said. He lifted her hand and kissed it, then turned away. His voice trembled. 'Go now, day is coming.'

Maimiti

Up in the mountains the pearl shell twisted in the gathering wind, turning, turning, turning, first one way, then the other, spinning, spinning, spinning. The moonlight it reeled in sprang back in flashing rays that pulsated at the edges of the old woman's fading vision. All her words had been spoken now. She had caressed for the last time the dry bone of Tetua's skull, and smelt the griefs of the flesh no longer. Now the world of light was reduced to a spinning globe, now time stood still, and the powers of her sorcery she released like eels from a trap, for her spirit had nothing to lose, and no need to return.

As the waterspout approached, the men stopped to watch on the deck. It was born out of the black clouds which had boiled up behind them, a cord of light, writhing in the squalling wind. Each saw in it the semblance of all the bog wraiths and bugganes, goblins and banshees he had ever heard of. Every hair of their necks sprang to attention. Yet the sweetness of that thing was unearthly too. Like a woman coming to him at dawn as he woke.

No man uttered a sound. It came so close they looked as one into its wheeling eye, and its keening rustle spoke to each alone. Only in the moment of their submission to its certain embrace did it turn aside, and pass them by as if it had lost interest in them.

A suffocating dread gripped Titriano, as if he had been struck a blow beyond which was not death, but a different kind of unknown darkness suddenly enveloping, the voice of the whirlwind sucking his blood.

The men were being bawled back to their stations, the ship springing to life as favourable gusts refilled the canvas.

Ned Young was at his shoulder. 'Unwell, Fletcher?' he breathed into his ear.

Titriano gripped the rail. 'How should I be unwell?'

'At the prospect of the voyage yet ahead, perhaps?' He took the spy glass and lifted it to watch the vanishing waterspout. 'Damn the bitches. They were full of mischief, were they not?'

The airs of Tahiti came flying on the wind that followed.

'Do you smell that, Fletcher?'

The men had a strange look to them as their nostrils filled and the sails bellied with the perfume of flowers and oils, the smell that lingered in the paths among the women's houses, the suffocating breath of desire.

Titriano could not account for the grief it aroused, for the crazy urge to throw himself from the rail and start swimming back.

A waterspout, nothing but a waterspout, a phenomenon of nature! Yet his blood was awake to something else. What stalking thing was it? Now he smelt the foul breath of rotten offerings on the marae, the odour of death. Soon his grief was followed by dread and in another moment fear got hold of his throat, the deck parted beneath his feet and the ocean seemed to yawn open for him.

Then again the longing for Tahiti was upon him, anger and humiliation at his helpless condition would set his blood to boil, until a man no longer had possession of his thoughts and could not sleep for the torments that pursued him, the memories that threatened to madden him.

✳ ✳ ✳

The storm that broke on Tahiti shattered a hundred generations. Nobody knew what direction to run in, or where was his home or who was his chief. Rain washed the blood from the women's faces; the banana leaves hung in ribbons.

Hungry on the spoiled shore, girls and women regathered at Matavai, to wait.

Teraura, sharpening herself on adversity.

Teio and her baby daughter, still nameless.

Tuaonoa with her proud tattoo, *A.S. 1789*, and her English name, Jenny.

Vahineatua, the quiet one with busy fingers.

Others too, manahune girls who hoped for their chance to join the white men on their ship.

Maimiti sitting alone at the end of the sand spit, day after day.

Maimiti. Sickness-for-the-sea. She who waits on the shore.
'It was Hinuia the priestess who gave Mauatua that name.'

'The old priestess who was the servant of her grandmother.'

'Her grandmother Tetua Avari'i who passed her dying breath to her.'

'And the curse of Matavai, they say.'

'A curse?'

'Vehiatua's priests cursed Matavai when her uncle was killed in battle and taken to the enemy marae.'

'Aue!'

'Another uncle, Tapuetefa, did not return from fishing. Itia took her to Pare for a tapairu and Matavai was Taina's for the taking.'

'Titriano will be her chief.'

'If he comes back.'

'He will return.'

'Is it true Teraura, that she dreamed of two ships, up on the mountain?'

'Sailing in opposite directions!'

'Then Titriano is certainly returning.'

'Aleck will also return.' It was Jenny who spoke, and the others saw from the lift of her chin that Maimiti was not the only one among them who had ambitions to power. Tuaonoa came from the noblest family of windward Tahiti. Everyone knew that her status was the highest among them, and as a tapairu in Itia's household, her fierce, haughty manners had attracted only the strongest of men. Now she insisted on the name the Englishmen had called her and they all bent their tongues on it.

'And Eti, he is coming back too,' added Teraura, quick to sense the rivalry.

'Eti is no white man.'

'But he is a chief on *Bounty*.'

'We will see who is a chief when they come back,' said Jenny.

When the ship reappeared at last on the horizon, dread and desire were hovering like twin ghosts above it. The chants are still on the wind that carries them across the ocean, the fleck of sail hanging forever at the margin of the sky, forever, forever, peeling like a scab that doesn't heal. The flesh falls from our bones, the sight from our eyes, ghosts ourselves we fly up like birds to guide them to shore with our wheeling and calling, forever, forever, haere mai, haere mai, haere mai!

It was soon known who was on board and who was not. They were halved in number, and more on edge than ever. Where they went the air seemed cut with knives, they were shadow men. A hundred rumours flew about them and the question was on every lip.

'Where is Parai?'

'They have killed him.'

'They fed him to a giant shark that followed them.'

'There was a battle on the ship and the others were thrown overboard, and Parai was killed in the head with his own gun, the big one.'

'No, he's remained at Aitutaki, that is what Titriano says.'

'Parai lied to us about Tute. Now Titriano lies about Parai.'

'Why, why do they lie?'

'Because they are afraid!'

'But what can they be afraid of, these white chiefs with their big guns?'

'Who is greater than them? Only their king, who is the owner of all their ships and guns.'

'And the owner of men.'

'Pah, their king is ten moons away.'

'Yet he has told them to go to Aitutaki.'

'Who will go with them?'

'Every last pig of Tahiti is being put aboard! As well to go with the pigs, otherwise who knows when any of us eats pork again.'

Maimiti

In Titriano's cabin everything could be heard – the squealing of those pigs and the bleating of goats and the loud laughter of men and women stowed in every available corner. Titriano wiped sweat from his brow with a cloth as I entered, but he could not erase the unspoken thoughts written thickly there. Now he would answer me at last.

'Where are we going, Titriano, you must tell me now, do we go to Aitutaki? I don't believe you.'

'Tupuai. We go to Tupuai, madam.' He attended agitatedly to the disordered papers which covered his table.

'Why Tupuai? Is Parai not at Aitutaki? He's dead, is he not?'

With wild red eyes he turned on me. 'If he is dead, it is not by my hand!'

Whose entrails were they then, spilling red across the ocean for the shark of longing to follow?

'By whose then? Tell me!'

'No, you are mistaken. Listen, listen to me. We argued. I put him off the ship.'

'You left him at Tupuai?'

'No, we gave him the ship's boat, the biggest one.'

Now in a flash the meaning of the dream came clear and my anger ignited.

'Is that a way to treat your enemy? You should have killed him!'

'He has a wife and children.'
'What of that?'
'I am a Christian!'
'Now he will surely row all the way to England to avenge you!'

He came to his knees then like a child who has been caught breaking a tapu; he covered his head and began to moan. 'You must help me, Mauatua,' he said.

Above decks the men were bawling out orders to each other. Jenny's strong laughter was heard above the other women's, and a baby was crying.

'That is no longer my name. Mauatua has gone. Nothing is the same any more, you understand.'

It is true, nothing is the same! All is lost!'

'Lost? No, we will come with you to Tupuai. We want to come. We are your friends.'

'They may never see Tahiti again. We can never return!'

'A Tahitian always returns to Tahiti, we are not afraid! To them you are chief Titriano. Why on your knees? Let us go up and stand together before them, and tell them where we are going.'

So must a woman grasp hold of her destiny, a woman whose cord was cast into the ocean.

Under the Wind

Heave up haul, o heave away
Weigh hey, roll and go
The anchor's on board and the cables all stored
To be rollicking randy dandy o!
Man the capstan and heave with a will

Weigh hey, roll and go
And soon we'll be driving her way down the hill
to be rollicking randy dandy o!

The laughter and singing on that flight to Tupuai! The women made harmonies for the sailors' chanties, and song after song was invented and embellished concerning the fate of Parai, the happy fortune of all on board and the glories of sailing *Bounty*. The blind man played the fiddle that set the Popa'a legs to leaping, and soon someone would begin beating the pahu, stirring the hips of all the women, and the rum would go passing from mouth to mouth, legs, hips, arms and drums conspiring to mutual frenzy, until finally men and women fell asleep in each others' arms on the moonlit deck.

A few men from Tahiti had even secreted themselves aboard to be sure of their places on this enchanted voyage. There was much jesting and feigned surprise when they emerged from their filthy hiding places below decks. Even the white men who, according to Titriano, wanted to go back to England, soon gave up their surly quarrels. The women knew how to overcome their perversity, the food was good and the sails were full. When the cursing and challenging began, someone started a song or made a joke. Titriano's men would spring to their weapons, but they were not needed and the anger flew away behind us like the spray.

Rehua stayed close to his new friend Titriano. In the hold were many pigs which Rehua had secured, with difficulty. In token of his esteem, Titriano had given him his three-cornered hat to wear, while Titriano himself wore the crown of palm woven for him by Maimiti on their last day at Tahiti. Side by side they were two navigators. Already he had pored over the charts in the cabin, beginning to decipher the mysteries of a world divided into squares that could be navigated by numbers.

The white chief was a proficient teacher, at first, but like his men he drank rum with abandon, mixing it with coconut water in the shell, sometimes passing into a deep sleep on deck. There were some aboard who would have liked to slit his throat then, if they hadn't been too drunk themselves, Rehua knew, but none brown or white would dare make any move while he himself was Titriano's taio.

Maimiti herself was like a fire rekindled, and hot as coconut husk. Now he could see that when she appeared on deck, Titriano's eyes would follow her. He prized her beyond anything. It would be a good exchange, Rehua thought, a ship for a woman.

Only first let the white chief taste the pleasures he craved. Next time he saw Titriano's eyes straying to her he made his offer.

'You know our custom, my friend. She is yours. I enjoy your ship, you enjoy my woman. You are taio Maohi now, it is correct.'

Titriano's smile was uneasy. 'Taio, she is a beautiful woman,' he replied. 'But in England a man may kill the friend who seduced his woman.'

'Kill him! This is customary?'

'Challenge him to fight. With sword.' He stepped back and demonstrated the method with an invisible weapon. 'Or pistol.'

'For a woman!'

'It's our custom.'

'Bad custom. Ours is good custom. She is related to all the important people of Tahiti. I am very happy for you. She makes you a chief of our people. It's my promise to you, my brother.'

Rehua called Maimiti over to them, observing how her eyes flew from one to the other as she approached. He reached out to her and drew her up against his belly, facing the white man. Their two faces seemed to look at him as one, a single, dark excitement in their eyes. The world was standing completely still around them.

With one hand Rehua freed the cloth she wore, and with the other he cupped her raho, parting her lips without shame. 'See how she wants you my friend,' he said, and the finger he held up was glistening wet.

Sweat broke out on Titriano's face, his eyes lost focus, and he lifted the coconut shell to his lips again as if to assuage a fire.

'Alone,' said Rehua. 'I leave you alone with her, maybe another time when you like we enjoy together.'

'Do it Mr Christian,' called a sailor who was lying nearby. 'Take her down below or I'll do it mysel'. The lassie's in sore need of it.'

'Hold your filthy tongue, McCoy. It's manners to ask the lady's opinion first.'

Rehua was pushing her up close to him, naked as she was, the delicious smell that had haunted him for weeks was warm in his nostrils at last, nor any taint of fear upon it. Titriano took her hand, as politely as if she were wearing silk gloves and a powdered wig. Hopelessly he fathomed her eyes for treachery, knowing that the urgency that now had him in its grip would overcome even the threat of imminent assassination. The momentary image of himself slaughtered on the deck, aslither in his own blood, vanished into the roaring miasma of lust and conceit that he knew now could be his ruin.

'Will you come below with me, madam?' he managed to whisper.

Teasing innocence and guileless invitation contested each other in the eager eye of her assent. Summoning up the final flourish of superfluous etiquette, he bent to retrieve her pareu for her as he steered her toward the hatchway. There was a roar of approval as they went from view, and the blind man set up another tune. Couples began caressing as if they had not enjoyed such pleasures for months, and few were sober enough to notice Rehua's smile of solitary pleasure at the wheel.

Maimiti

And so I learned at last how the white man likes to take a woman. With a fury and passion as if his life depended on it, with his lips covering every part of me, biting and sucking in new ways, his eyes ever holding to mine as if he would be lost there, foreign love words melting on his lips.

There was scarcely space to lie down together in that floating rat hole so we worshipped Tane on our feet, against the door, against the wall, on our knees, in ways never thought of under the palm trees with Rehua, and all the time the wooden ship rose and tipped and rolled beneath us, creaking and groaning. By the time we arrived at Tupuai we knew every wooden corner and metal edge of her, but never which angle it would appear at next. Or which creature might suddenly make its presence felt from behind some narrow partition – a cage of flapping chickens suddenly swinging, the haunted bellowing of the wretched cow, or once, the piercing glimpse of a rat's eyes in the very heat of my pleasure.

Of the smell, say nothing. But we were young and the power of our lust had its own intoxicating perfume.

It was not until later, on the longer voyage, that the women rebelled against that animal coupling between decks, closing ourselves in the great cabin and denying all access.

In that first time we did not talk much, we did not think, so great was our satisfaction. He liked to keep me close to him, within reach. His eyes would linger over me, I would feel his gaze, playing, waiting for mine, his hand reaching out for me. I would let it seek, silently, and then our eyes met and spoke, some ancient language of lovers, dark and exultant. Our tongues and lips we devoted to the foreign kiss, and the relishing of each other's tenderest parts, inflamed and seasoned with desire.

I began to feel something I'd never experienced with Rehua. More than the attachment of tight proximity, it was the conviction of my destiny, as if truly he had entered me even more deeply than his tireless ure, and set not a child growing – for I was mindful to prevent that – but something else, a spreading entanglement. What Hinuia had dreamed of when she cast a girl child's fate on the ocean, what I'd waited for, for so long! Prophecy fulfilled.

I did not even stop to wonder whether I had been bewitched myself, for if it was so, then I was grateful for that sorcery. Warnings and cautions had been useless: the moment had burst forth like a two-leafed seedling from the soil that had nested it, a flame leaping up from its tinder.

Whether we were hidden away together, playing love games in the narrow corners, or when we lived with the people, joining the singing and dancing on deck, we burned with that one flame, bright and strong. White and brown, men and women, were all briefly united in the blaze of light that surrounded us in those glorious days. The dolphins leaping through rainbows at the prow, the flying fish that showered the decks, the winds that blew so brisk and steady, everything was in celebration of Titriano and Maimiti.

And Rehua only smiled. Sometimes he lay down alongside on the deck, leaning on his elbow. 'It's good with Titriano, yes? You are happy now? It's long we waited, but now it's good, ne?'

He brought his friend the choicest food from the fire. Behaved like the best taio, sharing the woman in brotherly love. All the way now he was at the helm, holding the course to Tupuai, and casting nothing but glances of approval on us, the distracted lovers.

✖ ✖ ✖

When that island appeared ahead Titriano bestirred himself to speak to the people on deck. He spoke in English to his men, then Maimiti explained in Tahitian. Only her two lovers' high headwear gave them the advantage of height over her, the one in the salt-dried palm crown, the other under his hot three-cornered hat, its now-ragged trimmings tossing on the breeze. Bareheaded, straight backed, she stepped forward from between them. 'Mainmast', Titriano had begun to call her, for she was like the spar at the centre of the ship, whose topmost sails bellied high up in the dazzle of the sun. Mainmast standing tall at the centre of a new world.

'On Tupuai, we make a place to live,' she told them. 'Titriano is already known on Tupuai, and they will welcome us for we bring many good things to them, such as pigs, which they have none of. The white men now agree to peace among themselves. This is good. They wish to make a new home on Tupuai, and live as one tribe.'

The Tupuaians who came down to the beach had seen white men before, but never pigs. As soon as those creatures were unloaded and untrussed they ran off excitedly into the undergrowth, but the Tupuai people squealed louder and ran further.

Tamatoa was the chief there. It was proper for disembarking travellers to take gifts to the gods at the hosts' marae, but to Tamatoa, Titriano was himself a god. A white god, as Tute was to the old ones in their time, to be carefully respected. On the hot stones of Tamatoa's marae they exchanged breath, and names too, as if to be brothers.

'Maitai roa,' said Rehua to himself. It was good, here they would be able to live well for a while, repairing the ship ready to set sail again. From here he could set off across the beckoning ocean paths, feigning, perhaps, some convenient jealousy of this new contender for the white chief's brotherhood. He smiled to hear the white men breaking into the usual rowdy undignified cheering and shouting of their kind as the baskets of fish and fruit, bundles of cloth and dried 'ava roots, and stalks of fei bananas piled up.

They carried all the food back to the ship, and Tamatoa came on board too, full of awed admiration for everything he saw. He did not wish to leave, and in reverence for his new benefactor he spent the whole night by Titriano's side, in communion with his native gods.

� ✳ ✳ ✳

So cordial did the arrangement between the men appear, that when she heard Titriano ordering the sailors to man the capstan two mornings later, Maimiti dropped her coconut in mid-draught. Could she have misheard?

She watched them move lazily amidships, yawning and scratching their heads in the still rosy light of dawn.

Then, 'I thought we was stayin 'ere Mr Christian!' came the first protest.

'Do you want to be hanged from the yardarm, man? The next ship that passes will be upon us. We're moving somewhere safer.'

She was by his side in a moment and wasted no time to advise him. 'If we leave now, Tamatoa will be offended, and he'll avenge you!'

He laughed, held her by her shoulders and kissed her. 'Do you think me afraid of such a man's vengeance?' he said.

'No, but it's wrong. Wrong to offend a host.'

'What can he do to us?'

'He can call his gods down upon us. It is dangerous.'

'I am a Christian, Mainmast. I'm not afraid of his gods.'

She let his caress dissolve the narrow barb of fear that had entered her heart. As if the white god and guns could protect her too, here in the circle of Titriano's arms.

Rehua now came paddling alongside, and Titriano called over to him, 'Rehua, we must move the ship – go ahead and mark our passage through the coral.'

'Why Titriano? What is your intent?'

'To go east inside the lagoon.'

'The lagoon is dangerous! Shallow! Stay here Titriano, that is the word of your brother Rehua!'

'It is an order, Rehua!'

Maimiti was at Titriano's side, looking over the rail at Rehua. Wordlessly, she signalled her own incomprehension to him. Truly these white men were unpredictable and treacherous. Himself, he would be a loyal taio and look after his brother's ship. He plied his paddle ahead of *Bounty* all morning, guiding it safely among the coral heads which rose up in every direction. All morning the savage rattle of the iron chain grated on the tropical air as the anchor was cast out among the corals again and again, smashing them and scattering fish until it had fastened itself. Then the songs of the men at the capstan would float out across the water as they wound the heavy cable in again, the ship thus creeping forward over the shallows. On shore Tamatoa's men were following them. In the heat of the day, when those on board were resting and the ship stood exposed in the fierce light, the men on shore squatted among the shady undergrowth, barely visible, watching.

By evening the *Bounty* was beyond Tamatoa's boundaries and the warriors melted away. With apprehension Maimiti watched ahead. The evening was still and a shoal of cloud stood behind them in the west, slowly absorbing all the radiance of the sinking sun.

For Women and Land, Men are Lost

Maimiti

Fort George was the name Titriano gave to the place of our new home. George, which sputtered and hissed on the Maohi tongue, was the name of the English king, once described by Mai as a corpulent rascal with false hair, having less dignity than a court jester. It was a mystery to us why Titriano wanted to name our home to honour this king, for by now everyone had understood that the white men were fugitives who, if discovered, would be killed to avenge the stealing of the king's ship.

But it was our ship now, and fired with loyalty to it and the men who had risked their lives to bring it back to us, we threw ourselves happily into Titriano's service. His plan was to make a deep ditch, and within the ditch, high walls with the ship's guns mounted at the top. This, we hoped, would protect us not only from George's vengeful mariners, but the chiefs of Tupuai, who were certainly plotting against us by now, following Titriano's offence to Tamatoa.

Titriano sweated with the other men, and some of the women too, digging the ditch and building the walls from the soil they threw up. It was a low-lying place, chosen for its spring, but the mosquitoes and stinging insects were worse than any we had ever known. Our eyes returned constantly to the margins of the forest around us, where unseen watchers were surely observing. At night we were glad to return to the safety of *Bounty*, cramped as we were. At least we did not have to share quarters now with the animals, which had been released to run wild in the thick forest.

Now and then figures, a warrior or two, skin yellowed with turmeric, would pass along the edge of the earthworks with a disdainful gait. They did not want to cede any land, or food supplies, and least of all any women, to our men. Yet daily those women would flaunt their attractions along the margins of the forest. Titriano's men, enthusiastic for the possession of everything they set eyes upon, could not be warned of the impending danger. Wearing a minimum of brown barkcloth, the women flitted in and out among the trees, throwing incomprehensible jests and inviting smiles. We knew that those women were not just obeying the instructions of their own men to cause trouble, but were looking at our men, and choosing among themselves, just as we had on Tahiti.

We first saw Tinafanea when she was playing her part in these enticements, handsome and bold. Later, we found out she was also a talker, always at length in her own tongue. Her Tupuaian dialect was difficult for us to follow, yet after she came on board Bounty she talked to us volubly and incessantly. It was from Tinafanea that we found out what really happened the day the war between us and Tinirau broke out.

Blood had been shed already. Two Tupuaian men had died by the gun, and their women were sent to lure the men sleeping ashore as hostages. 'We had to make them follow us back to our houses, in the dark,' Tinafanea explained to us afterwards, as if we had not guessed their ploy.

'That must have been difficult,' remarked Jenny with fierce scorn, but Tinafanea was not embarrassed.

'Our men were coming later to take them captive. I had to lead one man to our chief Tinirau's house, and keep him there, that was the trick. He was easy to distract, his trousers were off very soon, and when he looked around for them later they had gone! He had to stay there all night.'

'Which man was that?'

'Oh, that one with a ship tattooed on his buttock, very nice.'

Aleck's ship tattoo was well known from his antics after he had been drinking rum. Although Jenny said nothing, her eyes blazed with fury. Tinafanea didn't notice and she kept on telling her story.

'He and I were waiting long for Tinirau, his ship was sailing big seas all night. Are all the white men so virile? Our men were supposed to come, they were going to tie up our unfortunate lovers, but they didn't come. All night long I listened for the alarm, but I heard only sounds of pleasure. I was glad.'

Now Tinafanea looked around at us all, her smile was very friendly but she was a pit full of dark Tupuaian treachery, and all eyes were on her.

'In the morning we wake to loud noise. Guns firing! We sit up, naked, and who do we find next to us, sitting up staring at us? Tinirau himself! His eyes very red. Outside someone shouting in English, calling for Aleck. The ship men, searching for their friends! Poom goes the gun again! We all three leap up to run, then suddenly Tinirau falls down again on the ground. I think he is hurt by the gun, which wounds from afar. Aleck is standing naked, he is shouting that he has no trousers, but what should I do, Tinirau's eyes and mouth are open, he is staring at me, groaning pitifully. I must decide quickly. I grab Aleck by the hand and pull him outside, his shirt barely covering his ship. I see Titriano's men rushing out from the trees to surround us, laughing and cheering like fools and firing their guns into the air. What a surprise when Tinirau comes running out too. Poom, Tinirau is so terrified that he gives one shriek and runs for the trees! What kind of a chief is that I ask you?'

Jenny was the only one who could resist laughing.

'Weren't you afraid of the guns?' asked Vahineatua.

'Yes, but now they will protect me. It's better.'

She was the first to speak this hope.

We knew that a bottle of rum was the most likely explanation of the failure of Tinirau's plot, and had saved our men's lives. The sailors could drink and drink it, but Maohi men fell stupid. We'd anxiously watched Titriano and his party go off in the morning in search of the missing men, and we'd seen them returning to Fort George late in the day with the three trouserless seducees, their hands unable to protect their genitals against our merciless laughter, for each was carrying not a gun, but something else that made our laughter run cold. Each carried a ti'i, like a child, one against his shoulder, one across his arms, one tied to his back. Titriano himself was swinging one as carelessly as a lump of firewood. They were the ancestor deities of Tinirau. Titriano had declared war by playing another one of our own favourite tricks.

The whole of this strange procession was accompanied by the triumphant Tinafanea.

How quickly she changed her little coarse brown pareu for a length of English cloth with yellow flowers on it, combing her hair, a chief's wife on *Bounty*'s deck.

'Now I am tired of Tupuai men,' she told us. 'They are very stupid and not interested in making love.' Her descriptions of their inadequacies soon had us laughing. It would be better to have her on our side than against us, as long as she was never allowed to go off anywhere alone. As for Jenny's pride, nobody was sorry to see it hurt. Among the foreigners good temper was valued more than good blood, we had realised.

Tempers became the bane of Fort George. Those ancestor gods of Tinirau sweated poison, the ship was full of their noxious breath. Some of the girls had bad dreams. Those things should not be there without priests to make them harmless, I warned Titriano. Hidden below decks they were silent and unseen, but their rage was heard in the voices of men like Churchill and Thompson, who became more than ever possessed by their black shades. They were the most troublesome of men, and they spread trouble among the others like a disease. Only Titriano could staunch the quarrels flaring up among them.

He threw his desperate energy into his plan, sweating twice as hard as the others from dawn to dark. At night he wanted to be seduced. His whole nature was to be seduced, and only in seduction could he find relief from the demons now in his pursuit. What strange groans of pleasure escaped his lips as he outpaced them in the throes of desire, his skin burning with fear and triumph. He gathered me under him like a valuable treasure, his sole salvation.

By day he glanced constantly over his shoulder at the shadows on the forest edge. I wanted to take Tinirau's gods out to sea and throw them away, but I was afraid to touch them. 'They are our bargaining tools. Tinirau will give us what we want in return for them,' he insisted.

'But what do we want? If Tinirau does not want us here it's useless for us to stay.'

'He'll understand the advantages for himself. He can come under our protection.'

'He is a very great savage. These people are not at all civilised. This is his land and he is the chief. He won't understand compromise, like my cousin Taina.'

'He'll come to his senses.'

'No, he will be very angry. You think everything can be won with your guns.'

'Is it not true, tell me?'

'He will not let you have any women. That is his power.'

'Other girls will follow Tinafanea.'

'She is treacherous.'

'Unlike you, my beauty. Come now, put off your shirt for me and let me kiss your sweet breasts.'

In his chest he had a gown such as English women wear, he told me, made of a soft fine white fabric, edged with intricate stitchwork and knots of red ribbon. He liked to see me dressed in it and then to take it off hook by tiny hook, kissing as he went, until finally crushing its fragile petals beneath us. 'Isabella,' he would whisper, 'Isabella, my love.'

That was the English name he gave me, and I liked it better than any of the names the other girls were given. Jenny, Nancy, Sarah. Teraura they called Susannah. And me, Isabella Christian. One afternoon he took me on deck in that dress. The day was just cooling, the people were stirring from out of the shadows where they had been sleeping when this vision appeared and startled them awake.

'No more work today,' Titriano announced. 'It's a wedding! Extra grog Mr Young!'

He had put on his officers' uniform, which none had seen him in for many weeks, the sword and hat complete. He brought out the big book, the Bible, which I had already discovered was a larger version of the book given me by Mai. People gathered curiously, the rum cup beginning to pass on its merry way around the company.

He put his arm about me, steadying himself. 'Ned Young, step up by my side and be my witness,' he cried. 'Susannah, come stand for Isabella's maid. This afternoon we will wed here before this company.'

'Aye sir, and who'll be the parson?' cried out the ever-ebullient McCoy.

'Not you my lad, for certain sure. I'll be my own parson, so God help us all. Get on your knees you filthy vermin and thank God for the day you set sail for Tahiti, for we're all free men now, no more bloody parsons nor prime ministers.'

There was an uproar of delight at this remembrance, and while none went obediently to his knees, some did begin climbing the rigging the better to see.

In the stir of announcement I was not quite sure what was happening, but Teraura was giggling at my side. 'Luckily Rehua went ashore to get firewood,' she tactfully informed me.

Titriano was opening up the book. Every kind of story pertaining to their gods and ancestors is in there. 'By this holy book,' he began, and he looked around at the crew. One by one they were removing their hats. 'By this holy book, I declare I will take this woman to be my wife.'

I was distracted by the sound of drums that came drifting on the evening breeze off the land. A priest's call to the marae perhaps, urgent and persistent. I tried to determine how far away they were, but they came and went like birds while Fletcher was reading and Teraura was performing.

'How beautiful are thy feet, o prince's daughter!'

She lifted up my long skirts and looked questioningly at my feet.

'The joints of thy thighs are like jewels, the work of the hands of a cunning workman. Thy navel is like a round goblet which wanteth not liquor, thy belly is like an heap of wheat set about with lilies.'

I could not understand what any of this meant, beyond the feet of the prince's daughter, but he was to explain to me very fully later on. He gave me instructions that I had to repeat, but I understood nothing of what I was saying, the drums were so distracting, being first from one direction, then another. He took my left hand and put a ring on one of my fingers. Afterwards he told me that it was made of gold. It is the purest kind of metal, he said, that will not get the tutae auri, the red decay that eats iron. The ring will last all my life, he promised.

It was over before I realised what had happened, and to wild cheering, kissed his mouth.

Eti Young then demanded that Fletcher marry him and Teraura too, for which Teraura wanted to wear the English gown, but everyone was so entirely absorbed in dancing and drinking that by the time she had squeezed herself into it nothing could be heard above the din.

I did not see Rehua that evening at all. But I found myself listening for the drums, guessing at the plots that were thickening ashore.

Friends and Enemies

Maimiti

When we sailed from that place three Tupuaians were aboard. Tetahiti, a chief's brother from the other side of the island; his companion, Oha, and the triumphant Tinafanea.

And Tinirau's vengeful ancestor deities. He could have had them back, but he lost them to his own treachery. He came with food and gifts to Titriano, proposed a truce in exchange for their return, and offered to drink 'ava on the deal. But one of the Tahiti boys had seen the Tupuaians hiding their weapons nearby, and word made its way to me. I gave Titriano the warning, in a code we had devised with the fingers of our joined hands. At Titriano's command the white men who had been lying atop the half-finished earth walls of Fort George stood up. Their guns were silhouetted on the sharp evening sky. Seeing his situation, Tinirau got up and departed without another word.

So we were left with his ugly ti'i on board. And Rehua. Rehua who by day was at his taio Titriano's side, working on shore with a spade and axe, sharing his rum on deck, but by night was seen sliding into the silent lagoon and heading for shore. Teraura was my eyes. 'What that Rehua doing, Maimiti? I am blacker than him in the night, I see him but he doesn't see me. You have to tell Titriano.'

But I could not betray Rehua.

'Titriano,' I said. 'Titriano, my husband, I fear those Tupuaians are going to kill us all, we shouldn't stay here. They're so treacherous, we know. Tinirau won't be afraid of the guns forever, he's already planning a way to get them from you.'

Still he talked of finishing Fort George, dismantling the ship to make houses inside the walls.

'This is not England, this is Tupuai. They are savage people, not afraid to kill us and take everything we have.'

He didn't want to hear me. So fierce his pain already. 'Isabella, Isabella, Isabella.' With biting lips and stinging tongue, driving his passion into me. Begging me not to leave him.

'Then we have to return to Tahiti. Get more women, otherwise your men will kill for their pleasure. Titriano, my husband, don't delay any longer.'

He called the crew together. 'Every man shall have his say!'

He told me this was the way on his Island of Man, the way of its chiefs. 'Nobody is higher or lower under the rule of our chief.' He told me about the way of his ancestors, who had sworn for twenty-five generations to deliver their law impartially. 'Like the backbone of a fish,' he described it to me, 'not to one side or the other.'

'Yes, that's good,' I agreed with him. 'The chief should be generous to all, especially to his family and taio.'

'But we don't share our wife there,' he added. 'Not even with taio.'

That taio, Rehua, was smiling. His lust for possession of *Bounty* was visible to me, if not to Titriano. He walked about on deck like its proprietor, like Parai used to, but smiling, his curling hair tied back with a piece of blue ribbon given him by Titriano, and blue britches. By night he slid into the water naked and swam as silently as a sea snake.

One day he came upon me briefly alone on shore. The fragrance of his Maohi skin, steeped in coconut since birth, enveloped me. Sweat beaded like dew on his oily shoulders. He had a flower in his hand and he passed it to me. A simple fau blossom, torn through to its red tongue. It was a question.

'Maimiti, are you happy? Do you like your white man now? Is he better than me?' The flower trembled in my hands. I could rip it apart entirely, turn my back, walk away.

He was closing on me with his sweet gaze. I thought of our son, who was the ornament of his grandparents' household on Aimeo, and of our two families connected for generations.

'No,' I whispered. For is one man better than another? Was Titriano's foreign smell and foreign tongue more pleasing? 'No.'

He brushed his palms across my breasts, stirring them to life, then slid them to my hips. Pressing his nose against mine, he inhaled my breath, I his. As if Titriano had never been, Rehua's potency reclaimed me; his blood connected with mine, the fau blossom pressed between us.

'Stay with me,' I said. 'The English men are very dangerous. We can't trust them.'

'But you women are so clever.'

I bit my tongue against myself and urged his heat upon me.

'He was your desire, e Maimiti. And this is also your desire.'

'Yes, but don't leave me alone with him.'

'You are always alone with him.'

From his tone, I knew precisely Rehua's intent. I remembered him drawing his finger across his throat. If he could not separate the ship from the man, the man would have to be sacrificed. I was Titriano's only protection.

'The Tupuaians are plotting, Titriano. They have a plan to take the ship and kill you. All of you.'

'Damn you scheming rascals!' he said. For a moment I thought he would turn on me, but instead he laughed, seizing my arm. 'What plot now? Who informs you?'

'There is a spy.'

'Why doesn't he come to me himself?'

'She speaks no English, Titriano.'

'You are all spies in my opinion.'

'We should leave in the morning.'

'It's impossible.'

'It's advisable.'

'I want to fetch the cow. That will distract them from their plotting.'

That was the kind of husband he was. I was clever, but he was more clever.

So now he called all the men together, the way of his ancestors. I didn't understand how letting them all argue for three days about what to do next was helpful. Chiefs should advise manahune and teu teu, not the other way around. We hung back, staying on board while they paced and ranted on the beach. There was no rum ration for three days.

On the third day the call of that rum was so powerful that a group of the men led by Thompson and Churchill came aboard with an axe. They began smashing the wood of the spirit-room door until they had pulled the lock out, rushing in with a cheer to release their beloved from imprisonment in there. After they had passed the cup, they behaved like old friends again. Hinuia had been right: There was a demon in that barrel, disguised as a friend.

They decided with their hands to return to Tahiti. 'All those in favour of Tahiti, raise a hand,' Titriano said. And at last they all did. He should have taken my advice earlier.

And still there was the matter of the cow.

Year of Our Lord 1831

'Now sit still, I tell you 'bout Captain Cook's cow, child,' began Granma. She settled herself in the sand, her long hands refastening the bindings of her white hair before she began the story.

They had walked along the shore from Papeete, leaving behind the misery houses of dying people, the lamenting aunts, and the curious English mission children who would have followed along if Granma hadn't shooed them away with a stick.

Passing among a herd of cattle wandering on the beach, Granma had no fear, not even of their long horns. The big beasts stretched out their necks, dripping strings of foam, their lashes curling, nostrils flaring. The black sand was puddled with their dung.

'Just speak them friendly,' Granma told Margaret. 'Like one sister.'

'I knew her long time, Captain Cook's cow, she long suffering like a woman. She came to Tahiti on his ship, last one, *Resolution*, all the way from England. Ten moons to cross that ocean. Ten!

'Her man cow came with her, rowed ashore on one boat from *Resolution*. Children gasped and shrieked when they saw the cow and her husband, for they got a big pair of curved tusks each atop their faces. Then we see the she cow have a teat bag all in a clump, not in rows like a pig, and the man cow got something hanging down there too, made everyone laugh again. English animals funnier than English people.

'That great English captain lead them up himself to chief Taina of Pare, just on some ropes they so nice and quiet those two. On their horns he tied up red and white ribbons with his own hands. Taina called for the priests to come put some sanctity on them, lot of people began to dance, treat them like two ancestors returning.

'People came from far around to see them. Taina supposed look after those two, but nobody know what for. Too big to kill, too strange to eat. After the captain left, Taina asked why didn't he bring horses for him to ride on like the English king. He let the cows wander away. Then come all the raiding and looting of Pare that time, they got separated, impossible to find in the thickets and abandoned gardens up the mountain valleys.

'But sometimes comes her mournful voice calling long long way, cross the lagoon, down the bathing pool, listen, that Captain Cook's cow. Other times the man cow heard replying from far away in the mountains to sunrise. One year they found each other because the she cow seen with a baby one, by some boys cutting bamboo cane one deep valley. But not again. Her baby must be died, for how her voice haunt those bad nights of girlhood, bad as ghosts, and remind me of the faraway land she from, land of the white men.

'When those white men coming again? When some great white ship appearing on the edge of the sky? Then I leave Tahiti and make a voyage beyond the horizon. That my secret vow, e hine.

'When *Bounty* came back to Tahiti a second time, we knew that ship full of slinking lies, smell the danger.

'But it was my ship, sent by the gods.

'The cows came a pair onto *Bounty* with us, both them raggle coated, burr footed, eyes astart. A crowd of shouting boys behind them, took three days to find them, bring them down the mountain, they after some rich reward.

'"Why we taking the cows, Fletcher, they too big," said I. "They eat too much, what for good are they?"

'"Milk, she'll have a baby and make milk."

'"But we have coconut, why take this big thing?"

'They were unwilling sea mates. Tupuai was far for those tethered creatures. Their feet slithered, they scrambled among nets of rolling coconuts and squawking baskets of chickens. They bellowed from their knees as the ship rose and fell across her ever-slanting path. Captain Cook must had some special arrangement keep them standing up all the way from England.

'One day the man cow would not get up any more, only pant on his knees. We women watched him nervously. Too much his suffering, we wanted to give him coconut water to drink, but only Teraura had the courage to get close to him. His big head now rolling on his shoulders, his eye staring afear, lips afoam. Careful careful, Teraura slid the dish of coconut near his mouth, those long horns so close. His eye fasten on her, he give a bellow made us scream and Teraura jump like a fish out a net.

'He drank a little but too late for him. His head fall down and his eyes blind over. Three men start clear the decks around him and push him to the rail. Captain's orders. Took three more to shove him over.

'They long time leaned after their deed with unclean hands. After he vanished from sight, they sluicing the deck, all slippery spittle and dung.

'Some of us began to feel sorry, aue, having heard his voice in the hills since childhood, we felt somewhat heartsick. The men just grinned at us, pass the rum cup. Rum soon made all forget.

'After that the she cow was doomed, for we understood she nothing but a feast in waiting without her mate. One of the white men, always the jester, declared her his true love. "My Sal's the loveliest girl on the ship ain't you my darlin'." He tie up some English cloth on her horns, kept the sun off her with that coloured stuff.

'Sometimes he brought her choice bites from his own portion, but other times making the fool with her he's lean his head into her shrunken belly and pull her dry teats, singing ridiculous songs to an uproar of approval.

'He had no wife of his own. Never enough women in that ship, while the condemned widow creature tolerating her misery with all dumb intelligence front our eyes.

'On Tupuai though, she set loose with the pigs and goats and they all disappear up the Tupuaians' gardens. They never had those animals there before, let alone one cow. She got away into wild country. She was getting fat on all kind of sweet thing there, some tasty little roots the Tupuaians grow, and that fat stalk taro. But when Fletcher decide we leaving, he sent the men to find her. He still wanted to keep her. "What for now, she makes no milk without her man."

'"Roast beef," he said.

'"What is that?" I ask, but I know already.

'For three days they fought about that roast beef, everybody want her. There was one Tupuaian chief, name Tinirau, who made a lot of trouble. He didn't want us there, just make trouble for us. Your grandfather Fletcher, he didn't understand island diplomacy, how to treat a chief. He wouldn't listen me. First he offended Tamatoa, now he's fighting Tinirau.

'Everybody doesn't want anybody else have that cow. They fought for her up into the sloping country, scrambling the rocks and back down them ravines full of slashing green. Finally the Englishmen got backed into a taro patch, go down in the ditches, one man fainting from a spear wound in his ribs.

'Smelling blood, like lizards, Tinirau's men waiting at the edge of the forest. Patiently, they wait. Sometimes the guns don't fire when the ground is wet like that taro patch, so they wait. Our men lying in the juicy stalks, also waiting. Mosquitoes very bad there, hard to not slap. Last Tinirau's men run out, spears lifted, and straight away come flash the gunpowder. No, not too wet after all. The blood wet there, one taro patch ruined, tapued.

'Fifty, sixty Tupuai men killed that day. Victorious party returns the *Bounty* led by one Tahiti boy carrying its red English flag above their heads. God save King George, they shouting, forgetting King George their enemy, they so victorious. They minds on the rum kegs.

'The poor cow, she driven alongside crying low, make us girls feel sad, make us homesick.

'That her last day. Moon rise she hanging in one aito tree with her face dragging on the ground.

'They own faces all red with fire and rum. Dark spirits coming crowding in the forest behind us, attracted to the butchery. Those men so pleased with themselves, shoot sixty

Tupuaians and carve pieces off the she cow, cook them on the fire. Even the one said the cow was his true love.

'What powers and protection the white god giving them, we would see. Nobody saying any prayer to Him.

'That night most the girls falling drunk with two husbands, but your grandfather already the only one for me, we were vowed together. I feel his afraid, he need me, that's why I stay beside him.

'Yes, that was a bad day and all badness sprung from it like a gushing wound. Turn away your ear now my child.'

Betrayal

Back at Matavai Bay, *Bounty*'s one good boat shuttled laboriously back and forth all day from ship to shore, rising and disappearing between the rolling swells. Black clouds were snarling around the two peaks overhead as the men who wanted to stay on Tahiti were put ashore. Bad ones, good ones, each equipped with a musket and a pistol, the blind musician with his instrument, and on the last trip, Tinirau's ugly ti'i were finally disembarked.

Maimiti watched the boat going with relief. Without all those disruptive elements, there was a better chance for their venture. A few canoes rode near the ship and people had been coming aboard all day, making themselves comfortable below. Aimeo was swept by veils of purple rain and the ship creaked underfoot.

Rehua came up beside her at the rail, shoulder to shoulder. 'Trouble comes, trouble goes, ne?'

Her fears started up again at the smell of his skin near her own. Of the two men, he was the more dangerous, she was certain, but her instincts clung to him although his familiar cunning had lost its appeal. 'And you,' she said, 'do you come or do you go?'

'It's a good wind to reach Aimeo.'

The good wind was running loose in his hair, tossing the feather pennants of a sailing canoe that lay alongside. His eyes were in the clouds. How many friends and relatives he had who would back him for the ship, the muskets, the glory of conquest!

Their son was the only foil to his treacherous enterprise that she could think of. 'Will you bring our son back with you? He should come on this voyage with us. Fetch him from your people, Rehua.'

How eagerly he accepted her commission. 'Yes, you're right, he should come with us. And you'll wait here?'

'With the ship, until you bring our son.'

'Two days.'

'I won't leave without him.'

A squall was coming down on them and the decks were suddenly cleared, men and women hastening down the hatches. Not bothering with further talk, Rehua let himself over the side and swam for the canoe. She could hardly see his head through the sheeting rain, disappearing and reappearing among the swells.

✖ ✖ ✖

Fletcher saw the canoe beating across the lagoon, and followed it carefully in the rain-specked spyglass eye, until he had seen the stiff sail deftly trimmed in the pass. Only Rehua would take a pahi beyond the reef in that weather.

It would be dark in two hours, and already there were a dozen women below decks, the usual uproar. Would there be no end of it, he wondered.

By the midnight hour, when he looked into the galley on the way up the main hatch, there appeared to be at least one woman to every man and some were evidently already retired together into the hammocks. He'd spent himself with Isabella. The memory of her flesh now burning in him would be alight through the shadowy hours of the middle watch. His own flesh was raw with passion, and the sight of the stars as he came up reminded him that all was not yet lost. The clouds were breaking up and the wind was dropping. He took a sip of rum from a flask and counted himself fortunate not to be suffering the lash of Bligh's villainous tongue somewhere in the stinking East Indies, sharing his bunk with half a dozen potted breadfruit trees and dining on rotten yams. He took another sip and congratulated himself heartily. The woman was his, the ship was his and the remaining men were loyal. He had only to find some suitable place, and he had a vast ocean of islands at his disposal.

No other watch mate appeared, but the prospect of a quiet flask alone under the stars allayed his fear of disorder. He hunkered down in the lee of the wheel where he could still hear the bursts of laughter and drunken singing beneath him. The ship moved noisily on the swell, shuddering in her bones and creaking along every seam, stretching and groaning, familiar as an old wife. Let them carouse and sleep and womanise, let the poor bastards. There was nothing more for them in this life except he find them a home. Somewhere they could live like men. A free society based on equality. That was something to drink to. And every man should have a woman his own. Monogamy, in his case, would be a virtue. At least one he could salvage. A drink for monogamy.

When the ship had fallen silent at last and the stars were bright between flying clouds, he took up a heavy knife which lay among a heap of coconuts, and leaning out from the rail he released the anchor cable with several fierce strokes of the blade.

Bounty gave a leap as if of recognition. She was free again, although her timbers were shrunk and cracked, her sails ragged, every spar and rail of her weary, her decks still crowded with animals and crates and plants. Like an old mare limping out of the stable she got under way again, her captain hauling on the sheets himself until McCoy showed his ragged head unexpectedly. 'Are we off already Mr Christian, it's no mornin' yet is it?'

'Square the yards, McCoy! The wind is fair, and a Manxman does not share his wife with anyone, do you hear me!'

'Aye aye, Mr Christian! Nor a Scotsman neither.'

※ ※ ※

At dawn the first wail disturbed their swift progress. Tahiti was slipping out of the mist behind them, and to starboard Aimeo's western peaks were still unlit when one woman leapt from the rail. She was under for a few moments, her friends on deck standing heart-stopped. Then she reappeared out of the wake and began to make for Aimeo, her hair plastered to her shoulders. It would be a long swim.

Now Aimeo seized Maimiti also, Aimeo's limpid wreath of light, Aimeo's perfect mirrored cloud, Aimeo's dark roaring centre, the eternal voice of water, the source. It tore from her like a limb, like an organ plucked. And Rehua, left behind, their betrayal complete, finished and over. Unless. She scanned the distance for a sail, but there was none.

'You didn't tell us, you didn't tell us the ship would leave in the night!' came the accusing cry, the other women crowding the stern in disarray. 'We have left our families, our children!'

'Where are we going on this ship of rogues? They have tricked us, aue!'

'Maimiti, tell Titriano we must go home, let us off!'

'Won't you swim like your cousin?' came Teraura, who wouldn't have left the ship if it was afire. 'Why go back, come with us, this is our good fortune. Roving the islands, East and West. We can reach Aotearoa in this ship, maybe we are going to England!'

'What do we want to go to England for? Some of us are grandmothers! Maimiti, we entreat you, tell that chief of yours to turn back and land us or we are lost on this desperate voyage. Who are these fiends? Maimiti!'

Maimiti, Maimiti! Isabella Isabella Isabella. Rehua, Hinuia, Mauatua, Tetua Avari'i ... the wake unrolling like a fern, a hypnotic trick, like the spinning of Hinuia's pearl shell, like the drumming from the high marae. Haere, haere, haere! We two are no more! The sun rising behind. The ragged sails bellying. Maimiti, Maimiti!

In the tiny cabin she found him sleeping, snoring. She could have ignited his breath, like McCoy did for a trick. Sitting beside him, she turned his face this way and that. His eyes opened once but he didn't see her. 'Wake up, captain,' she tried. No response.

There was a craziness on deck, the women who wanted to go home were wailing in the stern, and others were starting to join in. The men, including the Maohi men, kept to the foredeck and watched. When Maimiti stepped up to Eti Young the wailing stopped but the groaning of sail and mast seemed to heighten as if the wind had suddenly picked up.

She stepped up to him like a man. 'Eti, your captain say to put about and leave these women outside the reef at Aimeo.'

Eti laughed. 'Does the man give his orders to you now my lady?'

'Don't waste any time, that's what he say.'

Eti's laughter was ear curling. When he and Teraura laughed together they were like two noisy birds out of the same nest. 'What his problem today? He drunk?'

She made no reply. Eti Young's profile was very dark against the light-filled sail, tangled black locks flying up round his head, whites of his eyes bright, shoulders still heaving with laughter.

'It's an order!' she shouted.

'Aye aye Mrs Christian!' he shouted back, still laughing. 'Why not? We not good enough for these ladies, that's for sure.'

When the women saw the men go to the ropes to put about there was a noisy outpouring of gratitude and relief, but Maimiti went swiftly below, calling Teraura after her. 'I am going to Titriano's cabin. If Rehua is seen approaching come and warn me straight away. But if he is not seen, tell the women to pass on the news that I jumped overboard at dawn and was making for the pass at Afareaitu.'

Now it was Teraura's turn to laugh. She and Eti would laugh at anything; they would never stop laughing.

Maimiti sat behind the bolted door of Titriano's cabin with his pistol. It was a heavy, ugly thing and she didn't want to use it, although he had showed her how. The measure of grey powder carefully tapped into the chamber, and the lethal ball which would break open the flesh and cause a horrible death. Near her hand she also kept his sword whose deadly blade could fell a man as easily as if he were a banana tree.

Titriano snored and sometimes he mumbled and cried out. His head was wet. From beneath in the holds came the smell and noise of the pigs and chickens still captive there. She strained her ears to hear whatever might be happening above her, but the ship had become so noisy and the sea groaned so heavily against her sides that there was nothing to be discerned.

When she next came on deck, Aimeo was far behind.

Hiti a Reva Reva

Maimiti

The world of light is not controlled by the spirits, or the gods. That's what he say. He say it hang together in the sky like a spinning top and there's this law and that law acting on it. Gravity, that's one. 'Who is this Gravity?' I ask. Make him laugh.

Make him laugh when the cold wind's in our face day after day, no land in sight. Nothing but ocean. A whole moon afloat, then another and another yet ...

They were the worst kind of men. It was Vahineatua who first spoke this aloud. Varua 'ino, bad spirits.

That day a man had died. We had come close to the land of Purutea and a canoe had come out to greet us, with great excitement and exclamation at the sight of *Bounty*, the pale-haired men with us and the animals and plants overflowing from our decks. One man climbed aboard, wild eyed with amazement at the things he saw. It was Titriano's coat he liked most, Titriano gave it to him, and strutting in it he reminded me of Mai. He climbed up on the rail, showing his friends below his prize. Why did someone fire his musket? Why did the man of Purutea fall forward in the blue coat and splash into the sea? We rushed to the rail and saw the red cloud spreading up around his sinking body. His friends were already paddling as fast as they could to get away, in the shouting and shrieking of that moment was only confusion. Titriano was ordering the sails set, I saw the look on his face. The grip of demons.

'No demons,' he say to me. No demons. 'Only stories of old women.' He tell me about some demons living on his island. Half woman half fish, and sea men that come ashore to lure girls to a drowning. Old women by the fire telling them stories, he say.

'O Titriano, take me one day to your island, to your faraway island, see your people and the hills and rivers of your ancestors.'

He turn away from me then. His back so strong, the shoulders of a chief. I press my cheek between them, feel his heart. 'O Titriano, tell your wife.'

'The ship must be repaired before we can go to England. We need to find a safe place, repair the ship.' That's what he say to me. An island of our own.

But no island our own with those demons in pursuit.

Together in the great cabin we counted ourselves.

Maimiti.

Teraura, called Susannah. Vahineatua, Teio and her baby daughter they called Sully.

The cousins Mareva and Faahotu of Matavai, and the other manahune girls Puarai, Teatuahitea and Tevarua, who could beat good cloth, carry heavy loads and knew the best moons for planting all kinds of foods.

Proud Jenny, who had not spoken to Aleck since we left Tupuai, was seasick without cease, and her Tupuai enemy Tinafanea was similarly afflicted.

Stranger to us all was Toofaiti, a shy girl from the island of Huahine who was following her tane, Tararo, a chief of Raiatea.

Four women had left the ship when it made the last return to Aimeo and now we were fewer than the men by three. There was no need to speak of what this must mean, unless we were to find some other women somewhere, but our daily progress against the east wind carried us ever further from the islands any of us knew.

We had last heard of Rapanui from Mai, but only legend told us of Hiti a Reva Reva, Border of Passing Cloud, lost in the east.

Rehua may have known the pathway to it, which currents, winds, clouds, colours, would carry us there. Titriano had rolls of paper, weighted at the corners, heavy instruments and mysterious calculations. Our island had to be found.

It was Vahineatua who recounted the old story of Hauvana'a.

Hauvana'a was given in marriage to the chief Tu i Hiti, who came to Tahiti to get a wife. He was handsome and noble, but Hauvana'a pined for her family, turned away from him, and went back to her parents' household. Then in her separation from him she felt love pierce her heart. Her parents sent for Tu i Hiti and told him, 'Now your wife has become attached to you.'

Vahineatua was a good storyteller, and we were all eager to hear the old story afresh.

'Tu i Hiti was preparing to return to his own home, Hiti a Reva Reva, far beyond the horizon. He was loading up his big canoe when she came to him. "Aue, husband, I have been weeping for you," said Hauvana'a.

'"Why have you been weeping for me?" he replied. "When I was with you, you spoke unkindly to me and then you left me to return to your parents. Now I am taking leave of you and returning to my own land."

'Hauvana'a pleaded with him. She saw him handsome, she saw his strong muscles as he loaded supplies on that canoe. She had left it almost too late, she had to beg him now, which a woman does not like to do, especially a proud ari'i like Hauvana'a. "Don't forsake me, I beg you," she had to plead with him.

'"Then will you come with me?" he asked her. "For if you do, you must bid goodbye to your parents and sisters."

Some of the women began to weep and sob now, thinking of their own parents and sisters. The baby, Sully, was handed from arm to arm, breast to breast, the tears falling on her head.

'So,' Vahineatua continued, 'Hauvana'a went to her parents. Her father, seeing her tears, asked who had beaten her.

'"Nobody beat me, father," she told him, "but I am leaving you now, to go with my husband, who wishes to return to his own island."

'"Ah, you see my daughter!" he said to her. "I advised you not to spurn your husband, because he is a chief from the far Border of Passing Cloud and you might send him back there. Now look what dangers you will face in reaching that place. Many are the foes of the deep!"

The foes of the deep! Vahineatua began to list them.

'Ahifa-tu-moana, the sea serpent. Are-mata-roroa, the long wave. Are-mata-popoto, the short wave. Pahua-nui-api-taa-i-te-rai'i, the giant clam that opens against the sky. Anae-moe-oho, the shoal of monsters. Aue, aue, aue!

With every wave she mounted the ship moaned and shrieked, and we could hear the never-ceasing clank of the pumps below the waterline as they emptied out the hungry ocean.

'"So will you go with your husband, or will you stay here with your parents?" Hauvana'a's father asked her.

'"I shall by no means stay," she told him.

'"Will you not weep for us?" he asked.

'"Yes, I shall weep, but I would weep more for my husband."

'"Go then," he said to her. "You have a royal will and you cannot be persuaded to stay."

'So Hauvana'a went to Tu i Hiti, and he also advised her to stay. "Stay here with your people," he said. "Behold your own parents, your own mountains, and hear your praises sung by your own people."

'"I shall by no means stay," said she.

'"Stay, for as soon as your land is lost in the distant haze your eyes will begin to weep, and never will you behold Tahiti again," he said.

'"I will go with you," she said.

'"Then fetch your mats and garments," said Tu i Hiti, "and let us depart."

'So it was that Tu i Hiti and his new queen set sail to the southeast in his double canoe, and were soon out of sight of Tahiti.'

Aue, aue, aue.

We took our turn at the pumps, knee deep in the stinking hull in darkness.

If the water began to rise above our knees we had to pump harder. The men had pumping songs that went on night and day.

Oh I hope that we will never see,
Leave her Johnny leave her,
A hungry ship the likes of she,
And it's time for us to leave her.

Leave her Johnny leave her, o leave her Johnny, leave her,
The voyage is done and the winds don't blow and it's time for us to leave her.
The starboard pump is like the crew,
Leave her Johnny leave her,
It's all worn out and it will not do,
And it's time for us to leave her.
Leave her Johnny leave her, o leave her Johnny, leave her,
The voyage is done and the winds don't blow and it's time for us to leave her.

On and on and on those songs went, night and day. The sun rose ahead and sank behind, we hung in the centre of the empty horizon, and by moonlight we sailed steadily on, homeless on the glittering ocean of night.

III
The Talk of Women

Vahineatua

McCoy up the top mast looking out. Everyone looking for signs. No more talking, only watching, waiting. Nothing but burning points of light all round. No giant clam rising up, no bird, no stalk of weed. No Border of Passing Cloud.

Not knowing what god to pray to under the burning moon. Everyone listening, even the remaining animals fallen silent.

Clanking, creaking, shuddering, *Bounty* straining beneath us.

That's how it was. Let me speak now. I was there.

Afraid. Yes, that the truth. I, the orator's daughter, Vahineatua the pure, was afraid, finding myself on that ship of wild men.

Why hadn't I returned to Matavai and my people after the bad events that took place on Tupuai?

I could have gone ashore with the others, but not even Maimiti guessed that Titriano would leave Matavai in the middle of the night. She was the worst surprised, for half the women aboard wanted to get off, and everyone looking to her for what to do.

When I saw her tell Eti Young to take the ship back to Aimeo, I knew I had to stay with her. Our eyes met across the deck. She trusted me to stay with her. She was my distant cousin, with many shared ancestors, and although her bond friend Teraura was with her, sometimes a cousin is better.

Mills was the oldest man on *Bounty*. Other girls had the better men — Maimiti and Teraura the best. My own choice, James Morisson, had been left at Matavai.

After we were ashore at Pitcairn, Mills claimed me as his own, same as Quintal claim Tevarua and McCoy, Teio.

Prudence, he called me. That a name meaning caution, he say. 'Ye're a good girl, a good, quiet girl,' and because he was older, I hoped he be wiser, more fatherly to me. But I don't know what kind of fathers those white men had. Only thing they knew about fathering was one thing.

On *Bounty*, we kept Teio's baby Sully below in the big cabin with us most the time, but sometime we come up for fresh air. Eti Young the only one like to dance that baby girl and play games with her. Swing her out over the water, make her mother scream with fright, but Sully laughing, she love the ship, never cry on *Bounty*.

When we landed at Pitcairn we swam ashore, too impatient to wait for the little boat to come back and forth to *Bounty*, swerving over the dangerous rocks into the tiny bay. Eti Young helped Teio surf to shore with Sully in a barrel. 'She didn't utter one cry! Came out laughing!' Teio boasted ever after.

Must have been the daughter of a merman, that little sullen.

We came ashore at the bottom of a steep ascent, and looked up its raw ragged flanks, no other way up. That was the Hill of Difficulty, but Teio had those strong legs to go up a hill with a baby on her back, and Sully grew them too.

That day just the beginning of climbing up and down hills on our new island. That day the track untried, a slippery red knot of roots and rocks between the toes. But we knew it was a track, others climbed this way long before. The chiefess Hauvana'a, arriving with her husband, with her mats and her ti'i tied to her as ours were. Hauvana'a, Hauvana'a, Hauvana'a, I heard in my breathing, grasping for handhold and footing. This was the standing place of that courageous chiefess, the place her legend came to.

Hiti a Reva Reva, Border of Passing Cloud, we set foot upon you at last! O fenua maitai, the good land that fed and clothed and swallowed Hauvana'a's blood and bones without trace! Mother to our children, grave to our husbands! Hiti a

Reva Reva, I salute your wet red paths, your unassailable cliffs, your heights and depths, your fresh-flowing spring of water, your green thatch and abundant larders. I salute you, home of my hina tini, hidden treasure of the sunrise!

Yes, she had appeared like a promise of tomorrow, silhouetted in the last rays of the setting sun. Hiti a Reva Reva! 'Land ahoy!' McCoy was shouting up the top mast, and all was impatience on board that night, no sleeping.

Morning the island burst out of the dawn, bristling with sunrays like a vision, so beautiful was Hiti a Reva Reva, some of us began to weep. All eager to get ashore and taste her sweetness.

Soon we stretched out on her green and breezy heights. We, breathing her air and smelling her smell.

Through the trunks and fronds of the groves we spied *Bounty* below, riding the swell on her anchor. Titriano had ordered some of the men to stay there and begin to unload, but the three Tahitian men had climbed up with us. Now we stood surveying our new home. The fenua maitai, the good land.

It was Manari'i who said, as if to joke, 'Now is our chance to kill the white men as they come up the hill.'

'Don't be a fool,' Teraura said. 'They will have their muskets ready to fire even as they climb. Do you think they trust you so much? You should be husking coconuts for them to eat.' She herself was already plucking a chicken.

That night, the men ate with the men, according to our custom. We women took our own food separately.

Later, years gone by, our daughters came to eat with their fathers and brothers at the same table, according to Christian ways, but in the beginning we could not eat with the men, the way they slurp the food and suck the bones. We ate quietly aside, from our own end of the oven. Through the palm tops the stars were our own stars, the moon our same moon as always. 'It's a good land,' we agreed. 'Fenua maitai. We can live here.'

We walked and climbed all over our new home next day and next while the men emptied the ship. Every kind of good plant for weaving baskets and mats was there – the aute tree was there for cloth beating, and tu'tui for lighting. The breadfruit groves were thick, untended maybe two, three generations. The cane meadows covered the slopes of our mountains, all kinds bananas and plantains springing from the tangle of vines and weeds. The pigs and goats would soon begin to clear it. From the treacherous ridges that hang like ropes between the peaks, no other land is seen in any direction. O fenua maitai!

But the gods of the vanished people of that land were not pleased by us. At their marae above the bay, four tall ti'i were turned inland to watch us with stony eyes from its corners.

Maimiti and I were the only ones bringing our own ti'i with us. So sudden our final departure from Tahiti that all were unprepared. We should have had stones from our own marae, and sacred feathers to offer to these occupying gods, and prayers to chant to the deities of Hiti a Reva Reva. The correct way to arrive at an uninhabited land, please its spirits.

Instead we had to improvise with offerings of withered plants and roots carried from Tahiti, and the insignificant prayers of women and manahune boys, all under the disbelieving eyes of the white men, who had no fear of any gods and mocked our ways.

It was the white men who threw the ti'i over the cliff into the ocean below. We knew it was a bad thing, but we couldn't stop them. 'Ugly bits o' stone, starin' at us. Good riddance tae them!' said Mills.

They never listened to our warnings. Even the bones of a chief, buried under the marae stones with a huge pearl shell for a pillow, they threw over the cliff onto the rocks below.

Then we women knew there would be trouble, and we listened at night for the voices of angry ghosts. Aue.

Tevarua

Matiu hit me the morning I died.

That's why I lost my footing on the cliff edge that day, reaching for gull eggs.

He's hit me over the cheek make my ears ring, and as my fingertips almost touching those eggs, suddenly the ringing began again and nothing to grab for but the rocks that came loose under my hands as I began to slide, eggs crushing, skin burning. Then all the seabirds rising up, crying and screaming above my breaking bones.

Tevarua! Tevarua!

Strange I'm hearing my mother at home by faraway Matavai. And my daughter running along the cliff top with hair unbound and arms wide as if she'd catch me. But I am gone for sure. The surf rearing up, smashing down, seabirds whirling overhead. Gone for sure.

Matiu Quintal was the man who claimed me, Tevarua, for his.

All the men wanted to be like Titriano, keep himself one woman and share her with no other. All white men picked one woman, but Maohi men got to share. That's how the trouble start. Begin the killing years.

Matiu the same one set the ship alight. We were all living on the hilltop by then, under *Bounty*'s canvas. A great pile of things been hauled up the track. Timber, tools, sails, barrels, iron cookpots, trunks, boxes, lumps of metal, ropes, and all 'em remaining pigs and goats. Only them goats need no help to climb up the hill, jump away like fleas. Five days we were crawling up and down the bleeding track. Lucky the cow wasn't with us any more.

We didn't notice any smoke, because a cooking fire was smouldering in the rain, and we were taking shelter of the canvas roofs, the rum cup passing around. Matiu was gone for a time, then he slip back in against my side, wet and smelly as a fish.

Was Teraura first saw the flames. She came running and shouting, and we all crowded to the cliff edge, see down there our ship smoking, see flames leaping up through the smoke.

Titriano's shouting for who did it, who was it, but everybody's talking at once and nobody's saying anything. Our eyes can't leave that sight, soon the masts and spars all aflame, the hatches gushing like volcanoes, a dancing ghost of fire writhing all around on the water, pieces falling from aloft, trailing showers of sparks. When the wooden woman figure under the bowsprit plunged in like a diver, lighting up the sea with a fountain of sparks, my eyes overfilled with fire and all the women starting to wail, fearful.

Then Maimiti's raised up the first notes of a song. One favourite from home that all the girls knew, and we sang that song, and then another and another and another, watching until sunrise, our ship dissolved in flame, gone forever under the reddy waves.

Then we knew we had to live with the men, have babies.

We gave birth and gave birth. The fenua maitai sucked up all the blood like a thirsty god and gave us back the next generation. They were our hope. Every birth a promise. Matt, George, Charles, Daniel, then Jane and Polly and Dinah. So many sprouting up strong from the fenua maitai.

Each one's coming out different, some getting blue eyes, some getting yellow hair, some getting red-colour hair, some getting brown skin, some pink. I had most babies, being five, but one of them boys died. I think Matiu frighten him too much in the womb. Didn't want to live on the fenua maitai with us. He knew what was coming.

Matiu was coarse, hairy, and scarred like a boar.

Even so, his son Matt, strong, dark, fierce browed, was next-born after Maimiti and Titriano's boy.

'What a daft name Fletcher's give his lad!' said Matiu. 'Thursday bloody October! The first son gets his father's name where I come from. We're calling ours Matiu, me lovely, give me another kiss.'

Always another kiss. Then another bite, another bruise, another punch. Matiu like that, full up of anger. Sometimes Tevarua envying Mareva and Tinafanea, who shared them five Maohi men between them. It a shame and a curse for a Maohi man to beat a woman over and again. But Matiu, he got no gods to answer to and not one man stand against him though they see Tevarua's cut-up face, broken tooth.

Still, he got a curse on him in the end. Tevarua not the only one ghost silent witness to his skull crack, brains spatter, and his crazy soul expelled like a vile gas while the eyes of the living frozen by the sight of his spouting blood and convulsing limbs. Even the little sullen Betsy Mills, she there, one little girl, when the killing done.

His killers, Aleck and Eti, threw his body down a valley. Sinking slowly through the vines. Maybe one pig eat it. Then Eti wash the axe and grind it on the stone, grind it grind it, feel it with his thumb, hide it away in the rafters. But the spirits were satisfied at last. Matiu's blood was what they wanted.

Began with axe, end with axe, the killing years. Toofaiti knows. She will tell you.

Toofaiti

Why does black man sharpen axe?
To kill white man.

Toofaiti knows.

I, Toofaiti, the one Williams want for his own after Faahotu died.

Poor Faahotu, she died from something come out her throat like poison. Filled her ears and her nose and her eyes with poison, the itching, burning, weeping poison we call tui heanano. Poison her whole head, she lose her senses and fall sick. Soon she was buried in the soil of the fenua maitai, the way of the white men, and before the place got one blade of grass growing on it, Williams is coming for Toofaiti.

'Nancy, Nancy!' he's calling to me as I walk past the forge. 'Nancy won't you be mine?' He's beating hot iron on the anvil there, bang, bang, bang, and sparks flying out of the shade. Flying from his eyes too. He was slim as a girl, but with muscles gleaming from his work at the anvil, and long hair tied down his back. 'You can call me Jacky!' he call after me, his big teeth bright in the firelight.

But I was handsome Tararo's woman and Tararo was a proud Raiatean — claimed he was a chief of that island, too proud to share his woman with anyone, so even though I heard Williams, I didn't reply to him. Just give him one eyeful, so he knows. I was so lustful for that boy I couldn't stop thinking about his fiery limbs and how his eyes would shine in the dark when they were finally alone together. Couldn't see the danger.

That kind of sinful woman was I, before I knew the laws of Jesus. Oh dear Lord I pray. Every day on my knees to pray, kind Jesus to forgive me for those sins. Aue.

I stole Maimiti's mirror, such a sinner was I. Stole it from where she leave it by the door of her house. Maimiti never said anything about that mirror, who took it. But she knew who.

Used to comb my hair by it in some quiet place, nestle a row of fresh white nono flowers there. I'se afraid one day, thought I saw someone coming behind me in that little round door of light. Threw the mirror among the leaves and stones where it broke in pieces and had to be buried in a secret place.

Plenty of bad spirits were creeping up on me that time, vain Toofaiti looking at her pretty face.

Williams was becoming crazy with desire.

'Why he must have you?' protested Mareva. 'Why not Mareva.'

'Girls from Huahine are most desirable,' I told her. 'Huahine is the shape of sex, the lagoon there is the lake of love. Every day my whole life I swam in that lagoon.'

Mareva only gave me a look of disbelief. She said she would rather live with any white man, even Quintal, than three squabbling, giggling Tahitian men. 'They say they won't work any more, even though we women are slaving all day. They just want to live easy same as on Tahiti. The white men work in the heat of the day and they curse our men for resting in the shade, so they should do like the white men. That Temua just wants to play his nose flute all day and play with me all night. Too many men on this island.'

Tinafanea, the Tupuai girl who had caused so much trouble, encouraged the three Tahiti men to be lazy. Performing very fancy Tupuaian dances at any time of day, keeping them entranced, but all the time she's got her eyes on the white men.

It's going on like this.

Then Puarei was lost. She gone over the cliff edge, same as Tevarua in her turn. Was the devil spirits of the old ones pulled them over, the ones whose bones were disturbed when we came to the fenua maitai. Bones thrown over the edge. Aue. Nobody see her fall, or hear her cry out, we never see her any more.

Two white men, Aleck and Williams, now got no woman. Everybody's coming to an arrangement among themselves. Without a word Tinafanea rolled up her mats and went to stay at Aleck's house, leaving Mareva alone among the scheming Maohi men.

Williams got me in return for his skills at the forge. He said he would not work the iron in the fire for them, making all the tools and blades they wanted, unless he could have a woman, the one he wanted. They all come to our house to enforce this decision, Titriano looking as if he would weep, the others behind him with their muskets. They all sat down there on the paepae of our house, and Titriano spoke. Sweat was dripping off his brow, off his cheeks, off the end of his nose, his whole face was crying. He say, now on, Toofaiti be Williams' woman.

Tararo was a jealous, proud Raiatean. He stood up, shouted a curse in his own dialect, and walked away. We could hear him raving and howling as he went, and the white men smirked among themselves. They didn't understand Tararo was a chief, they were humiliating a chief.

The first night, after Williams had fallen asleep, I thought I could hear Tararo weeping on the night wind, but maybe was the ghosts that were thick around us.

Oh sweet Lord Jesus protect us from the ghosts. Oh sweet Lord Jesus forgive Toofaiti her sins.

We didn't see Tararo for three days. Then I'm on the way to get water at the spring, just near dark, he jump out silently and block the path. 'You'd better come with me, e hine,' he says. He making a horrible grimace like a warrior. 'White men are going to die.'

Such a dangerous position Toofaiti saw herself in.

'Let me come a little later,' I say, thinking fast. 'If Toofaiti disappears now they will all guess she has run to you. Let me come after dark, when Williams is sleeping. Then we have all night to get away.'

So he's agreed and we arrange a meeting place.

'Bring as much as you can, bring knives, bring a musket!' he ordered. 'You'd better come, e hine.'

I returned to the others with the water gourds, composing a song, my heart banging like one hammer. I walked past Titriano's house, singing that song.

Why does black man sharpen axe?
To kill white man.

Maimiti came out of the door, with her pregnant belly. 'What's that song you sing e Toofaiti?'

I sang it again, in our Huahine tongue that she would understand a little. Then I walked on to prepare the evening food. The roasted breadfruit were all skulls to be peeled, and the song burned on my tongue as I poked the fire while Williams looked on smiling with satisfaction, rum cup to his breast. When darkness came he was too deep in his own pleasure to feel the wild beating of my heart. When he slept, I crept. I fastened on his belt with the long knife on it, but did not dare to get down the musket from above his head.

By moonrise the island was spread below me as I stood with Tararo on the high ridge south to rest awhile.

Oh rest awhile dear heart. Rest awhile and pray for us. Jesus is the fountain of mercy, pray to Him for our souls' release.

✖ ✖ ✖

Toofaiti's hair is all colourless now, she is an old bag of bones, full of memories and stories she doesn't want to tell. O my grandchildren, my hina tini, pray for us, for we have sinned and the sins of the fathers will be visited on the children. This horrible sickness the Lord has sent to punish us, taking sons and daughters, mothers and babies. Aue, things I don't want to remember my child.

Ask Tevarua. But ehi, Tevarua is long gone to hell with all the other ancestors, wrapped in sin and misery.

Tevarua Again

Let Tevarua speak again. Tevarua who hides in the branches of fruiting trees, she who hangs above the roofs in the wind, lies below the surf-dashed rock pools where they fish. She who walks with the ancestors and whispers with the unborn, let her voice be heard again.

✖ ✖ ✖

Tararo, and Oha, who had run into the hills to join him, were first to be slain. We heard the shots, echoing across the ridge.

Titahiti was sent to do it. That's all I know.

Titahiti, like Tinafanea, was a treacherous Tupuaian, not afraid to kill a noble Raiatean like Tararo. He should have given up his own life, rather than kill them, but he had no courage. He became worthy of nothing but death himself, and finally it was I took his fate in my hands.

The fenua maitai was hungry for blood, thirsty for blood, she was devouring our flesh. She took my last baby, wrapped in a banana leaf like an offering, and made orphans of the other four. Ghosts' children.

But I was flesh and blood the day those shots sounded from the hills. Got baby Matt at the breast. 'Just shooting a pig,' I tell myself. I start thinking how the pig will taste, turned over and over above the fire the way the English men like best. And let the women eat the meat too, not like Tahiti.

No roast pig that night, but Titahiti seen creeping back alone after dark. Tararo and Oha never seen again. So many deep valleys on the fenua maitai, so many ghosts.

White Blood

Maimiti was standing in the doorway of her house in a such a strange way as Toofaiti came running, that for a moment she thought someone had wounded her too, that every man on the island had gone crazy at once.

Then she realised they were not death throes she was seeing, but Maimiti's labour pains. Of all days for a birth! Joy and horror curdled in Toofaiti's heart.

How did she suddenly remember the little coloured image, bound in metal and glass, that Jack Williams had locked away in his chest? That woman with upturned eyes, sorrowful and tender, her heart a pure flame in the middle of her breast.

'Who is she?' Toofaiti had asked.

'Mary, most blessed of mothers,' Jack replied, and he put her to his lips. 'Mother of Jesus,' he added confidentially, before putting her back among the jumble of treasures he kept locked in the chest.

Toofaiti knew Jesus was the one nailed on the cross. Mary, she remembered, Mary with her heart on fire.

Maimiti was bent double at the entrance of her house, bracing herself in the heavy timber door-frame. 'What is all that shooting?' she asked as Toofaiti came running up to her.

'Oh they're just killing a pig, Maimiti,' Toofaiti lied. She remembered the shots ringing in the hills two years ago, when Tararo and Oha had been killed. Now her second husband was lying dead.

'So many guns for just one pig?'

Before Toofaiti could answer another birth pain flowed over Maimiti's features like a wave, and subsided again.

'Are Teio and Vahineatua coming?' she asked.

'Yes, yes, everyone is coming. Let's go inside to wait, it's very hot today.'

Maimiti was reluctant. 'We should have a birthing house, a proper sacred place,' she said. 'I should have made one, there's still time. Take my knife and cut some palm fronds, e hine. If we neglect the proper ritual the gods become angry.'

Toofaiti tried to stall her. 'Why not let this one be born in the house like a Christian?'

Maimiti laughed. Then she closed her eyes and was lost again in the contraction of her womb.

'You see, it's late, come into the house now. Let's pray to the white God for this baby. I think our gods are already angry – let the white God have this one, it's better.'

Such a strong contraction now seized Maimiti that she could not argue, and let herself be helped into the cool shade of the house, where she leaned up against one of the roof poles.

Toofaiti knew what needed to be arranged. Bowls for coconut oil and water, rolls of clean cloth and mats. She saw her arms doing the necessary things.

Could it be true what she had seen just since? Or had she dreamed it? Had she really seen both Titriano and Jack lying dead in the moist red earth of their garden plots? Was that blood dripping off the glistening banana leaves? The fern-frond wreath she had put on her husband's head that morning, mashed into his shattered skull? His long black plait matted with flies, his hand twitching?

The smell of gunpowder and blood returned with a rush so strong that her stomach heaved once again and she ran outside to vomit, although there was nothing left in her belly. She picked up a pail of water left by the door and threw it over herself. O Mary mother of Jesus, she heard herself saying. She looked around, scanning the bushes and trees for men with muskets. She almost cried out with fright when the two little Christian boys appeared on the path. Charles the tottering baby was trying to help his big brother, both of them naked and laughing, Thursday shouldering a branch of coconuts cut down by one of those same men early that morning. Their laughter ignited Toofaiti's heart. She let them run, so proud of their prowess with the coconuts, running into her open arms. A flame of love leapt up so pure and bright it engulfed them all three. 'O Mary Mary Mary!' she heard. 'Mary is coming!'

The boys were laughing and wriggling in her wet embrace.

'Ehi, you're both so big and strong,' she praised them, 'but listen now, Mama's baby is coming and you must help us.'

'Shall I run and tell our father?' said Thursday.

'No, e tama, first you run very quick and find one aunty, and tell her the baby is coming. Tell her come to Maimiti's house. Don't tell any men, just aunties. Don't stop running till you find them. Quick!'

She watched him run away down the leafy pathway, wishing Titriano had not built his house so far from the others. She took Charles inside and latched the heavy door and the window shutters. Jack Williams had told her that demons were afraid of Mary and Jesus, and ghosts and bad spirits could be driven away just by repeating their names. Mary Mary Mary, she began to whisper.

It occurred to her that all the things in Jack's trunk would be hers now, if only she could find where he had hidden the key when he left the house that morning. Mary of the burning heart would protect her. Mary Mary Mary!

'Where is Fletcher? Does Fletcher know?' Maimiti was asking.

'Fletcher!' She had to check her tongue. 'He and Jack were planting yams, Thursday has run to tell everyone.'

'A good husband, very good, he works hard. This is a good land for our children.'

'Ae, all good men Maimiti. Except maybe Matiu. It is the Maohi men who are dangerous, jealous, like wild beasts.'

'They have reason,' said Maimiti. 'So many times I'm telling Fletcher.'

She was crouching on the floor now, her back pressed into a corner. 'Where is everyone? Have you cut the palm fronds for the birthing hut yet? Be quick!'

'Maimiti, let this one be born in the house, there's no time for the birthing hut. Let me put down the clean cloth here.'

'It is bad luck!'

'Bad luck!' Toofaiti stopped her own words by gripping her throat with her hand. What misfortune could follow now? 'No, the white goddess will protect us,' she remembered. 'The white god and goddess are very powerful.'

Maimiti gave a sudden gasp. 'Aue! Look, the waters, inside the house!'

A glistening puddle was already soaking into the earth floor. Toofaiti acted without thought. She gave the baby a piece of sugar cane to chew on, and set him among the sleeping mats. She unrolled the bundles of thick rough cloth Maimiti had beaten for the birth and laid them out on the floor, helped Maimiti onto them and positioned herself behind her, ready to brace her. She had done it for Tevarua and for Vahineatua too. She pressed her own spine against the wall and adjusted her grip under Maimiti's thighs, ready for the wave which came surging out of her belly.

By the time the other women arrived, in a staring-eyed group, some already bloodied by their paoniho, clutching their children to their breasts, Maimiti was too deep in toil to be distracted by anything. They took their places around her to deliver the baby, fighting back the gagging cries of anguish that rose in their own throats, trying to forget what they had all seen and heard and smelt this hour. The children, silenced by the strange, suffocated atmosphere, crawled in among the sleeping mats and fell asleep in a pile like puppies.

Leading the birthing chant, Vahineatua drew every woman slowly into the circle, the old words of Tahiti reassuring, the chants each had heard at her own birth, inviting her out of the womb into te ao marama, the world of light.

But the relief of the newborn girl's first cry had barely been felt, the rituals barely begun, when came a violent pounding on the door, and groans like a dying animal.

'Where's Fletcher?' Maimiti suddenly cried.

'God help us, open up Mrs Christian! God help us all!' the man at the door began to shout.

'Is that Aleck? Is there rum again? Where is my tane!'

'Aleck's drunk, that's all,' Toofaiti tried to reassure her.

'Ae, throw a bucket of water on him!' suggested Teraura.

'Let me in Mrs Christian, I'm a dying man!' bawled Aleck.

Toofaiti peered through a crack in the timbers. The blood-streaked mask of terror which met her eye caused her heart to leap now in horror and compassion. As if controlled by an invisible hand she pulled the latch and slid the heavy door open, letting Aleck fall in and collapse at their feet.

Now Maimiti began to call out in panic for her own husband, and Jenny in anguish for hers, so the names of the newly dead began to resound and children began to cry. Now the women told Maimiti what had happened that day already, gathered round her like the living dead themselves, their tears beginning to flow. Someone pulled Aleck onto the mats she had vacated, ripped the shirt away from the gaping wound in his shoulder, and began stuffing his raw flesh with the oil-soaked cloths prepared for cleaning the newborn.

Then came banging on the door again, even louder, wilder, the wooden battering of musket butts. Someone looked through the crack and shrieked that it was the murderers. The children began to howl in terror, the new baby crying, Aleck moaning in agony on the floor, the fresh-cut widows wailing and sobbing, while the door resounded in its frame. Finally the latch gave way and the four Maohi men, their naked torsos smeared with gore, came rushing into the house brandishing muskets and blades. Toofaiti and Tinafanea threw themselves on top of the wounded man on the floor, but it was Jenny — whose husband was one of those lying slaughtered in his own yam plot – who leapt between the four men and their last victim.

'Enough!' she shrieked. 'It's enough now, no more! We are women and children here. Are you all possessed by demons? Go and wash yourselves, then hide your faces in shame. You have murdered our friends and husbands and the fathers of our children, go, go, go, before we kill you!'

As one body, they turned and ran out of the house. Out there, night had fallen.

Teio

Mrs Christian became like one ghost for long time.

Whole island like a death place. Nobody leave the house at night. And nobody go near those gardens for months, just letting the bodies rot there, eaten by pigs, covered up by weeds and yam plants.

Until one day I heard Mrs Christian and Vahineatua got their husbands' skulls hidden in the rafters, and Eti Young's trying to take them away and bury them, Mrs Christian's shutting him out her house where he's becoming accustom to pass the time, and threatening to cut off his head too. She got Titriano's long knife in her hand.

All these sorts of things going on.

And worse.

One time soon, killing the Maohi men too. Manari'i kill Temua and run away up the hills, go hiding with Wim and Matiu up there, never coming back alive. Then Titahiti, that dangerous rogue, and Niau, died one same night, that the work of Teraura and Eti. Better not remember that one time. Too much blood, too much shouting, better not look again those days. Aue.

Now only four men walking alive, and nine men ghosts, and those four alive more frightening than the dead ones, way they're walking about with their guns and knives, way they're quarrelling and disputing every little thing, and Matiu's biting off Tevarua's ear and Wim McCoy's growing crazy, crazy in his own house, and Eti and Aleck too, roaming about the island, never know what corner they'll come around, got one musket on their shoulder make your heart jump.

And Maimiti's like one ghost too, never say anything. Got Eti Young going to her house every day, while Toofaiti gone to live in Eti's house, and Teraura's moved over to live at Matiu's house, try to protect Tevarua from his fists.

Jenny's the one try to take a lead. She wouldn't go with any man after the killings, stayed in her own house and any man comes near she comes out with a musket. One day I come her house and she's pulling it apart. She's got tools from the forge and she swinging them full force at the walls, sweat's running down her naked breasts, her hair's loose, her arms and legs all streaked with mud and dirt. When she sees me she points another tool and says, 'Help me Teio, I'm going to build a boat and get off this cursed place.' She swings her tool again, smash the corner of the house, loosen another plank and start pulling it with her bare hands. 'I won't die here like the lowest of wretched dogs! Not Teehuteatuaonoa of Paea, I'll build a boat and sail back to Tahitinui! Do you think I'm afraid of that ocean, do you Teio? Are you afraid of it? Will you die here and rot without ceremony rather than face the ocean? Better to die at the marae of our ancestors, better to drown, better to be swallowed by the sea monsters than live with these white-dog tyrants!' She wrenched the plank from the wall and heaved it towards me, almost land on my foot. I jump and grab that tool she pointed to, start swinging it too, otherwise I think she's so crazy she'll kill me.

Soon every girl's there, hear the noise and everybody's agreed, make a boat. Make a big canoe, take us back to Tahiti, yes, yes, yes.

Not long before we hauling the planks to the cliff edge, sliding them down the Hill of Difficulty, land in a big heap among the rocks there. Then the men coming too, looking at that heap, looking at us, looking at each other. 'How will you make a canoe, you don't know how. You got no canoe builders, just women and babies, crazy for think you going to get off this island!'

Jenny jump up in front of them, big as a warrior. 'Eight of us, four of you,' she say. 'Better you help us.'

Even Mrs Christian's come along to see what's happening, got that unlucky girl baby on her breast, got her hair all cut off with the scissors, wearing some shirt belong her dead husband with the two boys hanging off the end of it. Eti Young's go over to her, take her by the shoulder, gentle gentle. 'Don't you be feared Mrs Christian my lady,' he's saying. 'Just these girls want to make a boat.' Then he's lead her back to her house, carrying Fletcher's boys one on each arm like that.

Isabella

Isabella. Never I hear him whisper that magic name again.

Isabella Isabella. I whispered it to myself, those long nights of grief. Every time the baby stirred, I started up in the anguish of remembrance. My husband, my husband! Claws of fire would rake my heart. If not for our three children I would have willingly thrown myself from the cliffs. My scalp was stiff with scabs and scars of the paoniho, blood and tears would drip on the baby's face as she fed.

She was light skinned. She looked up at me with pale sea-green eyes full of miserable comprehension, as if to say, I am only a baby, but I know everything. So unfortunate she was, born in the midst of that massacre, with no proper ceremonies, no rites. I loved her, but every time I looked at her she reminded me of that day, and I would hear again the banging on the door and the screams of terror which announced her father's death. Again and again, and in the night I would wake in a panic and remember yet again, yet again, over and over, night after night, lie by the flickering candlenut light and remember. He is dead. He has left me here in this madness all alone. O Fletcher, Fletcher, Fletcher, I cried, night after night, aue, aue, aue, wishing I could die too. My heart was a rock, weighing in my breast. In the morning I wanted to lift it out of my body and walk without it, but I had to carry it everywhere.

Mary, she was called. I didn't have any name to give her myself, I asked Toofaiti to decide her name. Mary was the name of the white goddess, but I only remembered Venus on her shell, born when her father's seed was scattered on the ocean. Toofaiti said Mary was the mother of Jesus, in spite of being a virgin. She said Jack Williams told her, and she showed me the tiny picture of Mary that she had from his sea chest. It was a good name for that baby, who never smiled for a year, although she was not troublesome.

It was Vahineatua who came with me to the yam patch to get Fletcher's skull. So thick everything grows on that island, out of blood and bone and grief. It was hard to even find him there. With his own knife, while Vahineatua improvised the necessary chants, I cut the remnants of skin that held the bones together and dragged his skull out of its tangled nest of stems and roots. The worms had finished with his brain, his eyes, his lips, his nose. Only his matted hair remained attached to its shrunken scalp, and his teeth bared to an unfamiliar grimace.

Then Vahineatua got the head of Mills, and together we completed the task of cleaning them. That was the way of our ancestors. Through his skull the dead one may bring messages from the land of the ancestors.

High in the mountains above Matavai, the priestess Hinuia must have kept my grandmother Tetua Avari'i's skull carefully bundled at the back of the cave. Now Hinuia's own bones would be lying there, untended. This I remembered as I scraped and pulled at the white man's remains.

But the white man does not speak after death. Or he has nothing to say. Fletcher has been silent all these years. He abandoned Maimiti, and Isabella died with him. Only Mrs Christian remains, the ghost wife.

'Mrs Christian is the oldest lady on the island,' Aleck always introduce her.

Oldest she may be, but Teraura got more teeth then her! Heii. Wish we could get up and dance again together, but we got so much sin on our shoulders that we lucky we can walk. That's what Aleck say. He still hiding one bottle in the bushes though.

He used to climb to that cave up there, Mr Christian. After the killings began. Used to leave his family for days at a time. He didn't play any more, no more singing and dancing the babies any more. The way to the cave was steep and windblown, only the goats skipped along it. Too hard for Isabella to traverse with two little sullen. Only she go to him at night when the sullen asleeping, carrying him water pots by moonlight, take care her husband and get another one sullen in the belly, come to be little Mary, born the day her father's dead.

'Come you down now. Enough hiding your head up here, I won't bring any more the water and food.'

He shrugged his shoulders, his hair was long and his beard rough.

'We need you Fletcher. We all afraid. I your wife asking you, please come for your children.'

'We'll all die,' he said.

'Why you say this my husband? We have children, we need you.'

'We'll be punished, by God's will.'

'They won't find us here Fletcher, nobody find us here ever, this your island you wanting for.'

'God will find us, don't you understand, God will find us and destroy us Isabella, oh Isabella!'

Then he's crying on my breast, he's choking on his tears. 'You are my only friend Isabella, what must I do without you?'

'Don't be talking such. We got our children to care for, got everybody needing you.'

'I only want you my Isabella, I don't wish to see any other face ever again. I'm a wretch beyond description, I have broke my mother's heart and ruined my family name forever. It's a mercy if God will strike me dead.'

And he's sobbing like a baby and taking the teat in his mouth; he's sucking the baby's milk while I'm stroking his head and singing to him and soon we're moving together on the stony ground high, high above the restless ocean, can see over his shoulder the empty horizon of the dawn, not land nor sail to be seen.

That's how I got little Mary, got her in tears, bore her in tears, child of sorrow.

Sully

I landed on Pitcairn in a barrel, and never left alive, except swim around the whole island for sport. That one good swim. All my life I was climbing up the Hill of Difficulty and the other steep places of the fenua maitai, wet hair drying on our backs as the hot sun scanned the empty horizon looking for something to burn.

I remember the boat sinking. I'se just a little sullen then, when they built that boat. Was Jenny's idea, she was allus wanting to leave. Everyone was bailing, the water was sparkling all around us, I was never afeared of the sea. The boat rolled over and vanished from under our feet. Cocknuts floated, chickens sank. I'se swimming in the women's arms. See the big surf smashing up white on the rocks from far away, all around the sea glittering alive and I like one fish in it. The women were laughing and calling to one another as they swam, and holding up the babies, taking turns.

At the landing place our fathers were waiting, all four of them. All them laughing too. Jenny was angriest. 'That's my whole house sunk!' she say.

'Crazy women!' they say.

Some things stay burned on the memory. It's like a tattoo in there, always see the same picture.

See the same picture of Wim McCoy. Got stringy hair, eyes all reddy, and he's offering me the rum cup, and I'se taking it from him.

See that one over again. Stringy hair and eyes all reddy, holding out the cup.

I knowed him all my life, Uncle Wim. He and my mother Teio came to the fenua maitai together, Dan McCoy's my brother. So I just take one fiery sip afirst, just to please him, make him happy, be kind to me. Make him laugh, talk about his home place, bonnie Scotland. Ae, bonnie Scotland, he'd be saying, and he'd tell me all about his ma and his wee brothers. 'I wonder where they are now, ae do they ever think aboot their William, wonder if I'm enjoyin' a fine life on a South Sea island. Wish I were aback there now, ae, wi' a dram o' best malt by my side. Will ye no take another wee sip lassie? It's a fine dram if I say so mysel'.'

So I'm taking another just to please him, and he's telling me all bout Scotland which is all paved in stone and tis so cold their feet stick to the ground, but their bellies are full of fire. Sometimes he sing one or two songs with his head tipped back and his eyes closed. 'But then I wouldna' be here by your side lassie,' he'd say. 'Have another sip.'

My throat was so numb I could not speak.

'Ye're a braw lassie ae, a braw wee lassie, will ye no give your uncle Wim a wee kiss?'

We lay down in the bushes, the way the sky and the earth were moving it was like being on a boat. Then Uncle Wim fall asleep and I get up and walk away, wiping the sticky stuff off my legs with a bunch of leaves.

Like a tattoo on the memory.

Then Uncle Wim's gone. My mother Teio say, 'It's a good thing he gone. He was getting too crazy.' She didn't know I'se a drinking from his kettle too, and he's showed me how to make that rum with roots of ti plant mashed up. She didn't know bout Uncle Wim playing those games with me. She didn't know I seen him the day he died, choosing a big rock with a narrow part on it, looping a rope around there. 'What for you tying one rope on that rock?' I asked him. He's just look at me eyes all reddy, got his hair all bushy wild, can't hardly stand upright but make a sailor's knot in the rope, and another one the other end.

'Goin' to Davey Jones, lass. A sailor shouldn'ae die on land.' He gestured out over the cliffs with a shaking hand, past the white curling surf on the rocks below and the constant heave of blue water that surrounded us day after day. He put the loop of rope round his neck and took another swallow of his dram with the rock in his lap. His eyes rolled up in his head and he gave a moan. I squatted beside him, curious at this new behaviour. He didn't even pass me the cup, he pressed it fast to his breast. 'Uncle Wim?' I said.

He opened his eyes and stared at me as if he'd forgotten I was there. 'Run away lass!' he said.

Afeared of one of his rages I jumped up and ran. I ran home and played with Dan McCoy all afternoon, taking good care of him. My mother had our sister Kate in her belly that time, and she was making fresh cocknut pilhai that day. 'Grate the nuts for me,' she say, 'be a good girl and grate the nuts, my belly too hard today.' I grate the nuts and say nothing, and when I go asleep that night, Uncle Wim's not come back to the house, and when I wake up in the morning, he's still not there.

'I know where he is,' I told my mother. 'I know where he's a hiding.'

I led her there, under the fallen tree trunk and down the slippery path and up the edge to his place he kept the rum kettle. But he wasn't there. My mother looked over the cliff edge, holding to a bush while she leaned right over. 'We won't see him any more,' she said to me. 'He's gone to Davey.'

She never cried one tear, my mother Teio.

Not like Mrs Christian. I don't remember Mr Christian. He was dead long afore. But Charles Christian I knew my whole life. Up the bush we all lived together, all the mothers and children. After the boat sinking, they carried us up there into the hills, where we lived in shelters made of cocknut fronds. Hiding from the fathers we were, one long game of hide a seek.

They come looking for us sometimes, mothers hear them coming, they calling our names. 'Matthew! Daniel! Charlie! Where are ye? Come out now!' Mothers hushing us up, climbing up under rock ledges, pulling the greenery down around us, squatting in the rustling bushes.

Jenny's putting the powder in her musket. 'You no answer they call, never!' says she. Mrs Christian she's a weeping again, all a time weeping. Charles and baby Mary holding on her dress. Charles got big brown eyes wet and shiny as a starfish, smooth his baby backside as a brown egg.

That's the same kind of babies we made together, Charles and me, when he grew big enough to be my man, and I his wife. Eight little sullen we got, last one only a baby himself when the fever take me from my body.

Lived my whole short life on the fenua maitai, got buried there after that bout of fever, but never cease to hear the scratching of the cocknut fronds above my head and the voices of the living passing by.

Teraura

I, Teraura, the last alive.

I, a murderess.

I seen it all. The ship in her sails, the men and women, the fenua maitai, the dyings and birthings.

God must have kept me alive to tell all this, even though I so burdened with sin I can hardly stand upright.

Outlived Mrs Christian, and all the other girls who left Tahiti that strange day. Outlived three husbands. Eti Young and Matiu Quintal and Thursday October, all died afore me.

Outlived two my sons, Joseph and Charles, Maimiti's grandsons, who died that terrible time we returned to Tahiti. Outlived Mr Adams who saved my soul.

Outlived Tetahiti, whose neck I smote with an axe while he lay sleeping.

Aue, the axe, the axe of the white man, rubbed with a stone till it sharp. When I see an axe I shiver. 'Don't bring any axe near me!' I tell the little sullen, I tell the boys going for firewood.

'Why not Granma Susannah? Es good'un, sharp sharp, cut plenty a wood!'

'Sharp sharp cut your neck! Be careful with that one.'

Blood was flowing like water that dreadful time. First Tararo and Oha, slaughtered in the hills, bang, bang, bang. Then Mr Christian and Jack Williams murdered in their yam patch, along of Isaac Martin, John Mills and Wim Brown the one same day.

I was living with Eti Young then and I telling you, not one drop of blood on him that day. Nobody touch him. He walking round without a scab or a scar while his friends' bodies rotting where they fell. While Aleck close to dying from his wound, and Matiu and Wim hiding afeared in the bush, Eti Young got his own plans, never tell anyone.

Soon he's going to the dead man's house.

'To look after Mrs Christian,' he told me.

He's looking after her so much he's most the night there. He's chopping her wood and carrying her cocknuts and playing with the fatherless children.

'Maimiti's long time my good friend,' I reminded him one day under our roof. 'Like a sister to me.'

'Fletcher was long time my good friend,' he replied.

We looked each other. He still had that spark in his eye, and the tight curled hair like a Paumotuan, and a dark nose bent from breaking, all his teeth black and brown, but still used to make my heart smile. Could feel his laughter coming. Raising his eyebrow, his sinewy arms fold cross his chest. See that tattooed heart on his arm, said he put it there for me, and I was the dart that pierced it. Underneath like this, *E.Y.*

Lifetime ago on Tahiti.

But Maimiti the real dart. I had no babies with Eti, didn't know he was keeping those babies for Maimiti. Maybe wanted Maimiti all the time, just waiting for his chance, keeping close to me so he's close to her.

That doubt entered Teraura's mind like a big shark. 'Go to her then,' I said. 'You were waiting, now she is yours.'

He seized me by the waist, picked me up and embraced me. 'You Tahiti girls are so, so fine!' He began to sing, making up his words like that. He was a clever singer. He danced me till I fell down laughing.

Next day I left Eti's house, went to live with Tevarua and her babies. Her man Matiu was hiding up the bush with Wim McCoy that time, living like boars in the wild, afraid to come down. It was better for Tevarua – she was happy with her babies. 'Look, they are so sweet these white man's babies,' she would say. 'Look what he has done, my little Matt.'

Little Matt had skin as black as Tevarua's and eyes as blue as his father's. He could make an arrow from a sharpened stick when he was still running naked, and a bow to match. He could shoot a bird out a tree, and when he got bigger he pierced fish in the rock pools with that weapon. Tevarua so proud of him, even though his father beat and bullied her.

Aue, white skinned or brown skinned, they were the blackheartedest of men, and this Teraura, she the blackheartedest of women, may the Lord save my soul.

Seeing us without any man, Temua and Manari'i – who were manahune boys I would never have looked at in Tahiti, except maybe in the dark – began to hang around Tevarua and me. That Temua got a little nose flute, heii he's playing it all day long. He could make it sing with his breath, said things no white man could understand. Used to listen with him, on the paepae of Tevarua's house, oiling my hair in the evenings. Tevarua's sitting behind, feeding her little sullen. Temua never looked at me, just play the flute, his own hair falling loose like black ferns from the knot on his head, and one white feather trembling in the evening breeze. He's playing this way and that way, and I'm running the strands of my hair through my fingers over and over, combing to that twisting, wandering voice, running after it into some nice forest full of fruit and birds, and I'm thinking this Temua is so sweet, so sweet with his calling voice and hidden eyes, surely I will succumb to him. I won't go with these crazy white men any more, I'll stay with this Tahiti man and he can play his flute to me all night all day, forget everything, forget all that badness.

That's what I'm thinking one day, when I see bang, a flash of fire the corner of my eye, bang! Last note of the flute is lost in the blast of death. Temua is arched up on the step, all legs and arms shaking, his chest torn open, blood pouring. Baby's crying, Tevarua's sitting with eyes wide open astare. I see the blood on my hands, I feel something sticking on my face, bits of Temua in my hair. Little flute's in my lap, I pick it and fling it away in horror. Tevarua's starting to wail.

Jealous – those men were all so jealous they would bite like sharks, and when they had been drinking, there was nothing they would not do. Manari'i so afeared after he shot Temua, that he ran away up the hills, joined up with Matiu and Wim McCoy up there. Left only Aleck and Eti, Niau and Titahiti living in the houses with us women and children.

Rum was the biggest demon on that island, and now it began to stalk Teraura. When Temua dying like that beside me, something going sour in my heart, and I start to drink rum too. I found Matiu Quintal's supply, had it in the dark-colour bottles from the ship. Began to drink it sip by sip from their long, black necks. Just one sip each bottle, then another.

Soon, yes, the heart is numb, not asking any more why. Just grating the cocknut, and feeding the little sullen, and carrying water. No crying, no remembering, just slip into the bushes near the house for another suck at that long neck. Just fishing on the rocks and pulling down the breadfruits and bananas, lighting the fires, scorching the candlenuts for lighting, beating the barkcloth, digging the taro, filling the earth oven. No time to think any more why we only left with these few useless men, and doing everything ourselves. No belly for love. So many sweet fruits the fenua maitai, but we eating the dry hard one, aue.

Then one day I'm standing with the long pole in my hand for getting down breadfruit when I hear the little flute, Temua's flute. My blood's running cold. Pole's stuck in the tree, legs won't move. 'Who's that?' I want to say, can't speak, like in a bad dream. Little flute saying things no white man can understand. Then I'm feeling my legs all wet, and suddenly they starting to run, leave the pole hanging in the tree. I'm sliding down the slippery paths and ducking under branches and jumping over edges, and I'm running to Tevarua's house. 'Tupapau!' I'm crying, 'tupapau!' I'm run for hide.

I never had any trouble with tupapau before that, but that island getting so full with ghosts. Daren't walk alone any more the night time, not down Brown's water, not over Maimiti's house, not one foot outside the door.

Daytime, I'm thinking, is a ghost? Maybe it's one them other Tahiti boys, he's playing tricks on me. Couldn't be any white man. I'm thinking, if I hear that flute another time I'll say, Manari'i! Tetahiti! Niau! Stop that fool around!

So I'm walking about, putting my eyes in all directions, looking behind me. Carrying one gourd topped up with rum. Thinking I'm hearing, but no.

And again, what that footstep? Tetahiti? I'm calling. Not any answer, my voice sound foolish. Then again, what that?

I'm watching Niau and Tetahiti in the day. Ask, 'You find Temua's flute in the bushes?'

'No, where you throw it?'

'You should have buried that flute,' said Tevarua. 'That's the only way stop a ghost getting it. Should've thrown it in the sea.'

I'm start to not go out the house alone. Only with Tevarua or one the other girls. Everybody crazy in those times. Maimiti, she crazy sad; Toofaiti's crazy praying to the white goddess; Jenny's crazy pull her house down, build one useless boat.

Sometimes we singing and dancing like old times, try forget the ghosts. Not much of Matiu Quintal's rum left. Sometimes we telling old-time stories, but those old-time stories too full with ghosts. Scare us so we have to stay all together in one house.

Then comes that sound again, whispering out of the leaves! And again my legs are stuck, and I'm trying to call out, Manari'i, stop that fooling! But my voice not coming. My feet grown roots.

Tupapau!

One day Eti Young find me on the paepae and sit down nearby. 'Where you hiding that rum?' he ask me, he giving me the mischief eye.

'Should I be telling you?'

Then he's making the sweet talk, how we always laughing and playing together on Tahiti, and I know he's just wanting something from me, and I'm thinking maybe I'll give it to him.

'Only bring me a bottle and we'll take a sip together,' he say.

So I'm agreeing, thinking to find out what Eti Young got on his mind, and I pass him the gourd.

He's taking one sip, then I'm taking one, and he's laughing low, put his arm on my shoulders, like old times. 'You wenches full of mischief,' he say. 'What do you want? Do you want white husbands or brown ones? I got a message.'

'What message?'

'Your white husbands won't come down from the hills until the brown ones are dead.'

'What colour are you?' I asked him.

'Most exactly my own colour,' he reply. 'Not brown, not white.'

I'm thinking Eti Young got his own plan, not brown, not white. It's a black one. Take another sip the rum.

'There are three white men and three brown men alive. Who's to die next?' he say.

I'm thinking Matiu and McCoy and Manari'i up the hills. Sometimes we hear shots. They killing a pig for eat. It's hard to find those three, but they know where we are. And I'm hearing that flute, turning my belly to stone. Got to be Manari'i, taunting me. Or Tetahiti, he's looking strange at me sometimes.

We pass the gourd back and forth. I'm remembering *Bounty*, and Eti at the wheel in his blue coat and hat, so handsome and fine, his hair bound up in a black ribbon.

'Susannah, my Susannah,' he say. He start to laugh again and kiss me.

'What you wanting not getting from Maimiti?' I ask him.

'Susannah,' he say. 'Susannah, help me. Matiu and McCoy want us to send up the Tahiti boys' hands for proof they dead.'

'Aue!'

'Otherwise they coming down to do the work themselves. And kill me too.'

'What for they want to kill you, Eti?'

He spat into the bushes. 'Treacherous dogs. They know I promised Fletcher to look after Mrs Christian. They kill me, what happens to her? Quintal is no better than a dog.' Now Eti's become very agitated and begin to laugh and sob all at once, saying, 'Help me Susannah!'

We passed the gourd till it empty.

I must have agreed to help him.

But I don't remember taking the axe he had sharpened, don't remember lifting it above Tetahiti's sleeping head. Don't remember anything. Just sometimes wake up to a horrible sound. The dead thwack of iron on bone. Comes down on my breast. Aue.

Never hear the flute again. That's one good thing.

Epilogue

Under the Banyan Tree

I will extol thee my God, o King, and I will bless thy name for ever and ever!
Every day will I bless thee and I will praise Thy name for ever and ever.
Great is the Lord!

In the centre of Adamstown stands one big banyan tree.

Roots of that banyan tree hanging down all around, joining to the ground. The big leaves are thousandfold, sun and rain can't reach beneath.

Every morning we unroll the mats there, and kneeling we begin.

Suffer me not O Lord to waste this day in sin and folly
But let me worship Thee with much delight
Teach me to know more of Thee and to serve Thee better than ever before
That I may be fitter to dwell in heaven
Where Thy worship and service are everlasting.
Our father who art in heaven ...

First there was Mr Adams. Our father on the fenua maitai. The only man we'd ever known, one father, liken the Bible. Obey your father, says so in the Bible.

Some obeyed, some didn't.

Mr Adams became our father one day under this tree. You can ask Granma Susannah, she was there. You can ask Granma Christian, she was there, but she's not talking so much now.

Granma Susannah, she's a funny one, sometimes don't know if she's telling stollies. She say came one angel to father Adams.

'An angel!' Aleck's a-crying that morning. 'Wings like this!' He's throw up his arms to show us, see the ragged armholes of his worn-out English coat. 'Light flaring out all around!'

His eyes as red as blood, hair sticking out in points. 'He's told me to cleanse your souls. Your souls, for ye're all covered in blood and gore. Sons and daughters of drunken bastards all of ye! Afloat on the 'igh seas without a master!'

We eyeing the foam on his lips a little fearful. Could be he going to lay about himself with the nearest axe. Could be fall down and vomit. We holding our breath.

'No more!' He pulling himself up on his fallen bones. 'The master 'as come. The Lord in 'is mercy has sent us the Lord Jesus Christ to instruct us in 'is ways!'

He point his stick at the nearest boy. 'Bring me the Bible young Quintal, from out o' Ned Young's box.'

Quickly now, Vahineatua's daughter Rachel running over to him. 'Father, are you well?

'Couldn't be better, unless you was to sit down and listen to the word of the Lord my girl.'

We stayed fixed to the spot. What thing's he about?

Matt's running with the big book, carrying it like a rock on his shoulder. Aleck's lay it out and open it and dip his crooked fingertip into that teeming nest of words. He's give a moan like a sick man, for taking too much rum day and night, then a belch.

Then he's begin, like the orator on the marae, ''Ear my cry O God! Attend to my prayer! From the end of the earth I cry unto thee, when my 'eart is overwhelmed. Lead me to the rock that is 'igher than I, for thou 'ast been a shelter for me and a strong tower from the enemy!'

We full of admiration for his speaking. The words of that book were just like insects to us, but Aleck could tell them off his tongue. He's looking around at all us, like he want some answer.

It was Toofaiti went first to her own knees, but the little sullen were quick to the same. Soon everyone kneeling, their palms together. Some looking out the corners of their eyes.

Our father, who art in heaven,
Hallowed be thy name ...

We knew this one, but Aleck had extra relish on his tongue. We followed him curiously, like a goats on a hillside.

Thy kingdom come
Thy will be done on earth as it is in heaven
Give us this day our daily bread
And forgive us our trespasses...

After the amen we stopped and waited.

Our father, who art in heaven! He's begin anew, louder than the first time.

Hallowed be thy name!

Sometimes we saying that prayer fifty sixty times on Sunday, even after he's teach us some other ones. But never telling us His name. That God of Gods, I'm asking, what name shall we hello?

× × ×

Mr Buffet stood back and curled his left whiskers with his right hand, looked hard at every girl and boy. Especially the girls. Was as if he knew everything going on outside the classroom as well as in. Knew we'd been breaking open cocknuts on a fast day, forgotten to wash behind our ears, told lies and disobeyed our mothers.

'Heathens!' he suddenly announced. 'Your mothers were all heathens and your fathers not much better. But now you know the favour of the Lord. You know what is right and what is wrong, do you not?'

He looked about again at our carefully composed faces. Nobody wants to be a heathen.

'Do you know right from wrong?'

'Yes Mr Buffet,' the reply.

Nobody wants to be a heathen but Kitty Quintal can't help it.

Mr Buffet's opening up the book and clearing his throat. 'Yes indeed! The Bible has in it everything a young person needs to know. Today we will read from Matthew chapter 25. Who shall begin?'

It was Kitty started the giggling and set cousin Mary off. Their fresh memory of Matthew McCoy's stiff ure, and the unmentionable things he had promised he could do with it was too much to bear straight face.

Mr Buffet cleared his throat again, and a secretive smile began twitching beneath his whiskers.

'What impudent young heathens you are, come up here at once and stand before the class. What do you know that the Bible did not teach you? You first Mary Christian, speak up.'

Propelled by gales of helpless laughter, the wonderful secret was out.

'Why 'em boys like girls Mr Buffet!'

'And why is that young lady?'

Kitty was stifling her giggles on Mary's shoulder

'Come now, can't you tell me?'

We couldn't tell, and the harder we tried the more we laughed.

'Recite the Lord's Prayer three hundred times. In the corner!' said Mr Buffet.

He crossed his arms and watched us with satisfaction, we're looking out the corners of our eyes. Kitty's breasts were still jiggling with laughter under her chemise.

Lead us not into temptation and deliver us from evil
For thine is the kingdom, the power and the glory
Forever and ever
Our knees all hard as bark.
Amen
Amen
Amen

※ ※ ※

Was Eti Young that taught Mr Adams to speak out of the book. Still called him Aleck in those times, before the first ship came and he changed his name to John Adams, Mister. Charles and little Matt were sitting close by that day with ears wide open.

'We going to begin the beginning,' say Eti. Open first page and point. 'First word. Genesis. G E N E S I S.'

Aleck's scratching his head like he's got them kooties bad.

'That's the g, that's the e, that's the n,' Eti's pointing. 'Repeat the sound, man.'

We waiting and watching.

Bit by bit the word come out.

'Very good. Now, in the beginning God created the heaven and the earth.'

Charles was creeping close up to Mr Young's elbow, getting a good look.

'Es a big un book. Es gwen ter take all day,' he said.

Mr Young reached out and tweaked his ear. Didn't hurt.

He stayed there all day and filled his ears. Next day and next day too. He's repeating everything he hears. 'You'se telling stollies!' say the others.

'No! Es in the book. I seen it.'

Mr Young was coughing all a while. Sick in his chest. After a while see he's gwen fer die too, coming all blood out his mouth. Put blood spots on the book sometimes even though he's cover up his mouth with a piece of cloth.

We only on Joshua by then.

✖ ✖ ✖

'Matt Quintal said Mr Young killed his father. That's what Betsy Mills telling him. Betsy Mills says she was there seen it all and they cut Mr Quintal to pieces, Mr Young and Mr Adams. She said she seen the house all dripping with blood. She showed him how with a stick, how they chopping up Mr Quintal, just like one stack o' firewood she said.'

'She's telling stollies. Mr Quintal fell down the cliff too. That's what happened Mrs Quintal too, and that's what happened to Dan McCoy's father.'

'Mr Adams our only one father now.'

'And our father who art in heaven.'

'Hello be thy name.'

'Stop that fool around.'

Then came Mr Buffet, and not long before Mr Adams died came Mr Nobbs. Mr Buffet came on a big ship, so many masts and sails. 'Sail ho! Sail ho!' That's the cry on Pitcairn. How many times we're rushing to the edge, counting the horizon, see that little speck of excitement far away. We're trying to catch it like a fish on a line, bring it to Bounty Bay. See its treasures, talk to its men.

First all we say prayers under the banyan tree, got our clean cloths on and our mothers cover up their breasts and light the oven fires to feed the guests. Soon they climbing up the Hill of Difficulty, we sing hymns to them, then feed them. Big dishes of yams, cocknut pilhai cooked in banana leaves, one two pigs, roasted breadfruit, sweet cane juice. Mr Adams says, 'Gentlemen, we take no hard spirits on this island, please be considerate of our little children and their mothers and keep the sanctity of the Lord upon us all, amen.'

He's very strict when a ship's visiting, better behave or else.

We kept a fast every three four days, sun'sarise to sun'saset, by Mr Adam's instruction. 'Then ye'll have the Lord's redemption for all your sins,' he promised us.

One time a ship came on our fast day and the mothers complained for all the cooking and nothing to eat. 'If we not getting to eat today we going to tell the captain where bout you got your rum hidden,' they told him.

How they knew was because his married wife Teio Adams was now blind, and he's hide it in the house thinking she can't see. But she can see with her ears and she's listening where he's put it so she can have a sip sometime. So he's agreed to let us break fast with the guests, and nobody mention the rum bottle.

After the eating, there were more hymns, then everyone saying prayers by moonrise. Our hearts all full by bedtime, of songs and stories and psalms. We feel the Lord so kind to us. The Lord protecting us. The Lord our saviour from the hell awaiting sinners. The Lord our friend and father. The Lord an ocean of mercy. We sleep with the songs in our ears.

Alone O Love ineffable
Thy saving name is given
To turn aside from Thee is hell
To walk with Thee is heaven.

Sail ho! Sail ho! The boys are out fishing, Thursday October and George Adams and Eti Quintal. From the Edge we see them paddling fast out to sea to meet the ship. It's a fine day, the ocean is all flashing light in every direction, the little canoe goes up and over the swell, up and over. Mr Adams is beginning a prayer. Then he's sending Hannah to meet the sailors at the top of the Hill of Difficulty, with flowers in her hair and all kind words of greeting on her lips. Sometimes weary, hungry and sick they arrive, staggering over the top, and lovely Hannah's there smiling.

'The angel of the Lord encampeth round about them that fear Him, and delivereth them. O taste and see that the Lord is good, blessed is the man that trusteth in Him.'

'What can we send for you, what are your needs?' the captains would ask.

'Send to us one person to teach us to read and write and do what is good towards God, because we don't know enough,' we replied. 'That is our wish.'

Mr Buffet was the Lord's first answer to our prayers. He was good for reading and writing. Soon all the little sullen could make their names with a blackend stick, or if a lucky day Mr Buffet's sharp pen and ink.

Pen and paper was Margaret's secret longing. Not allowed to tattoo her hands, she wanted to fill pages like the book itself, with everything she knew. Granma Christian was discouraging. 'You just a little sullen, don't know anything,' she said. 'You wait till you older, then maybe someone's gwen fer listen you. Better you write out what's in the Bible.'

She beat out sheets of fine white tapa cloth for Margaret to practise on and kept the completed sheets in a roll to show visitors from the ships. Sometimes she gave the sailors a sheet in return for something particular. Cloth with coloured flowers on it, a whalebone comb, or a cooking pot. Once she got another book, a small one with pictures in it of children and strange animals. 'Mother Goose' it was called. 'That's the bird Captain

Cook brought to Tahiti,' she showed Margaret. 'You can write with one her feathers.'

'Mrs Christian, these children need nothing but the good book,' Mr Nobbs told her when she showed him her prize. 'Any other writings will simply spoil their temperaments. They are true children of God.'

Mr Nobbs came on one small small ship, just Mr Nobbs and Mr Bunker, who was crazy sick, scare us all with his long beard and ghosty eyes afore he died.

Mr Nobbs got whiskers even bigger than Mr Buffet, and his voice bigger too. Mr Buffet married Dolly Young and Mr Nobbs married Sarah Christian. But when Mr Nobbs found out who's the father of Mary Christian's little sullen, baby Mary, he's aroaring angry, say John Buffet's not fit to teach us, John Buffet's a sinner of the first order, and he won't ever speak to Mr Buffet again. Soon we got two schools, Mr Buffet's school and Mr Nobbs' school.

Forgive us our trespasses, some saying. John Buffet's one good man. No harm done, Mary's a sweet child, a blessing.

But Mr Nobbs' voice is very fine, Mr Nobbs can write poems and songs and he is a righteous man, hallelujah. Which school to go to?

Mr Nobbs broke his boat to planks and built a new schoolhouse by the banyan tree. All day long, hear the little sullen singing, reciting and counting, their voices lift up like kites on the whirling ocean currents overhead.

All day long the black ancestor goddess, hidden snug among the banyan's slowly strangling roots, hears the voices of her hina tini.

'The Lord doth build up Jerusalem, he gathereth together the outcasts of Israel. He healeth the broken in heart and bindeth up their wounds. He telleth the number of the stars, he calleth them all by their names. Great is our Lord and of great power, his understanding is infinite.'

The white fairy terns that flit and glide among the trees are the ears of spirits listening. Their bright black eyes look down upon the white-clothed girls between the leaves, generation after generation they return to their favoured branches to lay their eggs, watching the people and listening.

'For the Lord is a great God and a great King above all other gods. In His hands are the deep places of the earth, the strength of the hills is His also. The sea is His and He made it and His hands formed the dry land. O come let us worship and bow down; let us kneel before the Lord our maker.'

The black ti'i clasps her belly as the great tree engulfs her. She holds her secrets tight behind her closed lids. Long is her waiting.

Year of Our Lord 1831

Extract from Pitcairn Island Register, in the hand of George Hunn Nobbs.

    April 21st Thursday October Christian died
    25th Lucy Ann Quintal died
    29th Prudence (Vahineatua) a native of Tahiti died
    May 4th George Young died
    15th Kitty Quintal 2nd died
    16th Polly Christian died
    June 3rd Edward Christian died
    4th Jane McCoy died
    6th Mary Quintal born
    8th Kitty Quintal 1st died
    9th Nancy (Toofaiti) a native of Tahiti died
    25th Charles Christian 2nd died

27th Daniel McCoy 2nd died
27th Hugh McCoy died
August 7th sun eclipsed
12th Charles Driver Christian born
18th Robert Young died

September 2nd Our remaining numbers safely returned to Pitcairn aboard the *Charles Doggett*, a brig from Salem. Thanks given to the Lord for our island home.

Glossary of Tahitian Words

Tahitian is not as difficult to pronounce as it looks. The vowels are sounded as in Italian: a as in art, e as in epic, i as in machine, o as in orb, u as in ruby. Every vowel in the word is pronounced. Two or more vowels together are run into a smooth combination, unless separated by an apostrophe, which represents the glottal stop. The plural is generally the same word as the singular.

To Tahitian-speaking readers, I apologise for any mistakes I have made.

ae	yes
ahi	fire
'ahi	sandalwood
ahia hia	longing
ahime!	alas!
ahufara	barkcloth shawl
'ahune	plenty, bounty
aita peapea	never mind, no problem
aito	ironwood tree
Aotearoa	New Zealand
ari'i	aristocrat, person of high birth, descended from the gods
arioi	old Tahitian religious sect devoted to pleasure and entertainment
aroha	love,
aroha nui	all-embracing love

'ata	laughter
atua	god
aue	an exclamation used in many circumstances
aute	paper mulberry
'ava	mildly narcotic beverage brewed from plant root
fa'a'aro	barkcloth, now called tapa
Farane	France, French
fare	house
fare tupapau	a shelter for the embalmed corpse of an important person, lit. ghost house
fau	red hibiscus
fe'e fe'e	elephantiasis
fei	mountain banana
fenua	land
feti'i	relations, family
haere mai	a call of invitation and welcome
hara	wrongdoing, shame
hau	wind, breath of life
hei	garland, necklace or chaplet
heiva	festivity, party, celebration
himine	hymn (transliteration)
hina	woman or girl
hina'aro	desiring admiration, admiring desire
hina tini	descendants
hine	girl, young woman e hine form of address to her
Hina te marama	the moon

Hiti a Reva Reva	old Polynesian name for Pitcairn, lit. 'border of passing cloud'
i'e	cloth-beating mallet
ihu	human life force
'iore	small native rat
kaue	no (Pitcairnese)
maeva	welcome
mahu	a male who has lived as a female since childhood, from his own inclination
mana	spiritual power, prestige
mamu	quiet
manahune	the common people
Maohi	Polynesian
mape	Tahitian chestnut
mara'amu	south-east wind, trade winds
marae	outdoor temple
maro ura	A long belt or girdle, stitched with sacred red feathers, worn by the high chief at his inauguration ceremony, and added to with each generation
mati	Tahitian fig
mauriuri pee va'a	a wind of ill omen, lit. the wind that detaches canoes
mauro	longtailed tropic bird
Matari'i	the Pleiades
miro	tree, held sacred, often growing around the *marae*
moia	pandanus weaving
monoi	perfumed coconut oil

mo'o	lizard
ni'au	coconut palm
nono	plant used medicinally, with perfumed white flowers
opuhi	scented ginger flower
Oro	old Tahitian god of war
paepae	house terrace
pahi	large double canoe
pahu	drum
paoniho	shark's-tooth scarifier
paoti	scissors
pareu	length of cloth worn as skirt or dress
pau	finished, over
patea	form of address to older woman
Paumotuan	native of the Tuamotu islands
Peretane	Britain (transliteration)
pia	arrowroot plant
pilhai	Pitcairn word for a sticky pudding baked in banana leaves
pirimomona	virgin
Popa'a	foreigner
pua	flowering tree, sacred to Tane
puaru	infanticide, practiced as a form of population control in pre-European Tahiti
purau	beach hibiscus
ra'atira	underchief, of lower rank than ari'i
raho	female genitals
rahui	a prohibition on food supplies, for sacred or practical purposes

rama	rum (transliteration)
Rapanui	Easter Island
re'a	turmeric, native to Tahiti
revareva	a decoration of fluttering white strips worn on special occasions
tafifi	native jasmine
tahua	priest, person who communes with spirits
tahua mori	healer or doctor who uses massage
tahua ra'au	doctor who uses herbal medicines
taio	a friend with whom names were exchanged, and everything shared, including hospitality, gifts, and even sexual partners
tama	boy
tamanu	tree used medicinally
tane	man, men, also *Tane*, god of pleasure
tapairu	handmaids and companions of a chiefess
tapu	sacred, taboo
taro	starchy root vegetable
tatau	tattoo
tau' arearea	carefree years of youth, lit. 'yellow years'
Ta'urua e hiti i Matavai	lit.'Ta'urua rising over Matavai', the star Venus
te ao marama	the world of light, this world
te oho matamua	first fruits, a sacrifice
te po	darkness, the afterworld
teu teu	servant
tiare	Tahitian gardenia, scented flower
ti'i	carved image which can be inhabited by a spirit

tiputa	barkcloth cape
tiri a pera	secret pit where a family threw its personal discards, such as hair, nails etc
to'erau	north, or the north wind
to'ere	slit gong
Tohu	old Tahitian god of tattooing
tou	cordia tree
tui heanano	an eczema-like skin condition which can become severe
tuna	eel
tupapau	ghost
tupu	discarded items of a personal nature, such as nail clippings, hair or uneaten food, all of which could be used for sorcery and therefore had to be carefully secreted
tutae auri	rust, lit. iron shit
tu'tui	tree with oily nuts which can be burnt for light
upa upa	pleasure, especially sexual
ure	penis
uru	breadfruit
u'upa	native pigeon
va'a	canoe
vini	native Tahitian parrot, now extinct